INNOCENT TEMPTRESS

"I wondered if you'd be staying here," Tara said softly.

"Does it matter?" His voice was like velvet and he drew a little closer.

She could feel her pulses race and sensed they matched his. Slowly he reached a hand to delicately trace her lips with his fingers. "Does it matter?" he insisted in the same sultry voice. He watched her answer in the trembling of her soft, inviting mouth, felt her answer in the quivering warmth of her body.

"Yes," she whispered, "it matters."

Then, to Tara's surprise, his mouth moved to hers, tasting gently. He made no move to embrace her, but their mouths fused in a kiss that shook the foundations of their souls.

"Go back to those you belong to, Tara. You're a wide-eyed, innocent little girl who's going to get hurt."

She tried to twist away, but he grabbed her shoulders. His voice rasped in her ear as he pressed her against him. "I could take you here. Take you because you're a sweet, gentle believer. Love demands a whole lot more than a quick roll in the hay."

Tara gasped in shock.

"You don't know or understand what's at stake here, and you're too damn sweet to believe it. Get out of here, Tara, before I regret my own stupid streak of gallantry and make love to you like I want to."

LOVE'S BRIGHTEST STARS SHINE
WITH ZEBRA BOOKS!

SYLVIE F. SOMMERFIELD

AUTUMN DOVE

ZEBRA BOOKS
KENSINGTON PUBLISHING CORP.

ZEBRA BOOKS

are published by

Kensington Publishing Corp.
475 Park Avenue South
New York, NY 10016

First printing: January, 1989

Printed in the United States of America

Prologue

1865 Kansas-Colorado Border

Zachary Hale rode very slowly toward the camp whose smoke he had seen some distance away. He rode carefully, keeping an eye on everything about him. He smiled when he remembered the words he had said to a friend a few days before at Fort Lyon, that the last persons he had trusted had been his mother and father. There had been no others since he was a babe. . . . He'd been careful ever since.

He was careful now, knowing the men he rode toward might be a whole lot more than they appeared to be.

Several Indian raiders had attacked wagon trains on the Santa Fe Road east of Fort Lyon. While the commanders at the fort favored a policy of harsh reprisals against the Indians, Zachary Hale wasn't sure that the Indians had not been enticed to do so. He was one of the few who suspicioned the Indians had been armed and led by someone who was not of their blood—for Zachary Hale bore the blood of the Cheyenne as proudly as he did his white blood.

A treaty had been signed with the purpose of moving the Indians south of the Arkansas River and keeping them away from the overland routes. One of the major weaknesses of the Treaty of Little Arkansas was that the Indians who signed it

5

represented only a fraction of the many tribes of warriors who did not feel bound by it.

What was worse, he knew, the more warlike portions of the Cheyennes, notably the Dog Soldiers, had not even been at the council.

Zachary Hale-Windwalker was a man who stood with a foot in each camp, who understood each camp, and who suspected there was a third force at work; one who played one against the other in the hope of profit. Yet, he could not trace this elusive plot down, nor could he name the profit expected.

But somehow the guns had been brought. Again and again they had slipped by him. His anger was growing, for he knew someone played him for a fool and over this his white and red bloods no longer warred. . . . They joined forces to find the man or men responsible.

He neared the camp and sensed the moment they knew he was coming. They were alert as he rode closer. The camp was occupied by three men, and it was not until he came close enough that he could see them clearly and they could see him that a call of recognition came to him.

"Zach, boy," a man's gruff voice called, "come on in and sit. We got a lot to tell you."

Zach dismounted and strode to the low burning fire. He squatted on his heels by the fire and gazed across it at the three men. "So Mackie," Zach said quietly, "you said you had something to say."

The person Zach spoke to was a grizzled man of undeterminable age, with white hair and a white beard to match. His eyes were a pale blue and held Zach's.

"Shore boy," he grunted as he reached behind him to lift a rifle and toss it to Zach, who caught it in a quick reflexive move.

"Good stock," Zach said shortly as he examined the rifle then laid it aside. "But you've got more to say than that."

"Yep, shore do. Somebody wants to bring this kettle to boil out here."

6

"Who, Mackie, who?"

"I can't name any names. I wish I could. But I'll tell ya that these rifles came in on a wagon train. They came across from Ellsworth and down the trail past the fort."

"How do you know?"

"Found some good trail and tracked 'em for a spell. Then I run across this place where there must have been a meeting. Apparently it was a place to unload. Found an empty box and it was marked."

"Marked?"

"Well, the box was burnt. But not enough to blot out one name . . . Banning."

"Banning, who is he?"

"Trader, trapper, he brings people from St. Louie across the trail. What better way to bring guns. Who checks on the wagon trains? Why, the army even guards them."

Zach rose and lifted the rifle to carry with him.

"Where are ya goin', Zach?" Mackie asked. "You gotta walk careful being . . ."

"Being a half-breed?" Zach questioned mildly.

"You know it's so, Zach."

"Yes, I know that. But I know a lot of people both Indian and white are going to die if something isn't done."

"You be careful," Mackie warned. "Your life won't be worth a nickel if this . . . Banning, whoever he is, finds you sniffin' for rifles." Mackie stood to face Zach. "What are you going to do?"

"Now, Mackie, don't worry," Zach smiled. "I'm going to go to Ellsworth and hire on as a guide. Who knows . . . I might just run across Mr. Banning."

"And get yourself killed."

"Now why would anyone want to kill a half-breed guide?"

"You're asking for trouble."

"Maybe," Zach said thoughtfully, "but someone has got to put a stop to what's building. This Banning, if he's the one, he's going to make a hell of a lot of profit off of the innocent blood

7

of both whites and Indians. I'm going to Ellsworth, Mackie, and I'm going to do whatever it takes to find him . . . and to stop him."

Zach returned to his horse and mounted while Mackie walked over to stand beside him.

"Zach, boy, have you been out to talk to your pa about this?"

"Waiting Wolf would have me put away my mother's blood. He would have me lead people to fight each other."

"His people."

"My people," Zach added.

"And kill the whites."

"My people, too," Zach replied softly. "Mackie, I can't separate them. I'm Zachary Hale . . . and I'm Windwalker. I don't want rifles to separate them for me."

Zach rode away, and Mackie's eyes followed him with sympathy he would never show Zachary Hale.

"I hope you survive, boy. I shore hope you survive."

Chapter 1

The carriage careened down the hill completely out of control. The horses, wild with fear at the loud noise that had startled them, had the bits in their teeth and would not be controlled by the man who pulled at the reins without result.

The man's fear was not for himself but for the terrified woman who sat near him and clung to the carriage sides with white knuckled hands.

He pulled at the reins with all the strength he had, but the terror of the horses was beyond his strength. The next curve was too sharp and approached too fast. The carriage overturned and the occupants were both thrown clear. They lay like silent broken dolls.

The day was bright with sunlight and the air clear and warm. It was not a day for tragedy . . . but tragedy struck.

It was several hours before a passing carriage saw the wreckage and the occupants stopped to lend assistance, only to find assistance no longer needed.

Tara Montgomery ran lightly down the stairs. She had heard the pounding on the front door and knew there was no one in the house except herself. Her father and mother had taken the carriage earlier to go for their usual afternoon drive.

Tara was sure it was because they wanted to be alone. It always gave her such a warm feeling to know her parents still loved each other so deeply. It delighted her to see them reach to touch each other or to catch them looking at each other lovingly.

Now she was running to the door, wondering if somehow they had fogotten their key. She turned the knob and pulled the door open, to be faced by two of her father's best friends.

Their solemn looks made the smile die on her face. Something stirred within her, telling her this visit was not one of a friendly nature.

"Mr. Jacobs," she tried to smile again. "I'm terribly sorry my father isn't home. He and Mother have gone for a carriage ride."

"Tara, my dear," Reginald Jacobs said seriously, "may we come in, please? We must talk to you."

"Yes . . . yes, of course." She stood aside to let the two men walk past her. She found herself trembling as both men turned again to face her. She read things in their eyes, and her strength seemed to drain from her.

"Tara," Reginald Jacobs said gently, "I'm afraid we have some grievous news for you. Is there anyone here with you?"

"No, I told you, Mother and Father . . ." She stopped speaking, feeling her mouth go dry and her heart begin to pound fiercely. "Mr. Jacobs, whatever you have to say, please tell me. Is it Mother? Father? Is one of them hurt? For God's sake, Mr. Jacobs, tell me!" Her voice cracked and she clenched her hands together before her.

"It . . . it's both of your parents, Tara."

"Both?" she whispered through stiff lips. "Are they hurt? Where are they, Mr. Jacobs? Please, where are they? They aren't? . . ."

His face spoke volumes she wanted to deny. It could not be! They were happy, they were in love, they were all she had!

The words tumbled through her mind as she backed away from the two men slowly and shook her head negatively. "No," she whispered, "no, it cannot be. How? . . ."

10

"The carriage, my dear child," Reginald Jacobs said, his voice heavy with sympathy. "It seems the horses went crazy. The carriage overturned. I know it's no consolation, but they did not suffer any pain. They died instantly."

She made a soft whimpering sound and turned her back to them, burying her face in her hands.

Both men were silent, feeling the girl's heavy pain. There were no words they could say to ease her grief. It was a terrible blow to lose both her parents. She was only nineteen, hardly a woman to face life alone. But neither man knew quite what to do.

Tara straightened her shoulders and turned her tear-stained face to them again.

"Thank you for bringing me the news," she said softly. "I want my parents brought here. I will see to—to the arrangements."

"Tara," Reginald Jacobs spoke gently as he went to her to touch her hand, "my wife and I are deeply grieved. Your parents were very dear friends of ours. Please let us help you with whatever needs doing. I will tell my wife to come this afternoon. We cannot bear the thought of you being alone."

"Thank you, Mr. Jacobs, but I will be all right now."

"Amelia will be here as soon as I go home," he insisted quietly. "Your father and I were too close for us to desert his daughter now. I shall go and tell Amelia. She is anxious about your welfare."

"I'm grateful, Mr. Jacobs."

"Will you be all right until Amelia gets here, or would you agree to come home with me now?"

"I will be all right," she insisted quietly.

The two men were still uncertain, but they turned and left the house.

For a long moment Tara stood in the center of the quiet room. Then she sagged to the floor, allowing the hot tears of misery and loss to overcome her.

*　　　*　　　*

11

Her black dress billowed about her ankles and the veil cast a grayness before her, as Tara stood with her parents' friends and watched the caskets being lowered into the ground. She had found the past two days an unbelievable nightmare. Now her loss had culminated in emptiness and a terribly lonely feeling.

It seemed to her as if the preacher went on and on. His words were drowned in her thoughts as she reached for any and all memories that would help wipe away these terrible last minutes when she must say good-bye to the two who had been her whole life.

Finally it was over. Finally she could return to the quiet seclusion of her home and decide what she was going to do.

Of course she had the house, some money her father had left, some paintings, and her mother's jewelry. She would manage.

She tried to be reserved, polite, and grateful for all the expressions of sympathy. But what she needed most was to be alone to gather what reserves she had to face a future that was, at the least, frightening.

When Tara arrived home, she stepped down from the carriage and walked up the steps to the door where the wreath with black flowing ribbons still hung. She opened the door and went inside. As she turned to close the door, she noticed the envelope on the floor. While she was gone, someone must have delivered a letter. Finding her out, they had pushed it under the door. She bent to pick it up, and when she read the front, fresh tears started. The letter was from her brother, David. In the midst of her grief, she had not thought to ask if someone had sent him a message, although she knew he was so very far away. He was at Fort Lyon, in the wilderness.

Her brother, David, had been a graduate of West Point and had been sent to Fort Lyon over a year ago. She and her parents had both been very proud of him.

12

She sighed, supposing she would have to go on maintaining the family home until David could return. She knew society would frown upon her living alone, but now she could not think of sharing the house with anyone.

She sat down, tore the envelope, and began to read. Again, she was choked with grief as she realized that when David had written the letter he had not known of his parents' death. The letter was in answer to the last one she had written to him.

Dear Tara,

Sorry I wasn't there for your birthday, but I'm sure you had so many beaus at your feet you hardly had time to miss me.

I really do miss you, Tara, and Mother and Father too. But it won't be forever. If I want to get those promotions, I must take what the Army offers.

It's truly not that bad here at Fort Lyon. I've met someone who's very special. I have to think over this situation. I'll say a lot more in my next letter. It is a tremendously different world out here, Tara. It is a world that demands such strength from people. I'm finding it's building something in me I never knew I had.

If everything works out, I may get leave and come home for Christmas. I'll write and let you know. For now I have to go. I'm on duty in a few minutes.

Give my love to Mother and Father, and of course I love you too.

David

She would have to write to David herself. But she couldn't do it today. Today she had all she could do to handle her own grief.

The next three weeks were allowed to slip through her fingers. She moved through the days as if in a dream.

Tara awoke early on a bright Sunday morning. She dressed and sat at the dining room table to sip her tea. She had to make decisions about herself. The money in the bank would not last forever. She would go to the jeweler tomorrow and sell the jewelry her mother had left her. At least that would last until David could get home. She had not written to him yet, but she planned to do so today.

The knock on the door came as such a surprise that at first she didn't move. The rap came again, and she rose and walked to the door. When she opened it, she was surprised to see Walter Bradley, a banker who had been friendly with her father. It was a surprise to find him at her door on Sunday morning.

"Mr. Bradley?" she asked.

"Miss Montgomery . . . Tara, may I come in for a moment? I'm afraid I have some . . . ah . . . important business to talk over with you.

"Can it wait until tomorrow, Mr. Bradley?"

"No, Tara, I'm afraid it can't. I'm afraid there are some things that need to be tended to before the bank opens tomorrow."

"Come in," she replied. When he was seated in the parlor and had accepted a cup of tea, Tara sat down opposite him. "Now what is this business, Mr. Bradley?" she inquired politely, ignoring the warmth in his eyes as they moved appreciatively over her. He smiled.

"Can you call me Walter?" he asked gently. "I would really like to be a good friend to you, Tara."

"I'm sure you would, Mr. Bradley," she responded, trying to ignore the sudden sense of alarm. "What is this business you have to discuss?"

"I'm afraid there is some problem with some . . . ah . . . rather large debts your father had. They are quite large and I'm afraid, now that he is deceased, they must be honored."

"Honored . . . by what? I have very little money."

"I'm afraid the house itself must be sold to honor the

outstanding debts."

"The house!" Her alarm was evident in the expressive widening of her eyes and the way she stiffened in her chair. "But I cannot do that," she cried. "It is almost all that I have."

Walter Bradley smiled. He had seen in her eyes what he had come to see—fear and uncertainty. Now was the moment he had chosen three weeks ago, when he had watched her at her parents' funeral. Even then her beauty had been breathlessly outstanding. Even the drab black dress and veil could not dim the emerald of her slightly slanted eyes or the soft cream of her complexion. Her copper-red hair had been drawn to a chignon at the nape of her neck, but he could envision it loose and flowing about her shoulders.

He imagined the glow of her soft skin. His vision had stripped away the horrid black gown that had covered obviously ripe and luscious curves. His fantasies had brought her to his bed, to his arms, and his dreams had carried him here, where he was sure he had her at his mercy.

He stood up and placed his cup on a nearby table. Then he walked to stand very close beside her. He rested one hand lightly on her shoulder.

Tara was trying to control both her fear at his words and her aversion to his touch. She remained still.

His hand slid across her shoulder, and the tips of his fingers lightly touched the smooth skin of her cheek.

"Your father's debt was quite large, but I feel, if you desire me to do so, that I could be of some help to you in . . . handling this debt."

"You can take care of it?" She looked up at him, and he wanted to grasp her in his arms and kiss her lush pink lips until she satisfied the burning passion that had dwelt in him from the first moment he had seen her.

"I'm a very wealthy man, Tara, my dear," he said softly. "And I'm more than sure we can make some satisfactory arrangement that will give us both what we want."

Tara could bear his touch no longer. She rose to her feet and

15

moved a few steps away from him. Then she turned to face him again.

"And just what is it you expect in return for your so generous offer, Mr. Bradley?" she asked in a voice she held in fragile control.

"I expect just a small amount of generosity on your part, my sweet Tara. We could have a lovely relationship. I could see you are well cared for."

"And what of your wife?" Tara asked sweetly.

"She need never know. It would be a very . . . quiet and comfortable arrangement."

Tara's rage was so complete she was momentarily speechless. Then she tried to gather some semblance of self-control. She walked slowly to her father's desk and opened a drawer. She reached in and took out a small derringer, which her father had kept there, and pointed it at Walter Bradley.

"That is a disgusting proposal, Mr. Bradley, and I would like you to leave at once before I decide to shoot you and claim you attacked me in my own house."

"Don't be foolish, Tara. If I walk out of here, your house is lost to you. What will you do? You'll be on the street. Being my mistress is much more reasonable."

"I would rather sleep on the street," she snapped angrily. "I am becoming both very nervous and very angry. I am warning you to leave before I lose control of this gun," she smiled. "I might miss your heart and shoot off something you seem to consider very important."

"You'll regret this," he snarled as he began to move toward the door. "I'm leaving. You have two weeks. Either you come to me . . . or you get out of this house. The decision is yours."

"I've made my decisions."

"Then you live with it," he replied coldly. He left the room, and in a minute Tara heard the front door close.

She laid the gun on the desk because she was shaking too much to hold it any longer.

Two weeks! What could she do? Where could she go? There

was no one to turn to. She had two weeks to make a choice.

At that moment, her attention was caught by her brother's letter that still lay on the table.

David! David, of course. She need only get to her brother and he would see that she was safe. They could stay together, travel together, and wherever they went she could make a home for him, at least until one of them decided to marry.

But Fort Lyon was so far away. In fact, she really had no idea just how far it actually was. Of course, she reasoned, she need only buy a railroad ticket and it would most likely take her somewhere near Fort Lyon. Surely she could find some transportation from the railroad depot to Fort Lyon.

She looked about her. It would be heartbreaking to sell the things she had lived with and loved for so long. But she had to. It was the only way.

The next morning she went to the train station, to be met by her first disappointment.

"Fort Lyon, miss? No, there's no train that goes anywheres near the fort. The best I can do is get you to Ellsworth, Kansas. From there on, I expect you'd have to wait for a military escort that might be going that way or find a wagon train goin' west. Them's the only means into Fort Lyon."

Her obvious disappointment urged the man on. "That ain't no place for a pretty young thing to think of going. There's still wild Indians out there and I hear tell they're still warring on us and scalping people right and left. No, sir, you oughta just stay right here in Washington."

Tara had no way to tell him that staying here was just as dangerous for her. She simply smiled politely. "Please give me a ticket to Ellsworth. I'll be leaving some time next week."

The man sighed, raised his eyebrows, and shook his head negatively in the face of what he considered a typical female reaction to reason. Then he prepared the ticket and gave it to her. She paid him and smiled again, knowing that his avid curiosity would remain unanswered.

From the train station she went to Reginald Jacobs's home,

17

where both he and his wife were shocked when she told them her plans. She refused, in her own pride, to speak of Walter Bradley's offer.

Reginald Jacobs objected strenuously, but Tara was adamant. "I'm going to my brother, Mr. Jacobs. I've already bought my ticket and I leave next week. I need your help to facilitate the sale of everything, so I can take as much money as possible."

"But the house . . ." Reginald began.

"I'm afraid the bank owns that," she said dryly. "I just have the possessions in the house and my mother's jewelry. Will you help me?"

"Since you insist on having it this way, of course I will help you. I will take care of everything as rapidly as possible. But in the meantime, I insist on one condition."

"A condition?" she said warily.

"Until you leave, you stay here with me and my wife as our guest. It is bad enough that your things must be sold, but to stand and watch it being done is unbearable. We want you to stay with us until it is time to go."

"You're both so very kind," Tara said, with tears glistening in her eyes. "I would be delighted to stay."

"Good," he smiled. "Now come in and let us discuss the sale . . . and your plans."

Chapter 2

Tara watched all her worldly possessions being sold. She tried to control her anguish and shed her tears only at night, when she was alone.

The time drew close for her to leave, and she began to go through her clothes, discarding some. She realized she could take only a limited amount of clothing with her.

Finally the day came, and Reginald Jacobs and his wife took her to the train station. They had grown quite fond of Tara during her stay with them, but they could not seem to penetrate her determination to go to her brother. She kissed them both a fond good-bye, amid tears and admonitions to take good care of herself and please write. They waved farewell and watched the train chug from the station. Tara stood on the back platform and watched Reginald Jacobs and his wife slowly recede until she could see them no longer. She suddenly felt the terribly oppressive feeling that she would never return home and never see her friends again. She inhaled deeply and clenched her teeth. She was not one to weep over unhappy wishes. She would face whatever life had to offer. After all, she thought, she still had her brother.

She and David had been very close, and Tara knew he would more than welcome her. It would be quite a surprise, but she knew he must have been informed by the military of their parents' death. Surely David would get her letters before she arrived, and he would be waiting for her.

She went back into the train and settled herself in for the long ride to Ellsworth. Knowing she must make traveling plans from there, she was secure that she had enough money to buy passage to Fort Lyon.

As the conductor came past to take her ticket, Tara questioned him.

"How long will it take us to get to Ellsworth?"

"Oh, I reckon, barring any trouble, it'll take 'bout four days."

"Four days!" She, who had never given a thought to the immense distance between her home and Ellsworth or to the tremendous size of the wilderness she was going to, found it rather difficult to imagine.

"Yes, ma'am, four days. You'd best be grateful for the cars old George Pullman rigged up. At least you'll be able to get some rest on the way. Still, it's a pretty hard trip for a woman."

"Can you tell me a bit about Ellsworth?" she queried, ignoring his words of caution. She had no choice in traveling, but she did not feel she had to explain that to him.

"Well, Ellsworth is kinda rough. In fact, it's a rollicking, riotous, trail-end town."

"Trail-end?"

"That means Texans bringing herds north. After months on the trail, they kinda let loose in Ellsworth. There's probably several hundred parched and well-heeled cowboys there, 'bout this time. I hope someone's meeting you, miss, because Ellsworth can be a real wild town."

If Tara was afraid, she had absolutely no intention of letting him know it.

"I'll be fine, really. Tell me, how does one make arrangements to get from Ellsworth to Fort Lyon?"

"Fort Lyon is another long pull. There's usually a wagon train goin' 'bout this time of year, or maybe some of the military might be in town and you could travel back with them.

20

You got kin at Fort Lyon?"

"Yes, my brother."

"Maybe he'll come to Ellsworth to meet you."

Tara doubted if David had enough time to do so, but again she smiled. "Most likely he will. Thank you."

Slightly worried about this very beautiful and somewhat delicate, helpless-looking girl, he spoke again. "Miss, you'd best be careful. This town can be mean. If you need help, old Marshall Morton and his boys, Crawford and Brown, should be told right away."

"I'll do that. I'm grateful for your concern."

He nodded, smiled, and moved away, still worried about the stubborn set of her chin.

Tara returned to her contemplative look out the window. It was certain she must find a wagon train going west that would take her to the fort.

Oh, well, she thought, that is four days away. Right now I have to worry about today.

The four days of travel had sapped her strength and her resolve. From the window of the train she saw civilization slowly disappear and the wilderness just as slowly grow.

She was more than pleased when the conductor, now a very friendly face, came by to inform her that they would reach Ellsworth before sunset.

"You best see that someone gets your baggage to Drover's cottage. It's pretty good there; they got nigh onto eighty rooms. Run by Mr. and Mrs. Gore and Mr. George. You can get settled before the sun goes down, and you'll be away from the streets come night."

"I will, Mr. Grove," Tara smiled. "You've been so very kind to me. I shan't forget you."

"Well, I wish you well, miss," he laughed. "Although I expect the 'miss' will be changed just as soon as these boys out here get a look at that pretty face. There's not too many nice women like you hereabouts. Yes, sir, someone will snatch you up right quick."

21

Tara smiled, not caring to inform him that she was not quite willing to be "snatched."

The train slowly chugged to a halt and Tara saw her first glimpse of Ellsworth. She faced the business section, which was about three blocks long. The store buildings, mostly one-story and two-story frame structures with wooden awnings on the front, lined the outer side of the street and faced the railroad. Here and there structures of brick had been erected. Board sidewalks were generally in use. The main street ran along both sides of the railroad, making two streets called North and South Main.

When Tara disembarked, she stood on the wooden platform and looked about. She stood almost directly across from Beebe's General Store. From where she stood, she could read some of the identifying signs of D. W. Powers Bank, Minnich and Hounsons's brick drugstore, and John Bell's Great Western Hardware Emporium. She could see four saloons and a furniture store, then the sheriff's office.

She was about to enter the railroad station when a young man appeared at her side. He bowed slightly and smiled.

"Mr. Grove said you'd be needing some help to get to the hotel, miss. My name is Timothy Harper. I've a wagon here, and I can carry your baggage down."

"Why, thank you. That was very nice of Mr. Grove to tell you."

"He's sort of related, ma'am. He's my uncle by marriage. I have a small place on the other side of those hills. But I'd be right pleased to drop you and your belongings at the hotel."

She agreed, and he immediately secured her baggage in his wagon, then aided her in climbing to the wagon seat.

The drive down the main street was slow, and she again took the time to absorb the activity about her.

The resident population of Ellsworth in these cow-town days was about one thousand. Their chief business was trafficking in cattle and trade with cattlemen.

Tim informed her that when herds came in from Texas,

22

there could be as high as one hundred seventy thousand head of cattle in the pens outside of town and in the areas just beyond. The population would grow accordingly.

"Tell me, Tim, if I wanted to go on to Fort Lyon, what would be the best way?"

"Fort Lyon, miss?" He whistled. "That's sure a long haul. But you might just be in luck. I hear Caleb Banning is taking another wagon train out pretty soon. He is most likely on the way to California. He might just consider takin' you."

"Where can I find him?"

"Right offhand, miss, I don't know. But you can check with Sheriff Whitney. He knows just about everything that goes on here."

They had reached the hotel, and he and Tara carried her baggage inside. She thanked him again and made her room arrangements. Her baggage was deposited in her room, and she took the key and put it in her reticule.

When she came down the stairs of the hotel, again she stopped at the front desk and requested guidance to Sheriff Whitney's office.

"Sheriff Whitney, ma'am?" the clerk responded with curiosity in the depths of his eyes. "Is something wrong?"

"No," she smiled. "I just want to talk to him. Where can I find him?"

"He'll be in his office, I suppose. If he's not, his deputy can tell you where to find him."

"Thank you." Turning away before his burning curiosity could be put into words, Tara left the hotel. She stood on the boardwalk for a moment to locate the sheriff's office. Then she walked toward it. Quite aware of the eyes that followed her progress, she did her best to ignore them. She stopped only for a moment outside the sheriff's office, then with a determined firmness, she opened the door and walked in.

The room was not large, containing only a potbellied stove on which sat a pot of coffee, a desk cluttered with papers, and a low bench that rested against the wall. Beyond the desk was a

23

wooden door, behind which were three iron-barred cells. Behind the desk sat a tall, extremely thin man. His hair was dark, and he wore a short beard and full mustache. His eyes were clear blue and crinkled at the corners as he smiled and rose from his chair.

"Sheriff Whitney?" she requested quietly.

"Yes, miss. You're new in Ellsworth. Is there something I can do to help you?"

"Yes, please. I'm looking for a Mr. Caleb Banning."

"Caleb Banning," his brow furrowed.

"Is he here in Ellsworth?"

"Yes, he's just getting together the last of a wagon train."

"That's exactly what I want to see him about."

"Oh, I see. Are you and your family moving west?"

"I'm afraid there is no family, Sheriff Whitney. I'm going west."

"Alone?" he queried. Now he was frowning deeply. "A wagon train is no place for a lady alone. I'm not too sure Banning would even take you."

"I'd like to ask Mr. Banning if I might. I can most certainly pay my own way."

"I don't think money would be the problem. You're a woman alone. That has a lot of dangers. It's kind of hard to explain."

"If that is meant to frighten me, Sheriff, it's unsuccessful. I have a brother at Fort Lyon. He's all the family I have left since my parents both died in an accident a short while ago. I must get to my brother."

"Why, Miss . . ."

"Montgomery," Tara supplied.

"Miss Montgomery, you can just stay in Ellsworth. We can send someone for your brother, and he can come and fetch you."

Her annoyance was gradually growing into anger. Still she did not want to fight with him.

"I've been taking care of myself for quite some time, and I

24

intend to continue to do so even when I get to my brother. If you will just be so kind as to tell me where I can find Mr. Banning, I'll be grateful."

He did not doubt the stubborn set of her shoulders or the uncompromising eyes that held his without moving. He sighed.

"If you leave my office and walk down South Main to the end of town, you'll find a gathering of wagons. Ask around there, and someone will point out Banning to you."

"Thank you," she said quietly. Then she turned to the door.

"Miss Montgomery?"

"Yes?" Tara replied as she turned again to face him.

"I wish you would reconsider. You'll be a whole lot safer here in Ellsworth. The Indians out there are not exactly in a friendly mood."

"I'm sorry, I must go. I'm sure I'll be as safe as anyone at the fort."

She left, closing the door gently behind her. He stood and looked at the door for a moment, then shook his head negatively. "That might be just what I'm afraid of," he said softly to himself.

Following the sheriff's directions, it took Tara very little time to find the large gathering of covered wagons. People milled about in an almost orderly confusion. She stopped the first man she saw and asked where she could find Caleb Banning.

"Mr. Banning? He ain't here right now. We don't expect him until tomorrow night. I reckon he's checking on the last of the supplies and some beef we want to move along with us."

"Tomorrow night? But I thought you all were leaving soon."

"We are, as soon as Banning gets back."

Tara knew if she had to wait, she might not have time to prepare for the trip. As if the man could read her thoughts, he smiled. "You wantin' to go with this train?"

"Yes, I do."

"Well, where's your man and your wagon? I guess we could

help you get ready."

"I don't have either one," Tara replied, knowing now the reaction she was going to get. "I'm going to be traveling alone."

"Ma'am, I don't think any wagonmaster has ever taken a woman alone before. It's a hard trip. Besides, who would you bed down with if you don't have a wagon of your own?"

Tara was determined she was not going to be defeated by all the people who kept telling her what she could not do. She meant to be leaving for Fort Lyon on this train no matter what she had to do.

"Is there someone else I can talk to, some second in command?"

"Well, I guess so. It might be best if you talked to Zach Hale. He's sort of the chief guide out on the prairie. I guess we most like take orders from him. But I wouldn't get my hopes up with him."

"Where can I find him?"

"He's clear down the other end of the wagon. The last one is his. There'd be his driver and him."

"But I thought he was the guide."

"Sure, miss, but he needs a place to sleep and to store his own supplies. Although, I'll admit Zach Hale ain't one to spend time in that wagon. Sometimes he just eats there. His driver is his cook."

"Why doesn't he eat with everyone else? I'm sure you all eat together."

The man looked uncomfortable for a minute, then he replied gruffly, "I guess he just wants to be alone." He walked away before she could question him further.

Tara walked through the tangled group of people, making her way slowly toward a wagon that sat a little apart from all the rest. It seemed to her this Zachary Hale wanted to stress his solitary inclinations.

As she drew closer, a man walked around the wagon and stood with his back to her. His attention was on something he

26

was placing within the wagon. She stopped for a moment to examine him closely.

He was quite tall, and she could see the breadth of his shoulders were unpadded, for he wore only a buckskin shirt and leather breeches. He also wore Indian-type moccasins that enclosed his legs from below the knee and were tied with strips of leather.

His hair was dark, but the glint of the sun lifted the deep wine color to an auburn glow. It was long, touching his collar, and a band of red cloth was tied about his head. He gave the impression, even with his back to her, that he was immensely strong. His waist and hips were lean and solid.

She moved closer and closer, walking quietly. She was only a few feet from him when he suddenly sensed her presence. He spun around so abruptly that she gave a small cry of surprise and stepped backward a step or two.

If she had been seized by the wild untamed aura of him from the back, the sensation increased when she was caught in his penetrating blue gaze, which was so totally out of touch with the rest of him that she could only stare.

His skin was tanned a golden brown, but she knew immediately this was always his color and not the result of the sun.

She remained silent, quite unable to find adequate words under the intensity of his gaze.

Suddenly he smiled a white quick smile and moved toward her. She was crowded with the feeling that she was being stalked by some untamed beast of the wild as he moved slowly to tower above her.

"You look lost, little girl," he chuckled. "Can I help you with something?"

"I . . . ah . . . I'm . . ." She grew angry at the definitely unsettling effect he had on her and of his amused reference to her as a little girl. Her cheeks grew pink, but she clenched her teeth together and returned his gaze. She would most certainly mention his arrogance to whomever was in command. "I'm looking for Zachary Hale. I'm told he is the second in command here since Mr. Banning is not yet here."

"Well," he said softly, his eyes skimming over her, making her more uncomfortable and her cheeks hotter, "you're looking at him. What can I do for you?"

She felt a surge of dismay, followed quickly by a resounding surge of defiant stubbornness. He was not going to be allowed to intimidate her by that half smile and the knowing, almost inviting look she saw in his eyes.

"Mr. Hale, I've come to sign on with the wagon train."

"Now don't tell me," he laughed, "that I've the misfortune to meet the prettiest girl in six nations, and she's gone and gotten herself married to some storekeeper."

"I'm not married," she grated, "and it's none of your business if I were. I want to sign on and go west to Fort Lyon with this train."

"Where's your wagon?" he snapped. "Who's traveling with you?"

"Ah . . . I don't have a wagon yet. But I can buy one. And I don't need anyone to travel with me. I'm quite capable of taking care of myself."

Now he laughed aloud, and it took great effort to contain her urge to strike him.

"You have no wagon, no supplies, no driver, and you want to go west. My God, little girl, this is not a Sunday afternoon stroll. Go back east where you belong."

"I've enough money to buy whatever I need and more than enough to hire a driver. I want to sign on with this train. I have to get to Fort Lyon."

"Ah, I see," he said softly. "Did somebody kiss you and run away? I must say he had to be pretty special to get you to chase halfway across the territory to get to him."

Now she was well past anger. She sucked in her breath and held it only seconds before she lost control.

"There's not a man walking I'd chase anywhere. Why do simpleminded people like you always think a woman needs a

28

man to guide her around by the hand? Why I'm going to Fort Lyon is none of your damn business. From what I understand, you're only a guide. I want to sign on this train!"

His eyes grew brilliant, both with his own anger and a dawning respect for her.

"I'm the guide, which means I can say who goes and who stays. I'm here to see that what is done is for the best of the entire train. Taking along a pretty unattached girl like you means trouble. You have no wagon, no driver, and no supplies. So, the answer is still no. You can't go with this train."

"You are a stubborn, opinionated, arrogant, miserable wretch! Why can't I?" she nearly shouted. "I can buy whatever is necessary. And I'm asking for no help from you!"

'What's your name?"

"Tara Montgomery. Why?"

He came so close to her that she could feel the strength of him. She could smell the intensely male scent of him, and she looked up, startled, into eyes that promised more than her imagination could conceive.

"Because, little girl," he said softly, "you might be in more danger from me than from any threat on the trail. You're sweet and pretty . . . and the trail is long and hard. Men get ideas. You'd better think of that. The answer is still no. Go back home and marry some gentleman and forget this . . . or you might bite off more than you can chew."

She couldn't battle the words and the reflections in his eyes. His overpowering masculinity took away her breath . . . but not her grim determination that he would not best her. There was still Caleb Banning. Tara spun away from him, and she heard his soft laugh as she walked away.

Laugh now, you arrogant bastard, she thought. But the last laugh might still be mine.

Chapter 3

Zach stood and watched Tara walk away, her back rigid with her anger. What he had done was done deliberately. He had seen both her beauty and her vulnerability in one quick glance.

He was much too close to finding the answers he wanted. What he needed now was a smooth, uneventful trip, where he could keep close watch on Caleb Banning and find out how not only guns and ammunition, but also whiskey, were finding their way to the dissidents of the combined tribes, young men whose tempers could be stirred against the ever-encroaching whites. He had to find the reason for stirring the Indians into forgetting they could be reduced to an even worse condition than they already were. Someone wanted the Indians to join together and to fight. He was heartsick with the certainty that the purpose was to see them ultimately destroyed, or at least relegated to a place where someone's plans could not be interfered with. What did they have to gain? That was his unanswered question. He knew the white world too well. There had to be a goal that meant profit for someone. But who and what were answers he still reached for.

The very last thing he needed was a creature like this copper-haired beauty to add fuel to the simmering fire.

Zach knew Caleb Banning well. He was a handsome and completely conscienceless man. He liked his women. He had the ability to charm them until they were too lost to escape, when he chose to be rewarded for his efforts.

Zach was more than pleased that he had effectively stopped her from joining them before Caleb had had a chance to see her. She would never know that he had forced her anger for her own protection, but still he was relieved that he had.

"Tara Montgomery." He repeated her name, taking a moment to enjoy how pretty she was before he forced her from his mind. Much as he might have enjoyed pursuing her friendship just a little more, he would be damned if he'd lead one lone, beautiful girl into a danger she might not survive.

He went back to his work, prepared to put Tara Montgomery from his mind.

Tara was furious, and by the time she got back to the hotel, she could hardly contain her anger. Inside her hotel room she threw her reticule across the room.

"Arrogant bastard!" She satisfied her urge to vent her dislike of Zachary Hale. "You're not finished with me yet!"

She sat in deep thought for a while, then rose and went down to the front desk.

"Yes, miss, may I help you?"

"Yes. Do you know of Caleb Banning? The man who will take the wagon train west?"

"Know of him? Well, I know him a little. He won't likely be in town until later tonight."

"Does he have a room here?"

"Yes, ma'am, he does. He most likely will be here along about eleven or so, and he'll have a couple of drinks before he goes to bed."

"Mr? . . ."

"Dobbs," he supplied.

"Mr. Dobbs, if I make myself comfortable in that chair over there, will you be so kind as to point out Mr. Banning when he arrives?"

31

"Yes, ma'am. But it will be a couple of hours yet, at least."

"Can I find someplace to get a good meal?"

"The hotel dining room has good food."

"Thank you." She smiled again and he smiled back. Then he watched her walk to the dining room he had pointed out, with wishes in the back of his mind that might have startled Tara.

Tara finished a meal that she thought was quite good, even though they were so far from the fine restaurants of Washington. She returned to the hotel lobby, where she found a comfortable seat. She had a good view of the desk clerk, who smiled in acknowledgment of her presence.

It took more than an hour for him to arrive at the hotel. Tara felt she would have known him without the clerk's gesture toward her. She rose from her seat as Caleb Banning turned and walked toward her with a smile of pleasure on his face.

He was tall and well structured. She would have guessed he was at least six feet tall. His hair was pale gold and he had a mustache just a little darker. As he drew closer, she could see his eyes were steel-gray. He was quite a handsome man. The appreciation she saw in his eyes would, she fervently hoped, make her plans a little easier.

"Miss Montgomery?" he questioned in a deep voice. "Mr. Dobbs has told me you would like to speak to me."

"Mr. Banning?"

"Yes, Caleb Banning," he responded with an even warmer smile. "I should be very pleased if you would call me Caleb. And you are?"

"Tara Montgomery."

"Tara Montgomery, a lovely name for an even lovelier lady. How can I help you?"

Her first thought was that he was so much more the gentleman than the cold and arrogant guide, Zachary Hale.

"You can be of a great deal of help to me," she smiled as warmly as she could.

"Come sit down and we'll talk." He touched her elbow lightly as he guided her back to her chair, then dragged a

32

nearby chair closer.

"Mr. Banning," she began.

"Caleb . . . please." He smiled again.

"Caleb. Are you the man in charge of taking a wagon train west?"

"Yes, we're due to leave day after tomorrow. I have only a few last-minute supplies to arrange. Why?"

"I want to leave with you."

"Well, I see no reason why you cannot go. Just bring your wagon and your family. Make sure you have a very good driver. Of course, I'm sure you already have, but—"

"Mr. Banning, I'm afraid I have not as yet bought my wagon and supplies. I thought you might give me a little help with that."

"Your wagon," he repeated, then his eyes narrowed slightly, "and your driver?"

"I'm afraid there is no driver yet, either. . . . And there is no family. I am alone and I must make this trip. It is imperative that I get to Fort Lyon. You are the only train leaving."

"Miss Montgomery, this is a very dangerous trip for a strong man. But for a girl as—"

"Helpless?" she supplied. "I assure you, I am quite strong and not afraid to work. I'm sure I can hire a driver. I must go." She bent toward him, her eyes pleading.

"I never suggested you were helpless," Caleb said with a smile. "I suppose I could get you a driver, and supplies and a wagon are not all that difficult." He seemed to be considering. What she did not know was that Caleb had already decided to take her. But his decision was based upon ideas she had no notion of. Ideas that would blend with his plans and enrich his future profits.

"Please, Caleb, I'll be no trouble to you."

"All right," he said, as if he had struggled for a decision and had finally made it.

He knew she would not cause him any trouble, and he intended to eventually give her a great deal of pleasure himself.

33

When the time was right, she would be an asset he would enjoy, then be rewarded for providing to others.

"Do you agree?" Tara asked excitedly.

"You get some sleep. Meet me here in the morning and I will take you to get a wagon and the supplies you need. I personally will provide you with a driver."

"Thank you, Mr. . . . Caleb. I'm grateful for your understanding. I'll manage to take care of myself. I'll be no problem to anyone."

She stood and he stood beside her. Caleb was an extremely charming man, and he knew how to use his charm. "You are not to worry," he said soothingly. "I'm sure you will be well worth the effort." He patted her arm, enjoying her relaxed smile before she turned to go up the stairs to her room. Caleb stood and watched her go. What a lovely creature she is, he thought. She should make the tedious trip much more enjoyable, as well as more profitable.

He had much to negotiate with for what he wanted, which was whiskey and rifles. . . . But now he could add cream. . . . He knew only too well Tall Bull's delight in the possession of white women. Tall Bull would negotiate a lot for this one. Caleb chuckled, then he too went to his room. He sat down at a small table, checking to make sure he had tied up all the loose ends.

Tara rose very early the next morning. She dressed and went down the stairs to get information on Caleb Banning's room number. She was surprised to find him already waiting for her in the lobby.

"Caleb," she smiled. "I had not expected to find you here so early."

"You'll find, my dear Tara, that on the trail you will most likely be rising every morning before the sun does."

"Every morning?" she said, aghast at such a thought.

"Every morning," he chuckled. "And I'm afraid there will be very few of the luxuries you have been used to."

"I'm not a child who weeps for little things, Caleb. I need to get to Fort Lyon, and I'm quite willing to face whatever needs facing."

"Very good. Now, I have made arrangements with the shopkeeper to open early. If you have your money, let's get on with the purchase of what you will be needing. Oh, by the way, I've taken the liberty of getting a wagon for you."

"A Conestoga?" she asked, hoping to feel intelligent about a word she had heard someone speak.

"Where did you hear that?" he laughed.

She laughed with him. "I heard someone say it yesterday. Is that what I've bought?"

"Well, it's not a Conestoga. They're way too big for the roadless prairie. They weigh over a ton and a half. You'll have something just a bit smaller, but more maneuverable."

"Well, what do you call them?" she insisted.

He looked into her eyes and laughed again, his eyes glowing with humor. "A wagon," he replied. Tara had to laugh with him.

They walked together to the store where she would be able to buy the equipment and supplies she needed.

She was surprised at the amount of supplies she would need.

"Should I save some money for later?"

"Where are you going to spend it? If you run out of anything out on the prairie, there's no store to buy it from. Now, just take everything I recommend."

She nodded, realizing more and more that she knew so very little about prairie travel.

Blankets, flour, salt, kitchen utensils, clothes, water keg, cooking pot, ax, and folding camp stool were carried behind the store, where Tara was given the first view of the wagon she would call home for a long time.

The wagon had a billowing cloth top that arched above a sturdy frame of hickory boughs, which could be rolled back for ventilation. It was waterproofed with paint or linseed oil and made of heavy canvas. It had massive axles to support the

35

weight of the wagon and the supplies. On one axle hung a grease bucket filled with a mixture of animal fat and tar.

The large wooden wheel with wide iron rims would ride easily over humps and hollows in the trail and help keep them from sinking into soft ground. The lighter the wagon, the less likely it would sink into muddy stream-banks or prairie sloughs. Also, it wouldn't tire the long-suffering teams that pulled them such tremendous distances.

"There really won't be much room in there once all these supplies are packed," Tara said. "Where shall I sleep?"

"Well, Tara my dear, when the weather is favorable, you will sleep outside. You will sleep inside only when it rains."

"Outside . . . on the ground?"

Caleb laughed heartily. "Yes, my dear, outside on the ground, padded well with blankets, most likely under the wagon."

"Oh," Tara whispered softly.

"Just about everyone does, Tara. You won't be alone. All the women find their beds so. Does it upset you? Do you wish to change your mind?"

She could change it so easily, she was afraid. But what did she have to return to? "No," she said quietly, "I do not intend to change my mind."

"I knew you were a very courageous young lady," Caleb said gently. "It will be a very great pleasure to share this trip with you."

She knew he wanted to make her more confident, but she felt the first touch of early uncertainty . . . as if she were moving into something deeper and much more dangerous than the elements she would soon face.

"Ah . . . well, thank you," she responded, drawing herself a little away from him. His eyes had seemed to penetrate her, making her nerves shriek a warning. . . . But a warning of what? He had done nothing but help her.

"Now, while all the supplies you have just purchased are packed, you will return to the hotel and have breakfast, then

36

we can settle any other details during the rest of the day."

She nodded, wanting to be in the company of people. They walked back to the hotel and into the dining room where, to Tara's surprise, they found another man awaiting them.

He rose as Caleb and Tara approached him. He was dark, which seemed to overpower Tara. His eyes were black, his hair was black and long, his skin was dark, and the clothes he wore were also dark. He was an extremely large man and heavily muscled, with a powerful chest and arms.

"Tara, this is Brace. He will be your driver. He can handle a wagon better than any man I know. He will be able to take care of any . . . problems that might befall you on the trail. He's a dead shot in case of Indian attack."

"Indians! Attack!" she groaned. Things were rapidly going from bad to worse. She was truly frightened now, and she stood teetering on the edge of quitting. She turned to Caleb and was about to say the words that would keep her safely in Ellsworth . . . when another voice cut through the silence.

"Just what do you think you're doing? This girl is not leaving with our train. I've already told her she could not go."

Tara spun around to face a dark visage with crystal blue eyes, blazing with fury.

Tara turned back to Caleb, whose eyes were hard, even though his lips twitched with amusement.

"What is the problem, Zach?" His voice was biting. "Do you find it too difficult to add one more wagon to the lot? Is it too much for you?"

Zach was very obviously trying to control his anger. His eyes held Tara while he spoke to Caleb.

"I have already told her we don't take helpless females along. She's a woman alone, with no equipment. She doesn't go," Zach stated firmly.

"Well, I hate to upset you, Zach, but she has just bought all the equipment she'll need, and I've provided her with a driver. You haven't forgotten, have you, that you are only our guide, while I am the owner?"

37

Zach's face became suddenly very still and very unreadable. Those who knew him better would have told anyone that this was when Zachary Hale was the most dangerous.

Zach had to stay with the wagon train. It was the only place to find the answers he needed. But to do this he must endanger a girl so beautiful she took his breath away. It would be a contest. Could he find his answers and still protect Tara? Or would she be a price to be paid to protect so many more lives?

It was Tara who made the choice for him. She turned to Caleb and Brace. "Thank you for all your effort, Caleb, and I accept your driver gratefully. I'll be ready to leave first thing in the morning." She turned again to face Zach. "Since, as Caleb says, you are only the guide, then I imagine you have nothing more to say about it. I'll be leaving for Fort Lyon with you in the morning."

"You're making a very foolish mistake, little girl," Zach said quietly. "This is a trip filled with more danger than you can imagine. You had better think about your decision."

"I have thought about it," Tara said coldly. "I'm not afraid. I'm sure as a guide," she said bitingly, "you can protect us from Indian attack."

"Maybe you can, Zach," Caleb said in a taunting voice. "After all, who knows them better than one of their own?"

Tara's eyes widened, and Zach missed nothing about her shock. The angry bitterness filled him again. He had seen this look of arrogant white man surprise many times, but this time, to his own surprise, it stung.

"Don't worry about me, Caleb, I can get us through safe. But you're creating another problem with her that just might endanger everyone else on the train."

Annoyed that Zach spoke to Caleb as if she were not even present, Tara's resistance grew, smothering the feeling that there was some kind of electrical current between these two men. They were working together, but she still had the feeling they both disliked and distrusted each other.

"That responsibility is mine, Zach," Caleb said softly.

"Your job is just as a guide. I make the final decisions. So she goes. She has all her equipment, so we'll still be ready to leave first thing in the morning."

Tara watched Zach's eyes, which had become like chips of frigid blue steel. But he smiled and shrugged as if the battle, fought and lost, were no longer of concern to him.

"All right, Caleb, if that's the way you want it. It was my job to warn you about trouble."

"I consider myself warned." Caleb's smile was no colder than Zach's.

"Oh," Zach said as an afterthought, "she won't need Brace to drive. I just found out we have an extra driver already handy. Brace can ride with me . . . if you still want him to go along. He's not really needed."

If Caleb was angry at Zach's effort to rid the train of Brace's presence, he said nothing. He smiled and turned to look at Tara.

"That is up to Tara."

Zachary did not miss Caleb's use of Tara's name, as if they were developing some special friendship. That, too, annoyed him, and he couldn't believe his own reactions.

Not wanting to irritate Zach any further, in the hopes that they might at least develop some kind of fragile friendship on the trail, Tara nodded, "If Mr. Hale has someone in mind to drive my wagon, I see no reason why he shouldn't. I do thank you for the offer of a driver, though."

"Well, then," Caleb smiled, "it looks as though we're ready to leave in the morning. Tara, would you join me for dinner tonight?"

"Why, yes, I would be pleased," Tara responded. Caleb nodded, motioned to Brace, and the two left. For a long moment, Zach and Tara looked at each other in silence.

"Mr. Hale . . ."

"No need for words," he said roughly. "You've had your way, as I suppose you're used to. But you're in for a very hard time. You have tonight to think your foolishness over."

39

He turned and left her abruptly before she could snap back a retort. She could only inhale deeply as she tried to control the urge to run after him and strike him as hard as she could . . . only she wasn't too sure whether he would strike her back.

She returned to the hotel, where she made sure the last of her clothes was prepared for morning. She was frightened and excited at the same time.

When she went downstairs later after bathing and dressing carefully for her last meal in civilized society, she found Caleb already waiting for her.

They had a pleasant dinner, and even though they did not speak of Zachary, his presence hung in the air.

Caleb tried to tell her of the more pleasant aspects of the journey, such as the beauty of the untamed country and the friends she would surely make as they traveled.

Tara was quite relaxed and ready to face the trip as Caleb walked her to the door of her room. She unlocked it, then turned to face him.

"Thank you, Caleb, for a very pleasant evening. I will see you early tomorrow."

"Good night, Tara," Caleb smiled. "I'm looking forward to us becoming good friends on this trip too."

"Good night." Tara watched him walk away, then she turned to enter her dimly lit room. She had left the lamp burning low. As she turned from the door, she gasped in shock as the pale lamplight reflected in cool blue eyes.

Chapter 4

"Are you planning on screaming?" Zach asked casually.

It was the taunting voice, coupled with the smile, that told her it was exactly what he would expect from the naive little eastern girl. She could actually feel him as a force driving her to act like the foolish girl. She was determined not to give him that satisfaction.

She smiled. "Is this a social call?" she asked quietly. "Or is this a little trip to try to talk me out of going tomorrow?"

"You are a stubborn one, aren't you?" he chuckled.

"If I were a man, you would call me courageous. Since I am a woman, I'm stubborn. Did it ever occur to you that I can't afford the luxury of distinguishing between our genders? I must do what has to be done."

"What you did was to prove a point," he said, angry that she had responded differently than he had expected. "And it was a very stupid thing. You have no idea what you're up against."

"Can't you understand that it just doesn't matter?"

"Doesn't matter! You jeopardize your life to go to some godforsaken spot, and when you're told how dangerous it is, you shrug it off like it isn't important."

"Why do you think I can't handle the trip? Is it your judgment? Well, maybe you are wrong."

"I don't think so. You're used to comforts. You're a lady and

41

this territory is not for ladies."

"And what about the other women on the trip?" she challenged.

"They're married. They have husbands and sons to care for them. You don't."

"Then I'm going to be trouble for you? Is that it?" she demanded angrily.

"Yes, damn it," he answered, surprised that his anger was growing to match hers. Losing his temper was something he very rarely did.

"Well, stop worrying, Mr. Hale," she said, so angry now her voice was like shards of ice. "I would not ask for help from you if I were dying. But neither will I back away because you don't want any more responsibility. I will be quite happy if you keep as much distance between us as possible. . . . But I will go," she emphasized the last four words.

She watched his eyes glow with a blue brilliance, the muscle in his jaw twitching as he clenched his teeth. She was absolutely certain he would have loved to have strangled her. For a minute it gave her immense satisfaction.

Then the glow of anger was just as firmly subdued. His mouth twitched into a wicked smile, and he took a few steps toward her. She held her ground, refusing to be intimidated.

He reached out a hand to run the tips of his fingers down her cheek. "Look at you," he said quietly. "Your skin is so soft and white. You're beautiful . . . delicate . . . and alone. You're making a mistake that might cost you so much more than you bargained for."

"Stop trying to frighten me," she said, her eyes holding his. "You won't succeed."

"Won't I now?" he asked. "Tell me, little girl, what will you do if some wild frontiersman decides to take a liking to you? What will you do in that case?"

Before she actually grasped the meaning of his words, an arm reached out to pull her roughly to him. Tara gasped in shock, and before she could react, his hand caught her head

42

and he took her shocked, parted lips in a kiss of overwhelming force. She struggled and writhed in his arms, but she had no leverage to move the size of him. Slowly she realized he was forcing her to move backward toward the bed.

Her struggle increased but was still ineffectual. She felt the edge of the bed at the back of her legs, then suddenly she was tumbling backward. The weight of his body pressed her against the soft mattress. His hands, which were rough and hard, began to caress her.

A ragged sob escaped unwillingly from her as she fought valiantly. She was growing dizzy from the force of his mouth as he ravaged hers. Her body began to tremble as the realization of his intent filled her.

The front of her dress was torn open by a rough hand. She groaned softly as she felt his hand cup her breast. His knee forced her legs apart, and she could feel the length of him pressing intimately against her.

She struggled to regain command of herself, mentally forcing herself to remain still, as his true intent became clear to her. He did not intend rape. . . . He intended to frighten her so badly she would run.

Tara used all her courage to gather her strength of mind and purpose. She looked up into the startling blue of his eyes. With deliberation, she made her voice as cold and hard as she possibly could.

"You dirty half-breed," she sneered. "Get off of me before I scream and have you shot for this."

The words were like ice, and Zach felt the cutting edge of them. He also began to realize a fact that came as a surprise to him. If she hadn't stopped him . . . He had begun to feel much more than he had bargained for. He couldn't believe the tables had been so neatly turned on him.

He looked down into wide green eyes. He knew she was extremely frightened. He could feel her whole body trembling. But she continued to hold his gaze, and for a moment he was stunned into admiration.

43

"What does it take to scare some sense into you?"

"Certainly not this. I just don't believe there are any men on the train that would subject me to this. Most likely I am safe from everyone but you."

Her implication that he was the only man who would be so unkind and brutal was another stinging blow to his pride. Now he meant to prove another point. One that might frighten her more.

He caught her hands and drew them above her head, holding them firmly with one of his. Her eyes widened, but she refused to back down. The mellow glow of lamplight glistened against his bronzed skin and reflected in the shimmering blue of his eyes. Slowly he bent his head and gently kissed the corner of her mouth. He heard the soft intake of breath and felt her body quiver as he continued the gentle attack. He kissed her lips, her cheeks, and her eyes, again and again, until he felt her straining away from him in desperation.

This was something she had not bargained on. She was surprised at her body's sudden heated response. He was stirring awake an emotion she had never tasted. For the first time she felt fear . . . but fear of her own self.

Her lips parted in protest, but no sound was uttered as his mouth gently took hers. His tongue was probing lightly at first, then insistently, until her mouth softened in response. She had never been kissed like this, and she felt control draining away.

He felt it the same moment she did, and with a soft laugh he suddenly stood up. He stood for a moment by the bed to absorb the sight of a beauty he could only admit to himself was the loveliest he had ever seen.

Her green eyes wide with shock, her hair disheveled by his hands, her torn dress revealing her soft flesh, all made her look and feel vulnerable and helpless.

"Think about it, little girl," he said softly. "It's wild and dark out on the trail. There just might not be anyone around to run and help you if I decide to finish what I started. Think

44

about it," he laughed again softly and left, closing the door quietly behind him.

Zach was more than sure he had finally reached her. In the morning, she would not be with the train when it left.

But he hadn't stayed to see the shock on her face turn to fury. He had not seen her rise up in anger and throw a vase of flowers against the door he had just closed. Nor did he hear her last words grated through tears of anger.

"If you ever touch me again, I will kill you Zachary Hale. . . . But you will never stop me. I will go and there is nothing you can do about it. . . . I will go."

Zach walked down the back steps of the hotel as silently as he had ascended them a short while before. He had the ability to merge with the shadows, and no one knew that he left the hotel and returned to where his wagon sat prepared for morning travel.

He climbed into his wagon and sat down to remove his boots. Then he lay back on his blanket and clasped his hands behind his head. He was in a state of profound amazement. He could still taste the softness of Tara's parted lips and smell the scent of her perfume. His body tingled with an urgent reminder that he was closer to possessing her than he had ever planned to be, and he still wanted her. The desire was a wicked-toothed monster that gnawed at his vitals, being finally subdued by sheer strength of will.

Tara Montgomery was a silk trap in which he did not have the time to get enmeshed. She was a snag in his plans. Somewhere in the wagon train a cache of rifles was hidden. He had to find out not only how they were hidden, but where their destination was and who was to collect them.

He also needed to put his finger on the answer to what Caleb Banning had to gain by forcing an Indian uprising. When he thought of Caleb, he thought again of Tara. Caleb was charming and deadly . . . like a rattlesnake. And Tara might be a victim of much more than she was prepared for.

Thoughts of her once again reminded him of the feel of her in his arms, and try as he might, he could not seem to erase her from his mind.

Despite her vulnerability, she had fought him. He could still taste the fear in her and realized it was also fear of something she had never known. This thought did very little to calm the wicked, insistent flame that burned low within him. He could have taken her. He still felt the response within her that she fought as wildly as she did him.

This would not do, he thought angrily. The trip to Fort Lyon was going to be hard enough without thoughts of her tangling up his mind, which might make him less careful than he habitually was.

He was satisfied with two things. He could put many miles between himself and the tempting Tara, for he knew, whether he had aroused her or not, he had frightened her. She would not be going with them. Secondly, she was also out of Caleb's reach as well. He had to be on his guard with a man like Caleb, and a woman like Tara between them would make his plans doubly dangerous.

He laughed softly to himself. Caleb was in for quite a shock when Tara came to him the next day and told him she had changed her mind and realized the dangers of the trip. He couldn't wait to see Caleb's face.

"Serves you right, Caleb old boy. Little girls like her should be snatched out of your reach, for their own good."

This thought was snagged on an even more elusive one. Tara had said she was going to Fort Lyon to meet someone. Was it another man in her life? He could not help but be disbelieving of a man who would ride away and leave a lovely gem like Tara to follow. What kind of man would a girl like Tara follow in the face of danger and possible death?

She meant nothing to him but an annoyance, his logical mind claimed. Why then, his senses shouted, could he still feel her soft skin on the tips of his fingers and taste the sweetness of her mouth in that one fragile moment when she had hovered on the brink of surrender?

With grim determination, he tried to push Tara from his mind. He succeeded only until sleep claimed him. Then dreams beyond which he had any control allowed her to dance back into his thoughts like a wisp of cloud-touched beauty.

Tara sat on the edge of the bed still broiling with anger . . . and another emotion to which she could attach no name. She looked down at the torn front of her dress and a soft sound came from her, as she felt again the strength of his hands against her skin. She would never admit to herself the sensations his touch had created.

He had tried to frighten her on purpose and she knew it. What confused her was the desire that he had stirred awake within her. It had shaken her with the sudden wild fury of it. She had actually wanted . . . no! No! she thought miserably. She had just been frightened. She would soon make Zachary Hale understand she was not to be intimidated by him. She was not going to allow him to be laughing at her as if she were a little girl still afraid of the dark. He was the dark. She had looked into his eyes and seen something there she could not understand. But she was not going to let that vague something force her to run from him.

She could imagine what she was going to see in his eyes in the morning when she appeared bright and early, ready to travel. She knew there was nothing he could do about it then. It would be too late to stop her. She laughed softly when she thought of how angry he might be. But it would serve him right, she thought, for using such a crude and ugly way to try to force her away from the wagon train.

She undressed and prepared for bed, still trying to erase the lingering memory of his touch from her. But she, too, failed to sleep. She, too, was caught up in disoriented dreams in which she could again feel the hard mouth that had momentarily

47

softened against hers. She could still feel the touch of his hands, which were angry and forceful at first, then turned gentle and warm. In her dreams she lost her fierce control, which allowed a new magic to weave a web she would never know when awake, that she was in danger of being caught in.

Zach was up and out of his wagon long before the first gray streaks of dawn touched the sky. He felt quite pleased with himself. Within a few hours they would be leaving. The threat of a beautiful influence like Tara had been effectively eliminated, and he had only to concentrate on the task ahead . . . First to get these people safely to Fort Lyon, then to find out where the explosive danger of rifles was coming from.

He whistled lightly as he harnessed his horses to the wagon, then set about waking the others so that fires could be built and breakfasts eaten rapidly. He would eat a quick breakfast with one of the families. He knew that Caleb preferred the luxury of a hotel room to the wagons. But that satisfied Zach as well. It would be much easier for Tara to tell Caleb when they were alone.

He grinned, thinking of the look on Caleb's face when she told him. The more he thought about it, the more he enjoyed the thought. Finally he had to chuckle aloud. The sun had started to rise. Zach patted his horse's rump as he passed by. "Yes, sir," he chuckled, "it's going to be quite a surprise to our old friend Caleb. I hope he takes the disappointment well." He had never felt more pleased with himself, forgetting completely that pride often went before a fall.

Tara, too, unable to sleep any longer, was up and dressed for over two hours before Caleb knocked on her door. She had chosen a plain blue cotton dress with several less petticoats than usual. The few clothes that had not been packed in her wagon were already in a small carpetbag that sat near the door.

48

She waited impatiently for Caleb, not admitting to herself she wanted moral support when Zachary Hale saw her coming.

Finally the knock came and she gave a ragged sigh of relief, running to the door. Caleb smiled. Even in rough cotton and a wide-brimmed bonnet to protect her from the sun, Tara was an exquisite creature to behold.

"Good morning," Caleb smiled his most engaging smile. "I know it's early, but we expect to cover at least twenty miles today, so we have to get an early start."

"I'm ready. In fact, I've been ready for quite some time."

"No qualms or second thoughts?" he inquired.

This statement made Zach jump into her mind so swiftly she had very little mental protection as she thought of the fierce way he had tried to dissuade her from the journey.

"No—no second thoughts. I have to get to Fort Lyon."

"You don't have to worry, Tara," Caleb said gently. "Just put yourself in my care. I'll make sure there is nothing for you to fear. Whatever protection you need, you'll have."

"Thank you, Caleb. I hope I don't sound childish to you. This is really a large undertaking. I'm grateful for your kindness and your consideration. I don't want to cause you or . . . anyone else on the train any problems."

"You needn't worry," he laughed. "The responsibility is mine, and as far as I am concerned, you're no problem . . . no problem at all." He pointed to her bag, "Is this all?"

"Yes, everything is in the wagon. I guess I'm ready to go."

"Then let's get started." He took the bag from the floor, let her walk out the door ahead of him, then pulled it closed behind them.

After they left the hotel, they walked to the far end of the town where the wagons waited. Tara was caught in the same emotion again. It was as if she were closing one lifetime and beginning another. As they neared the wagons, Tara was sure they would come face to face with what would soon be a very angry Zachary Hale.

They drew closer. Tara nursed the wild hope that somehow

49

she would escape Zach's notice, and they would be well on their way before they came face to face. It was a lost hope.

Zach made it a point of knowing everything that was going on and who belonged to what wagons. He did so because, one at a time, he meant to question each family and search each wagon without anyone's knowledge of what he was doing.

Tara's wagon was the only one not hitched and ready to leave. Zach stood near it, waiting for Caleb, so he would have the pleasure of unpacking it himself. His arms were crossed and his hat tipped low over his eyes. He stood relaxed and braced against the wagon frame. He was prepared to enjoy Caleb's annoyance. He was not prepared for Caleb's satisfied voice as he called out Zach's name. Nor was he prepared to see both Caleb and Tara walking toward him. He saw the defiant lift of her chin and the way her eyes met his, and he had to smile both in disbelief and in an admiration he would never admit to her. He gathered his surprise behind a calm exterior. She was a challenge and she had defeated him . . . this time.

Chapter 5

Tara watched Zach's face closely. She saw the first shocked look, quickly covered by a smile that did not reach the chilled blue of his eyes. He moved a step or two from the wagon and took off his hat as they approached. His face was touched by the same teasing smile and a look that was less than flattering. She expected some form of attack and was not disappointed.

"I see you've had all your fears consoled, Miss Montgomery. I guess all it took was a strong shoulder to lean on. It's good to know you're so . . . capable."

Her cheeks flushed at the implication that she had found solace the night before in the protection of Caleb. But she refused to rise to his bait.

"Miss Montgomery is ready, and from the looks of everyone, I guess we all are. I think we'd better get started," Caleb said. "I'm afraid we'll be moving steadily from now until well after noon," he added. "Your driver's ready if you are. I must get to the head wagon and get them started."

Tara nodded and Caleb walked away, leaving her with a still dangerously silent Zach. She watched Caleb as long as she could, purposely keeping her gaze from Zach's. Instead of moving, Zach stood close . . . too close and too silent. When she could no longer tolerate his overpowering silence, she turned to look at him. He had been studying her closely, but his

51

face was unreadable when she gazed up at him.

"Mr. Hale, if you will please move out of my way, I'll get up on the wagon and get ready. I'm sure we're holding up the train."

"You'd better change your mind while you still have the chance," he replied.

"You'd better understand," she said coldly, "I'm not afraid of you no matter what you think. I don't appreciate your cheap, tawdry way of trying to scare me. It was not a thing a gentleman would do."

"A gentleman . . . like Caleb? Are you sure you know what a gentleman is?"

"Yes," she said sharply, "like Caleb. He most certainly wasn't atrociously cruel as to try to scare me like that. Well, you didn't succeed, so please get out of my way."

Zach laughed. "No, I suppose Caleb was just what you needed." He moved aside to wave her past him. "Go on, Miss Montgomery. We'll be moving pretty quick. You've made up your mind, and I guess it's too late to change it."

Tara wasn't too sure about this smiling and accommodating Zach. She started past him and he caught her arm, jerking her close to him. His eyes blazed into her.

"Just remember this. You're taking the chances, so be prepared to take the consequences. Don't come running when you find you're in over your head."

She smiled through gritted teeth. "As long as the consequences don't include your presence, I'd be delighted to face anything." She jerked her arm from his hold and climbed up on the wagon seat beside the driver Zach had chosen more carefully than she knew. She gazed straight ahead, refusing to look in his direction again.

Zach stood for a minute, looking at Tara with the deepest desire to drag her down from the wagon seat and kiss her until she could protest no longer, combined with an equal desire to beat her until she couldn't stand up.

Finally he walked to his horse and mounted. Then he rode to

the head of the train, and it began to wind its way slowly from Ellsworth.

Within three hours the jolt of the wagon had shaken every bone in Tara's body, making her stiff and sore. To make matters worse, they showed no sign of stopping yet. She squirmed in her seat and brushed sweat from her forehead. The old white-whiskered man who sat next to her, handling the four horses that pulled her wagon expertly, laughed softly.

"Are you kinda uncomfortable, little lady?" he inquired pleasantly.

Not wanting word of any complaint to reach Zach's ears, she tried to smile and to stifle the groan that almost burst from her when they hit another rut and the wagon jolted heavily.

"I'm fine Mr. . . . I don't even know your name." She turned to look at him in surprise. She had been so caught up in her own misery that she had forgotten to even ask.

"Wal, ah ain't a 'mister' to you, little girl. Name's Barrett . . . Tobias Barrett. But," he chuckled, "most just call me Mule."

"Mule?" she questioned in surprise, not wanting to laugh.

"Yep, Mule. It's cause I'd prefer to run mules rather than horses. Got the name a whole lot of years ago, and it's kind of hung on since then."

"I will agree, Mule," she grinned, "that I've certainly ridden in more comfort."

"Now, don't let that worry you, miss. Most gets a little sore and tired first day out. You'll get used to it. By the time we reach the fort, you'll be able to ride wagon or horse all day if you cared to."

"Lord, I'd love to have a bath," she spoke half to him and half to herself.

"Wal, lessen you finds a good creek or river, you won't be taking a bath from here to the fort. Yes, ma'am. There's only the barrels of water we carry on the wagons. Oh, you can wash

53

up, but you sure ain't taking no warm baths."

"Wonderful," she muttered, quite sure Zachary Hale would make a lot of her discomfort should she let him know about it.

"Mule, when are we going to stop to eat? I'm so hungry . . . and I'm dying of thirst."

"Oh, we'll be stopping right soon."

But "right soon" turned out to be another two hours, and by the time the wagons were stopped, Tara was truly miserable.

To make matters worse, as she climbed down, she felt a strong hand reach up to help her and turned to look into blue eyes that were decidedly amused. In fact, she got the distinct feeling they were bordering on laughter.

She jerked away from his hand, and the sudden move of an already stiff and sore body brought a cry of pain just as her foot slipped and she tumbled less than gracefully into a pair of strong and too helpful arms. Hunger, pain, and anger were enhanced by the certainty that he was laughing at her.

She was mistaken about the laughter. But no one would have ever been able to convince her of that. He knew from experience how she must feel, and he had come to see if she were faring well enough to go on or if she needed help.

He knew when their eyes met that the last thing she would do would be to admit how she felt or that she needed any kind of help from him.

"Please put me down," she said, biting her lip to keep another cry of discomfort from him as he let her feet drop to the ground.

"Sorry, I thought you might fall."

"Don't worry," she said scathingly, "I'll manage without your help."

He grinned again, touching his hat as he bowed slightly and walked away.

"Oh, that man is such an arrogant, conceited . . ."

"Zach Hale?" Mule questioned. "He's a good man, that one. If anyone can get you from here to the fort in one piece with no problems, it's Zach."

"Because he's half Indian?" she inquired.

Mule turned to look at her, all smiles wiped from his face. Tara was startled by his reaction.

"Now, I tell you something, little girl," Mule said softly. "Don't you go faulting that boy cause he's a breed. His ma and pa were both fine people."

"Who was? . . ."

"His pa is an Indian."

"Have you met him?"

"I've met him a few times. His ma was real pretty."

"Was she a prisoner?"

"Hell, no! Excuse me, miss, but you're sure green. His ma stayed because she loved his pa and him, and she didn't want to leave."

"Then why does everyone seem so . . . so . . ."

"Ignorant?" Mule supplied. "That's cause most folks are. But you look too smart to be taken in by such things. I can see sparks fly when you two get together, so it might be best if you just stayed away from each other. But don't go thinkin' less of him cause he don't rub you the right way. Zach's a damn good man, and I'm proud to be a friend of his."

Tara smiled. "I'm sorry, Mule, I didn't mean to sound . . . ignorant. I'll do two things. I'll stay away from Zachary Hale . . . and I'll try to be a friend you'd be proud of, too."

Mule smiled. "I think you'll do, little girl," he said softly. "Yes, sir, I think you'll do."

Tara watched him walk away, wondering why she felt so pleased at such remarks from a rough old man called Mule.

The meal, laughingly called so, was short and, as far as Tara was concerned, hardly edible.

Long before she was prepared, they were given orders to make ready for travel again, and Tara was back atop the bone-jarring wagon and moving slowly forward. Her only consolation was that by the time she found sleep tonight, she would be one day closer to her brother and some semblance of security and safety.

*   *   *

55

Zach had tried to keep from looking back down the long line of wagons to find the one he sought. He tried but he failed. He turned in his saddle often but could barely make her out. He had known how difficult the first few days of travel might be for her, but their stop at noon had made it quite clear that she would absolutely not accept a kind word or offer of help from him. He had to chuckle at his own self. Why should he care how she managed? It was her own damn stubborn fault that she was in such a position, and she deserved whatever she got.

Zach watched as Caleb rode near her wagon and talked to her for a few minutes. What had started as suspicion and distrust of Caleb slowly and insidiously began to grow into something Zach would not have recognized if he had faced it. But he refused to face it.

The day dragged by and Zach knew they would not stop until the sun was only a red rim on the horizon. He found himself stirred by his impatience.

Their final stopping place for the night was near a small stream. The wagons were drawn into a protective circle, a position they would assume every night. A fire was built in the center and a communal meal was cooked by several women.

Mule unhitched and cared for the horses while Tara, who had completely lost her appetite, spread a blanket and sat in the shadows of her wagon. Mule knelt near her when he returned.

"Are you all right, little girl?"

"Oh, Mule," she half sobbed and half laughed, "I simply must have some water. I'm so exhausted and I hurt so much."

"Wal, there's a stream nearby, just beyond those trees. How about I get you something to eat first and some hot coffee."

She nodded without really hearing him, and Mule tramped away.

Tara felt a deep black well of self-pity swelling up inside her. She wanted to cry but didn't even have the strength for that. She gave a thought to the wonderful idea of a deep pool of water in which she could immerse her bone-weary body. She struggled to her feet and fished around in her wagon until she found a blanket. Then she made her way to the stream, which was a greater distance from the wagon than she thought.

Zach had come to her wagon minutes after she had gone. First he looked inside and then under it, in case she had decided to go to sleep. But he was puzzled when he couldn't find her. It was then that Mule decided to return with a dish of food and a cup of steaming coffee. For a minute they just looked at each other, both expecting the other to clear up the mystery of where Tara was.

"Mule," Zachary said quickly as he scowled darkly at his somewhat amused friend, "I made you her driver so you could keep an eye on her. Where is she?"

"Last I seen her, she was sitting right there waiting for me to bring her this." He set the plate of food and the coffee down. "And she wasn't feeling too good, either. You pushed her pretty hard today, didn't you? I think you knew damn well she was a greenhorn, and you meant to teach her a lesson or two."

Zach's guilt made him turn away from Mule's scrutiny. "Well, she has to be here somewhere."

"You goin' lookin'?"

"It's my job," Zachary said gruffly. "I can't just let her go wandering around alone. Don't you have any idea where she is?"

"Wal," Mule scratched his head thoughtfully, "I seem to remember her saying something about water. . . . Hey, where you goin'?"

But Zach was already disappearing around the end of the wagon and striding into the darkness.

Tara found the stream more by accident than anything else. Every move, every step took a great deal of effort. When she found the stream, she laid her blanket on the bank and removed her clothes, tossing them upon the blanket. The water did not have a swift current but eddied in pools near the edge. Not caring about the depth, she waded into it and found it just below her waist. She closed her eyes and eased down into it until the movement of the water against her began to loosen

57

tired muscles and relax her body. The water, warmed by the heat of the sun during the day, had just begun to cool, but it still felt welcome to her tangled muscles. She sat in the water, feeling it slowly cool her fevered skin.

"Come out of there." The voice was harsh and demanding, and for a moment she was disoriented. Then she recognized it. Her eyes searched the shadows, but she did not have to look long. He stepped down into the pool and grabbed her arm, yanking her up from the water.

She gave a squeal of outrage as he pulled her upon the bank, but before she could gather enough wit to fight back, she found herself wrapped in the rough wool blanket and being massaged briskly.

"Damn fool, don't you realize you could die from staying in there? It's cold in that water, no matter how good it feels. Your body would have started to cramp soon, and by morning you would be sick."

She could feel the stimulation of his hands slowly returning the life to her limbs . . . and was just as slowly beginning to gather her strength. He stopped rubbing when she abruptly stepped back from him and gathered the blanket closer about her.

They stood close . . . too close, for it was at that moment that the rising moon decided to spread its rays through the trees. Now she felt the night chill and began to shiver. "What do you care if I'm sick or not?" she whispered. He could see her clearly now and realized she was on the verge of tears. She had uprooted herself from her home to travel more than halfway across the country to find a man who obviously didn't care much. She had faced the rough day's travel with more spirit than he had thought she would show.

Now she was tired, travel-weary, lonely, and frightened. He overlooked the fact that he had told her not to come, accepting that she was now here and was, despite the courage she possessed, extremely frightened. He knew she would die in a huddle at his feet before she would admit that. This was not the time for "I told you so."

58

"Look," he said gently, "I know how you feel. The first day's travel is hard on anyone, even a seasoned traveler. You just need a little rest and some food. Tomorrow you'll be stiff, but in a day or so you'll forget all this and you'll feel much better."

The gentle touch of his voice, combined with her discomfort and loneliness, finally reached a point beyond what she could control. With a choked sob, she bent her head and allowed the threatening tears that had filled her to surface. She trembled as she wept, never even realizing that his arms came about her and that he pulled her against his chest, rocking her gently, whispering soothing and consoling words against her hair.

Zach was profoundly aware that he held a nearly naked and very vulnerable woman in his arms. In fact, under any other circumstances, he would have found the embrace a prelude to much more.

"It's all right, little one," he murmured against her hair. Gently, his hands began to soothe her. They changed from just holding her to a soft caress of her blanket-wrapped form.

Slowly, her tears were gotten under control. After a few minutes she stood silent, her cheek resting against his chest, and the firm beat of his heart was a solid relaxing sound.

Neither wanted to move; neither had the strength to break the tenuous touch. Then, slowly, Zach tipped her head up. He looked into her tear-washed eyes, saw the moist trembling mouth inches below his, and in that moment resistance was forgotten. It was a force neither of them could control.

He bent his head to taste lightly, meaning only a touch. But the intent got lost in the volatile flame that suddenly ignited within him.

Her mouth was soft, still wet with her tears. He could taste the salt of them as his tongue gently caressed, then with a seeking need, parted her lips to enjoy the sweet moist caverns of her mouth, until he could hear the soft sound of pleasure Tara never knew she had uttered.

One arm held her now, molded against him, while his other hand slipped under the blanket to touch the warm smooth

59

flesh beneath.

Tara felt as if a torrent of liquid flame was flowing through her. His mouth played softly on hers until her response began to match his. Slowly, the blanket was dropping away, and his hands were expertly stroking her body until she wanted to pour herself about him and feel the strength of him fill her.

"Tara!" The call of her name from some distance away shattered the moment and jolted them both back to reality. With a soft cry of distress, Tara bent to grasp the blanket and draw it about her. Her eyes met his in near panic. The voice was Caleb's and he was obviously searching for her.

"Get your clothes and go over there and dress," Zach whispered. "When you're finished, get back to the wagon. I'll make sure nobody knows you were here."

"If—I never meant—Oh!"

"Don't worry, Tara," he replied coolly. "No one will know you were swimming in the nude. It might draw too much attention. I'm sure old Caleb would love to join you."

"God, I'm sorry I was so foolish! This was just another part of your little idea of fun, wasn't it? What a stupid baby you must think I am. This will never happen again, that I promise you." She snatched up her clothes and faded into the darkness.

Zach fought the urge to go after her. He wanted to tell her it had never been a game, that he had been caught in the same force as her. But he knew that not only would she never believe him, but he would also make her distrust him more.

But something had been stirred to life that he could not so readily kill. His whole being sung with the desire to have her. He could not deny it at the moment, but he was determined that he would. She would be a sweet interlude, but he was suddenly shaken with the subtle idea that she might not be an interlude. She might develop into something he could not easily rid himself of or forget. Grimly, he turned from the direction Tara had vanished in and walked toward where he heard Caleb approaching.

Chapter 6

Tara groaned awake at dawn the next morning to the bustle of the train making preparations to leave. She sat up in the still-dark interior of her wagon, disoriented and uncomfortable. It took her a few minutes to reorganize her thoughts and realize she truly was over twenty miles away from Ellsworth on her way to Fort Lyon.

Memories of the past night crowded her thoughts with more misgivings. She had been sitting in her wagon by the time Caleb had returned from his search for her and his subsequent meeting with Zach. He had stopped by her wagon to check on her and Mule, who was lying on his blanket by the wagon. Mule blithely lied, saying Tara had returned and been asleep for some time.

Tara missed seeing the look of amused satisfaction in Mule's eyes. It seemed Mule was not too fond of Caleb, either.

Now she dressed hastily, knowing she would have to find some privacy in the brush, then wash quickly to be ready to leave on time. . . . And she had no plans on being late and having Zach come to see why. Tara was ready on time, and the wagon train again began to wind its way slowly westward.

Mule and Tara became friends during that second morning ride. She laughed at the wild stories of his forays in the wilderness, and he listened to her talk of her parents. He felt sorry for her only for a moment, until she explained that she didn't want pity. She wanted only to be reunited with her brother.

Mule was pleased with one thing that Tara revealed. He could now tell Zach about the man who was drawing Tara westward. He knew, despite Zach's efforts not to look interested, that he was more than interested. Mule chuckled to himself. He had a suspicion that Zach was much more interested in Tara and her welfare than he would ever admit.

They ate another rapid lunch and were on their way again. Tara was becoming more accustomed to the movement of the wagon. Mule watched from the corner of his eye and was again satisfied to see Tara's gaze constantly searching the riders to find one broad-shouldered form.

"I kinda expect we'll be stopping a little early tonight," Mule said casually.

"Early? Why?" Tara questioned.

"It's the second night out."

"I don't understand."

"It sort of takes the edge off."

"Mule, what are you talking about?"

"I reckon a pretty city girl like you would have a pretty dress in that wagon of yours, now, wouldn't you?"

"Of course I have a dress."

"Well, tonight there will be a big campfire. Zach will have a good meal fixed, and the boys will bring out their fiddles. We'll have a little party. It'll be the last one until we reach Fort Hays. There will be some drinkin' and some dancin'. Everybody will have a slam-bang good time."

"Oh, I see. That sounds like fun. When will it be?"

"I'd say just about dark."

"It will certainly be a welcome change."

"Yes, I reckon it will. It will make everybody a little more relaxed and a little easier to get close to each other. Ya see, out here folks have to be close to each other on a train. . . . It's all they got."

Tara began to think that Zachary Hale was an excellent judge of people. He seemed to know exactly when to do whatever was needed.

The day began to ebb away, but Zach made no effort to approach her or to even look in her direction. To her, it looked as if he had completely forgotten she was there. But that was far from the truth. Zach had not missed a move she had made. He had watched her relax and laugh with Mule. This pleased him, for Mule was more than a friend, and would fill him in on what Tara said and what she thought.

As Mule had said, the wagons were circled early and the large fire was built. Food was supplied by every family, and it turned into a veritable feast.

When the fiddles were brought from the wagons, everyone was laughing and sharing friendly conversations. When the music started, there were shouts of enthusiasm and people circled in the intricate square dancing.

Tara was caught up in the fun of it all and was enjoying dancing with the men from all the other wagons. When she wasn't dancing, she was clapping her hands to the beat of the music and just watching. She had not seen Zach all evening and was surprised by the fact that she missed him.

"Tara?" She turned suddenly to see Caleb standing close behind her. "I believe this is my dance."

The fiddles now had slowed to a somewhat screeching waltz, but Tara smiled and turned to raise her arms to him. He slid his arm about her waist, and they began to move into the ring of dancers, circling the embers of the large fire.

Tara began to grow uncomfortable under Caleb's intense gaze. She suddenly felt threatened, and she had no idea why. Caleb had never made an overt move toward her.

"You are exceptionally lovely by firelight," Caleb said. "You are much too lovely to be traveling alone out here. Tell me, why are you really going to Fort Lyon?"

"To meet my brother." She went on to explain that her parents were both dead, and she had no other relatives that she

63

knew of.

Caleb listened with what Tara felt was sympathetic interest. His intentions were hidden by the chameleon's mask, and his interest had been honed to a fine point. Only a brother, he thought, and a brother who did not even know Tara was on her way.

He knew, when the time came to meet and negotiate with Tall Bull, he would have a lovely incentive to add to the negotiations. But that was in the future. For now, he planned the seduction of Tara Montgomery with a master's touch. He meant to enjoy this trip to the limit. When the dance had ended, Caleb stood with Tara in the shadows near her wagon.

"You are so lovely, Tara," Caleb said softly. "You don't belong in this rough, untamed country. You belong in a beautiful mansion with lovely clothes and servants."

Tara laughed softly. "I'm afraid that will never be part of my life, Caleb. Between David and me, we do not have much in the way of material things. We have only a little bit of money and a few of Mother's things I brought with me. I shall have to settle for much less."

Caleb reached out and gently drew her close to him. "But I can offer you so much more. I have a great deal of money, Tara, and after this trip I will have a great deal more. I can offer you laughter and fun and pretty clothes."

He had been steadily drawing her closer and closer, until Tara began to resist.

"I'm not sure that's what I want, Caleb."

"It's what every woman wants," he chuckled. "And especially a woman as exciting as you. You are one of the most exciting women I have ever seen," he said, his voice lowering to a whisper. Tara felt trapped, and she couldn't understand her sudden feeling of fear.

Caleb was a strong, handsome man who had been kind and generous to her. Now he had offered her even more. Then why did she feel like running away? Why did she feel this strange resistance?

His arms were about her now, and she knew he meant to kiss

her. His mouth hovered close to hers, and she was mentally preparing for a struggle when a soft voice interrupted them, causing Caleb to spin about, a muffled curse on his lips.

"Tara," Zach smiled lazily, "I think this is the dance you promised me."

"Forget it, Zach," Caleb snapped. "The lady isn't dancing any more tonight." Tara's eyes jerked up to Caleb and denial was on her lips when Zach spoke again.

"I wasn't talking to you, Caleb, I was talking to the lady."

"I said to move away," Caleb grated.

"Caleb," Tara said firmly, "I make my own decisions. If I promised Mr. Hale a dance, then I shall honor my promise." Tara would never tell Zach that she was relieved to see him. She started toward Zach, but Caleb caught her arm. His smile, as he looked at Zach, was deadly.

"Do you really believe these people will accept a half-breed dancing with a lady?" Caleb asked softly. "Do you want to ruin her among all these fine upstanding folks?"

Zach's eyes had never left Tara, and now her startled gaze met his. The half smile on his lips never changed, only the challenge growing in his eyes as he looked at her.

"I think the lady can choose to say if she feels it's beneath her or if it will do her any harm. The choice, Tara," he added softly, "is yours."

There was a moment of breathless silence as Caleb glared at Zach and waited, assured that she would refuse. After all, Zach had been the one to give her trouble from the beginning.

Zach searched Tara's face, looking for one moment of denial, one thought that told him she meant to refuse him.

What shattered Caleb's anger and pierced Zach's uncertainty was when Tara smiled and extended her hand to Zach.

"I would be most pleased to dance with you, Zach, and the devil can take anyone who is childish enough to believe it wrong."

Zach found he could not quite believe her at first, then he smiled. She had even more courage than he had thought. He reached to take her hand, drawing her away from Caleb and back to the ring of dancers. Then he turned and took her in his arms.

There was a sudden hush among the dancers and the watchers, but Zach and Tara ignored it. Heads bent close together and whispers passed between a small group of older ladies who sat on the sidelines of the dance. They buzzed with the first touch of anything interesting or exciting that had happened since they had joined the train and the realization that it might be the last.

"But, my dear, you need only just look at him to know."

"Know what, Agatha?" came an answering whisper.

"Why's he's half Indian . . . a veritable savage."

"He does look rather interesting," came a wistful reply.

"Interesting! Good heavens, he's so—so untamed. If I were a pretty thing like that, I declare I wouldn't be playing with such fire. He looks dangerous to me."

"Yes . . . he does."

"And look at the way he's looking at her! It's almost scandalous."

"I don't know why it's so scandalous. He seems like such a nice young man, Agatha, he's been exceedingly charming to us," Bertha Mendle inserted. Bertha was a small, delicate woman who usually kept her own counsel and was not one to either defend or condemn others.

"I know," Agatha said with raised brows and a pursing of her lips, as if what she were about to impart was of extreme value. "But Mr. Banning says you can't trust Indians. They're sly and sneaky. Why, he said sometimes unsuspecting white people have been killed right in their own beds. And young girls have suffered worse fates, I'm told."

Both women nodded their heads in mutual agreement, returning their eyes to Tara and Zach, as if expecting Zach to throw Tara to the ground and ravage her before their eyes. But one might have seen the twinkle of enjoyment in the eyes of Bertha Mendle, who had a few memories of her own that made her interest in Tara and Zach more sympathetic than most of the onlookers.

66

Of course Zach looked like the very wilderness in which they traveled, but Bertha saw the strength in him and the sense of belonging to where he was. This man could take and hold what he wanted, and Bertha wasn't too sure that, despite what she felt, Tara wasn't filling Zach's scope of vision right now . . . whether he even knew it or not.

Zach was well aware, not only of the eyes that surreptitiously watched them, but of the thoughts that were in their minds. To him it meant very little, but he wasn't too sure about Tara.

He had done what he had done because he had watched Tara's face. He had stood unobtrusively in the shadows and watched Tara laughing and dancing. He enjoyed her pleasure, until Caleb took her in his arms. He was surprised at the surge of primal violence that blazed in him. He knew Caleb much too well, and Tara would be just another victim. Still, Zach would have stayed out of sight if he had not caught a moon-touched glimpse of Tara's face. It was filled with resistance. He knew she was not quite the helpless little girl he had first thought her to be, and his move to her aid was as much to annoy Caleb as it was to rescue Tara.

Once he had done so, he found himself asking her to dance, another thing he had not planned on.

"So, you're scandalizing the entire train again," Zachary chuckled.

"Again?"

"Traveling by yourself sounds an awful lot like being too independent to suit most of the ladies."

"I can't apologize for that. Surely they can understand that I had no choice."

"They can't understand it or forgive it," he replied. "It's . . . different, and differences are hard to tolerate."

She sensed the bitterness that lay behind the words and began to wonder about what kind of man lay behind the wall of his blue eyes.

"And you're dancing with the savage half-breed. You might not be easily forgiven for that."

Tara smiled, but her eyes held his. "I don't recall," she said quietly, "asking anyone to forgive me for anything. I'm a woman who is quite capable of making my own choices in life."

What leapt into Zach's mind was most certainly not what Tara had meant. He thought of the man who was drawing her across the wilderness to meet him. He realized there had to be a tremendous force between them to make Tara do something so dangerous. Why it should irritate him was a mystery, but it did.

He laughed softly and saw Tara's eyes darken.

"Is that so amusing?"

"It's just that you remind me of a child whistling in the dark to prove he isn't afraid of shadows."

"I really resent your constantly referring to me as a child. I most certainly am not."

"No," he smiled. His eyes were warmly suggestive as they raked her. "From what I remember from last night, you most certainly are not."

Her cheeks flushed with the same remembrance, but she refused to let his knowing smile intimidate her.

Zach again thought of the force that drew Tara. Either the man in question was a fool, or there had not been enough between him and Tara to make him believe she would go to him. Zach found his curiosity more alive than it had ever been.

They had not been on the trail long enough for Zach to have made a thorough search of the wagons. Having had her wagon supplied by Caleb, Zach thought there might be a box or two containing rifles packed among Tara's things. One way to find out would be to search the wagon personally, and the only way to do that was either to find a way to get her away from it . . . or to find the answer to the subtle question of Tara at the same time.

The music stopped at this moment and people began to mill about. No one seemed to notice the fact that not only did Tara and Zach move away from the firelight as all the dancers had done, but Zach continued to draw Tara with him beyond the shadows of the wagons and into the pale moonlit shadows toward the nearby trees.

Tara stopped not too far from the wagons. She knew it would be more than dangerous to go any further with this man, yet something within her urged her on. It could have been her defiance at his attitude of amusement and his calling her childish that made her want to prove him wrong.

"Surely you realize you're giving the gossips much more fuel," she protested. "Or is that what you have in mind?"

She could see the white of his smile as he stood close to her. "Afraid?" he asked softly.

"Of you?" she replied coolly. "Hardly. What could you do to me except give the women a little more to talk about?"

"Then take a walk with me. It's a beautiful night."

"All right," she agreed. The cautious woman within her screamed danger signals, but the disobedient, curious girl whispered against the warning, telling the subtle lies that led her to move to his side and walk beside him toward the trees.

They walked in silence for some time, feeling the quiet peace of the surroundings. Zach stopped beneath a huge tree, leaning one broad shoulder against its trunk. Tara moved to stand near . . . but not near enough that she would be inviting any ideas he might have.

"You are a strange man, Zachary Hale," she said curiously.

"Strange, how?"

"I don't understand you at all."

"What is it you have to understand? I'm a man like any other."

"No, I hardly think that's true. You are different than any other man I have ever known."

"And you've known so many," he chided gently. "How am I different than all the men you have known?"

She could hear the amused tinge in his voice, and rebellion rose again to extinguish caution.

"Why must you treat me like a little girl? What pleasure do you get out of making me feel foolish and innocent?"

His eyes melded with hers, and she felt her heart skip a beat at the depth of his searching gaze. "Because that's what you

69

are. You play with fire like a child, with no real idea of the results. Besides," he chuckled, "it is a pleasure to see your eyes catch fire like that."

She turned her back to the tree and rested against it, then turned her face away from him. "I'm not the infant you would portray me, and I hate being laughed at as if I had no understanding of anything."

He seemed to move only slightly, but suddenly he had braced one hand on each side of her against the tree. She found herself looking up into eyes that had darkened with an emotion she could not even begin to understand.

"I have two choices, Tara Montgomery," he said gently. "Either to laugh . . . or to show you all the things you don't really understand. I told you, you play with fire, Tara. . . . You can get burnt."

Something quickened to life in the depths of her being, calling to her in the way of passion from times beginning. She did not know this force, but she held it, nurtured it, and felt the responding glow of warmth from its flame.

She looked up at him and felt the urge to put her arms about him, to feel the hard length of his body against hers. It was a strong and overpowering urge, and Zachary did not miss its look.

He saw her lips part slightly, while her body trembled, as if caught in a storm. He heard the increase in her ragged breathing.

Tara would not run from this strange and violent tumult. She was afraid, yet she was almost mesmerized by the intoxicating man who towered over her.

Slowly he moved to press his body against hers, and his mouth parted to capture her trembling lips.

It was cataclysmic; both of them reeled under the explosive thing that ignited within. He heard the soft murmuring sound from the depths of her as his arms came about her, and he molded her body to his.

Tara needed no guidance. Her arms went up and about his

70

neck. Her one hand pressed against the hard breadth of his back, while the other tangled in his thick dark hair, urging his total possession.

She had never been kissed with this near-violent passion, nor had she ever felt the power that surged through her. One of Zach's hands pressed against the center of her back, while the other skimmed down her curved back to caress her buttocks and force her body tighter to his. They blended together, forged momentarily by a power stronger than either of them could ever hope to conquer.

Zach had not intended this. He was not prepared for this. But once he felt the magic of her in his arms he could not let her go, even though his slowly disintegrating sense of good judgment was clamoring to be heard. There was no turning back for him. Once he had felt the heated brilliance of the wild possession she had created, he wanted it completely. He released her lips reluctantly and again their eyes met.

"I want you, Tara, you know that. Do you hear with a woman's fire or a little girl's heart?"

Tara knew little of what he asked, and the shock of it all was that she wanted him in a way she could not explain even to herself. She could not deny it. She was a woman, and the need called out to her to know and to taste the passion of a woman.

"I want you too, Zach," she whispered.

"Do you know what you're saying? Don't play games. They have rules."

"I want to know," she whispered. She put her hands on each side of his face and drew his head to hers.

As their lips met again, she suddenly felt exultant, as if a power had swung open a door . . . a door that could never be closed again.

"So the child would be a woman?" Zachary whispered. Before Tara could answer, he was drawing her into the deeper shadows of the trees. Her heart pounding with a fury, she went with him.

Chapter 7

The place in which Zach chose to stop was secluded and kissed by moonlight. In its glow Tara could feel the warmth of his gaze as he again drew her slowly toward him.

She was like a fragile bird, ready to fly away at any sudden shocks, but Zach had no intention of letting her go. He drew her into his arms and again his mouth claimed her willing, parted lips. His tongue intruded into her mouth, lacing with hers, drawing hers into his, until he heard her catch her breath and felt the quivering of her body in his arms.

Time seemed suspended as he held her crushed against him and kissed her endlessly, deeply, until she was dizzy and clinging to him for support.

He eased himself down, drawing her with him, until they lay side by side on the soft, sweet-scented grass.

His arm was about her waist and his other hand was tangled in her hair, imprisoning her in a hold that kept her soft mouth molded to his.

She was aware of the penetrating warmth of his body as he crushed her to him, its mystery drawing her to press even closer. Her breathing was erratic, and she felt the moist warmth like a small flame, igniting and beginning to grow within her.

Slowly he gently caressed her, feeling her body quiver

beneath his touch. His hands moved from her waist to cup her breast. Even through the fabric of her dress he could feel the crest harden. He kneaded with a soft circular motion until he could feel her strain toward his pleasurable touch.

She was not conscious of when or how the buttons of her dress were opened. His rough, calloused hand touched breasts that seemed to ache with the need of something more.

The dress was pushed aside as was the camisole. Then he bent to lightly run his tongue across one nipple, then the other. As she arched against him, she could have cried out at the sudden ecstatic delight that moved through her.

He caught one nipple in his mouth and suckled gently, circling it with his tongue until she whispered his name. Her head was thrown back, her eyes closed as she was caught in the luxuriant delight of his touch. She had never been so alive! She had never felt such a fire to the very depths of her being.

Nimble fingers loosened clothes deftly. Had Tara been more versed in lovemaking, she might not have been so startled when she felt the electrical shock of his hands stroking her body.

Within minutes, Zach knew that she was not versed at all, but he was caught up almost as deeply as she by the open and free way she returned his kiss and by the sweet, giving way her body moved to meet the touch of his hand. He could hear her ragged gasp for breath, could feel the pulsing beat of passion that was new and vital.

He stroked her softly with his hands until her body was afire with wanting more to release this surging heat. It was a delicious, mind-searing pleasure, and Tara was sure there could be nothing more exquisite. Then his warm mouth began to torture her body, teasing and enticing a response. She felt as if the core of her was melting, flowing through her like a river.

Abruptly Zach moved from her, and in a lethargic haze, she saw him removing his clothes. As if in a dream, she was held suspended in a mystic world. All she could think about was how gracefully beautiful he was. Like a tawny lion, his hard muscles rippled under taut flesh.

He returned to her side, and now her hands moved with their own volition, stroking his hard body. He was warmer than before, and when their bodies touched, she felt almost drugged by the sensation of flesh against flesh.

He knew she was going to be startled and hurt, but he felt a desire he had not felt with his other women who had been random conquests, which he still felt Tara to be. He wanted her to enjoy this to the fullest and hurt her as little as possible. He could have taken her then, but he chose to lift her to the pinnacle of desire.

He let his hands and mouth explore every curve and hollow of her body, using his tongue to trace delicious patterns until he felt Tara losing her hold on reality.

He separated her legs and moved above her, letting his passion-engorged shaft gently slip against her warm moistness. She was wet, sensitive, and swollen with passion, yet he did not penetrate. He continued to use himself to massage in slow strokes until Tara arched against him momentarily, feeling she would go mad. He moved within her a fraction, feeling the barrier. His mouth met hers, and he gathered her to him as he thrust deeply, wanting to end the hurt. He heard her startled moan and felt her stiffen slightly at the suddenness of pain that followed exquisite pleasure. He sensed when most of the pain was gone, and then he began to move slowly.

Tara quickly forgot the brief pain as her body soared, and Zach began a slow and methodical thrusting. Something fierce and volatile seemed to be gathering in a heated ball in the center of her, as the driving pleasure of the hardness of him filling her body seemed to be reaching to touch the exquisite heat.

Tara did not understand this first taste of such magical sensations. She only knew her body had a will of its own and she did not want it to end.

The fiery strokes increased in depth and sureness, and the delightful sensations made the gathering heat expand until she

74

was moaning softly. Her legs had entwined about him, and her hands clung in wild desperation, as if she were drowning and he was the only solidity. Suddenly the fiery center exploded in one contraction after another. An explosive and fulfilling orgasm rippled through her.

Zach had sought this moment; he had held himself back with iron will. But now that he knew her release was here, he could hold himself back no longer. He thrust to the very depths of her, feeling the soaring pleasure as they became almost one, melted together by a fury that lifted them both to a profound fulfillment.

Zach rolled to his side and gathered Tara close to him, sensing her need to be held as the realities hit her. But the recriminations he expected didn't come.

He had prepared himself for the tears of a girl who had suddenly been made a woman. But he was not prepared for her to curl close to him like an affectionate kitten. He also didn't expect her to rest her head on his shoulder, her soft hair gently caressing his chest, her warm tears slowly trickling against his skin.

"Oh, Zach, I never knew there was anything like this," she whispered.

This sensual pleasure had been part of Zach's life for so long he had forgotten his first time. Now she seemed to be renewing something within him, replacing a well-tasted cup with a new wine, more potent and dangerous to his peace of mind than anything he'd ever tasted. A warning jolt struck him that Tara was more than a threat, she was a danger he couldn't afford. But he seemed helpless, at this moment, to let her go. His hands softly stroked her flesh and he kissed her tenderly.

What shook Zach's resolve was the fact that he was more than reluctant to let her go, that he would have liked nothing more than to renew their passion.

Women had been useful objects for Zach from the time he was fifteen, and he was unprepared for this wisp of a girl, all innocence and sweet giving, to find the minute crack in his guard and wriggle inside. He couldn't afford such an attachment—not now. He knew Caleb's danger, and he had a job to do that did not include a moment to romance a girl who would possibly end up in the center of everything and get hurt badly in the process.

He was puzzled by his own self. Not one to walk so casually into such a situation, Zach was, in fact, a man who had kept as much distance between himself and innocent virgins as he could. Now he was immersed in a tantalizing new emotion, one he just could not afford as much for her sake as for his.

Tara did not fit into any plans he had made, and she most certainly could not remain with him once this trip was over. He knew the heartless attitude that so-called civilized society would have. Had it not been a traumatic lesson to him? He did not want Tara to suffer the stigma of being with a half-breed. They had never seen him as a man, and they most certainly would not accept what she had done gracefully. She would be bitter and angry and most likely disbelieving, but he had to end what was between them before it was beyond his capabilities to do so . . . Yet he wanted to hold her just a little longer, feeling that this night would most likely be the first and last they would ever share. Despite his self-confidence at the beginning, he was not quite sure how to let her down easily. He could face it only one way: He had to make her understand the truth as quickly as he had made her accept the first thrust of passion, in this way saving her later pain—if he could be sure what the truth was.

Lost in a beautiful warmth, Tara half dozed, sated and complete. In this dreamlike state she enjoyed the soft caresses of Zach's hands and the warmth of his body that held her like an enclosing cocoon. She did not want to ever move for fear of breaking some magic spell.

She had not yet begun to question herself or to question Zach's absolute silence. For this fragile moment, the spell was woven about her like a spiderweb mist. Very slowly a type of uncertain reality began to work its way through her haze. Zach was more than silent; he had withdrawn to a place where she could not follow.

Tara raised up on one elbow and looked down into his eyes. The pale moonlight behind her made her only a shadowy form. But it touched his face with its light, and she found his eyes filled with an unreadable look.

"Zach, I—"

"I think it's best for both of us to get back to the wagons, Tara, before Caleb comes to look for us again." He laughed softly, "Much as old Caleb would love to join you here, he'll have to understand he's out of luck for this trip."

For this trip! The words shattered her euphoria like breaking crystal. The ragged pieces slashed at her heart. This had been nothing but Zach's casual answer to the threat of Caleb. It had been some kind of contest between these two men to see who could defeat her defenses first.

Zach knew what she was thinking, and despite his disgust at himself, he encouraged her thoughts. "I'll help you dress," he said casually, as if this were an interlude he considered best forgotten.

Tara sat up quickly and snatched her dress to her. Zach sat up beside her at the same time. When her face was touched by the moonlight, he could clearly see the look of hurt and betrayal in her eyes. They were moist with tears. "Don't bother," she said. "I can manage. I'm sure there's nothing to hold you here if you feel the need to rush back to the wagons before someone finds you out."

Now he laughed aloud. "A rendezvous with a pretty girl won't spoil my reputation. We half-breeds have a reputation already. They will just feel it's something expected. Come to think of it, I do have a difficult time ignoring beautiful ladies in need of being kissed. I guess it's my savage blood."

She couldn't berate him; he had told her no lies. He had said he wanted her, but it was a far cry from saying I love you. He had even warned her against playing games with him and of the burning regret she was feeling now.

77

She mentally groaned under the weight of shame at the way she had fallen so freely into his arms, like the foolish little girl he had named her. Only, she was a girl no longer. She was a woman who had, for a moment, lost her equilibrium. But now she found it quickly. She could not help the hurt or the tears, but her angry defiance was raised as a shield to protect her from any further damage.

"What's the matter, Tara?" Zach asked, as if he had no idea at all, even though he could read her anguish very well. She would never know the effort it took for him not to take her into his arms. He wanted to hold her, to soothe the hurt, and to tell her he had found something in her arms he would most likely never be able to forget. Surprisingly he realized he wanted to make love to her again, this time with infinite care, until she knew she belonged in his arms.

"You are a savage, aren't you?" she gasped. "You don't care who you hurt as long as you have your way."

"My way?" he chuckled softly. "From what I felt and heard, it wasn't all my way. I think you enjoyed it as much as I did. Nobody was hurt, Tara," he chided gently. "If you tell the truth, I think you'll admit you got as much pleasure out of it as I did."

She bit her lips against the tears and the knowledge, in the secret recesses of her mind, that what he said was the bitter truth. She wanted to scream, to throw herself at him and scratch the laughter from his face. Unashamed of his nakedness, he stood up. She was vibrantly aware that he still had an electrical effect on her. His body was graceful, clean limbed, and extremely masculine. He moved to her, and suddenly she found her dress torn from her hands. She had only time for a startled gasp before she was caught against him with arms that felt like steel. She began to fight, but he had caught her unprepared and her arms were effectively pinned between them. His mouth sought hers, but she turned her head away. Tangling one hand in her hair, he held her head immobile while he kissed her fiercely and possessively.

78

Tara was not about to succumb to the power she knew he could still wield over her. In desperation, she bit his lip until he jerked, shoving her a step or two away.

He touched his lip and actually laughed. The little witch had drawn blood. "Damn, if you're not as wild as I am. Maybe we'd make a good pair, Tara."

"Don't you ever touch me," she grated through ragged gasps. "Stay as far away from me as you can through the balance of this trip."

This was what he wanted more for her protection than anything else, yet he was surprised by the sting he felt. At any other time, he would have deliberately held her until he seduced her into admitting they had shared a miracle between them. But he knew damn well this was the moment he had to let go.

"You're really not going to be fool enough to run to old Caleb's arms for comfort, are you, little girl?" he asked tauntingly. "You'd better know he's as much a savage as I am. He'd like nothing better than to have the last laugh."

He had to know. He had to keep her safe from Caleb, even if it came to calling Caleb out sooner than he had expected. His taunt had been successful. At least if he couldn't have her, he had made sure Caleb never would either. He heard it clearly.

"I just want to get to Fort Lyon. You and Caleb can play your games with some other stupid girl who's foolish enough to believe there is one inch of manhood in either of you. Don't worry, I won't play victim again."

She snatched up her dress and Zach watched as she put it on, almost in tears. Her hands were shaking so badly that she couldn't close the buttons on the back of her dress.

Zach went to her and roughly turned her around. She stood in an agony of silence while he buttoned the dress. She didn't want to turn around to look into the challenge of his eyes again.

"Good night, Zach," she said bitterly. "I hope you're quite pleased that you made a stupid fool of me. I had hoped . . . I

79

wish I could never see you again, but I must. This trip will be over soon, and we will be free of each other. Until then, please . . . just leave me alone."

She walked away and Zach slowly gathered his clothes. He wanted to go after her, to tell her that he didn't want to let her go with this kind of hurt and rejection. With concentrated effort, he slowly dressed, assuring his mind that what had happened had been for the best, while his heart and his body sang a melody of denial. He wondered when he would be able to wipe Tara away completely.

He also wondered about the man to whom Tara was going. Tara had been a virgin, yet she was following a man who had obviously left her untouched. He knew for certain that if she were his, she would only have to reach out a hand and he would be beside her, not only making sure that no other would ever have her, but that she would know beyond a doubt that she belonged to him.

He made his way slowly back to his wagon, facing a night he was quite sure was going to be sleepless.

Tara stumbled toward the wagons, blinded by the tears she refused to shed. She was shaking with the violence of surprised anger and betrayal. How neatly she had walked into his arms! What a naive and simple fool she had been! She had known him for what he was. She had instinctively known he was a predator, yet the truth of her own self-deceit was the fact that, despite her knowledge, she had braved the flames. She had been devoured in the brilliant ecstasy he had ignited, and now she must nurse the burnt embers and heal her singed emotions. Once she did, she promised, she would never again allow her body and her emotions to control her common sense.

She climbed into her wagon and curled up on the blankets without undressing. After a while she could not control the tears. What she wept for she didn't even know herself. He had promised her nothing, offered her nothing, and led her to believe nothing. Why, then, did she feel as if she had lost a part of herself she might never be able to find again? Why did she feel that there was so much left unsaid and untouched between them?

She cried useless tears until finally she succumbed to both physical and mental exhaustion. She slept, fighting the dreams that she had fought when awake.

Mule, who lay awake beneath the wagon, heard and knew what had happened. He had seen Zach leave the circle of wagons with Tara's hand in his, and Mule had no doubts as to how the confrontation had resulted.

This was not like Zach to hurt another so badly, especially someone as sweet and gentle as Tara. Mule could not understand at first, then the realization came to him and he smiled. Zach had wanted to protect Tara, so he had pushed her away from him. But not, Mule figured, before he had reached to touch her beauty just once. Mule meant to tell Zach the next day, to look into his friend's eyes, to find out for himself if holding a beautiful woman like Tara in his arms would ever be enough for a fiery passioned man like Zachary Hale. Mule had some pretty strong doubts about whether or not Zach, once he had caught her, would be able to let her go. Morning would tell.

Chapter 8

The next morning appeared gray, with piles of blue-black rain clouds that obliterated the sun. Still they would move, and all involved with the train were making preparations. By the time the wagons began to move slowly, there was a steady downpour.

Tara rode inside the wagon, seated where she could look past Mule at the train ahead of her. It looked like a row of white-sailed ships on a vast ocean. She could see the riders and recognized Zach, even with his poncho covering him and his hat pulled low over his eyes to give him as much protection from the rain as possible.

Rumbling thunder in the distance and an occasional bolt of lightning made everyone concentrate on the control of the animals and the safety of the equipment. There was no time for random conversations, with everyone's attention on controlling their wagons and keeping moving. The rain did not slacken until well into the afternoon. By mutual agreement of all the leaders, they chose not to stop to eat. Mule assured Tara this was because they felt sure that by evening they might ride safely out of the rain.

Toward the end of the day, this proved to be right. The sky was already a dull red, while the billowing prairie grass was in shadow by the day's end. Large flocks of crows flew overhead on their way northeast to roost in the cottonwoods. The trees bordered a stream near where the wagons also intended to stop for the night.

It had been a long and tiring day, and even the teams that were in prime condition were exhausted. Tara wanted nothing more than to get out of the rolling, heaving wagon and stand on solid ground.

The wagons did not circle that night but pulled into random spots beneath the cottonwoods. There were fires being built and food being prepared, yet the camp was extremely quiet. Children slept beneath the wagons early, from exhaustion.

Zach moved from wagon to wagon to make sure there were no problems that might slow the next day's progress. He had not planned on going near Tara's, assured that Mule would have no difficulties. Yet, when he stood some distance away, he could see Tara and Mule by the campfire. Before he could change his mind, he was already walking toward them. It was his job, he thought defensively, yet he wanted to make sure Tara was all right. He wanted to see her again, even though he was quite sure of the reception he would get.

He stepped into the ring of firelight as quietly as a shadow, catching fragments of conversation before Tara or Mule realized he was there.

". . . so you don't need to worry about a thing, girl. Zach knows the land like the back of his hand. It ain't possible for that boy to get lost."

Zach chuckled to himself. Obviously the vastness of the land had begun to intimidate Tara as it did most people crossing it for the first time. It was then that Mule sensed his presence and looked up quickly. Then he smiled.

"C'mon over and join us, Zach boy. The coffee's still hot and there's a bit of stew left."

Zach walked toward the fire and dropped down to rest on his haunches. He was directly across the fire from Tara, who was making a studied effort to ignore his presence.

Despite all outward appearances of calm, Tara could not

83

ignore him. He was a force she could actually feel. Slowly and hesitantly, she raised her eyes slightly to just catch him in her line of vision.

"I'm not hungry, Mule, I just stopped by to see if everything was all right." Zach was sure that the last person to need any help would be Mule.

Mule wanted to scoff at this, but he kept discreetly silent. Zach's eyes had never left Tara, and Mule was entirely too observant to miss it.

"'Evening, Tara," Zach said in a voice kept in rigid control.

"Good evening, Mr. Hale. We're fine, I assure you. I'm sure we don't need any special attention. Mule is quite in control of everything. I'm sure you must have other things to worry about, so we wouldn't want to keep you here."

Mule could have laughed outright at this moment. Zach's little eastern lady had claws, and Zach had just been told to get out. Mule was quite sure this was a new event for his friend.

"It's part of my job, Tara," Zach replied coldly, assuring her this was no special stop.

"Then I'm sure you and Mule must have things to talk about, so I won't intrude."

Before Zach could think of any words to stop her, Tara had risen and walked out of the firelight. She disappeared in the shadows, and Zach watched until she vanished. He was brought back to the present by Mule's soft laugh.

"'Pears to me, boy, you got bee stung."

Zach had to chuckle. "The lady seems a little put out with me."

"I expect that's cause you keep treatin' her like she's an interference."

"She is, Mule," Zach said softly. "More than you know."

"She don't have any idea what's goin' on."

"No, but she put herself right in the middle of it no matter how I wanted her not to."

"Could be, boy, what's important to you just ain't important to her. Could be she's got some things important herself."

84

Before he could raise barriers to stop it, Zach's mind leapt to the man Tara was running to.

"I suppose you're right, Mule, but I sure wish she'd chosen another train."

"Any signs of guns?"

"I've searched about three or four wagons. No sign yet. He has a damn good way of hiding them. And I can't get near Caleb's wagon or those two that are close to him. He's watching me close, too, but I don't think he really has any idea what I'm up to. In fact, I think it's Tara that has his back up."

"Could be. He's taken a real shine to the girl."

"He hasn't bothered her, has he?"

"Nope, I'd blow off his head if he tried climbing in her wagon. I can't stand the man no how, and I'm getting right partial to her."

"Keep a close eye on her, Mule, especially if I'm not around."

"Could be I need to keep an eye on her especially when you are around."

"Just what's that supposed to mean?"

"Well, the other night she comes back to her wagon. Now, I'm half sleepin' under her wagon, but I shore can't help hearin' her cryin' her head off. Now, I say to myself, what could make a pretty young thing like that cry like she was hurting real bad? I just couldn't figure it out . . . maybe you have an answer."

"Sorry, I don't. Maybe she's just lonely for home . . . or for whomever she's running to."

"Whomever? . . . Boy," Mule grinned broadly, "I guess you don't know she's runnin' to her brother. He's in the military at Fort Lyon. They lost their parents, and he's all the kin she has left."

"Her brother," Zach repeated slowly. He kept his face immobile, but his heart pounded against his chest in a surge of pleasure he refused to acknowledge. It made no difference to him whom Tara was going to, he professed. But the subtle voice

85

kept calling, Lie, lie, lie. "Well, I think I'll stretch my legs, then get some sleep," Zach said as he rose. "See you in the morning, Mule." He walked away and Mule smiled to himself in satisfaction. He had never seen Zachary Hale run from anything, and he figured this time was as much a shock to Zach as anyone. Mule curled in his blanket and soon slipped into contented sleep.

Tara had walked away from the wagon and into the darkness, where she could control the mixed emotions she felt. She stood beneath a tall cottonwood, blending with the tree and the night. She didn't know why Zach made her feel empty and alone, why he had such a devastating effect on her peace of mind. She knew there could be nothing more between them. Hadn't he given her sufficient reason to know that? And yet she could still feel the intense magnetism that drew her eyes to him even against her will.

She was angered at the way her pulses pounded fiercely, and her body grew warm with a memory she preferred to forget. It had meant nothing to him and she would not allow it to mean more to her.

Lost in her thoughts, she was not aware of approaching footsteps until a twig snapped sharply. She turned her head toward the sound.

Zach was as unaware of her presence as she had been of his. She watched him step out of the shadows of the trees and stand near the stream. Obviously he was also in deep thought, so Tara remained silent, cloaked by the darkness beneath the tree, and watched him.

He knelt and swooped up a handful of pebbles, tossing them one at a time into the stream. He was half shadow and half moonlight. She controlled, with a great deal of effort, the sudden urge to walk to him and put her arms about him. That was the last thing she could ever do.

So Tara was on her way to her brother. That thought had no

business pleasing him as it did. His mind had certainly not been on guns and disaster for the past twenty-four hours. That was not healthy in the position he was in. Yet, guns and disaster were what he knew was coming unless he traced down the supply source.

Tara still slipped within his mind no matter how hard he tried to push her from it. Mule had said that she had cried as if she were hurt. The thought of this left a bitter taste in his mouth and the ashes of remembrance stirred to life. He recalled the feel and the taste of her, until he was completely immersed in something that had been so exquisite. He allowed the memory only for this moment, this one vulnerable moment. Then he would store it away permanently.

His instincts, honed by the danger of the wilderness in which he had had to survive, suddenly came alive. He became aware that someone was standing within the shadows of the trees only a few feet away.

"Damn," he muttered. He had made himself an open target, and if Caleb were wise to what he was doing, he might just be walking close to death. Slowly he turned his back to the tree, feeling the twitch between his shoulder blades, as if a knife blade could already be aimed his way. He walked a step or two upstream, then eased toward the shadows to blend with them and disappear.

Tara breathed a sigh of relief when she saw him turn his back to her and move away. Evidently he was on his way back to the wagons to sleep. She was both disappointed yet relieved that he had not known of her presence.

She relaxed, unaware that Zach had moved silently through the shadows to circle behind her. If it were someone intent on his life, he had a whole lot of questions to ask.

Zach could see the dark shadowed form, and he moved to within a foot of Tara. Then he reached out and circled her body in one arm, clamping his hand over her mouth to prohibit any calls for help. It took less than seconds for Zach to know he had captured a woman in his arms. His responding senses, along with the feel and scent of her, told him who the woman was.

Tara was so startled that she was, for a moment, paralyzed by fear. By that time Zach was already releasing her. Her fear turned quickly to anger as she spun about to see him grinning broadly.

"Sorry, Tara, I thought you were someone else."

"You could have asked who it was," she choked angrily. His sudden laughter did little to ease her fury. "You find that funny?"

"More than you can imagine," he replied.

His laughter died to a smile, and he folded his arms across his chest and leaned his shoulder against the tree.

"You shouldn't be walking around out here alone. Some uncivilized savage just might come and grab you up to carry to his lodge."

"I think the only savage I have to worry about is you," she snapped, still irritated at his look of amusement.

"You might be right about that, too," he replied wickedly.

"Don't try to frighten me, Zach. Mule said I was perfectly safe at least until we pass Fort Hays."

"I just don't want you to create a habit."

"Don't worry about me. I don't need your protection."

She was such a combination of a scared little girl and a defiant woman that Zach was drawn closer. This small movement seemed to suddenly make Tara aware of the situation in which she found herself now. For several seconds they stood in a silence, which soon began to grow in power.

Zach reached out a hesitant hand and caught a few strands of Tara's hair between his fingers. Her hair was soft like silk and curled about his fingers. It smelled clean and whispered of wild flowers. His eyes swept down her body as if he were drawn by a force that he was powerless against. He remembered too how soft her skin was and how she fit against his body as if they were two parts of a whole.

Tara wanted to push his hand away, to deny what was stirring to life within her. But she couldn't. It was as if she were

88

frozen both in time and place.

Despite all his vows of staying away from her and of never touching her again, Zach seemed temporarily unable to honor them. He reached out and took hold of her shoulders, drawing her to him.

Her lips parted to deny him, but they uttered no sound as his mouth touched hers. She felt as if she were melting about him like warm honey, as if all her bones and sinews were liquid. His arms were hard and strong, filled with the power to make her forget all words and warnings.

Their mouths parted, leaving both breathless. He caught her hair with one hand, drawing her head back so he could press searing hot kisses on the soft flesh of her throat.

He murmured her name softly as his kisses gentled and moved from her throat to her cheeks, then her forehead, her eyes, then back to her responding mouth that had lost all resistance.

She was again responding in a haze to the exquisite sensations he was evoking. All her senses were heightened by his touch. She could feel the rough stubble of a day's beard against her cheek, the warmth of his breath against her sensitive flesh.

She inhaled the combined scents that enhanced his aura of complete masculinity, felt the hard strength of his hands as they moved down her back, catching her buttocks and pressing her more firmly against him.

She could feel the surging of his passion-hardened manhood as it pressed insistently against her. The touch seemed to ignite her until she felt moist and throbbing in response.

His hand slid down to catch the hem of her dress, which had ridden up to her knees. Slipping his hand beneath it, he caressed her thigh, drawing his hand slowly and enticingly upward until he cupped the warmth between her thighs. Even through the cotton pantalets she wore, Tara could feel the erotic pleasure his slow, stroking fingers elicited. Then his hand left, causing her to arch involuntarily after its pleasure-giving touch. She could feel the band of her pantalets stretch as he sought softer, more intimate contact.

Zach felt the warmth of her against him, and he let his hands trace the fine molding of her body. He couldn't believe so slim and soft a body could have a force that drove him wild. Zach could not get enough of the taste and feel of her. He kissed her over and over and over, drugged on the magic of her being.

The forbidden brilliance eclipsed all emotions within Tara, except the sudden overpowering heat that flowed through her. As she opened her mouth to catch her breath, his open mouth closed over it. His tongue caressed hers, drawing hers into his mouth. She was drowning and could not battle the flood of passion.

It was only when she felt the cool night air against her flesh, felt the touch of his hand, that a sudden reality shattered the fantasy world and violently shook her. She was actually succumbing to his touch as easily as she had before! My God! He must think her completely wanton, or else so enthralled by his touch that she couldn't resist him. The truth of this was ignored as her anger rose to smother it. With an exasperated groan, she pushed him away from her, clutching her dress to keep it closed.

"No, don't."

"Tara . . ." he began, but her own self-recrimination was overpowering all other thoughts.

She almost leapt to her feet, buttoning her dress as fast as her shaking fingers could manage. Zach rose to stand beside her.

"Stop playing your little games with me! I know how you feel about my being here, that you think I'm nothing but trouble. But I'm doing just fine, so please let me alone and stop trying to make a fool of me." She was in tears and very near hysteria.

Zach wasn't going to force the situation. He most certainly hadn't been any more prepared for what had happened than she was, and he didn't want it to go any further than it already

90

had. He watched her disappear in the darkness with a tinge of regret, but feeling it was most likely better this way. He could only mean trouble for her, and for him she was a danger he couldn't afford. . . . But he was just as certain the balance of the trip was going to be more trying than anything he had bargained for. He couldn't stop the uncomfortable feeling that Tara was in much more danger than that of just being seduced by him. There were people who would give a great deal for a white woman as beautiful as Tara Montgomery—and he was almost certain Caleb was one. Only, Tara would not end with just Caleb. Maybe he could put the two together somehow. Possibly, Tara might be the path that would lead to Caleb's downfall. He'd watch carefully and wait for Caleb to make the mistake.

Chapter 9

Zach rode away early the next morning, while the preparations were being made for the wagons to roll. He would scout on ahead at least until after midday, then return with an evening's destination in mind. This way the entire train would be assured of the best possible camping place. It also gave Zach freedom of movement and time alone to sort out his thoughts. He had gotten off track, drawn from his goals by a girl who could cause him nothing but trouble.

It would take them another two days before they reached Fort Larned. In those two days, he intended to put Tara Montgomery from his mind. Too much depended on him finding out how the guns were delivered, by whom, and to whom. So far Caleb had made no moves to meet anybody, but Zach was watching him closely, and when he made his first mistake, Zach intended to be there to put a stop to Caleb for good.

But another goal was close to the first. Whoever dealt with Caleb was one of his father's people. Zach had to find out who had so little care for his own blood that he would stand by and allow them to be massacred, for a massacre was what it would inevitably be. Even with guns, the Cheyenne out here would be badly outnumbered. Since the flow of ammunition would be erratic, they could never hope to succeed. He was scared of the result, for it might mean the final decimation of his father and

92

all the people in Waiting Wolf's village.

By the time Zach returned to the wagons he had chosen a place to camp and made his instructions clear to the train leader.

With grim determination he kept himself active as they headed toward the evening's campground. He kept his eyes away from Tara's wagon, but was having a great deal of difficulty keeping his mind and his imagination from wandering to shadowed memories that could never be anything more.

Zach succeeded in at least keeping himself away from Tara's vicinity for the two days it took to get to Fort Larned. They would remain only as long as it took to replenish supplies, and although he kept both Caleb and Tara in his sight, he made no move to come any closer.

From Fort Larned the train wound its way slowly to Fort Dodge. From there they would follow the Arkansas River to Fort Lyon.

Tara was frustrated by desires she refused to acknowledge, angry at Zach for reasons she could not face, and annoyed with him for not approaching her again and giving her the satisfaction of cutting him off coldly as she had planned. He had just stepped out of her life, leaving a void whose presence she fought.

It had now been over fifteen days since they had left Ellsworth, and the train continued to snake its way along the course of the river.

Mule was well aware of the simmering atmosphere and watched with amusement as it grew. Tara and Zach continued to skirt each other, and Mule began to wonder what they were going to do once they were confined to the area of Fort Lyon and could not escape coming into contact with each other. Besides this, he was thoroughly taken with the idea that this was most likely the only woman Zach Hale had ever run from, and he was quite certain this was aggravating Zach as well.

* * *

Word streaked through the entire wagon train. In two more days they would reach Fort Lyon. The days of uncomfortable travel would be over for some of the families, although a few were still planning the extended trip to California.

The night fires crackled and voices were tinged with excitement. Tara and Mule sat beside their fire after having eaten the evening meal. They sat in a companionable silence, comfortable with each other after the long hard days had shown them that each could depend on the other.

Mule was surreptitiously watching Tara, who sat in a quiet dreamlike state. He had read her face well a few minutes before, when she had caught sight of Zach in conversation with a family some distance away. Before she could control it, he had seen longing, fear, and puzzlement. Tara could not understand a man like Zachary Hale, and Mule, for Zach's safety, could not enlighten her. He chafed under this restriction, but he valued Zach's life too highly to jeopardize him.

Tara had picked up a stick and was gently poking the embers of the fire. They cast a red-gold glow across her face, catching in her brilliant coppery hair. Her skin was glowing from the daily touch of the sun, but her green eyes were thoughtful and introspective.

"What ya thinkin' about, Tara, us gettin' to the fort in a couple of days?"

"Oh that," Tara sighed, "and I guess a lot of things. I haven't seen my brother for so long. I wrote and told him about our parents. I guess it's going to be a whole new way of life, and maybe I'm a little scared."

"Rattlesnakes! You ain't scared of much. I been watchin' ya this whole trip. Ya got a lot more spunk than most girls your age. Just makin' this trip all by yourself was a big bite to chew."

"Not really, when you consider I had very few choices. I couldn't stay in Washington alone, and David was the only family I had left."

"This trip hasn't been an easy one, girl, and Zach hasn't

94

made it any easier, has he?" Mule questioned quietly.

Tara's eyes leapt to his; he saw the uncertainty and she saw the sympathy. Tara turned her head away, unprepared for his sympathy and not wanting him to see the unwelcome tears that had sprung to her eyes.

"Why is he so—so hard and unfeeling, Mule? Why does he dislike me so?"

"He ain't a hard, unfeeling boy, Tara, he's just a little more scared than you are."

"Zach?" she said in a disbelieving voice, turning to look at him again. She laughed bitterly. "I doubt very much if Zach has ever been afraid of anything."

They were silent another long moment, then Tara spoke in a near whisper.

"Mule, tell me about him. What's he really like? What makes him so—so unapproachable?"

Mule seemed to ponder this carefully. When he spoke it was very slowly, as if he didn't want to make a mistake that might mislead her thoughts. "His ma came out here when the mission school was here. She was a teacher. I guess she took a liking to the young Indian children and that didn't sit too well with some of the white folks. Then when Karolyn met Waiting Wolf, well, I guess most considered it bad. But those two, they loved each other. Anyway, when the mission school closed, his ma chose to stay with Waiting Wolf."

"Is Zach the only child they had?"

"Yep. His pa took it real hard when she died. Cut his hair and mourned something fierce. Then he turned all his attention to Zach. Zach's ma had taught him to read and write. . . . But she didn't have the answers to how he was supposed to live half in one world and half in the other."

"He must have been unhappy."

"Not always. After his ma died he got kinda wild, then he straightened out and been doin' all right."

"Mule?"

"What?"

95

"Why does he resent me so much when his own mother was white and chose to stay with his father?"

Mule found it difficult to answer this without revealing why Zach was with the wagon train. "I don't think he resents you, girl, he's just worried some."

"About what?"

"There's a lot of trouble brewing out here. Most of the Indians are pinned to reservations. Still, there's a lot of hot heads stirring up trouble."

"Zach never married?"

Mule contained his pleased smile. "Nope, guess he never found a girl that made him want to settle. I guess you're some of the reason he's jumpy. We're sitting on a powder keg, and he's afraid something will happen. Besides, you got his dander up when he couldn't scare you off. I guess he's used to women being a little easier to handle."

"I still find it hard to believe he's any way near being civilized."

"There's a lot to be said about being civilized. I'd say it's how a man feels about all the other humans in this world of ours. There are some who are careless about bringing pain and trouble to others and still call themselves civilized. Then there's some, like Zach, who do more than they brag about. You want to find out the better man, Tara, don't look at his face to see if he's handsome, look at his heart to see if it's honest."

Tara sighed, wondering if it would ever be possible to find what was truly in Zachary Hale's heart. She contemplated all that had happened and, after a while, turned to Mule with more questions on her lips, only to find he had curled up in his blanket and gone to sleep. She returned her gaze to the fire and her thoughts to Zachery Hale.

Fort Lyon was a few short hours away. They would reach it before the day was ended. Tara could feel a tumultuous excitement course through her. She sat on the seat of the wagon beside Mule and tried to contain her impatience as they slowly wound their way up the last hill.

The sun set behind the fort itself, casting it in shadow. In the vast sun-kissed land, the fort looked small from the distance.

"Fort Lyon, Tara," Mule chuckled. "We made it all in one piece."

"I can't wait to see David."

"Well, 'bout another two hours will see us riding through those gates."

He turned to look at Tara, who was shading her eyes against the red glow of the dying sun and looking from their position on the hill's crest to the valley floor, where an easily identified rider was racing toward the fort.

"Mule, will he stay at the fort, or will he just ride away?"

"You want him to stay?" Mule returned his gaze to the horses but listened for her reply.

"Yes," came the whispered reply.

"I don't know what he'll do, but it sure as heck is going to be danged interesting if you was to ask him to stay. 'Course, he'll go visit his pa sometime soon. His family means a lot to him."

"I thought he just had his father."

"No, got a stepmother, Singing Grass, and a half brother, Little Raven."

"Little Raven." Tara was surprised by a new thought. "Does Zach have an Indian name?"

"'Course he does. He was given both names when he was born. His ma called him Zachary, and his pa called him Windwalker."

"Windwalker," Tara repeated softly. "It sounds—it sounds just like this land. So—so big, and so free."

"Yes, I guess you might say he is like this land . . . free. I hope," Mule added almost to himself, "that he can help keep it that way."

Mule whistled to the horses and slapped their rumps with the reins as they followed the wagons into the fort.

The fort was much larger than it first appeared. There were over three hundred cavalry men in the barracks and nine officers besides the commander. The officers, several of whom had wives and children, had small quarters of their own. Then there were separate quarters for the commander, several warehouses filled with supplies and ammunition, a small center for social affairs, stables, and storage rooms. All were built around a center square in which the flag was raised every morning. The entire area was surrounded by a high wall of logs with a platform that ran around the entire wall, four feet from the top, on which sentries walked slowly, keeping their eyes on the vast area about them.

The wagon train entered the fort through a large gate. Its door swung wide to give them entry. There was a bustle of activity while shouts of welcome mingled with laughter and voices of children. The coming of a wagon train was an exciting experience in their otherwise dull lives.

Tara was anxious to find David and nearly leapt down from the wagon seat. She was met by the only three unmarried officers, who had the ability to spot a pretty girl for miles.

"Welcome to Fort Lyon, Miss—"

"Montgomery, Tara Montgomery," Tara replied with a smile that drew them closer.

"Montgomery. We have an officer here with the same name," one was quick to observe. "I do hope you are not going to tell us you're his wife."

"No, I'm his sister. Where is he?"

"Sister," the third grinned happily. "Best news I've heard in months. But I'm afraid, for a short time, you'll have to allow us to make you welcome. I'm afraid David isn't here."

"Isn't here?" Tara questioned, her alarm growing. "Where is he?"

"Gentlemen!" The voice was deep and stern. All four had their attention drawn quickly to the man who strode toward them, accompanied by Zach who, without realizing his own reasons, had taken the best way to separate Tara from the three young officers. He had brought the commander of the fort to

98

meet her. If Tara had known the truth, she might have been surprised at Zach's satisfaction. It pleased him when they found it difficult to control their disappointment at Tara being so quickly snatched from them.

The three saluted sharply and Tara became aware, in a subtle way, that this commander kept his forces under complete control. But he was young, she thought, not much more than thirty-three. He was quite handsome as well. His hair was a deep gold and he had a full mustache. His eyes were forest-green and were smiling warmly now.

"Please allow me to introduce myself. I'm Major Aaron Creighton. I'm the commanding officer here in Fort Lyon. Zach had just told me you're David Montgomery's sister. I'm terribly sorry to disappoint you. David is away on a mission for me in Denver, and I don't expect him back for at least a month."

"A month!" Tara repeated.

"You needn't worry, Miss Montgomery. You will be quite comfortable in David's quarters until he returns. Do you plan only a visit, or are we to be allowed to hope you plan to stay with us?"

"I'm afraid, Major Creighton, that I'll be staying with David. It is obvious he did not receive my letter."

"There is mail on the table in his quarters, but I'm afraid most of it came since he has been gone. Is there something wrong?"

"I'm afraid . . . David doesn't know that our parents were killed in an accident. It looks like David will have to put up with me for some time."

"Let me extend my sympathy and show you to David's quarters. The wagon will be unharnessed and lined along the outer wall so you can unpack your things at your leisure."

"Thank you." Tara spoke to the officer but was aware of Zach's silence and his position, a few steps away from the group, as if he knew he would not be welcomed within its circle.

Major Creighton extended his arm to her and she took it, still wondering, as they walked across the compound, why Zach had been so silent. She looked back over her shoulder and saw him still standing where they had left him, his eyes following her.

The accommodations for the officers were under one roof, as was the barracks, but separated into quarters consisting of four rooms for each officer. Tara was comfortable with the thought that at least there was enough room for her, since many of the others had wives and families in the same amount of room.

Aaron reached to open the door for her, and as she stepped inside he followed. She was surprised at the coolness inside in comparison to the heat on the outside.

David was Spartan in his tastes, yet the place was neat and well kept. There was a table just to the side of the door and Tara recognized her own letter on top of the packet of letters left for David in his absence. Their parents' death would be a terrible shock when David returned, and she too would have to live through the loss again. She held this thought at bay as she turned to face Aaron Creighton again.

"Thank you so much for your concern. I'm sure I shall be quite comfortable here. I've brought a few of Mother's things with me, and I can brighten the place up while David is gone."

"You alone will be a very bright addition, not only to David's quarters, but to the entire fort. I can already see all my young lieutenants will be falling all over themselves to see that you're comfortable."

"Thank you," Tara laughed softly. It had been some time now since she had heard such flirtatious flattery. Her ego needed it after her trip with Zach. "You're very flattering."

"Well, we haven't much social activity around here, but you are in time for the annual officer's ball," he laughed. "If you can call it that. Anyway, it has always been an enjoyable occasion."

"When is it?"

"Next week. I should like the privilege of escorting you." Again his smile was boyish and full of amusement. "Rank has

100

some privileges, so I've outmaneuvered the men who will soon be pounding your door down."

"Everyone is invited?"

"Oh, yes, it's the one time a year the officers host a party for everyone in the fort."

"I imagine Mule and Zach will enjoy it after our long trek."

"Zachary Hale?"

"Yes, our guide."

"Oh, I know Zach . . . it's just that he won't be there."

"He'll be leaving here so soon?"

"No, he'll still be at the fort. You have to understand, Tara. We can't invite Indians to the ball. Why, the whole fort would be up in arms. There's been too many problems out here with those red devils for me to go and invite one to a party. Besides, I don't think such a subdued celebration would be to Zach's . . . ah . . ."

"Savage tastes?" Tara replied coolly.

"Yes, you might say that. Tara, there are some wild hot heads among Zach's own tribe, and I feel sure he knows who they are, but he won't give me one name so I can put down this damn uprising."

For a moment Tara was stunned by what this civilized "gentleman" was asking Zach to do—to betray people of his own blood.

"You are not very fond of the Indians, are you?"

"Fond of them! They're a bloodthirsty lot of savages and we'd sleep a lot better if we could just control them. We have to do what we can to rid ourselves of the troublemakers and the ones who would believe they have one slim chance of survival. After that, we could deal with them on the proper reservations, contained where they belong."

"I see," Tara replied, remembering many of the things Mule had told her about Zach and his people. "But," she added quietly, "I was under the impression we were the trespassers, that this was their land before it was ours."

Aaron flushed, but his mouth grew firm. He attributed

101

Tara's words to the fact that she was a gentlewoman not long in the West, and that she knew very little about the Indians. After a while she would grow to understand what he said, after she understood what devils these savages were. He would allow her the time to learn.

"Either way, Miss Montgomery . . ."

"Tara, please."

"Tara," he smiled again, "I'm afraid it is not in my power to invite Zach. But I will say that he would most likely refuse. He has a damnable . . . sorry . . . amount of pride. He just wouldn't be comfortable there, and I'm sure he would cause a whole lot of discomfort among all the others."

"Yes," Tara said softly, "I imagine he would."

"I knew you'd understand. Now, I'd best go and see that everyone else gets settled."

Tara closed the door behind Aaron and stood in thought. Somehow she could actually feel the way Zach must feel. To be a guide and a supplier but not considered good enough to socialize with the white people at the fort must leave a bitter taste in his mouth. She tried to push thoughts of Zach from her mind as she watched Aaron walk toward him again.

The commander walked across the compound to where Zach and Mule were standing, engrossed in conversation that might have made Aaron more uneasy than he already was. Mule spotted Aaron as he approached and whispered to Zach, "The big white chief is comin'."

Zach didn't turn around and could hear Aaron stop behind him.

"Windwalker," Aaron said coldly.

Zach smiled at Mule's closed face and turned slowly, "You don't have the right to use that name. I don't want it dirtied on the white man's tongue. The name is Zach. Now," he grinned, "what can I do for you, Aaron?"

102

Chapter 10

Aaron walked closer to stand beside Zach. One of Aaron's biggest battles was to fight the respect and sometimes admiration he felt for a man whom he had considered beneath him. Aaron had to chuckle aloud. Zach was the only man at the fort that dared call his bluff and get away with it. He motioned Zach to walk with him and kept his voice just within his range.

"You son of a bitch, why the hell did you bring a pretty thing like her out here?"

"Why, Aaron, isn't it safe here with all these big brave blue shirts to protect her?" Zach chided with a glimmer of humor lighting his eyes.

"Very amusing, Zach. Your sense of humor leaves a lot to be desired. You know we're sitting on a powder keg and it's about to blow at any time."

"I didn't plan on bringing her here."

"Course not. You snatch up every pretty face you see, but this was a big mistake, Zach."

"I know, and I didn't plan on bringing her, Banning did."

Aaron stopped, turning to look at Zach who smiled benignly. "What's Banning up to?"

"Want me to take a guess?"

"I wouldn't mind."

"Rifles. He's arming my people and hoping for an all-out war."

Again Aaron's piercing gaze held Zach's, "How can he get rifles to them? Who's buying them? Just what the hell can I expect? I have to know where they're going."

"So you can strike first like the rest of the whites and wipe out the 'savages.'"

"Zach, I won't have a war out here. I have to do something fast. All you have to do is name me some of the hot heads and I'll put this insurrection down."

"It's not an insurrection. My people, for the most part, don't want a fight. They just want to be left in peace. I'll find out about the rifles . . . but I won't name you any names."

"So it's Banning bringing the rifles?"

"Right."

"You wouldn't have anything to do with it?"

"Don't let your prejudice jump in front of your good sense," Zach said coldly. "I'd bring my people a lot of things but never rifles."

"As far as the military is concerned, Zach, you're as suspicious as Banning. It's my job to keep an eye on both of you and I intend to do just that. One slip, Zach," Aaron said gently, "one slip and I'll make sure it's your last."

Although Zach seemed to be untouched by Aaron's words, a cold, helpless rage ate at him. Aaron had one blind spot—the conviction that all Indians were devious and untrustworthy. He knew Aaron would not be watching Banning as closely as he was him. Yet Zach knew Aaron was a man of strong convictions and even stronger capabilities. If he could just learn not to hate everyone who had a drop of Indian blood . . .

Zach smiled an aggravatingly calm smile, which he knew infuriated Aaron.

"I'll keep that in mind, Aaron, be sure of it."

"I'd still like to know why you let that girl come here alone. She'll have this fort turned on its ear, and I've got enough troubles already."

"I tried to warn her off, but as you'll find out, she's as

104

stubborn as they come."

Aaron chuckled, "Don't tell me you've found out firsthand. My, my, I thought you were irresistible. What happened? Did you find out she had no taste for 'savage' blood?"

"Aaron, old friend," Zach said softly, "one of these days I'm going to take offense," he grinned, "and maybe—just maybe— I might decide your scalp might look real good on my war lance."

Zach walked back toward Mule without waiting for Aaron's answer. But he knew Aaron was watching him with a close-to-murderous look. It gave him a small amount of satisfaction.

"You and that ornery cuss lock horns again?" Mule inquired with a broad grin. "Iffen you two could stop spittin' at each other, you'd probably be friends."

"Could be you're right, Mule. But until he can stop seeing red and white and start seeing me, I don't think there's a chance of that any too soon. Come on, let's go have a drink."

They walked through the bustle of unloading wagons toward the only place within the fort that served liquor.

Zach slid into a chair with his back securely protected by the wall, and they ordered drinks. Fragments of conversation drifted their way and most of it was about the coming ball. Mule was more than certain Zach heard and knew he had been deliberately ignored. He also wondered just what Tara was thinking and if she would prove to be the woman he thought she was.

By nightfall, campfires were lit by the travelers who would soon be moving on and hadn't unloaded their wagons. The ones who were to stay had lined their wagons against the wall of the fort and were trying to begin making their new quarters comfortable.

Tara had taken possession of one of the rooms in her brother's quarters and set about unpacking what little possessions she had brought with her. She was surrounded by the confusion of petticoats, shifts, and other sundry objects, when she heard the knock on her door. She stood from her

105

kneeling position before one of her huge trunks, dusted her hands together, and walked to the door.

"Aaron." She was surprised but smiled warmly.

"I know there are no provisions here since your brother has been gone so long, so I thought I might invite you to join me and a few others for dinner."

"How considerate of you all. I would be more than pleased. I was wondering where I was going to scrape up some food."

"We'll see you're supplied with provisions tomorrow, but for tonight we would really be honored if you would join us."

"Thank you, Aaron."

"I'll be by around about seven-thirty to escort you, if that's all right."

"I hate to inconvenience you. If you will tell me where to go, I'm sure I can find it."

"I'm sorry, Tara, but I can't have you drifting about the compound alone after dark. You are too young and much too pretty. I would hate to have to punish one of my men for making a foolish mistake."

"I'm sorry, I hadn't thought of such a thing. I'll be ready at seven-thirty."

"Fine. I'll see you then."

Tara nodded and Aaron smiled. He touched the brim of his hat in a half salute and walked away. Tara stood in the open doorway and watched him cross the compound. After a few minutes she felt the tingling sensation that someone was watching her. She scanned the area and suddenly she saw Zach, standing on the porch of the only saloon, one broad shoulder against the roof pole. His fingers were hooked in his belt and he seemed totally at ease, yet she sensed he was watching her closely. She swung the door shut.

Zach watched Aaron move from Tara's door as she stood framed in the doorway. He could feel his pulses race and his loins tighten, and he cursed himself again for allowing Tara Montgomery to reach in and touch him in a way he couldn't understand and found unwelcome. He watched her close the door, knowing their separation was better for her and knowing just as certainly that it was going to be some time before he could succeed in wiping her from his mind and his memory. His eyes drifted to the line of wagons against the wall of the fort, guarded by Banning's men. Mule came to stand beside him.

"What you thinkin', boy?" he asked gently.

"That he's got a hell of a lot of guards for a line of empty wagons. What do you suppose he has in there that's so valuable he has to guard it?"

"Wal, Zach boy, we can't just saunter over there and take a look now, kin we?"

"Not now. But after things settle down for a couple of days, maybe the guards will get careless."

"And some soft-walkin' Injun is just goin' to take hisself a little peek."

"Now, Mule," Zach said mildly, "that's trespassing. If a red man was caught doing that, he'd be shot without mercy."

"Then a white man can peek."

"Well . . . maybe I'll convince my red half that my white half should do just that."

"Want me to?"

"Nope. I just want to see them."

"Then what?"

"I'm going to trail them to the buyer, and when I find him I'm going to drag both Banning and whoever he is before my father's council. We're going to stop a blood bath . . . if we can." His eyes returned to Tara's door. "No matter what might stand in the way, we're going to stop a blood bath."

Tara had bathed and put on her second best dress, saving the only pretty gown she had for the coming ball. The dress was pale blue, its sleeves long and fitted and the bodice molded to her slim frame. The skirt was full and, with several petticoats, was wide enough to accent her waist and soft curves. She had coiled her hair at the nape of her neck, brushing it back from her face with some tendrils freely escaping. Tara was pleased with her reflection in the mirror and with the fact that she was ready when the knock sounded on her door. She grabbed up a white shawl from the back of a chair as she passed and opened the door to smile brightly up at Aaron, who was momentarily speechless at her beauty.

"Tara, you are absolutely beautiful."

"Thank you, sir," she replied.

"Shall we go?" Aaron extended his arm and Tara pulled her door closed, tucking her arm in his as they started across the compound.

It was a wide area of over a hundred yards of hard-packed dirt. The commander's quarters were directly across the compound from Tara's. From the lights and the murmur of voices, Tara could tell the guests had already arrived. She was both a little surprised and flattered that Aaron had come for her himself, when he was the host.

Aaron opened the door and escorted Tara inside. The guests ceased their conversations and turned toward them. She could feel their assessment of her.

The three young officers who had been the first to welcome Tara stood impatiently waiting for the formal introductions to be over, so they could swarm around her.

"Ladies and gentlemen, I'd like to introduce our newcomer, Tara Montgomery. She is Lieutenant David Montgomery's sister, recently coming from Washington. Of course you know Caleb Banning." Caleb smiled, but his eyes swept over her appreciatively.

"Tara, this is Lieutenant Samuel Duboise and his wife, Charlotte"—he waited until they exchanged greetings—"and this is Lieutenant Rodger Foster and his wife, Joan. Next to them is Master Sergeant James Braughn and his wife, Carina." They smiled and wished her welcome. "Next is Sergeant Charles Murphy and his wife, Bridy." Aaron smiled, knowing he had deliberately saved the three young officers for the last.

"These three," Aaron's eyes sparkled, "are the ones I must warn you to beware of, Tara. I'm afraid all three are still single. Lieutenant Ian McIver."

"Good evening, Miss Montgomery," Ian bowed slightly. He was handsome in a brawny Scottish way. His hair was a deep flame and his eyes a penetrating green. "It's a welcome that you are in this dreary place. You've surely brightened it."

"Thank you, Lieutenant McIver."

"I'd be pleased if you'd call me Ian."

"And I will remind you to call me Tara."

"Tara," he grinned, quite pleased.

"This is Lieutenant Sean Callihan," Aaron motioned toward the next. "Beware of his Irish charm, Tara; he's a dangerous fellow."

"Sure now, Colonel," Sean grinned, "you'd be misrepresentin' me, givin' the lady wrong ideas. I'm as mild as a newborn lamb, and I'm pleased to make your acquaintance, Tara Montgomery. It's a fine Irish name you have."

Tara was well aware of the wicked Irish charm of Sean Callihan.

"And last, but just as dangerous," Aaron chuckled, "is Lieutenant Randolph Brighton."

"Charmed. Tara," Randolph Brighton murmured, "you are most welcome here."

"Thank you," Tara replied as she withdrew her hand from his, feeling his reluctance to let go.

"Tara, may I get you a glass of wine?" Aaron questioned.

"Wine?" Tara seemed surprised, and soft laughter rippled through the group.

"We've not gone past all the amenities, Tara," Bridy Murphy smiled. "Charles has some very good wines sent occasionally by his brother, and we're more than pleased to share them with everyone."

"I would love a glass," Tara replied.

By the time they were seated at the dinner table, Tara had had two glasses of wine. She found herself between Sean

Callihan and Ian McIver, who vied for her attention.

The dinner progressed with laughter and amusing anecdotes that kept Tara engrossed. But despite all the pleasantries, Tara was subtly aware that part of her was detached, having drifted to thoughts of Zach and his exclusion from all of this. She wondered what he was doing and if he were with someone else, annoyed with herself for caring. She looked across the table at Caleb, unable to read the thoughts behind the warmth of his smile. Those thoughts might have terrified her had she known.

Tara was receiving a warm welcome. She was being invited into a circle of friends with whom she might be sharing long years. Why then did she feel alien, incomplete, as if there were something yet to be done that would change her life and make it forever different?

At the close of the evening, there was a mild discussion on who would walk Tara to her quarters. Ian's determination won out, and he grinned broadly as she slipped her shawl about her shoulders and tucked her hand through his arm. They walked across the now-silent compound, guarded by the sentries who walked their posts on the platforms near the top of the protective stockade. The night was still warm and Tara looked up, amazed at how close and brilliant the stars seemed to be.

Ian flirted shamelessly with her, and she had to laugh with him at his obvious flattery.

"Do you ride, Tara?"

"Oh, yes, I love to."

"Then you must let me take you out of the fort and show you some of this territory."

"But I thought that was dangerous."

"Dangerous?"

"The Indians. Caleb seemed to think . . ."

"There's no problem. They're unarmed and scattered. The danger is all in Caleb's mind. Maybe he was trying to frighten you."

"I'm not frightened, just careful. I wouldn't want Aaron upset with me."

"He is a formidable man, but anyway, if you will agree to a ride soon"—his green eyes warmed as they looked down into hers—"I'll make sure I take especial good care of you."

"I shall think about it, Ian," Tara smiled. "Ask me in a few days, when I'm settled."

"All right, I'll do that."

They had reached Tara's door and she turned to extend her hand out to him, "Thank you for walking me home, Ian."

"My pleasure, Tara. I'll see you tomorrow."

"Good night."

Tara watched Ian walk away, then reached out to open her door. Her hand paused as her eyes caught a movement near the stable door. She looked closely, in time to see Zach reach out and pull the stable door closed. She didn't even realize she was moving slowly toward the stable until she was almost halfway there. She stopped, surprised at herself and surprised again that, instead of turning back, she continued to walk. She had no idea what she might say to him, but she sensed she wanted to make him know that, despite all that was between them, she could not exclude him from her world as the others had done.

Within the stable one lantern was burning, spreading a vague mellow light and creating shadowed corners. At first Tara could not see Zach, and she stood motionless until the low murmur of a masculine voice identified his position in one of the stalls. She moved toward it on silent feet.

The last thing Zach expected was to come face to face with Tara as he exited the stall. For him it was as if one moment she was in his thoughts and the next she was standing before him. It took him a moment to understand that she was real and not a figment of his imagination.

"Tara, what are you doing here at this time of night? And alone! What stupid jackass let you go wandering around by yourself in a fort with so many woman-hungry men?"

"I'm quite capable of taking care of myself," she replied, annoyed that, just at the time she wanted to make peace, he had to be the heavy-handed male again.

111

"I remember you saying that once before, and I don't believe it any more now than I did then." His eyes were sparkling with the taunt.

"You're such an obstinate man!" Tara exclaimed angrily. "I came here to talk to you. Why do you have to be so—so damn ornery!"

"Watch your temper," he teased with a broad and very aggravating grin.

With forced concentration, Tara held her tongue until she was again in control. She was not going to give him the satisfaction of her continued anger.

Zach's eyes raked her and glowed with a deep appreciation. "That's a becoming dress, Tara. I thought you were pretty, but I'll change that: You're beautiful." His voice was deep and pulsed with warmth.

Unprepared for the sudden compliment, Tara's lips parted in surprise. This man was so unpredictable. She never knew quite what to expect from him. On top of that, the warmth in his eyes was eliciting a physical response that shattered constructive thinking. He had moved closer, and she found herself looking up at him and feeling her heart begin to pound.

He wore a buckskin shirt, loosely laced at the front to expose a bronzed chest with a mat of dark hair. His breeches were snug-fitting buckskin, and Tara was frightened to look down, knowing his physical arousal matched the heat that sparkled in his blue eyes. A red bandana had been rolled and tied about his head, giving him a rugged appearance, and his thick black hair, curling against his neck, enhanced his aura of powerful sensuality.

"You said you came here to talk to me?" he questioned softly.

"What? . . . Oh, yes . . . I . . ." She fumbled for the words she had planned to say, while his intense blue gaze seemed locked on her mouth. "I just wondered if you'd be staying here."

"Does it matter?" His voice was like velvet and he drew just a little closer. He was close enough to see the pulse at the base of her throat throb wildly.

She could feel her pulses race and sensed they matched his. Slowly he reached a hand to delicately trace her lips with his fingers. "Does it matter?" he insisted in the same sultry voice. He watched her answer in the trembling of her soft, inviting mouth, felt her answer in the quivering warmth of her body, so lightly touching his, and the way her eyes seemed to darken, the lids growing heavy with passion.

Tara fought the emotions that seemed to surge through her in wave after wave. They broke against all her senses, and she became acutely aware of the sheen of perspiration on his skin, of the scent of him, manly and virile, and of the warmth of his body.

"Yes," she whispered, "it matters."

"Why, Tara?" His hand traced the fine contours of her jaw and the tips of his fingers moved lightly down her throat. "You and I both know that these people will never allow it."

"Doesn't that bother you?"

"Not anymore," he lied.

"What matters then?"

"That my people don't die. That they're not bloodied by people like Caleb Banning. That no one . . . like Aaron Creighton . . . finds a reason to kill them all."

Tears filmed her eyes and caught on her lashes, and she couldn't understand them. It was as if she felt a great deal of futile pain.

"No tears, Tara." He bent his head and brushed his lips across the tears on her cheek, tasting their salt. Then his mouth moved to hers, tasting gently, his tongue probing until her mouth accepted it. He made no move to embrace her, but their mouths fused in a kiss that shook the foundations of their souls.

Then, to Tara's surprise, he took hold of her shoulders and reluctantly broke the kiss. He turned her around and pressed close to her.

"Go back to those you belong to, Tara. Better yet, go back home where you're safe. You're a wide-eyed, innocent little girl who's going to get hurt. Reach your hand for the fire, Tara, and you're going to get burnt."

She tried to twist away, to turn in his arms, but his hands were immensely strong and she couldn't move.

His voice rasped in her ear as he pressed her back against him. "I could take you here. Take you because you're a sweet, gentle believer. Love demands a whole lot more than a quick roll in the hay." Tara gasped in shock but he was remorseless. "You don't know or understand what's at stake here, and you're too damn sweet to believe it. Get out of here, Tara, before I regret my own stupid streak of gallantry and make love to you like I want to."

Finally she twisted free and spun about. He saw the hurt mingled with the anger in her eyes, and he was pleased, for it was his only defense. He wanted her so badly he could feel it burn within him like a forest fire.

She was panting and her eyes sparked with flame. "I came here because I felt sorry for you! How foolish. You're a savage just like they say you are, and I don't care what happens to you. You're right, I was stupid. Stupid to believe you had one honest feeling in you. God, I hate you! I hate you!"

She spun away from him and ran to the door, pushing it open and continuing to run until she crossed the compound and found, through the mist of tears, her door. Once inside she bolted it, leaned against it, and gave way to the tears that threatened to choke her.

Zach followed her as far as the stable door. He stood in the doorway and watched her until she disappeared.

"Tara," he whispered, the ache in him growing to proportions he couldn't believe. He could feel the emptiness she left behind her, like a dark void, and the taste and scent of her would remain with him for much longer than he could imagine.

But he couldn't bring her down into the dark confusion he

114

was involved in. She was bound to get hurt, and he felt this hurt now was better than what would happen if he ever let her begin to care for him. At least now she was only attracted to what he was, and the difference excited her. He was sure that was all it was for her, but he was shaken by what it had become to him. She was a danger he couldn't afford.

He pulled the door closed and was just about to turn around when a slight rustling came to him. His hearing had been developed as protection and it was keen. He stood immobile for several minutes, then he smiled and, without turning around, spoke softly, "Little Raven, what are you doing here?"

Chapter 11

Little Raven had stepped out of the lodge he shared with his parents. Word had come just the night before that Windwalker was back and that he slept in the white man's fort. Windwalker was the brother who had been Little Raven's whole life from the time he could remember. Even though they did not share the same mother and Windwalker was nine years older than Little Raven, they had been as close as brothers could be. Windwalker had taught Little Raven to hunt and to ride.

Impatient to see his half brother, Little Raven had moved quickly to his pony, and in one fluid motion he mounted and was riding away from the village of Waiting Wolf.

At sixteen, Little Raven was more man than boy. He was tall for his age, standing nearly six feet, and he was heavily muscled yet graceful. His bronzed body exuded good health and signs of regular physical activity. He rode with an easy rolling motion, accustomed to the gait of a horse since the age of three, when Windwalker had sat him astride one for the first time.

His face gave promise of great strength, the cheekbones high and the nose straight over a wide mouth that boasted firm sculpted lips, given to smiling often. His eyes were clear and black as night, as was his glossy hair that hung in two braids to his shoulders.

Given to lightheartedness and often to humorous mischief, Little Raven found his world most satisfying. He had parents who gave him strength and a half brother whose moccasins he wished to walk in. A pretty girl could catch his wandering eye easily. The only cloud in his blue sky were the white men in the fort that stood too close to his village, and the knowledge that Windwalker didn't trust them either, even though half his blood was theirs and he often chose to live among them.

The last thing he planned to do was to ride up to the fort and request entry. He knew he would not be welcomed, even though he would be admitted. Besides, it did his sense of humor good to gain admittance without the knowledge of the pacing sentries. He had done it often, filled with satisfaction each time he did. It gave him something to boast about to the other young warriors. He frowned with the knowledge of what was growing, not only in his village but in many others. A force was slowly building that would require only one spark to set it off. Lately, the words of Tall Bull had promised there would be guns—guns that would mean trouble. He needed to know Windwalker's thoughts on this matter.

When he reached the fort the day was just beginning to fade, and he dismounted and prepared to wait. Soon would be the time when father sun slept beyond the horizon, and mother moon had not yet risen in the night sky. It was the time he would find his way into the fort and seek out his brother. He waited with infinite patience, remaining immobile and watching the comings and goings in the fort with a keen eye. His smile curved his lips at the challenge facing him. There were at least eight sentries pacing the wall. Little Raven chuckled softly to himself, considering the eight-to-one odds in his favor. He fed his horse a handful of grain that he carried in a pouch hanging at his side, then hobbled the animal carefully to make sure he did not stray too far, in case Little Raven needed him quickly. Then, on silent feet, he made his way to the wall of the fort, moving from shadow to shadow.

Scaling the wall took little effort but some very careful

timing. Then he slipped silently to the ground within the fort. Again his smile twitched his lips. If the white man was always so self-assured and careless, then it would be easy to defeat him.

Little Raven's meandering had taken him into the fort, but only as far as the stables and his brother's room nearby, plus the storage rooms where he had often snatched bits of food for his always-grumbling stomach.

He moved like a shadow to the back of the stable and then inside. He froze as the murmur of voices came to him. He kept in the shadows, watching the confrontation between Tara and Zach. He heard only snatches of their words, but he heard enough to know something unsettling existed between his brother and this white woman. He realized they were battling somehow and yet drawn to each other at the same time. What disturbed Little Raven more was the look on his brother's face when the pretty white woman fled the barn. He had never seen his brother look so shaken and so unhappy.

He had moved only slightly but knew in an instant the moment Windwalker became aware of his presence. He watched him grow tense and alert, then he heard the soft chuckle.

"Little Raven," Windwalker said without turning in his direction. "What are you doing here?"

Zach slid the bar across the door as he spoke, making sure they would not be intruded upon. Little Raven stepped from the shadows, and Zach turned to face him. Both men smiled. There was no outward sign of emotion, yet each knew he would give his life for the other if the need came.

"Word came that you were back, Windwalker. I would welcome my brother home."

"You are the first to speak words of welcome, little brother, and they sound good to me. Is our father well?"

"He is."

"And your mother?"

"She is also well."

118

"You came for another reason besides seeing if you can still slip in and out of this fort. You've been playing that game for a long time."

Little Raven laughed softly, "And still they cannot catch me."

"Be careful. One slip and they might give you cause to regret it. There is always great fear among the whites. That is why they cannot live with the earth and must hide behind walls."

"You are right as always," Little Raven added. "Our father has sent me to ask you to come to him. He would speak with you."

"Something wrong?"

"There is much"—Little Raven shrugged—"unrest. Some of the young men want to band together and chase the white men from their fort and back toward the rising sun from where they came."

"And you, little brother, are you one of these?"

"No . . . I would hear your words on this before I think of what to do. Already our father is alarmed. I would not want to add to his worry. That is another reason I wanted to be the one who came for you."

"You are growing in wisdom as well as size, Little Raven. It is a wise man who takes council and thinks carefully of how his deeds will affect others."

Little Raven felt an immense pride. As far as he was concerned, one compliment from Windwalker was worth all the words he could hear from any others.

"You will ride with me now?"

"Do you think you can get out as easily as you got in?" Zach laughed. Little Raven's laugh blended with his.

"They will never know I was here."

"Where is your horse?"

Little Raven told him the location, then Zach replied, "I'll saddle up and meet you there."

In minutes, Little Raven seemed to fade into the dark, and Zach set about saddling his horse. He unbolted the stable doors, led his horse out, and walked to the gates of the fort.

All the men in the fort knew Zach came and went as he chose. The sentries opened the gate, and Zach mounted and rode out, laughing at the thought of Little Raven's ability to come and go as he chose without one sentry realizing their fort had been penetrated.

It took Zach very little time to find Little Raven's horse, and just a few minutes later his half brother appeared with a wide grin of satisfaction on his face.

Little Raven mounted and they moved away together. They rode side by side for a while before Zach realized Little Raven was occasionally casting a puzzled look in his direction.

"What's on your mind, little brother?"

"I would not anger my brother by speaking of things that do not concern me."

"I don't know of much in my life that does not concern you. Speak of what you will."

"The white woman at the fort," Little Raven said softly.

For several minutes Zach was silent, then he spoke. "What of her?"

"I watched her face when you were . . . speaking. She felt much pain. It seemed . . . confusing, for you touched as if she were . . . someone special, then the touch turned to something else. I don't understand. How can one love and hate at the same time?"

"Nothing is simple, Little Raven. But . . . I don't want to see her hurt."

"But you hurt her; I could see it in her eyes."

"But not as badly as she could be. I know you don't understand that either, Little Raven, and it's pretty hard to explain."

"Is it because," Little Raven asked softly, "your blood is not of hers? Does she feel shame that you are half blood to us as well?"

"Again, brother, you are wiser than I thought."

"I do not believe this."

120

"You don't?" Zach laughed.

"No, you were seeing your own heart maybe. I saw her eyes. I do not believe her heart is so. Maybe, brother, she is a woman like your mother. Maybe . . . it is you who are blind."

"Now," Zach chuckled, "we will speak of something else."

"Yes . . . but as you told me once when I was a child, problems do not run away and hide because we do not want to look at them."

"She is not a problem, Little Raven. And I will explain this much to you. When you hold something close to you—when it is important—there are times that you must do what looks cruel for its protection. And that, my young brother, is the last we are going to say about it."

Little Raven remained silent but Zach was amused to see his half brother's disagreement written plainly across his face. He ignored it and gave himself over to his own thoughts.

Tara . . . Loving her would be so easy. . . . Love! Where did that thought come from? He couldn't fall in love with Tara Montgomery. It was beyond any kind of reason. They could never be together at the fort, and she would not want to live in his father's village. Most likely, she could not. After all, she was recently from the East and her head had been filled with stories of the "savages." But the soft scent of her perfume was in the air and the feel of her warm pulsing body in his arms refused to be banished. His mouth grew grim. He would push Tara from his mind if it were the last thing he ever did. He and Little Raven continued their ride toward the village in silence.

Little Raven and Zach slid from their ponies before Waiting Wolf's lodge. Their feet had barely touched the ground when Waiting Wolf stepped outside. Zach could clearly be seen in his father's face, with the exception of the fine lines at the corners of his eyes and the deeper grooves about his firm mouth. They stood the same height, and Waiting Wolf still had the same hard-muscled body of his youth. Their only differences lay in the slightly lighter color of Zach's skin and the deep blue of his eyes. Waiting Wolf and Zach had not seen each other for nearly a year, and the reunion was joyful. Waiting Wolf placed both of his hands on Zach's shoulders. "It pleases me to see my oldest son return. It has been too long since you began your journey."

"Any time away from you, my father, is too long," Zach replied. "And Singing Grass, she is well?"

"Yes, she is well."

"Father, we must talk of many things."

"I know. I know why you are here and the questions you must ask. But the answers will not be easy. Come, come and sit in my lodge and we will talk." Waiting Wolf turned to Little Raven, who had never been invited to sit in council, or to supply any thoughts or plans. "Come, Little Raven, sit with us and talk."

Little Raven had never been prouder or loved his father and brother more than he did at this moment. Too choked to speak, he simply followed them both inside.

Once seated about the small fire in the center, there was another moment of silence. Little Raven and Zach both would wait until their father chose to speak.

"Your journey was safe and . . . successful?"

"The journey was an easy one. There were no problems," Zach replied, neatly dodging his father's subtle questions. "Father, I hear of things that make me fear for us."

"You speak of promised guns. Such words have set the young men on fire. I have tried to warn them that the promises can be lies. The guns are a dream that will not come."

"They are worse than that. They are a disaster if they do. I have been working for months to find where they're coming from and who is planning on receiving them," Zach said.

"You would stop us from having guns? With the white man, it is now the only way we can hope to fight back."

"To hunt with, for protection, but you and I both know if we let it go, there are those who won't stop there. They would use

122

the guns to make war—and a war with the whites is one we cannot win."

"A man cannot bow to the ones who come to take the food from the mouths of his children and the land from beneath his feet."

"I do not ask us to bow, Father, I ask us to try to live together. It will be hard enough to control the wild ones on both sides, but if you agree, our people are lost."

"I have not made a decision. I have not seen the guns, and I don't even know if they are real or not."

"Who in our village would deal with someone for guns? Who is stirring up the young men?" Zach asked softly as he bent toward his father.

"Do the white men want this information?"

"Father, do you think I would betray one of my own and bring the whites down on us?"

"I speak not of your betrayal, my son, but I would not put you in a position of choice. The day may still come when you will be forced to choose a side. It is hard belonging to two worlds."

"I would do nothing that would bring shame to you or to this village. Nor would I dishonor my mother."

Waiting Wolf reached a weathered hand to rest on Zach's arm. "We will not argue over this, my son. I tell you that the guns have not been brought here. I will also tell you that if they are brought to me, I will send for you."

"I am worried that they will not be brought to you. That others may take them and lead raids that will bring the whites down on us. Father, if I find those who are guilty and bring them before you and the council, will you do all you can to control anything that might happen? It is all I ask."

"Then I will give you my word. If you bring them to me, I will do all I can to keep peace."

"That is all I ask. That you won't let any of our people begin something that only their deaths will end."

Little Raven had not spoken and prayed he would not have

123

the attention brought to him, for should either his father or brother ask him for names, he would have found it difficult both to lie and to tell the truth, as he knew names and he knew more about the promise of guns than his father did.

"You will stay with us tonight?" Waiting Wolf questioned. "There are many who have missed you." The words were said by Waiting Wolf with a twinkle in his dark eyes, but Zach knew whom he meant.

"I have not seen Morning Sun for a long time. Surely she has found a warrior to her liking and is ready for marriage."

"I think the warrior to her liking has been gone from our village."

"I will stay the night, but I must get back to the fort before midday tomorrow."

"There is someone who draws you back?"

"Uh . . . no, no one. I'm tracking some information and I don't want to lose the trail."

"Then you must eat and drink and speak to all the others."

"Yes, there are many I would like to talk to."

As they rose to their feet, Zach became aware that not only had Little Raven been very silent, but his eyes refused to meet his. He promised himself another talk with his now-too-silent brother.

Tara awoke just before dawn, slightly disoriented and tense from unsubstantial dreams that had plagued her sleep. There was a pitcher of water on a nearby stand, and she poured a little in a bowl and sponged her face and body free of sleep. She dressed slowly, forcing the dreams from her mind and wondering just how she was going to spend her day and how, in the confines of the fort, she could keep from crossing Zach's path again.

Her cheeks grew warm with the shame she had felt when he had implied she had sought him out so he would make love to her, when he had told her how easy it would be to take her. But

124

worse than that was the memory of her response to his kiss, to his tremendous physical magnetism. She had wanted him. It was impossible to deny it to herself as she vehemently would do any others.

She had to forget Zachary Hale. She had to remember that he truly was half savage, and she had to remember that he was quite capable of using and discarding her if he felt she were in his way.

By the time she finished dressing, the sun was forcing beams of light through the shutters that covered her windows. She went to one and pushed it open, inhaling the fresh warm air and feeling the pleasure of the warmth of the morning sun on her face.

Her appearance at her open window drew Caleb's attention from halfway across the compound. He walked toward her, taking the time to enjoy a beauty he planned one day to have for himself.

"Good morning, Tara. Did you sleep well?"

"Yes, Caleb, thank you. My, it does get active around here early in the morning."

"Well, the military is always up by dawn."

"And what about you?"

"Oh, I'm an early riser too. It's a beautiful day. Would you like to go for a ride?"

"I'd love to. What shall we do about breakfast?"

"Over in the mess hall would be your best bet. It looks like you're in need of supplies."

"Yes, Aaron said he'd see to my provisions today."

"Well, I'll tell you what. You change so we can go for a ride, and I'll go see Aaron. Then we'll get us some breakfast and be ready to go."

"All right. Thank you."

"Think nothing of it. It's my pleasure to help you. Who knows, you might be a great help to me one day."

"I'll be ready in no time, and Caleb, I'll be delighted to return your kindness."

125

"Yes," he said softly, "I'm sure you will."

Caleb moved away toward Aaron's office, and Tara returned to her room where she hastily changed into a riding skirt. At least, she thought, it would take her away from a chance meeting with Zach.

Caleb and Aaron arranged for provisions to be put in Tara's quarters, and less than an hour later, Tara and Caleb left the mess hall and rode out the gates of the fort.

"You fit well in this territory, Tara," Caleb said as they rode slowly. "I'm glad I brought you, even though Zach was dead set against it."

"Is Mr. Hale this way with all women or did he just take a dislike to me?"

"Zach!" Caleb laughed. "Zach certainly doesn't dislike women, especially if they're as pretty as you. But word has it he has a little dusky-skinned gal in his village just waiting for him to get home so he can get hitched."

"Hitched . . . married?" Tara could not believe the wrenching inside that made her breath catch.

"Yep, married. Of course it won't mean much to him, I suppose. These Indians are not exactly the domestic type. He'll visit her now and again, enough to leave her with a papoose or two, then he'll go on trying to collect every pretty girl he sees."

"I hadn't thought of him . . . I mean . . . he just didn't seem . . ."

"Tara, don't let these savages fool you. He's a handsome one, and he hates the whites out here. We're a threat to him. There's been raid after raid on the white settlers that live in the territory. Whole families are just butchered. Did you know these bucks think it's just fine to scalp any white man, woman, or child. They wear the hair on their belts or on their war lances."

"How—how awful."

"There's a lot of rumors going around now about someone bringing guns to the Indians, but if you do some right figuring, you can be pretty sure who's doing the gunrunning."

"I don't understand."

"Look, Zach has been happy here until the whites moved in. Then he gets mad and decides to do something about it. So the white side of him takes over, and he goes back and buys some guns that he's going to bring back and turn on the whites."

"But why would he lead all these people out here and be so protective of them? If he wanted them dead, he could have had them attacked before they got here."

"Because his guns haven't arrived yet, and he figures the more whites in the fort the more will die as soon as he can whip up his redskin brothers to a frenzy. Once he gets them on the warpath, there won't be a way to stop them. Especially if he's armed them."

"But what can we do?"

"We have to just wait and watch until he makes a mistake. Then the military will have him where they want him."

"What—what will they do if they catch him bringing guns?"

"They will hang him—after a trial, of course."

Tara was silent, and Caleb was satisfied that she was stunned and confused.

But Tara was finding it hard to believe what she had heard. She couldn't equate the Zach who had held her and made love to her with the man Caleb had described.

They returned from their ride by midday, and Tara went straight to her quarters. She had to close the door between her and the world and sort out her thoughts. She didn't want to believe what Caleb had said, remembering Zach's coldness toward him. Was it because Zach didn't trust Caleb, or he knew Banning didn't trust him?

Tonight was the ball, and she planned on listening closely to all conversations. She knew Zach was less than welcome in the fort because of his Indian blood. But surely they could not believe him guilty of such atrocities as Caleb had described.

But the wait would be oppressively long, and she wanted to give Zach some benefit of the doubt. She had no idea where he

127

might be, but the stable seemed a good place to start.

She half ran, half walked to the stable and went inside, closing the door after her. She spun around when she heard Mule's voice.

"What's the trouble, girl? Some of those randy boys chasin' ya?" he chuckled, but the laughter died when he read Tara's face. He moved to stand close to her. "Something is the matter, isn't it? What is it, girl?"

"Mule, I've got to talk to Zach."

"Afraid ya can't right now."

"Why? In heaven's name, why? Mule, it's really important."

"Well, I'd like to help ya, girl, but it seems he's gone."

"Gone?"

"I came over here to talk to him late last night, and I found his room empty."

"But where? . . ."

"If I was to make a guess, I'd say he had a visitor sometime last night. Most likely a messenger from his pa, and he went right off to talk to him. Iffen his pa sent for him, Zach wouldn't waste much time gettin' to him."

"You mean someone from his tribe was actually in here last night? Would they let them in at night?"

"Not so's you'd notice it," Mule laughed. "Whoever came, came right over the wall, and I'd bet I would be safe in sayin' it was Zach's kid brother, Little Raven. He's got about as much nerve as Zach does, and he'd probably get a right good laugh out of it. I expect he'll be back right soon. You want me to tell him you were looking for him?"

"No—no, never mind. It wasn't important at all."

Before Mule could speak again, Tara turned to leave. Her mind was in a turmoil. She couldn't trust Caleb, so Zach said, and Caleb said she couldn't trust Zach. But so much pointed to Zach's guilt. Who else would have a better reason to wipe out the whites? Who else would have a better opportunity? All evidence pointed to Zach, and yet some deep part of her refused to accept this.

She returned to her room and bolted the door, then she lay across her bed to think. Nothing had been rational from the first moment she had met Zachary Hale. He had confused her and stirred to life emotions she could not believe. Because of the callous way he had treated her she should be able to believe in his guilt, but she couldn't. She had to face him; she had to read his eyes and listen to his answers before she would truly know. Another thought lit deeply in her mind. Had Zach returned to his village, as Caleb had said, to marry? This, above all things, she had to have an answer to.

Chapter 12

Zach rose from his seat by his father's fire, but before he could speak, the door flap was pushed open and Singing Grass came in. Her smile was quick and warm. Waiting Wolf was the entire center of her life as was her son, Little Raven. But Zach held a spot separate from everything. When she had come to Waiting Wolf's lodge as his wife, she had been frightened that his firstborn son would find her distasteful. At first Zach found it hard to accept a woman whom he felt was trying to destroy his mother's place within Waiting Wolf's heart. He had been lonely and filled with sorrow after losing his mother. It had taken a long time before they became tentative friends, but it was the coming of Little Raven that had built the bridge between them. Zach suddenly became the leader, the big brother, and he fell into it with a passion that pleased both Waiting Wolf and Singing Grass. He had guided Little Raven's first steps, ridden with him on his first pony, and had been so engrossed in his growing affection for his half brother that he forgot his own pain in the process.

"Singing Grass, it is good to see you again."

"And to see you, Windwalker. You have been gone from this lodge much too long. I hope you are here to spend some days with us?"

"Not this trip, Singing Grass, but I hope to return for a stay soon."

"If you are finished speaking to your father, Morning Sun would like to speak to you."

"Where is she?"

"She waits by her father's lodge."

Zach turned back to his father. "Is there more you wish to say to me?"

"No, my son, go and speak with Morning Sun."

Zach nodded and left the lodge to the three silent people who prayed something beyond them would keep their wandering son in their village.

Zach walked between the lodges, thinking of Morning Sun. He saw her standing before her father's lodge. She was small and slender, with her long hair braided in two waist-length braids. Her smile was quick when she saw him and she moved toward him.

"Windwalker," she spoke in a warm voice, "it has been long since you left."

"The trip east and back has been a long one, but it was necessary, Morning Sun."

"You will stay now?"

"I cannot. I must go back to the fort in the morning."

"But why must you always go to the fort? Do you not like our village and our ways any longer? Does your white blood call so strongly?"

"That is not the reason, Morning Sun. You know my life here has been good."

"I miss you very much, Windwalker."

"I know. I have been gone long, but one of these days I will come home for a long stay."

"Is—is there something . . . someone special at the white fort that—"

"There is no one special. I just have things that must be done. I cannot speak of them to you or to any others. You must understand."

But he had seen Tara's face flash in his memory and knew he had skirted the truth. He found it difficult to reason it out in his logical mind. Tara was nothing but a threat to his peace of

131

mind and even to his cause. Yet he had to do everything that would keep her and the others in the fort safe, even though he knew they were the intruders. Still, he knew whatever vague things were in his mind could only result in problems for his people. The same old problems faced him. He felt the same tug of war between his white and Indian bloods. His father's people could not win a war, and he would do all in his power to make sure the means to war never arrived.

"You sleep tonight and leave at dawn," she pouted. "When do you have time to share with us?"

"We have shared years closely as brother and sister. We will have many more years together when I return. For now, there are things that must be done. I must return to the fort in the morning."

"Tall Bull speaks to my father of marriage," she blurted suddenly.

"Tall Bull!" Zach repeated in surprise. "Surely your father would not marry you to him."

"He thinks on this matter." She shivered and her eyes glowed with a fear he hated to see in someone he cared so much for. He and Morning Sun had been as close as possible, playing as children. There was a bond between them he could not deny, and he refused to evade what he thought was a responsibility.

"And you, what do you think?"

"I think I would not care to be his wife."

"Then we must speak to your father. You are not a woman to be given to a man like Tall Bull. He abuses all who pass before him, even his animals."

"You—you care enough to speak to my father?" she questioned hopefully.

Zach took hold of her shoulders, and she felt her heart quicken only to have her dreams dashed by his next words.

"Morning Sun, you have been like a sister to me for many years. I would speak to your father as a brother would. Do not worry. Rest tonight, and we will talk later." He kissed her cheek and left her. She gazed after him, her heart in her eyes.

132

Zach gave some thought to Tall Bull. He couldn't imagine any father wanting to marry off his daughter to a man like him. From the days of their childhood, Zach remembered well the streak of cruelty in Tall Bull. He had found him abusing Little Raven once when his half brother was no more than six. Their first confrontation had led to many more, and the mutual dislike grew like a wall between them.

At this moment, Zach's first thought was to talk again to his young brother. There were things he had seen in his face that had stirred a feeling of unrest. Surely Little Raven was not involved in the gun shipment? He didn't want to believe that, but worse he didn't want to believe his brother had chosen this time to break the confidence that always existed between them.

As was custom, Zach had a lodge of his own because he had found it better to allow Singing Grass her own home and family. He went to his lodge, hoping, as was habit, that Little Raven would come and sit with him to share the long talks.

He did not have long to wait. He had built a small fire and seated himself comfortably when the door flap was pushed aside and Little Raven entered. His smile was quick, and he dropped down across the fire from Zach. There was mischief in his brilliant black eyes.

"You are here, brother. I am surprised."

"And why would you be surprised?"

"I had thought a girl as pretty as Morning Sun would hold you longer. In fact, I had doubts that you would return to your lodge this night."

"Jumping to conclusions can be very misleading, little brother," Zach grinned.

"I think maybe returning here was your idea alone." Little Raven laughed.

"I would speak of other things as well. Is it true that Spotted Bear considers letting Tall Bull have Morning Sun as a wife?"

"It has been spoken of, but Morning Sun does not choose it so. It is her father. Tall Bull makes him think he is a mighty one. He fills him with promise . . ." Little Raven stopped

133

abruptly, knowing, in his freedom with his brother, that he had walked into territory he had not planned on. He was young and had made a fatal slip. Zach was too attuned to him not to know at once that Little Raven withheld words.

"Promises of what?"

"Well . . . ah . . . just big promises. You know how Tall Bull has always been. He boasts to those who don't understand him as well as we do. His boasts mean nothing."

"Little Raven, we have never been false with each other. Your words don't lie to me, but your thoughts do. It has never been this way and I would not have it so now. What is it that is so difficult to tell me when we have shared everything?"

"I would not lie to you, Windwalker."

"I know. But don't leave empty places in your words."

"I do not know all the truth of things. I do only know what I have heard. I cannot accuse anyone of anything."

"I know that. I want to hear what you have heard."

"I must ask you some questions first."

"Ask."

"Why is it wrong for us to have guns? Many of the warriors have them. They are gifts from trappers or those they had traded for. Why is it wrong for all of us to have them? I would like to hunt with the long rifle."

"I never said it was wrong to have guns."

"But you seek those who would bring them to us. You want to stop them."

"It isn't just that way, Little Raven."

"Then speak to me of how it is. I would understand."

"The guns themselves in the hands of warriors like Father, you, and many of the others are a good thing, but in the hands of some, the long guns turn into something else. They turn into a weapon of death. There are those who would bring war to our people."

"Is it wrong also to drive away the people who would take from us the land and even our food?"

"I have been across the big river to the place where the sun

134

rises, Little Raven. I have seen the numbers of the bluecoats. Where we number hundreds they number a hundred times more. If we kill, these greater numbers will come, and it will get bigger and bigger. By numbers alone they will destroy us, unless we learn to live beside them."

"There are truly that many of them?" Little Raven said in wonder.

"There are even more than I can describe. It is like a great flood, and I would not have our father and our people washed away in the waters. I know that guns must come, Little Raven. But we must put them in the hands of the right men and not in the hands of those who don't care about the future of our people."

"But we cannot say this is so. These men speak other words. They say if we can take the forts and chase these whites away, the others will feel fear in their hearts and will not cross the great river again. Our land will be ours again."

"They speak lies! I have seen and I know it is not so. They will come, and before they do, we must learn many things. The first is we must learn how to live with them, and we must learn quickly. Little Raven, I don't ask you to betray anyone. I know that your friends must number among these men. But I ask you to think very carefully and make your decisions without the promises of others. You are a man, and a man must be careful because his decisions not only affect him, they affect everyone who loves and depends on him."

"I will do this. Windwalker, I am grateful you do not ask me to betray names. I cannot do this yet. Not even for you."

"I understand. But use your head and your heart. I must go back to the fort. If you want to talk, come and send smoke. I will see, and I will join you. Don't try to come in anymore. They are touchy, and their commander, Aaron Creighton, is a man with a hard heart when it comes to our people."

"I will do that," he sighed in relief. Deceiving his brother was a mountain he was grateful to see dissolved. "Windwalker, do you go back to the fort only for the guns?"

"What's on your mind now?"

Little Raven smiled. "I thought you might be going back to look into the eyes of the very beautiful white woman."

"Again you jump to conclusions."

"She is still very beautiful."

Zach's face became closed. "But she is not for me, brother. Think on this. Would it be a good thing for my people if I were to take her, to convince her to come with me? It would rouse their hatred more, and I don't think she could live among us. It is too much to ask. So the barriers between us are too big. It is best if I do not look into her eyes again. I must go back to the fort, but it is only to find how the guns are coming. Once I do, and I can find a way to stop what is growing, I will come back here to stay and help. Maybe then there might be time to marry within the tribe, but that is a thought for much later."

"It is good to have you to talk with, Windwalker. I have missed you."

"When we get this problem settled, you and I shall go on a hunting trip for a few days. It will do us both good."

"Good. I must go now."

Zach looked at him in momentary surprise but said nothing. Little Raven was too old to be told what he could or could not do, or the friends he could keep. He was old enough to make decisions for himself.

"I would ride with you in the morning as far as the fort," Little Raven offered.

"Good. We leave early."

"I'll be ready."

Little Raven left, and Zach was alone with his thoughts. He could present a cool demeanor to anyone else, but he couldn't lie to himself. Dangerous as it was, Tara drew him back to the fort with more force than the guns. It was a war he would have to fight alone, for he could not make her a casualty of it. He lay down to sleep, forcing Tara from his mind in self-defense.

*   *   *

136

Morning Sun rose early and walked to the stream for water. As she walked back toward her father's lodge, she was so deep in thought that Tall Bull was standing in front of her before she realized it. She nearly collided with him before she became aware of his presence.

"Tall Bull," she gasped.

"When you become my woman, Morning Sun, you will not run after the half-breed who chooses his white people over you."

"I am not promised to you yet," she said coldly, "and until I am, I will do as I choose!"

"It will be little time until you are, and I know how to make you understand how an obedient wife behaves."

"I will never be your woman, Tall Bull. If the day comes that my father is foolish enough to agree to it, it is the same day I will put an end to my life."

Tall Bull's face drew down in a dark scowl. "The day will come when I will be a very powerful man in our tribe. You would do well to marry me."

"And how will you become so powerful?" she sneered.

"That I cannot say now, but you will see. When I am, you will be given to me as wife. Your father will be more than pleased to do so."

"I do not believe you. Leave me alone! I will never come to you of my own free will."

She pushed past him, fear lending wings to her feet. Deep within she felt a certainty that if Tall Bull did gain stature in the tribe, her father might agree to his wishes to have her. Only, now she had become curious as to what devious plan lay behind his words. She would find out, and when she did, she would take the truth, first to her father, then to the man she loved . . . Windwalker.

Spotted Bear was more than surprised when Zach requested permission to speak to him. He too had hopes that Morning Sun would find favor in Zach's eyes and that he would take her as wife. For his daughter to marry the son of their chief would

137

bring honor to them all.

He told Zach to enter, and when Zach was comfortably seated, Spotted Bear chatted for a few moments about unimportant things. While he spoke he could hardly keep his eyes from the beautiful rifle Zach had laid across his lap. Finally, Spotted Bear could retain his interest no longer.

"The rifle you carry is very beautiful. You are a lucky man to have such a weapon."

"Yes," Zach agreed. He lifted the rifle carefully. "It is a possession I am very proud of. But," Zach added casually, "I could be persuaded to part with it."

Spotted Bear held his breath, but Zach could see the light of excitement leap into his eyes.

"And what force could persuade you to be separated from such a weapon?"

Zach casually handed the rifle to Spotted Bear, wanting to whet his appetite for its possession. Spotted Bear took it and examined it carefully, brushing his hands over it as gently as he would a woman.

"It would take only a word from Spotted Bear to have such a rifle."

"What word?" Spotted Bear looked at Zach intently.

"I have known Spotted Bear for many years. You are a man of honor. If you give your promise to anything, I know it will be kept."

"You want a promise from me?" Spotted Bear said suspiciously.

"Yes, I do."

"What is it that you want?"

"Tall Bull has spoken to you of his desire to have Morning Sun as a wife."

Spotted Bear nodded, pleased that Zach seemed to be leading up to his own proposal. "I would have you deny him," Zach finished.

"He is a strong warrior. Why should I deny him?"

"Because Morning Sun does not want to marry him."

"I know," Spotted Bear said quietly. "It is another she wants."

Now was Zach's opportunity. He could claim Morning Sun as wife, settle in his village, and forget the white world. But a force called to him that, no matter how he battled, he could not fight. He named it responsibility, but the deep inner voice whispered Tara's name in his ear like a devilish taunt.

"I want Morning Sun to be given the freedom to make her own choice. That is all I ask. Do not give her to Tall Bull. Let her take the husband she wants when she chooses."

"What if she does not choose?"

"Then let her remain in your lodge to care for you in your old age. But let the final choices be hers."

Spotted Bear knew now that Zach had no intention of taking Morning Sun. He was disappointed, and he knew Morning Sun would be as well. But the request was very little compared to the reward.

"It is done, Windwalker," Spotted Bear said finally. "Morning Sun will make her own choices and Tall Bull will not be her husband."

"Then Spotted Bear's word is enough. I leave you with a happy heart, Spotted Bear, that my sister will also be pleased at your generosity. May the rifle bring much meat to your lodge and may you live long and prosper."

"My daughter should be grateful for the love of such a brother as well," Spotted Bear replied.

Zach rose and spoke the polite words of departure. When he had gone, Spotted Bear gazed at the closed door flap for a while.

"I wonder if my daughter will be grateful or if what she feels is for a brother. I hope one day you will come home and look into her eyes and see where your place should be."

He returned his attention to the rifle.

Zach and Little Raven rode toward the fort in companionable silence, broken only by an occasional observance of a wild

139

animal or by short casual remarks, of little importance. Zach and Little Raven rested their ponies midway to the fort, and they chewed on pemican and dried beef, washed down with cool water from the stream where they had stopped.

"We'll reach the fort by the time the sun goes down," Little Raven supplied casually.

"Should. But you turn around at the top of the hill. I don't need any more problems than I already have."

"I told you, they will never see me," Little Raven grinned.

"Why doesn't that give me any peace of mind?" Zach replied with a laugh.

"Don't worry. I'll send smoke if it is important that I see you."

"Okay. Well, let's get going. I want to get back in case Caleb has decided to make some kind of a move."

They rode again, and their judgment of time had been accurate. The sun was just rimming the horizon when they crested the last hill that led to the fort. Drawing their horses to a halt, both men gazed down on the large wooden edifice that had changed their lived so drastically. To them both, it was a blot on the face of the earth, and Little Raven especially could not understand men who could live so confined or in such fear that they had to barricade themselves behind walls he had found as penetrable as if they did not exist.

Zach turned to face Little Raven. "I leave you here, brother. Tell our father, should he need me, to send word and I will come."

"Any words I should take to Morning Sun?" Little Raven grinned.

"I'm not giving you such an opportunity. I spoke to her last night. That is enough until this problem is settled."

"You believe I would bend your words?"

"Definitely. Now get going before our commander gets wind of you and sends a few bluecoats out to see why an 'Indian' is sneaking around his fort."

"I could give them quite a chase," Little Raven replied hopefully.

140

"Just get out of here."

He could hear Little Raven's chuckle as he spun his pony about. There was a quick wave and he was gone. Zach sat for a few more minutes, and as dark clouds gathered to herald the night, he rode down toward the fort.

Tara, with the help of Mrs. Murphy and Mrs. Braughn, had gone to a great deal of trouble to look her very best for the ball. Her brilliant hair had been, at first, argued over delightedly by both women, who finally agreed and styled it atop her head in a mass of blazing red-gold curls. Her one and only ball gown was a deep emerald that exposed soft shoulders to an advantage, making both women caution her not to breathe too deeply, or she was likely to cause a stampede. Her deep green eyes were made more brilliant both by her excitement and by the nearly matching color of the gown, with its fitted bodice and very wide skirt.

She was excited, all the while denying to herself that she hoped Zach could see her. Of course he would not be there. He could not be there. And, she had to chastise herself, why would she even want him to be? Caleb had said that Zach had a woman in the Indian village he planned to marry. How could he have treated her as he did and gone to the arms of another woman just as easily? Savage! Wild savage! she thought angrily. He had made a fool of her and she never intended to let it happen again. . . . Still . . .

She rose and joined both women, who walked with her across the compound to the place from which the sound of music already came. What Tara did not know was that Zach stood just inside the dark shadows of the stable door and watched her move across the compound. He watched her as a man would watch a vision that had just stepped from one of his best dreams.

He stood in a breathless silence as he enjoyed the moonlight lightly caressing soft skin he would have given anything to touch again. But she walked into the ballroom and out of his

141

life, without ever knowing of his presence.

Again he felt the bitterness of the thought that the blood of such great and good men like Waiting Wolf could be the barrier that would forever stand between them.

"You're a damn fool!" The voice came from behind Zach, and he turned quickly, not surprised to see Mule behind him. Mule was the only person who would ever stand a chance of getting this close without Zach knowing he was there.

"Mule, what are you talking about?"

"You. You're lettin' those soldiers push you around. That don't sound like you. Why don't you go and clean up and go in and have a dance with her if you want to?"

"To what use, Mule? It don't mean a damn thing to her, and I'm not going to let it be that important to me."

"Don't mean a thing to her, huh? Wal, you tell me why she came looking for you the night you left, all bright-eyed and pretty. She said it was important, that she had to talk with you."

"You told her where I went?"

"I told her where I thought you went. You slipped out so slick I didn't know. I had a feeling Little Raven was here."

Zach grinned, "You were right. My father wanted to talk with me."

"That boy can sure as hell slip in and out of here like a shadow. I hope you warned him about what can happen. If Commander Aaron Creighton ever finds him goin' in and out without a by-your-leave, they'll nail his hide and throw him behind bars. I have an idea how a free spirit like Little Raven could stand that."

"I've already warned him. It won't be happening again."

"Real good. Now, what are you goin' to do about that little gal?"

"Mind your own business, Mule."

Mule spat a stream of tobacco juice and grinned, "Ya are my business."

"You don't understand."

142

"Don't, huh? Wal, I don't think you're playin' fair. Besides, a lot goes on in there with Caleb Banning that you ought to know about."

"Like what?"

"Like he's fillin' them with wild Indian stories and likely fillin' Tara with a few choice lies too. How are you going to put a stop to it if you don't go into the lion's den and defend yourself—and your people, I might add. Seems to me there ought to be someone who could stand in there and defend what you think is right."

"Mule, I—"

"I know, boy. You been split down the middle and hurt from both sides so often you're a little wary of walkin' into it again. But there comes a time when you can't work in the dark, and you have to stand up and get counted. You have to play their game and play it better if you want to stop them."

Zach stood in a deep silence, and Mule knew he was considering his words very carefully. Only after several long minutes did Zach turn to him and smile a smile that made Mule chuckle, for it was decidedly wicked.

Tara was surrounded almost immediately by Ian, Sean, and Randolph, who fought amiably over whose dance was the next. She was having fun but was still feeling as if she were poised on the edge of some kind of precipice. Zach hovered on the edge of her mind, eating away at her reserve and nibbling just as harshly on her jealousy—a jealousy she would never admit to herself. Let him have his Indian squaws! After all, he was more their kind than hers. What did she care?

Tara had just finished a dance with Ian, and they had walked back to the group of merrymakers. Someone had just said something amusing and there was a lot of laughter.

Suddenly, the room seemed to grow quieter and quieter. The stillness rippled through the air like a wave, as the band screeched to a halt piece by piece until the fiddle player pulled

143

his bow across his fiddle in one long drawn-out note. All eyes swung to the door, and Tara turned around to follow their gaze. She sucked in her breath harshly as she saw Zach framed in the doorway, looking more handsome and untamed as ever, with a smile on his face and a look in his eyes that told her he was in a devil-may-care mood. His eyes were on her, and she found it difficult to breathe. She felt as if she were being drawn toward some inevitable thing about which she had no control at all. The feeling frightened her a bit, but not enough to make her eyes turn from Zach.

Chapter 13

Tara watched Zach move a step or two into the room. The look on his face was as cool and detached as if he belonged where he was. She had no idea that his heart was pounding with well-remembered feelings. They were feelings stemming back to the time he was a boy and was roughly tossed out of white gatherings. He looked about the room as if he were unaware of what had caused the strange silence.

Aaron stood with a grim mouth and total disbelief in his eyes. The three young lieutenants were frozen in the same immobility, waiting for a move from Aaron to tell them what to do.

Caleb watched from across the room, hoping Zach had overstepped his bounds for the last time.

Zach wasn't too sure the night wouldn't turn into a disaster. In a moment Aaron would rebound from the shock, and Zach would be faced with the shame of being ejected. His eyes searched out Tara's wide green eyes and held them.

Tara actually found it difficult to breathe as Zach held her gaze. He was so devastatingly handsome. He had changed from his rough buckskin to a white shirt and black pants, but the effect was just as breathtaking. The white shirt made his deep tan look deeper, and the black pants hugged his legs like a second skin.

145

Her eyes raised again to his. She didn't know what she was reading in them, but she felt the magnetic pull as if he were drawing her to him. He was! He was forcing her to decide something; she could feel it. Then the realization came to her. He wanted her to come to him! The nerve of him, she thought. She had felt shame and pain at his hand. He had offered nothing of himself and taken all from her, yet he wanted more. She could see him pay now. Pay for every moment he had caused her any distress. She would see how he could face the shame of being told to leave. She would not move! But she found herself doing just the opposite. As if her body spoke a language her mind did not understand.

There was a ripple of sound throughout the room as she moved slowly toward him, accompanied by soft gasps and intaken breaths. But still she moved slowly, until she stood inches from him. At that moment no one in the room seemed to matter.

Their eyes had never broken their hold as Tara came closer. She was aware of both the tumultuous emotions within her and some deep inner struggle within Zach. Mule's voice echoed in her ears. She smiled.

"Hello, Zach." Her voice was soft and slightly shaky, but at the moment Zach couldn't think of anything that had ever sounded better to him. "You're late. But I saved you a dance."

There was another gasp from most of the assembled ladies.

"Thank you, Tara." His voice was firm and deep, and there was so much there that Tara did not understand. Still, she felt as if he had touched her in some way that she might never understand.

Zach took her hand and drew her to the center of the floor. But there was no music as yet. Tara smiled and turned to look at Aaron.

"Aaron, could you please tell the band to play. The party has just begun."

Aaron meant to refuse—it was on the tip of his tongue— and if he had, there would have been an immediate ejection of Zach.

"Sure now," Mrs. Braughn spoke loudly as she nearly dragged her husband to the floor, "start the band playin'. 'Tis a party, isn't it?"

"I agree," Mrs. Murphy added swiftly. She walked to the floor, and her surprised but pleased husband followed.

Unless he meant to insult Mrs. Braughn or Mrs. Murphy, Aaron had no choice. He motioned to the band, who began to play a waltz while their awed eyes watched Zach and Tara.

Zach was still unsure, but it was Tara who stepped into his arms and spoke softly, "Shall we go on with that dance?"

For the first time Zach realized he had been holding his breath. He put his arm about Tara and began to move slowly. They did not speak again.

Tara had no idea why this situation had come about. She was more than sure that if she knew the true facts of it, she might not be so pleased. But she could feel the strength of his arm about her, and she was aware of every move, every ripple of muscle as his body swayed with hers. He smelled clean and slightly of soap and leather, and also of a deep scent that was elusive but so totally masculine it enveloped her. The blue of his eyes was vivid and warm, and when he looked down into hers, she felt as if she were melting.

"You're absolutely beautiful," he said softly. "Mule said you wanted to see me the night I left. I'm sorry I wasn't there. What did you want me for?"

Thinking of what she wanted seemed so trivial now and rather embarrassing. How could she say that Caleb had told her about another woman and she was curious . . . no, jealous? She couldn't. Besides, the memory of her shame and anger at him from their last conversation began to flood back.

He watched her cheeks grow pink, and he knew she was remembering. He wanted to say he was sorry, but at that moment the music stopped again. He was struck by the sudden panicky feeling that what had started out well was going to disintegrate into something not so well.

147

Aaron and Caleb reached the couple first, and by now the commander's face was a cloud of anger. It was Caleb's smug smile that caught Zach's attention. This time he wasn't going to be pushed. Tara felt his arm grow tense, and she knew he intended to stand his ground.

By all standards she should have left him then. After what he had put her through, he deserved what might happen. She should be satisfied . . . but she wasn't.

"Aaron," Tara began as soon as Aaron and Caleb reached their side. "Now that Zach is back we can celebrate. It sort of makes my journey complete. He brought me safely all the way from Washington, and all those others as well. I certainly think it appropriate that he celebrate our safe arrival with the rest of us."

The obvious fact that Tara supported him left Aaron few choices, but he tried. "Of course, Tara, but I'm not sure Zach really intends to stay. Maybe he just wanted a word with you."

Tara looked up at Zach, whose arm she was still holding. "Is that why you came, Zach?"

"I'd like to say it was, Tara, but that wasn't my reason." He looked down and smiled at her. "But had I known how beautiful you would look, it would have been."

"Just what was your reason?" Caleb inquired arrogantly as he moved closer.

He was not the only one who moved unconsciously closer. Most of the people present sensed the beginning of a confrontation and waited for Zach's reply.

"I guess it's because I'm tired of a lot of things."

"You're tired," Caleb repeated with a derisive laugh. "And just what is it in the white fort that you're tired of . . . Windwalker?"

Tara could feel the ripple of tense muscle through Zach's whole body, but his challenging smile remained intact.

"I'm not ashamed of the name, Caleb, any more than I am of my white name. In fact, I think it puts me with a foot in both camps and able to say a whole lot more than any white . . .

especially one who seems to have an ax to grind."

"Meaning me?"

"If I was to put my finger on where all the rumors of 'savages' killing everyone they see and being like animals you can't negotiate with get started, I'll bet I'd be safe to name you, Caleb. You've had a lot to say to stir up trouble. You're a prime example of white ignorance."

"Are you trying to tell us you're an example of those heathens out there?" Caleb scoffed.

"No," Zach said softly, "I have yet to be the man my father is. But I know he wouldn't betray his own kind."

"Meaning I would? Do you have some proof of that, or are you just trying to convince these folks to let down their guard and just let those redskins in here? Maybe we should just open the gates and welcome them in, so's they could wipe us all out."

There was a soft murmur of voices filled with uncertainty and fear.

"You know damn well I don't have any proof. If I did, you wouldn't be standing here."

"Maybe it's just being clever. Maybe you think these folks are going to believe you. Maybe they won't be lookin' at you any more. Well, you can forget that. You're a half-breed, as loyal to your Indian friends as you can get."

"You men can hold it right now," Aaron interrupted angrily. "This is no place to be bringing your fights. I want it finished now."

The three young lieutenants moved forward slightly, as if only awaiting the order to throw Zach out. As far as they were concerned, he was the pauper looking at the princess, and they found it difficult to swallow.

Tara suddenly sensed Zach's alert command of his body. He was ready for them, and she began to wonder if he couldn't handle himself even at three to one.

"Stay where you are," Aaron commanded. "Zach?"

Zach smiled. "All right, Aaron. I guess I made my point.

149

That's what I came here for, anyway. Just to let these good people know that they have less to fear from my father and our people"—his eyes found Caleb's—"than from slippery snakes who lie and steal and bring guns to the people of my village. One of these days when he does, I intend to stomp on him just like I would any other vermin."

Zach walked away from them and was gone by the time the full realization of what he had said struck Tara.

She had thought him vulnerable. She had felt a silent call for help, and all the time he was using her again. He was gaining her help to get in. He had played her for the innocent fool again, and she could envision him laughing at her and the way she had climbed out on the proverbial limb for him while he casually cut it off. God, how many times could she be a fool for this man? Well, this was the last time. From now on, as far as she was concerned, Zachary Hale was someone who had ceased to exist. She turned to smile at Randolph, who had just asked her to dance again, and as she stepped into his arms, she firmed her vow to forget Zachary Hale.

Zach had stood outside the door for several minutes, trying to draw his frayed anger back into control. He'd allowed it to get away from him, a thing he seldom did, and in the process he'd alerted Caleb to what he was thinking and why.

What bothered him most was the way Tara had come to his aid, and then he had turned on her. All in all he had followed a desire to see her again, and in the process he had spoiled any chance of even a friendship between Tara and him, and now he couldn't do a thing about it. He had felt her stiffen, had seen her face go pale and her chin set stubbornly. She would be sure to doubt any kind of trust in the future. In fact, he was pretty sure she'd doubt anything he ever said or did. He walked across the compound and literally slammed into the stable, startling the horses and making Mule curse in surprise.

"What the hell!" Mule sputtered. Then he saw Zach's

150

scowling countenance. "What ails you, boy?"

"I made a damn fool of myself by letting Caleb know what was on my mind."

"What sidetracked you?"

"A pretty girl in my arms and too much confidence did it. I should have known Caleb was pushing me."

"It ain't that much of a loss, Zach. He had a pretty good idea you was trailin' guns. Maybe you'll make him move quicker than he planned to. If he does, we can catch him red-handed."

"Yeah, but he's wise now, and he might have an ace or two up his sleeve. I wouldn't trust Caleb Banning any further than I could toss him. We have to keep both eyes open now and be ready for anything."

"You think he might try to kill you?"

"I wouldn't put it past him."

"What about Tara, Zach?"

Zach was silent for about a minute too long, and his eyes avoided Mule's studiously as he stepped into a stall and brushed his hand down the silken coat of his horse. He made soft soothing sounds and the horse nickered in response.

But Mule wasn't about to be put off so easily. He knew Zach too well. He came to the stall and leaned against the wood frame.

"I said, what about Tara?"

"So, what about her?"

"Did she tell you what she wanted to say to you when she came here?"

"I asked, but she didn't get the chance to answer." Zach still refused to turn in Mule's direction. He chewed his lip thoughtfully, hoping Mule would give up on the questions and just go to sleep. But Mule was as stubborn as Zach and infinitely more patient. Zach turned to leave the stall and Mule held his ground.

"What difference does it make to you, anyhow?" Zach protested guiltily.

"It makes a lot of difference. Now, suppose you tell me just

151

what happened in there?"

Zach made an exasperated sigh, then reluctantly told Mule everything that had occurred. Mule's face seemed to redden and swell with each word until he finally exploded.

"You blamed young buck! You let that gal walk out on a limb to make things easier for you, then you left her just like that to face all those gossiping biddies and never even said one word of thanks or nuthin'! You didn't even give her the credit for what she had the backbone to do. You sure are an ungrateful young pup!"

"Look, Mule, it's better this way. Our worlds don't mix."

"But you'd use her to make a point. I just don't believe that."

"It's the best thing, Mule, believe me. There's no room in her life for a half-breed who can't give her anything permanent anywhere. You think the gossips are bad now. What do you think they'd do to her if she was seen often with me?"

"If I was asked, I'd say she has a right to do her own choosin'."

"Don't be crazy, Mule."

"So what did she do in there?"

"Whatever she did will pass. They'll credit it to her being new here and not knowing that you can't trust a dirty Indian. She'll probably learn pretty quick."

"You ain't been fair to that kid from the first minute you laid eyes on her. I never thought I'd see the day." Mule shook his head as he turned away to find his bed in the stacks of fresh hay. "No sir," he muttered, "I never thought I'd see the day. Knowed you since you was a sprout and knowed your pappy and never thought I'd see the day." He squirmed into a comfortable position and became quiet.

Zach left the stall feeling guiltier now than he had before. He had made the small room off the stables his a long time ago. It was Spartan in comfort and equipment, containing a bed and a collection of ropes, bridles, and two saddles. Articles of clothes hung on pegs on the walls and two pairs of high moccasins sat

152

on a small wooden trunk.

He sat on the edge of the bed for a minute, then lay back and braced his hands behind his head. There was no way he was going to do a thing about Tara. It was only asking for trouble. It would be better for them both if he just let her alone.

But in the stillness her voice came to him. "Hello, Zach, I saved you a dance."

She hadn't even known he would be there. Brilliant green eyes lingered before him and the feel of her in his arms had been destructive to his reserve. If he closed his eyes, he could still smell the scent of her perfume. He cursed and sought a more comfortable position. But he knew his discomfort didn't come from the bed. . . . It came from his conscience.

He rose to his feet, making his way in the dark through the stables and out the door, blending with the shadows. He was as soundless as the soft breeze. But on his bed of hay Mule grinned to himself and rolled into a comfortable spot. After a while he slept.

Tara was well aware of subtle differences in some of the women. They watched her with cool frowns, some of the men even remaining aloof. But she ignored them and enjoyed the balance of the party. At the end of the evening it was Aaron who walked her home, and he had pulled rank to do it. He felt it was his duty to again caution Tara about having sympathy for any Indians and for having any kind of feelings about Zach in particular.

They walked slowly, and Tara was the first to speak.

"Aaron, I'm sorry if I upset you . . . or any of the others tonight."

"Don't let it worry you, Tara. Everyone here knows you're new to our ways. You'll learn after you're here for a while. Once David returns, he can help you understand. I'll be the first to admit that Zach is . . . rather powerful in his ways. But he's gotten some kind of an idea that someone's leading his

153

people astray. No matter if he had a white mother or not, he's more Indian than white, and he has a hard way of continually proving it."

"He seems to hate Caleb."

"It's more personal than anything else, and they just rub each other the wrong way."

"Caleb really isn't selling guns to the Indians?"

"I don't see how he could do it without me or someone else at the fort knowing it."

"What will happen if they're armed?"

"We'd end up with some kind of a war."

"Why?"

"Waiting Wolf would like to see the forts gone from here. They consider all this land theirs."

"But, Aaron, don't they have a right to it?"

"No!"

"But—"

"I know what you're going to say. But civilization can't be stopped by some wild untamed natives who don't want any kind of progress. We bring them a lot of good things, Tara. But they're too stubborn to change and too stubborn to let us show them a better way to live."

"And if they're armed . . . then you can't talk to them?"

"Put rifles in their hands and you'll see a blood massacre. Once they have guns, you'll never get them to sit down to a council again. They'd be beyond talk." He stopped and turned to look at Tara. "Tara, if the truth were to come out, I have a feeling the guns might be being run by Zach, and he's trying to hide his tracks by making a lot of noise."

"That's what Caleb said," Tara declared thoughtfully.

"Caleb?"

"Yes, when we went riding yesterday."

"What did he say? Did he have any proof?"

"No. He just thinks it's Zach."

"I see." They continued to walk.

"Tara, I know this is hard for you, and I want you to try and

154

understand what I'm about to say."

"Yes, Aaron?"

"Zach is a man who has had to rely only on himself all his life. Although his mother was white, he has been raised like a wild animal by the Indians. His father has tried to keep him from any connections to us, but I guess he started coming here when he was just a boy. He got a few beatings and began to grow a deep hatred. What you saw tonight was just more of it. I'm afraid your attempts to be cultured and kind were wasted. I want to warn you, because he'll use you or anyone else to get back at the whites. He feels he should have been accepted as white and that can never be."

"How do you know all this? Did you know his mother?"

"No, my parents did," he replied grimly, "—before they were killed by an Indian raiding party and our homestead was burnt to the ground. My parents could never understand what Karolyn saw in Waiting Wolf."

"I imagine," Tara said softly, "that she must have loved him if she chose to give up everything and live with him and bear his child."

"Yes, I suppose she must have," he reluctantly agreed. "I think she had an idea to start a school. But she died before that idea got too far. She never knew that it would have been useless. They don't want civilization. They want us to go back east."

"Maybe . . . if we tried again to make peace . . ."

"How, when one of their own brings guns? What do you think those guns are for?"

"I suppose . . . but it's terribly sad."

"I think the saddest part of the story is Zach's mother. Maybe it's a blessing that she died before she could see what had become of Zach. I don't want you caught in a web of some kind that might get you hurt." He smiled, "Your brother would never forgive me if he returned to find a situation like what might occur if you let Zach's lies get to you."

"I can take care of myself," she replied, hearing Zach's

words in her mind and recalling how amusing he thought it was that she had so often made this same claim.

"Well, you'd best get some sleep. It's been a very eventful night."

"Yes, it has. Good night, Aaron. I'll see you tomorrow."

"Good night, Tara." Aaron bowed slightly, then turned and walked back to his quarters.

Tara felt depressed and confused. She found everything she had been hearing a little too much to digest after the night's events.

She went into her brother's quarters. In the main room she struck a match and lit a lamp. She sighed deeply and reached up to unpin her hair, letting it fall about her shoulders. She could not pull her mind away from the look in Zach's eyes when she had first seen him enter the ballroom. It seemed he was again the boy who had come to the fort seeking acceptance, only to be met by bitterness, distrust, and often punishment. So engrossed in her thoughts was she that Tara did not hear the door to her bedroom open. She heard nothing, until a familiar voice spoke.

"Hello, Tara, I thought you'd never get home."

She jerked about across the room, green eyes filled with surprise meeting cool blue ones filled with the knowledge of all that had been said to her—and all that he intended to prove wrong, one way or another.

Chapter 14

As suddenly as it had come, the shock of seeing him vanished. Why would she be surprised at anything Zachary Hale did? He seemed to do whatever he chose whenever he chose to.

"Zach, what are you doing here? I don't suppose there's any use in telling you what could happen to you if I should scream."

He grinned tauntingly. "Are you afraid enough to scream? Have they filled you with enough stories that you're prepared to be—?" He shrugged, but the challenging glow in his blue eyes made her temper flare. She was angry, but she was also surprised that she really wasn't afraid.

"I'm not afraid of you, Zach," she replied coldly. "But I would be grateful if you would tell me why you're here. Is it for—?" She mimicked his shrug elaborately enough to bring a touch of laughter to his lips. Damn, he thought, she's got a lot of courage to tempt me like she's doing.

"We never finished our conversation."

"Need we finish? After all, you got from me what you came for. That should be enough for you. You're a wonderful opportunist, Zach. You'll use anybody or anything to get your own way, and I'm a prime example of that. I have a habit of underestimating you, a habit I fully intend to break."

"It's because of the way you feel that I think we have to finish it. One-sided arguments are not very well balanced, are they? Or are you another one to judge by what others say, without finding the truth?"

"And what is the truth?"

"Before I answer that, maybe you can tell me what you think the truth is."

"How can anyone tell?"

"You mean you don't quite believe the great white soldier?" he chuckled.

"I believe that he believes what he said," she flushed under his intense gaze. "Maybe," she added softly, "you should take steps to convince him as well."

He drew his dark brows together, almost as if he were puzzled. "Do you really believe there's a way to make those Indian haters think that they have some misconceived notions? You are a romantic little girl, aren't you?"

"Stop it, Zach. Because of you, I am no longer a romantic, and I'm not foolish either. Aaron told me a lot of things but not malicious or hateful."

"What did he tell you?"

"He thinks you're more Indian than white, and that you say you think someone is trying to lead your people astray. But in reality it's you. He thinks that you and your people are too stubborn to change, and that in truth we've given them a lot of things, but they won't let us show them a better way to live."

"And?" he prompted.

"And he told me about your mother, and how she chose to live with your father despite what she knew it would cost," she added quietly.

"He's full of one-sided information, isn't he?" Zach said, his bitterness skimming the surface.

"How would I know if it's one-sided?" she challenged. "How would anyone who came out here know? If you want people to believe differently, why don't you do something about making things different?"

158

"You don't know what you're talking about." His anger was stung by her direct blow. "You want me to tell you some of the other side? All right, I will." He moved closer to her, and she could see the glow of roused emotion in his eyes, which she was somehow sure he hadn't meant to display. "I'm proud of my Indian blood as I wanted to be proud of my white, until they beat the pride from me. Until they made it clear that one drop of Indian blood made me a dog to be kicked from their camp. I earned brutally my right to walk in the white world. I fought for every inch of the path. Do you want to know why I fought? It was my mother's wish that I honored. She had carefully taught me to read and write, and she wanted me to be educated. Well, I was, but it cost a lot. I would never betray my people, and most certainly not my father who is a man with more honor than all the men who live in this fort. My people are not too stubborn to live beside you. And you are right, they did give us a lot. They gave us whiskey and guns to begin with. Then they gave us smallpox and measles. Oh, yes, they gave us a lot! And now we're asked to move to a reservation and give them everything we have left. Don't tell me about a better way to live. Our way was good for us for long generations before you came. If you want to give us something, make it self-respect and peace . . . only I don't think you know how to give that!"

The realization of his anger finally came to him, and he inhaled deeply and turned away from her for a moment. Tara could not deny the bitter hate he felt. She could feel it in the powerful current of his rigid body as he gathered himself into control. Again Zach turned back to look at her, and he saw pity and tenderness, two emotions he could no longer bear from Tara.

He moved a step or two closer, until they stood just inches from each other. An electrical current swirled about them and they stood in the vortex, suddenly aware of each other and the immensity of what stood between them. Who would be able to pick up the pieces if these two worlds were to collide?

159

"I would love to show you—"

"What?" she pressed, sensing he was about to say something she wanted to hear.

"Never mind. It wouldn't do much good. You will always be what you are, and there is no way I can change the path I must walk on."

"How do you know? You don't know what I am because you never really took the time to try."

"Sometime maybe, but there's no time for that now." He had his cool arrogance under control. "Although, I must admit, getting to know you better is interesting."

"That's not what I had in mind," she snapped.

"You're sure?" He sounded suggestively disappointed, only to watch the anger flare in her eyes.

"Zach, I think it's time you left."

Zach moved a step closer, and Tara found words dying on her lips.

"I came here because I wanted to say I was sorry for what happened tonight, and I wanted to thank you for making it a little easier for me." He moved even closer. "I watched your eyes, you know." His voice had lowered and became soft as velvet. He reached a hand to touch her hair. "You have the loveliest eyes." His fingers drifted into her hair, enjoying the softness of it.

"Don't, Zach. This is useless. We can't talk. . . ."

"You're right. I don't think words will ever be any good between us. But there's so much more."

"No." She tried to make her voice firm, but somehow the words sounded weak and defenseless. She backed up a step, but it was much too late for her to recognize that Zach was much more dangerous when he was stalking something he wanted. At this moment he couldn't seem to dam up the sudden flow of intense desire that swept through him like wildfire.

He reached out suddenly and gripped her waist, pulling her against him. "Are you afraid enough to scream?" he asked softly.

160

"Is that what you're trying to do, frighten me?" Her voice was as challenging as his had been. "If it is, you've failed," she added. Her chin tipped firmly and her eyes held his. She could lie with every part of her body, he thought, but pressed closely to him he could feel her heart pounding fiercely.

"What a liar you are," he chuckled. "Just think, Tara, if you called out, someone would come. This camp is heavily guarded. Within minutes I would be locked behind the bars of their jail, and you would be free to go on lying to yourself and believing that you feel nothing."

"I have the feeling their jail couldn't hold you, and you would return for revenge," she replied coldly. "This is what it's all about, isn't it? It's continual revenge. Who is it you want to use me as a weapon against, Zach? Is it all white men, or just those here at the fort? Aaron? Caleb? If you can't strike at them, then you search out what you think is their weakest spot. Well, don't underestimate me, Zach. Maybe I cannot battle you by force, but I will not play into your hands. Whatever you want you must take. I won't scream . . . but I won't surrender, either. So, you see, you will win nothing."

"I hear your words, Tara, and maybe you even believe them yourself. . . . Or do you? Would you like me to take what you truly want to give, so you can deny to yourself that you have been touched by a 'dirty savage,' and that his touch gave you pleasure that you continually deny?"

"Will you ever lose any of your arrogance?" she demanded.

"If they cannot beat it out of me, do you think you can succeed where they failed?"

Zach was pushing Mule's words from his mind as hard as he could. He hadn't been fair to Tara from the day he had met her, Mule had said. But even when he came to try to be fair, her delicious body and inviting lips seemed to destroy all good intentions. Combined with the challenging coldness in her eyes, which he wanted to change to a look he had seen before, he found it impossible to keep good intentions in mind. He had come to apologize, and now he wanted her so badly that his

161

blood sang in his veins and his senses were tangled around her slim lush body like vines about the trees in the forest. The sheen of her skin in the mellow lamplight was like burnished gold, and reflections of the same mellow light danced in her green eyes. Her body was warm and, pressed intimately to his, he could feel the sensuous curves, combined with the trembling that made him want to hold her even closer. He wanted the trembling of denial to cease and a new cause to replace it.

Reluctantly, Tara was just as aware of the virile strength of the hard, taut body pressed to hers, awakening sensations she had tried in vain to forget. No man seemed to have the power to awaken in her what Zach did. He was the one man it was totally wrong for her to respond to. Nothing could come of it but disaster, for their worlds could not mix. It was obvious to her even now, when her body quivered with desire and her struggling mind tried to deny it.

"I cannot tolerate this, Zach," she whispered. "I want to be something special to someone. You are a man who casually takes and smiles as he waves good-bye. We are more than a race apart, we are a world."

As my parents were, he suddenly thought. But he destroyed that thought at its birth. He did not dare hope or dream that Tara could be any more a part of his life than she was at this moment.

"In many ways you are still a child, impatient with those who do not see the world your way, at the same moment your eyes have only just been opened."

"Do you think I'm insensitive?"

"On the contrary. I believe you feel everything. But there is more to truth than simply feeling. Just as there is more to this. At least, face the truth in this one thing, Tara." His voice lowered to a soft breathed whisper as his lips gently touched her cheeks, then slipped to her soft, half-parted mouth. She inhaled with a startled gasp as his embrace tightened and his mouth seared hers. She felt as if the core of her were melting, flowing into her limbs. Her knees almost buckled, and she clung to him with the overpowering sense that she was drowning and he was the only stable rock to which she could hold. Her heart raced, sending her senses reeling, and he could feel the beat that matched his. Her mouth was soft, moist, and pliant beneath his, and he absorbed the sweet taste of her like the taste of water in the barren dryness.

One arm held her bound to him until she felt she must break, yet her body strained to his. His other hand skimmed down her back to pull her even closer.

By the time his mouth released hers, they were both breathless and caught beyond their depth in a surging river of scalding passion. Neither had the strength to escape the flowing need, the silent call that broke all other barriers.

Zach caught her face between his hands, threading his fingers in her hair. With infinite gentleness he kissed her forehead, her eyes, her cheeks, then again sought her mouth. There was a soft, inarticulate sound from the depths of Tara as his mouth again closed possessively over hers. No thoughts of right or wrong, or of the foolishness of what they were doing, were allowed past the barriers of their need to travel this road of passion to the summit.

Tara prayed only that this was different, that it meant more to Zach than before. He told her there was truth only in this, and she wanted desperately this time to believe that it was so. That he would know as well as she, that there had to be more than just passion alone.

She had only to cry out and this overpowering moment would end. But she couldn't. A flame beyond her control had melted defiance down to a need that was echoed in every beat of Zach's heart.

Again he broke the kiss, but only to let his lips press against the throbbing pulse at her throat and burn in scalding kisses along her shoulders and the soft flesh of her breasts.

Nimble fingers found the hooks at the back of her gown and released them, the thin material beneath hardly a barrier to his

163

seeking hands.

Her breath was coming in ragged gasps as she threaded her fingers through his thick dark hair to press him closer. The gown slipped to the floor, and his hands brushed her heated, pulsing flesh, lifting her senses higher and higher.

He swung her up in one fluid movement, taking a step toward the bedroom door, when the knock reverberated through the room, bringing Zach to a sudden halt and sending Tara into a panic of sudden realization of her vulnerable position. She was nearly naked and being held in the arms of a man who was not exactly the most popular person in the fort. She was utterly speechless. The knock sounded again. Tara jerked her head about to look into Zach's eyes. She could have shrieked at the amusement accompanied by a look of sheer deviltry.

"Put me down," she hissed.

"Uh uh," he chuckled. "Ask who it is," he whispered. Tara gritted her teeth and glared at him. The knock sounded more insistently.

"Ask who it is," Zach said softly, "or shall I answer the door?"

"No! Are you insane?" She raised her voice, trying to sound calm, controlled, and sleepy. "Who is it?"

"Tara, it's Caleb. I'd like to talk to you for a moment."

"No!" Zach said in a voice filled with suppressed laughter. "Tell him to go away."

Tara struggled, but she was in no position to get any leverage, and Zach was much too strong for her to get free of. She was furious now but powerless to do anything about it.

"Tara, are you all right?"

"Better answer him, Tara," Zach whispered again. "He might think you need help and come bustling in. The door's locked, isn't it?"

Now Tara felt real panic. She had not bolted the door yet. All Caleb had to do to walk in was to lift the handle. Zach saw this as quickly as she did, and his smile grew broader.

164

"You better say something really convincing to get rid of him."

Tara squirmed again, pressing her hands against him to get free. He slid her feet to the floor, only to capture her in his arms and hold her more effectively than he had before.

"I'm fine, Caleb, but it's really late, and I was going to bed. Could you talk to me tomorrow? I'm really tired." The last words ended in a muffled gasp as Zach took his time to leisurely press his lips in soft kisses down her throat, nibbling gently on her flesh.

"I must ask you for a small favor, Tara, and I need an answer tonight. It will only take a minute." Caleb's voice was insistent, and Tara was absolutely certain at any moment he might try the door handle. Still, Zach refused to release her, and the torment of his random kisses were driving her wild. She was caught between panic and passion.

"Tara . . . please."

"All right," she called, "I'll be there in a minute!"

Tara looked up into Zach's teasing, warm eyes and saw that he was prepared to call her bluff. Their eyes locked, challenging blue meeting shimmering green. Her lush body pressed to his, her soft, inviting mouth inches below Zach, Tara was prepared to keep control, to see how far she could go.

"Let me go, Zach."

"You don't want that any more than I do. Admit it, Tara. If he hadn't come, you would be in that bed with me and more than willing to be there. Tell him to leave, that you have something more important you have to do."

"I will not, and you won't stop me from going to that door. You also won't be here when I open it—unless you want to destroy me in this fort. . . . Unless you want me to taste their hatred and their revilement as you so often have."

She loosened slightly. She saw the surprise register in his eyes, combined with the beginning look of admiration and respect.

"Is that what you want, Zach? Because you are made an

165

outcast here, you want me to be too. You want them to say she is that . . . half-breed's woman. That she doesn't care for conventions such as marriage. That she is to be called whore from this night on . . . And Caleb would do that, wouldn't he? To hurt you . . . maybe, eventually, to have me." Her voice ended in a ragged whisper, and he could see tears, which she was too proud to shed, glisten in her eyes.

He let her go, and she ran to where her gown lay and put it on. Silently Zach came behind her and hooked it. He brushed a kiss on her shoulder. She remained motionless for a moment, and when she turned about, Zach had gone in the same mysterious way he had come, like a silent shadow.

Tara inhaled a shaky breath, then walked to the door to open it and face Caleb.

"Yes, Caleb, what is it?"

Caleb moved slightly forward, but Tara's immovable stance made it quite clear he would not be welcomed inside her quarters. Another day, he promised himself, you will not look so damned exciting and lock me out. One day I will have you—on my terms. Then we'll see what can be done with your disdain.

"I'm sorry to disturb you so late, Tara, but it is important."

"What is it?"

"Among the supplies we packed in your wagon are several boxes that belong to me. They are trading goods for the Indians. If it's all right with you, we will reload them in one of the empty wagons of mine."

"I didn't know there was anything in there of yours."

"They were very small boxes. I didn't think you would mind."

"No, of course not."

"Well," he smiled, "I figured if you saw some of my men climbing about your wagon tomorrow, you might be alarmed, so I thought I would drop by and tell you."

"You should have told me earlier."

"I planned to tell you at the dance, but your half-breed guide made his little ceremony and—"

166

"Zach is not mine," she said with the chill of anger in her voice. "And the way you say 'half-breed' makes it sound like something dirty. Zach's parents were different, but they were married and happy. He can't be to blame because one was white and one was Indian."

"It's not just me, Tara. If you play around with him, you're going to be courting a whole lot of trouble. I tried to warn you before."

"I'm not playing around with him!" she protested angrily. "But I don't believe he is as bad as you say he is. Maybe you and the people here don't understand what he's doing here. He's—"

"He's doing what?"

"Caleb, I'm tired, and I'd like to go to bed if you don't mind. Whatever there is of yours in my wagon, you're welcome to remove it tomorrow."

"I'm sorry if I made you angry." He tried to warm his smile, but Tara was reasonably certain where he intended it to lead, and she wanted no part of it.

"I'm fine. . . . Good night, Caleb."

"Good night, Tara. . . . Oh, would you like to go riding tomorrow?"

"Yes, of course. Being confined here is not exactly fun."

"Good night then. After I see to my things in your wagon, I'll come for you."

"All right. Good night." She made it final by backing up a step and closing the door. She heard him walk away, then slid the bolt firmly home.

Tara turned to face her bedroom door. Was Zach still there? Did he stand behind the closed door listening and waiting for her? Her heart began to skip as she walked to the door and pushed it open. The light from the main room made a path across the floor, bringing into relief her open window with the curtain still billowing from the night breeze. Zach was gone, and Tara wasn't sure whether she was pleased or disappointed. One thing was for certain: She wasn't going to find sleep easily tonight.

Chapter 15

What Tara didn't know was that Zach had stood behind the door. His purpose at first was to remain until Caleb was safely gone, not trusting the man at all.

Zach had heard Tara's defense of him, and a feeling he could not identify washed through him. He had attempted to take her as casually as he would one of the girls at the cantina. He had meant to complete what he had started, what his body still cried for, until she fanned the flames of guilt in him by defying Caleb in his name. He didn't understand Tara Montgomery.

He had become alert when Caleb talked of the boxes he had stored in Tara's wagon. This interested Zach. If they were not big enough for rifles, they might still be some kind of proof to link Caleb to them.

As Tara closed and bolted her door, Zach vanished through the window as quietly and soundlessly as the night breeze. He moved through the shadows toward the wagons. In the darkness, it took him some time to find Tara's wagon. When he did, Zach slipped inside. Very vague moonlight outlined what was packed. It would be extremely hard to find the boxes that belonged to Caleb. He would have to resort to trial and error.

It took him nearly a half hour before he ran across three small boxes. These boxes could hardly have contained rifles unless they were in pieces. The boxes were bound by heavy straps, and it took him several minutes to get them undone. Once they were, he opened the lid. It was impossible to see what was inside, so he reached in to feel.

Maybe his eyes couldn't see, but his experienced hands knew exactly what they felt: shells and rifle bullets. He smiled in the darkness. Maybe he didn't know where the guns were, but where there were bullets there were guns. It was only a matter of time until he could put the two together. Then he would have a score to settle with Caleb Banning.

His soft chuckle blended with the night breeze as another, more interesting thought came to him. He took several bullets from the box and put them in his pocket. He had a point to prove, but he also had to have proof of where he had gotten the bullets. He rummaged around until he found a piece of material that felt soft and feminine to the touch. This he put in his pocket, too. With a silent laugh, he left the wagon. His body had a long memory tonight of something incomplete. He also had something to settle with Tara Montgomery.

Zach made his way back through the shadows to his own quarters. There he examined the piece of cloth to find it was a silk scarf woven in a multicolored pattern. He raised it to his face and inhaled the soft scent of Tara on it. If anything, it heightened his urgency to see her again. But he would wait; it was something Zach did well. He lay across his bed and conjured up the shock he would read on her face. Surely she would believe the truth then.

The moon rose high, and even the guards were less wary, their eyes looking outward, hardly expecting activity inside the fort. It was then Zach made his way from the stable to the shadows beneath Tara's window. He had to smile again, seeing the window open. Tara must be confident that he would not return. He reached for the window frame.

Tara found her thoughts more than annoying when she found Zach gone. Surely she did not want him to be there!

Ignoring a vibrant answer from forbidden senses, she prepared herself for bed. It was a long time before her eyes grew heavy and she drifted into sleep.

She came suddenly awake when a hand closed over her mouth and a heavy weight pressed her to the bed. She was terrified, but only for a moment, for if her eyes did not know him, her senses did. She stopped struggling and heard his soft chuckle.

"Good girl. I only want to talk to you, but I can't have you calling out. Are you going to listen?" If she heard him out, maybe he would leave. She nodded her head. He withdrew his hand slowly, prepared in case she meant to deceive him, but she remained quiet. She was relieved when he moved from her, because her deceitful body was responding in a way that made her tremble.

He was a shadow in the room and she rose slowly from the bed. Suddenly he struck a lucifer, and the lamp sent pale light about them. Zach looked up from the lamp and the satisfied smile froze on his face. Tara stood before him, wearing a nightgown that to most would have seemed demure. The neckline was high and the gown long, but through its folds he could see the vague outline of her body—enough to set his pulses racing and detour his mind from its goals. Her voice brought him quickly back to reality.

"What are you doing here?"

"Come here, Tara, I want to show you something."

She came close, curiosity filling her eyes. "What is it?"

On the way to her room, Zach had tied the shells in her scarf. Now he withdrew it from inside his shirt. He saw recognition on her face.

"I heard Caleb say there was something of his in your wagon."

"That scarf is mine."

"I know. I took it to prove where I found . . . this." He handed the scarf to her.

She could feel the weight and she unfolded the scarf. The

170

shells lay in the palm of her hand.

"There is no ammunition in—"

"No, Caleb put these there."

"I don't understand."

"Why would he need to carry ammunition in your wagon instead of his?"

"He said there was no room in his."

"He lied."

"Why?"

"Tara, for God's sake, where there are shells, there are guns to fire them."

"What is this supposed to prove, Zach? Of course he is well armed. He needs to carry ammunition for the protection of the people he brings here."

"Protection! For their eventual deaths!"

"Zach, you don't trust Caleb, so you see everything the way you want it to be. No one here will believe this."

"Of course not." His voice was strangely soft and his eyes blazed with the realization that the same truth held for everyone at this fort. He was an Indian to them, trying to condemn a white man. He had hoped Tara wouldn't see him the same way, but his hopes had been dashed. "No, of course not," Zach repeated. "What I am doesn't give me the right to condemn him, does it? You find him so honorable, Tara."

"Zach, this has nothing to do with how I feel about Caleb."

That she felt anything for Caleb struck him with an almost physical blow. It was followed by a surge of intense desire, which lit his eyes like a blue flame.

What Tara read in his eyes made her quiver and take a step back. His emotions were battered enough for him to bury his good sense behind them. He wanted her—and he wanted to wipe the look from her face that said she didn't want him. He moved toward her.

For what seemed an eternity they looked at each other. She did not mean to bend, but the dangerous glow of his eyes should have warned her that Zach did not mean to bend either.

171

He continued to gaze into her wide green eyes and saw no fear, only defiance. Passion, awakening slowly, set the pulse of her blood coursing through her veins, making her stir against the sudden warmth that sent tingling sparks to every nerve.

Slowly, he enclosed her wrists in an iron-hard grip that numbed her fingers. Still their eyes held, hers defiant and his warming with the stirring need that was rapidly pushing all other thoughts aside. She felt the heat of her blood pounding through her. The roar of thunder echoed about them as their eyes battled each other.

His nearness and desire written plainly in his eyes made her whisper a silent word of resistance before his mouth touched hers. It was a soft, gentle kiss, his tongue tracing the outline of her mouth as if to seek entry, then gently finding its destination.

"No," she moaned against his mouth, but the word gave him the entry he sought.

He caught her head between his hands, and his mouth, hard and passionate now, closed firmly over hers, forcing her lips apart, his tongue thrusting deep, tasting her sweetness, and setting her head spinning.

She pressed both hands against his chest in a futile effort to stop the overwhelming sense of masculine strength that was devouring her resistance and stirring a volcano within her, sending the flames through every inch of her body.

A deep ache began to grow within her, an ache that blossomed into a surging heat, leaving her trembling and falling deeper into the magic he was weaving about her.

Deeper and deeper the kiss grew, his tongue daring, caressing sensuously, and wiping from her mind the existence of anything else but him.

They were alone in a cataclysmic universe, sheltered from all intrusion except that of the emotions neither could deny. A searing crash of thunder echoed about them as their lips met and their bodies forged together, forged to an intense desire by the strength of him that seemed to enclose her in a swirling

172

magical world.

She could not believe the ecstatic hunger into which she was slipping. She was touched by an exquisite power that set her body on fire and wakened every savage instinct that had lain dormant for so long.

They were barely touching, yet brilliantly aware of the tremendous power that seemed to be drawing them together. He put his arm about her and drew her against him.

They kissed frantically, unendingly, drawing life from each other. He tore down every wall of resistance she had formed as he pressed heated kisses along her cheeks and the soft texture of her throat. He traced a molten path downward until the neck of her nightgown forbade him the soft enticing flesh beneath.

He cupped one soft, rounded breast in his hand through the material of her gown, and he could feel its warmth. He touched the hardened nipple with a slight pressure and circling motion. It was an erotic sensation and she breathed a whispered moan. She could hardly believe the aching hunger that had set her whole body trembling.

Slowly his hands slid up her satin skin to touch her hair. Deftly he loosened the pins and watched it tumble about her.

His eyes darkened to an intense blue as he absorbed her beauty, drinking it in with a soft sound of appreciation.

She closed her eyes, feeling the heat of his gaze and his hands again as he removed the filmy material.

She opened her eyes when she felt his hand leave her, watching in utter fascination as he removed his own clothes. His body was sleek and hard, the long, flawless muscles rippling under taut, tanned skin.

How beautiful he is was the first thought that came to her mind. She wanted to touch him, to know him as he knew her. She reached out her hand and he remained suddenly still. Gently she touched his face, the square chin with a slight stubble of beard, then slipped through the thick black hair, marveling at how soft and smooth it felt. Tara slid her hands down to his shoulders and across his broad fur-matted chest.

173

How well proportioned, how taut and hard he felt. Her hands skimmed his narrow waist and rested on his hips. She raised agitated and uncertain eyes to his and felt the warmth of his gaze fill her.

With a ragged groan his arms came about her and his mouth sought hers in a kiss that exploded the fragile hold either had on reality. He lifted her easily and carried her to the bed. Slowly and almost reluctantly his mouth left the sweetness of hers to travel to her passion-hardened breasts. He caught one of them, then the other, tasting deeply, his teeth nibbling just enough to draw a gasp of sheer carnal pleasure as the sweet pain of it swept over her. She was startled when his lips left her sensitive nipples and began to touch the flesh beneath the curve of her breasts, then moved down to lightly catch the soft flesh of her belly.

An agonized groan of helpless, excited sensuous flame touched the center of her as his hands first caressed her thighs gently, then separated them. Through half-closed eyes she watched as he pressed his lips to the soft flesh of her inner thigh. Slowly . . . slowly, one kiss after another, he searched and then found the most sensitive and most heated center. The sensation was so wild and exotic that she wasn't sure she could bear it. Her fingers tangled in his thick hair and she cried out without hearing. She twisted and writhed as his tongue sent warm and nerve-tingling sensations through her. She fought both to resist and to search for more. Her body won out over her mind as it arched up, seeking more of the exquisite ecstasy his questing tongue gave.

He rose above her, bracing on his arms, his throbbing manhood barely touching the pulsing entrance. He looked down into her passion-blinded eyes. He wanted to see her face when they joined. He wanted to know their pleasure was mutual. He gave her all of himself with a completeness he had given no other.

He watched her eyes glaze with the heat of her passion. She could only feel now, for he was dark above her like a force from

174

beyond their world. Her body arched up to meet his, and both were beyond all thought but the pulsing life that was spinning their world beyond control.

More than one time he had to still himself to keep control, to keep from tumbling over the brink until he could carry her with him.

The core of heat building within her began to expand, and she was like a brilliant blue flame dancing in the center of a volcano. When it reached a peak the dazzling contractions rippled through them both, achingly sweet and totally consuming. They lay silent for a long moment, catching their breaths.

Tara lay in a haze of completed ecstasy, too shaken by the intensity of the orgasm to try to speak, not knowing words to speak even if she could. The tangled web of their relationship—if she could call it that—left her uncertain. Zach was tumbling back to the same unwelcome reality. If he had not been so caught up in the web she seemed to have the almost unbelievable power to weave about him, he would have had sense enough not to reach. But he had reached, he had touched, and he'd tasted a miracle. Now he had to face the fact that it could never be his. A terrible kind of pride thrust her claws into his heart and tore searing wounds. He would not look into her eyes and see what he had seen in so many others. She had almost said the words. She had said no one in the fort would believe him. He was certain that included her. . . .

The room was suddenly quiet, so quiet the night sounds could be heard clearly through the open window. Their breathing under control, they lay together, arms and legs entwined, pulses beating to the same rhythm, and yet a void was grow growing between them. Inches became miles, silence became condemnation and regret.

He rose from the bed and began to dress. Tara sat up, holding the blanket before her, suddenly more aware of her vulnerability and her state of nakedness. She saw the grim line of his mouth and the way his eyes avoided hers, not knowing

175

that he couldn't bear to look into the deep wells of her green eyes to see scorn and disgust.

When he was dressed he lifted the scarf and the shells from the table. He placed the shells in one corner of the scarf and tied it securely. Then he tossed it into her lap.

"Here's a reminder, Tara. Maybe one day you'll judge by different standards than you do now. Maybe one day you will be a woman who looks at life without the blinders of society." He walked to the bed. "For now, I guess it's your way. I can't seem to climb the white man's wall." He walked to the window.

"Zach!"

"Don't be upset, Tara," he laughed bitterly. "No one saw me come, and no one will see me leave. Whatever shame there is in lying with a savage will never be linked to your name. Your reputation is safe." With a graceful move he was a dark shape in the window, and then he was gone.

Tara stared at the window, shattered at the touch of pain that made tears spring to her eyes. "Damn you, Zachary Hale," she whispered. "Damn you."

Zach returned to an uncomfortable bed that felt extremely cold and empty. He cursed Tara, too, for the ability to reach him through the shield he had worn for so long. Those wide green eyes seemed to be able to find all his well-camouflaged weaknesses. He hadn't meant to do what he had done, and he denied the hurt he had felt at the realization that he could not make her look past what others said he was. Tara Montgomery meant only more problems for him and he certainly didn't need any more.

He demanded his body's control, but he had to force the idea of Tara from his mind, walking through his father's village beside him, seeing him and his people as they were and not as they were portrayed. It was an impossible idea and he wanted to destroy it at its inception, before it destroyed him. Because he knew, for that one wild moment, that he possessed her, the

176

thought was even more dangerous, for to admit that was to admit she had possessed him as well, and he could not afford that weakness.

Tara remained sleepless for hours, watching a patch of moonlight slowly work its way across her room to rest on the bed. She had left the scarf, with its knot of what Zach had considered evidence, on the bed, and now she looked at it lying mutely before her and tried to be logical.

Of course it was not enough evidence to condemn Caleb. It was Zach's hatred for Caleb that blinded him to all but the obsession to strike out at Banning. No man who knew this territory would travel without being well armed. But why put the shells in her wagon? Caleb seemed to be trusted by everyone at the fort. Then why the intensity of the hatred between him and Zach? Surely all the bitterness was in Zach's own mind. But she could only remember the intensity of his gaze as he seemed to be searching within her for an answer of some kind. This memory left her vulnerable to other emotions, emotions she found difficult to handle. He could touch her, and reason fled. He could kiss her and some wild thing within her was unleashed. This was the worst of all things, and her muffled groan touched the silence of the room even though she turned her face into the pillow to hide it. These forbidden memories filled her, and again his hands stroked her flesh and his mouth drained her of all will. She cried softly and did battle with these unwelcome thoughts until exhausted sleep finally claimed her.

But even here she was deceived and betrayed by her senses, for dreams will not allow escape and she became lost in them.

177

Chapter 16

David Montgomery set his drink on the bar and turned to face a table where three men sat, their voices loud and strong enough to be heard by him. While he listened to them talk, he realized he was glad that he would soon be returning to Fort Lyon. Denver was a military district of Colorado Territory and under the command of Colonel John Chivington, a man whom David detested for more reasons than he could tell.

Chivington worked together with the governor of Colorado territory, John Evans, and the two of them stood united in a policy of harsh reprisals against the Indians. Chivington was outspoken in his desire to exterminate all Indians whether innocent or guilty.

Lieutenant Nathan Hays was the third member who sat at the small table. He was as determined as the other two that his tour of duty would see the final elimination of the persisting Plains Indians.

David exchanged a look with a tall buckskin-clad man who stood beside him. Curtis Longstreet had lived among the Indians as a trader most of his life. The Indians had called him Long Rifle for years, out of respect. And David had called him Long from the time he could remember. The two had been in comradely conversation until Chivington's voice rose enough to carry to them.

"There can be no dealings with these people. They are ignorant and sly, and they wouldn't have the first notion how to honor a treaty."

"I agree, John," Evans added. "We've given these savages enough room already, and no matter how we try to talk they continue to kill and scalp indiscriminately."

"They've been raiding the settlements again, and until Washington understands that, the only way to deal with these people is with an iron hand."

"I hear you're gathering a regiment," Nathan Hays added.

"I most certainly am."

"Denver is rather isolated, and Washington doesn't realize what danger we're in from this murderous vermin. I agree with John. We have to attack and wipe them out before they attack us and it's too late," John Evans stated firmly.

"And that bastard, Black Kettle," Chivington exclaimed angrily, "wanting us to give him back the group of murderous heathens we have for some prisoners he says he has! I will hang them first and return their bodies. I don't believe he has any prisoners to exchange anyhow."

David nudged Curtis Long, picking up the bottle they were sharing and two glasses. Then he motioned Long to follow him, making his way to a table some distance away from the three so they could talk without their words being overheard.

"Stupid jackass," Long muttered as he sat down with his back to the three. David laughed softly.

"That he is, but he's a dangerous stupid jackass."

"He's really getting up a regiment?" Long inquired.

"Yeah, a bunch of barroom toughs and other riffraff. The worst crew in the world, and they're all spoiling for a fight," David added in disgust.

"And with a man like Major General Samuel Curtis behind him, he'll get it."

"I know. I remember Curtis. He don't want treaties and peace, he wants suffering and eventual extermination."

"I'm going to hightail it out of here and get back to the fort.

179

What about you?"

"I've done what I was sent to do. I'm going to do my best to get out of here pretty quick."

Long looked at David through narrowed but friendly eyes. David was a handsome young man of twenty-five. His lean body was well-set, used to strenuous exercise. His broad shoulders seemed suited for the blue military uniform, which made his copper-gold hair and brilliant green eyes appear even more startling. Having been west of the Mississippi for over a year now, he was tanned, an obvious foil to his light-colored eyes. He was usually a quiet but levelheaded young man, well suited, in Long's estimation, for command. Long also knew he was well liked by the men who served under him.

Long made few friends, being very careful of the ones he did. David was one of the few, and that was mostly because Long felt he was innately too honest and caring to be able to survive among the wolves who wanted to wipe the Indians out. The idea of such butchery was totally alien to David's nature. Long would have liked to see David in command of Fort Lyon instead of Aaron Creighton, whom he knew as a good soldier—if he could only have David's understanding and compassion for the Indians. He liked David despite the fact that he was military. "You goin' right back to the fort?"

He watched a muscle jump in David's cheek and saw the almost imperceptible tightening of his body. He was pretty sure his suspicions had been right.

"What's that supposed to mean?" David frowned.

"Thought I might ride back with you," Long grinned. "Man ain't safe with these bluecoats runnin' free."

"I don't mind if you ride along. I've got to make a stop on the way."

"How you riding?"

"Down along the big Sandy."

"I don't suppose your stop is going to be on Sand Creek—old Black Kettle's camp?"

"Might be. You have any arguments?"

180

"Hell no, I been trading with Black Kettle's people for a lot of years. Got some friends there. I kind of get the feeling you have a few too."

David remained silent for a moment, then he picked up his drink and gulped it down. "Yeah," he replied. But no explanation followed, and Long wouldn't press for an answer. An answer, he had a reasonable suspicion, that he already knew.

"When are you leaving?"

"Soon as I get the estimable Colonel Chivington to give me the sign. I've been after him for days to give me the dispatches. I've got a feeling he wants me to ride with him and his bunch."

"No luck, huh?" Long grinned.

"Hell no, I wouldn't trust him as far as I could throw the whole bunch. He's unstable enough to do anything, and I don't want to be with him when he does."

"Well, you give me the high sign when you're ready to pull out and I'll trail with you." Long sipped his drink, then set the glass down.

"Do you plan on staying out here much longer?"

Again David frowned and his eyes grew thoughtful. "I'm not sure yet. I like the duty here and I've got a lot of friends, but I've still got my parents and a sister I haven't seen for a long time."

"Something special holding you here?" Long added softly.

David looked at him again with his frown growing deeper. He and Curtis had been friends for a long time, but he still felt this was an area he couldn't confide in anyone. An area he had thought, until now, that no other human knew about.

"What are you getting at, Long?"

Curtis Longstreet was a bear of a man, with dark brown hair, thick and unruly, matched to a short beard. His eyes were a piercing slate-gray and had seen more of life than most men had seen in the same thirty-eight years. Usually a reticent man, he opened himself only to those closest to him—and those were very few. He seldom, if ever, intruded in another man's

181

life, but he liked David and had a feeling he was headed for a whole lot of trouble and grief.

"Look, boy, I ain't messin' in your life, and if you want me to get out, I will. But I got a feeling you're getting close to someone in Black Kettle's village. If you are, and you expect to still have a career and family, you better forget it. You know damn well just how a white officer and some squaw would fare out here with this bloodthirsty bunch."

"Small Fawn is no squaw!" David retorted angrily. Then, as Long sat silently back in his chair, David realized he'd made a mistake.

"'Course she ain't. Probably as pretty as they make 'em. But you got a lot of things to think about."

"How do you stand, Long?"

"Hell, boy, I guess you don't know. My wife is Cheyenne. I got a couple of kids. But I don't have the club hanging over me that you do. You got a career and a family at home. That's a lot to give up. I'm only sayin' you got to walk careful."

David sighed. He didn't have to be warned to walk careful; he'd been doing it since he'd met Small Fawn.

"Ride with me to Black Kettle's village. I want you to meet Small Fawn. Then you can tell me what I should do."

"I can't tell you what to do. Like I say, I did what pleased me and I'm happy. But you—you got a family to think of. One thing is for sure: You can't take Small Fawn home. She'd die there, and it would be worse for her to see what they could do to you. Your career would be dead. It's a hell of a choice, David. I can't give you any answers."

"Yeah, I guess this is something I have to work out. So you going to ride with me?"

"Yep, I'd like to meet this little Small Fawn. Maybe we can cut up to my place. I got a cabin on the small end of the creek. You can meet my woman."

"Well, I want to get out of here soon, so I guess I'll bang heads with Colonel Chivington in the morning and see if I can get those dispatches. If I do, how long before you can leave?"

"Couple of days."

"Then let's say a week if all goes well."

"Good." Curtis poured them both another drink. "And good luck with the charming colonel."

"If he don't eat me for breakfast, I'll be out of Denver in a week and glad to put it behind me."

They left the saloon, not stopping to talk to the three men who sat with their heads together, making plans that would affect David much more than he'd ever bargained on.

Zach watched Tara and Caleb ride from the fort. He had also watched Caleb's men carry the boxes from Tara's wagon to another one of Banning's. He had gone from wagon to wagon and found no sign of guns. But they had to be somewhere close and he knew it. He would simply watch Caleb until he made another mistake. His first, as far as Zach was concerned, was to reach for Tara. Maybe Zach couldn't have her, but he would die before he would let a traitorous man like Caleb have her. He was also just as certain that Tara might just be more trade goods for Caleb when the time came.

His sense of humor was suddenly combined with another more subtle feeling. He saddled his horse and rode after them, keeping enough distance so they would not know they were being followed. It would have been difficult for any other man with less expertise to follow Caleb without being seen. But his presence wasn't detected, and Caleb continued his subtle undermining of the Indians in general and Zach in particular. He also did everything to build a confident trust in him that he could use at the right time.

He watched Tara, her gold hair glimmering in the sunlight and her lips parted in appreciation as he looked about. He had to restrain the lust that tore through him.

"So you removed what belonged to you from my wagon?" Tara inquired.

"Yes, I know it was an imposition, but my wagons were so

183

full and it was only a few boxes, so I didn't think you would mind."

"Of course not."

"I imagine your brother will be returning soon?" It was important for Caleb to know when David was expected to reappear. He hoped to be prepared to move before that happened. Once it looked as if Indians had taken his sister, even David, whom Caleb knew to be bending toward sympathy toward the Indians, would be forced to pick up a gun and fight.

"I'm afraid, from what Aaron says, it might be several weeks yet."

"Too bad. I know he'll be put out when he finds you've been here all this time and he didn't know it."

"That doesn't bother me nearly as much as the fact that David doesn't know about our parents yet. It will be such a terrible blow."

Tara didn't say that she longed for the security she would feel when she had the only remaining person in her family near.

"Well, at least the two of you will be together."

"Yes," Tara replied softly. "Caleb, you are somewhat of a mystery."

"I?" Caleb laughed. "What's so mysterious about me, Tara?"

"Well, I'm sorry if I sound overly curious, but you seem to be . . . well, educated. Besides that, you just give me the impression of military."

"Military," Caleb repeated, startled at her acute observation. "I'll make claim to something of an education, but I'm afraid military has not been part of my background. Whatever gave you that impression?"

"I guess it's the order and command you had over the wagon train . . . and even here you're always in control."

"That's more habit than military training. I'm just a combination wagon master and trader."

"You trade a great deal with the Indians?"

"Yes."

"What do they give you?"

"Me?"

"I mean, what do you trade for what?"

"I trade cloth, iron kettles and pans, and a multitude of other things. What I get in return is passage over their lands and sometimes a few articles, but not much. It's the ability to cross their land in peace that I value most."

"I see."

She seemed to accept his explanation, and Caleb was relieved that she didn't push it any further. She was much too clever and her brother was no less so.

They reached a small stream where Caleb said they should stop to rest the horses and give them some water. Once they had done so, Caleb loosened the saddle girths so the horses could rest, then he and Tara sat side by side on a flat rock near the stream. Neither were aware of the intent blue gaze that followed their every move.

Sitting almost shoulder to shoulder, it was only moments before Tara drew her gaze from her surroundings and turned to look into Caleb's eyes, realizing he had been studying her closely.

She smiled to cover the sudden chill of fear. What did she have to be afraid of? Everyone had seen them ride out, so surely he could do her no harm without answering to many people. At that thought her mind leapt to Zach, who had claimed Caleb was not to be trusted.

He was handsome, there was no mistaking the fact, and he was charming enough to catch a girl's fancy. Yet she was still distinctly uncomfortable.

"You are so beautiful, Tara. You look perfect out here with the sunlight in your hair. You know the Indians are fascinated over people with golden hair. It's rare out here."

"Thank you, Caleb."

"I hope you decide to stay here for quite a while. I would like to take you to visit some of the tribes I deal with. You might learn a lot."

"I suppose staying or leaving will be determined by David. He's all I have now, so our moves will depend on his career."

"I'd like to think," Caleb said quietly, as he bent closer, "that I could help convince you to stay."

Their bodies were close and his mouth hovered too near to hers. One arm slid about her waist. Tara was gathering her wits and prepared to do battle. But at that moment a familiar voice, dripping with amusement, made them leap apart in surprise. Surprise, which Tara was soon aware, could look like guilt. She flushed at the thought, then realized angrily that might make her look even more guilty.

"Well, well." Zach's voice was taunting and his smile was worse. "Sorry if I'm intruding. I didn't know this was such a romantic meeting place."

"What the hell are you doing here?" Caleb snarled as he rose to his feet. Tara sat immobile, angry and frustrated at what this might look like to Zach.

Zach shrugged. "Just passing by. Thought I'd water my horse. Good thing," his voice was filled with laughter that grated on Tara's nerves, "that I didn't come by a little later. It might have been embarrassing for everyone."

Tara gasped and a brilliant rage filled her eyes. She nearly leapt to her feet. "How dare you say such a thing!" she demanded.

"He is what he is, Tara," Caleb said coldly. "What else can he think but the worst of others. I imagine he's conceived the idea of what he would do in my place without realizing 'civilized' men don't take advantage of women in such a situation."

Zach actually laughed, which did very little to ease the situation. Caleb's face was a mask of ill-controlled fury, and Tara looked as if murder were her greatest hope.

"I conceived the idea that you couldn't be trusted, Caleb?" Zach laughed again. "Not my conception, my friend. I think it began with your mother."

186

"You half-breed scum," Caleb snarled. "I could—"

"Could what?" Zach's voice was dangerously soft, and the smile was gone from both his lips and his eyes.

Being certain that Zach wanted him to push further, Caleb controlled himself with the promise that Zach would pay one day soon—and pay with his life.

"Don't!" Tara cried. She was angry at Zach and at herself for reacting to his challenge the way she had. Both men looked at her. "Take me back to the fort, Caleb, please," she said coldly. Then she turned her back and walked to her horse. She tightened the cinch herself, struggling for composure to contain her frustrated tears. Then she mounted, keeping her gaze from both men. She wheeled her horse about and started for the fort.

Caleb cast a scathing look at Zach and started for his horse, but Zach gripped his arm to stop him. Caleb faced Zach, and both men were restraining battle with much effort.

"Zach, you'd be wise to leave the fort and get back to your own people, where you belong."

"If I thought those people were safe, I just might."

"You seeing ghosts in the night, Zach?" Caleb smiled. "Some of your people's superstitions coming to the surface? Maybe you ought to go on a vision quest or whatever it is your red brothers do to get some 'medicine.'"

"You put a hand on Tara or make any moves toward her, and I'll practice some other traditions of my people. Ever been staked out in the hot sun naked for a few days, with your eyelids cut off so you can't close your eyes? Let me tell you, Caleb, old friend, it will start with frying your eyeballs and end up frying your brain. Anything happens to Tara, and that will be the best you can expect."

Zach swung up on his pony and Caleb cursed his saddle's looseness. He tightened the cinch and mounted, but he knew Zach would catch up with Tara long before he did.

Tara rode without looking back, not caring where either man was at the moment. She could hear a horse approaching from

187

the rear, but she refused to turn to see which one it was. Then Zach appeared beside her, and they rode in silence until Tara's curiosity got the best of her.

"Zach?"

"What?"

"What were you doing out there?"

"Like I said, just passing by."

"Of course. In hundreds of square miles of empty land, you just happened to be passing by that very spot."

Zach chuckled softly, and Tara could not control the twitch of her lips in a half smile. Zach's chuckle grew to a laugh, and in a moment Tara was laughing with him.

"So, I followed you from the fort," he admitted.

"Why?"

"Because romantic little girls shouldn't be allowed to wander into deserted places with a coyote. All she'll make is one healthy meal."

"You really hate him?"

"Hate's a small word when it comes to a man like Caleb."

"And yet you have no proof. You don't really know he's guilty of . . . whatever it is you think he's doing."

"Tara, I don't have to see a skunk to know he's in the vicinity; all I have to do is smell him."

"Zach, you have a lot of enemies at the fort."

"I know," he replied quietly. Then he turned to look at her. "What about you, Tara Montgomery? Friend or enemy?"

Before Tara could answer, Caleb's horse could be heard, and in a few minutes he was beside them.

The ride back to the fort was done in silence, each tied to their own thoughts.

For Caleb it was a cold, deathlike fury. He meant to have Tara, but now he intended also to make sure Zach paid for all he had said and done and for interfering in his plans.

For Tara the thoughts were more confusing. She had no idea who to believe. Caleb was a man trusted by many, a man who had led people across hostile territory safely, a man who seemed valuable to all in the fort. Yet Zach did not trust him. and Zachary Hale—Windwalker, they called him—was angry and hostile himself. He was a man few at the fort seemed to trust. A man who was not adverse to using anyone around him to meet a goal.

She was confused, but she planned now on keeping her distance from both men until she understood this wild and untamed country and its even wilder and more untamed men.

For Zach there was no less confusion. He found himself making promises to let Tara walk her own way and concentrate on what he had to do, while on the other hand he kept her in a corner of his mind constantly and couldn't seem to push her out. She needed protection whether she believed it or not. What worried him was whether, in her stubborn willfulness, she was going to accept protection.

All the arguments he made with himself were useless. There was something about Tara Montgomery that brought out a side of him he didn't understand.

Chapter 17

Tara, Zach, and Caleb rode through the front gates of the fort. Once they reached the stable and dismounted, Zach led his and Tara's horses inside to see to their care, while Tara walked across the compound to her quarters.

Caleb stood before the stable watching Tara until she went inside, his anger at Zach growing with each breath. He led his horse inside and gave orders for his care.

Zach smiled to himself but continued to finish the care of his horse and Tara's. He had pinched Caleb and made him angry. If he could keep it up, Caleb was going to make a mistake, and when he did, Zach would be there to nail his hide.

Zach wouldn't have been so pleased if he had known of the events transpiring some miles away.

Little Raven squatted on his haunches amid a small group of young warriors, some near his own age and a few a little older. He was watching Tall Bull with a small amount of fascination. Despite his distrust of the man, he knew Tall Bull had the power to sway younger and wilder men. The promise of guns and ammunition plus plenty of the white men's whiskey had them excited.

Little Raven was confused. Everything Tall Bull said seemed

right. It was truth—the white men's injustice and his eternal pushing.

"How much must we take from these white intruders?" Tall Bull questioned arrogantly. "How long will we sit in our lodges like women and listen to the old men who would give our land away?"

"We cannot fight so many," one young warrior offered.

"And we cannot fight guns with spears and arrows," another added.

"I know that," Tall Bull boasted. "But soon there will be guns for everyone. Then we will drive them back beyond the rising sun where they belong."

It was then that Tall Bull noticed Little Raven's thoughtfulness. If he could get the chief's son to fight beside him, he would have the power to sway the rest.

"Little Raven," Tall Bull began, "your heart tells you what I am saying is so, does it not?"

"My heart speaks your words, but my head still hears the words of my brother. He says it is wrong for us to pick up the white man's guns and fight. He says we must learn to live with each other."

"That can never be. We cannot live at their side. They do not want it so. They want to kill us. Well, I say we should kill them first!" Tall Bull was clever. "Your brother would keep you a boy when you should be treated like a man."

He had hoped to fire Little Raven's resistance, but what he saw was cold anger as the chief's son stood erect. "I am not a child. But I am also not a foolish man who shouts always for others to fight. I will speak with my brother and I will heed his words, for he is one who knows the white men well. He will speak the truth."

Little Raven walked away from the group sensing Tall Bull's anger. He would not let Tall Bull have the satisfaction of seeing his doubts. He would talk to Windwalker.

He rode, deep in thought, allowing everything to walk in his mind except the words of caution from his brother that he was not to sneak into the fort again. His mind was troubled, and he needed answers if he were not to make a mistake that would perhaps cost him his life, but worse, maybe Windwalker's love and respect as well.

When he reached a place where he could see the fort, it was already growing dark. He would not have long to wait until he could slip in and speak with his brother.

Zach had allowed the day's activity at the fort to flow about him. He lazed near the stable, keeping one eye on Caleb's activities and the other on the closed door to Tara's quarters. There was a feeling in the pit of his stomach that something was about to break. With any kind of luck, Caleb would make some kind of move tonight, and he'd be there to catch it.

The fort grew quiet, and mellow lamplight flickered from a few quarters. Sentries walked their posts, and all seemed to be well. Zach had sat before the stable with Mule beside him, pretending he was repairing a bridle. Caleb's quarters glowed with light, but at any time he expected it to go out.

"He's keepin' an eye on us as hard as you are on him," Mule offered.

"Maybe I ought to take a little stroll."

"Where ya goin'?"

"To see if any of his men are gathering around the wagons. If they are, then he's about to make a move."

"Watch out for yourself. One step and you're a dead man."

Zach went inside the stable, and any onlooker would safely assume he was on his way to his own room. But once inside, he moved like a swift, silent shadow. He exited the back door to the stable and stood quietly in the depths of the night's shadows to orient himself. Then he began to work his way toward the wagons.

Little Raven moved with his accustomed stealth. He made

no sound, moving from place to place and stopping each time to make sure the sentries had not become aware of him. But they continued to move in uninterrupted steps along the upper wall. Timing himself with a precise ability, he scaled the wall in the short moments when the sentry had just passed and had not had time to turn and retrace his path. In seconds he was over the top, dropping lightly to the ground and backing against the inner shadowed wall to make sure he had not been seen. He had dropped inside the wall, just behind where the line of barracks joined Zach's room. From past experience, he knew the less distance he had to cover the safer it would be.

The challenge of moving about the fort freely and even stealing a few supplies from the storage rooms had always been fun. But tonight fun was not what he had in mind. He had to find Windwalker. He made his passage as direct as possible, even though he scoffed at the white man's futile protection. He could move where he chose and when he chose, and no one could catch him.

Little Raven wasn't sure Zach would even be in the small room, for he knew it made his brother feel as confined as the white man's wooden walls did him. But Zach's room was his only logical place to start. He moved swiftly, and in a few minutes he found himself outside Zach's quarters. One quick look in the open window told him the room was empty. His next thought was of Mule, so he moved to the back door of the stable and slipped inside.

Mule always slept in the stable, proclaiming an affinity for horses that balanced his dislike and distrust of most humans. But Mule was still seated before the stables, his attention on the light that still glowed from Caleb's quarters. Alert as he was, Mule did not hear a sound from behind him until his name was whispered from just inside the darker area within the open stable doors. The name was repeated only twice before Mule recognized the voice. He didn't turn around but stood slowly, as if he were stiff. He stretched and yawned, then moved toward the stable doors as if he had decided to go to bed.

Inside he was met with what appeared to be emptiness, but Little Raven's chuckle was soft and teasing.

"You little devil," Mule whispered in a deeply aggravated voice. "What the hell you doin' inside this fort again? I thought your brother put a stop to your roamin' around in here like it belonged to you. Dad blame it, Little Raven! Don't you know if you get yourself caught, you ain't the only one in trouble? Your brother will pay for it, too."

"It is important, Mule," the voice came quietly from a dark corner. "I seek my brother. I must speak to him. Tall Bull speaks of guns and war. I must tell Windwalker and ask what is to be done."

"Guns and war," Mule repeated angrily. "Tall Bull. Zach should have known he was a troublemaker all the time. You suppose he's mixed up with Caleb?"

"I don't know. He will never say where he's going to get the guns. He only says when we are ready they will come."

"Zach's gone over to where the wagons is settin'. He's lookin' to see if Caleb makes any moves."

"Are the guns in the wagons of Caleb?"

"Zach said he searched 'em and they ain't there. But he's got a pretty good idea they're somewhere close."

"I must speak with Windwalker," the voice grew fainter.

"Little Raven? . . . Little Raven!" Mule whispered as loud as he could, but he was sure Little Raven had already gone. "That blamed kid is goin' to get himself hung yet."

Mule was frustrated. He couldn't go to the wagons to warn Zach without betraying his presence, and he couldn't stop Little Raven. All he could do was hope Little Raven was successful, and he and Zach would find their way back to the stable safely.

Zach had worked his way around the periphery of the fort carefully. He felt certain there would be plenty of time since, even if there was evidence in the wagons being transferred, no one would be moving until it grew late enough for even the

194

sentries to grow tired and lax. But he would wait. A small inner voice told him that he should be alert and ready for anything tonight.

By the time he reached the corner of the stables nearest the wagons, the moon had risen just above the wall. He swore lightly under his breath. Of all the nights he could have used some sheltering clouds, this was one. He prepared himself to wait and watch.

Little Raven, self-assured and casting both caution and his brother's warning to the wind, made his decision to move from stable to stable, across the compound and in front of the half-open gate.

The sentries at the gate stood just inside the closed doors and around a fire. Expecting trouble to only come from the outside, they paid very little attention to what might be occurring inside. The ring of light from the sentry fire made the dark shadows surrounding it even darker. Little Raven, in a half crouch, moved from the stable and worked his way slowly across the compound toward the wall on the opposite side, in what would have been full view of the sentries had they been looking.

Laughter and excitement bubbled up in him as he reached the wall safely and began to work his way around to where he could view the wagons.

Windwalker must be among the wagons, he thought at once. It would be interesting to see if this time he could catch his brother unaware. He had never done so before. Knowing the wagons must be empty, he was sure they need not be guarded too closely. He crossed swiftly from the corner of the stable to the first wagon.

Zach, from the shadows of the wall, saw the fleeting movement. Caleb's men were on the prowl. He was right. Tonight might be the night they found a trail to the guns he had been searching for in vain for so long.

At the same moment of Little Raven's safe arrival at the

stable wall, Caleb and Brace came outside from Caleb's quarters. They had extinguished the lamp first. Caleb felt confident that tonight would be the last night needed for him and his men to move the shells they had scattered through the wagons into the three that contained the rifles. Once this was finished, he would ride out to meet Tall Bull and find out about his progress in rousing the braves with promises of guns. Once they were set, it would only mean delivering the guns and watching the aftermath. Caleb was pleased that the man who had hired him would be well satisfied.

They moved slowly, not wanting to attract any undue attention. For all intents and purposes, they seemed to be headed for the stables.

Little Raven moved from the first wagon to the second, then the third. He could see a dark form before him by the fourth wagon and mistook it for his brother. He was about to move forward when the sharp click of a gun being cocked and the pressure of cold metal against his back made him freeze.

"You just stand still, Injun." The voice was cold and firm. "I don't know if you understand me, but you sure understand this." He prodded Little Raven in the ribs with the gun.

"I understand you," Little Raven replied.

"Well, well, an English-speakin' redskin. Hey, Joe, come on over and see what I caught me."

The shadowed form Little Raven had mistaken for his brother turned and moved toward him.

Little Raven was trying to think but at the moment he couldn't grasp a way out of his dilemma. There was no way he was going to bring Windwalker into this if he could help it. He wasn't afraid, and that was his undoing. He stood with a pride and self-containment that irritated the two men.

"Cocky little bastard, isn't he?" the second man snarled. "Maybe he needs to be taught a little lesson."

"I have done no harm," Little Raven protested, "I came only to see the white man's fort," he lied. "I will go."

"You will like hell," the first man countered as he jabbed the gun against Little Raven again. "Just how'd you get in here?"

Little Raven remained silent. He had sensed these men were going to pose a real problem. But he did not expect what happened. The second man struck fast and hard, and the blow slammed Little Raven back against the first. He would have fought back against them, angered at the surprise blow and the bitter taste of blood in his mouth. But the first man struck a glancing blow against his head with the gun, not enough to render him unconscious, but enough to drop him to his knees. Again the second man struck, kicking Little Raven in the side and knocking the wind from him. It was his first contact with the whites who inhabited the fort, but it brought out clearly what Windwalker had meant when he told him to stay away. For the first time he felt the touch of fear and that was potent for a young man with Little Raven's pride.

This was the scene that met Zach's eyes when he rounded the corner of the stables. It took seconds to realize who was being beaten. Like Little Raven, he forgot to use his judgment. Zach ran toward the two who bent over his brother and he leapt, bringing one down with the force of his attack. His fist jolted the prostrate man into unconsciousness, and he turned to face the second who had already drawn his gun. They stood only two feet apart, Zach prepared to attack and the other man unsure, since he recognized Zach as wagon guide, whether to shoot him or not. He might have had Caleb not spoken from the shadows.

"Well, what have we here? Zach, old friend, just what kind of mischief are you up to?"

"Call off your dog, Caleb. They were trying to beat up Little Raven."

Caleb's eyes swung to Little Raven, who was slowly getting to his feet, holding his injured side and clinging to Zach to help himself rise.

"Little Raven? An Indian! Here in the fort?" Caleb chided. "Now, Zach, you and I know that's against the law here. Just what was he doing here . . . and . . . who let him in?

197

"He's young. He just made a mistake of curiosity. Let him go. He won't be back."

"Oh no, no," Caleb laughed. "I do believe that you were passing him guns to carry back to his friends." His voice was triumphant and filled with mocking pity. "Now, Zach, you know that's pretty bad. I think Aaron is going to be mighty, mighty put out."

"Caleb, that's a lie!"

"Oh, you know that and I know that, but Aaron doesn't. And I think he'll believe me when he finds you . . . and him . . . and a few guns to make it look good."

"Little Raven had nothing to do with this. He's a boy," Zach protested. But Little Raven was having none of this. If Zach were to pay, he would most certainly pay with him.

"I am a man," he argued arrogantly, "and the dog is a lying snake. You—" he said to Caleb, "you are the one who promised Tall Bull guns."

"Tall Bull?" Zach looked quickly at his brother.

"I do not know for certain, but Tall Bull promises much."

"So the young one wants to stand with you, Zach," Caleb taunted. "Tell me . . . Little Raven, is it? Tell me, do you know that you will be hanged for this?

Little Raven was shaken. To die as a man in battle or on a hunt was one thing, but to be hanged in the white man's fort was a terrible thing. He would have no medicine, no way to join his ancestors once his body was left behind. He was struck to silence, and Zach knew the fear that quivered within him. But he moved to stand closer to Zach.

Caleb gave a short nod of his head, and Zach realized he had been so intent on Banning that he had forgotten the man with the gun. The gun butt caught him on the back of the head. Everything went black before him, and he slumped to the ground. Little Raven gave a cry of fury and tried to grab the one who had struck Zach, but four to one were too many and soon his unconscious form lay beside Zach.

*　　　*　　　*

Mule was the first one to realize something was wrong. He had tried to wait for Zach, but when the wee hours of the morning began to turn to dawn, he began to wonder what might have happened. He stood up from his bed of straw and made his way to the stable door to peer out. He expected to see a still-sleeping fort and was both surprised and nervous when he saw the glow of light from Aaron's office. He knew beyond a doubt something was drastically wrong, and he had a pretty good idea what it might be.

The rest of the fort slept, and only the sentries saw Mule walk slowly across the compound toward Aaron's office. But Mule was a familiar form who caused no alarm, and he walked up on the porch quietly. He wanted to hear what was going on before he walked into something. There was a window to the left of the door that was partway open. Mule moved close to it and squatted down so he could hear.

"So where did you find them?" It was Aaron's voice and it was grim.

"I tried to tell you, Aaron." Caleb's voice was smooth and smug. "He must have passed the rest of the rifles out because we searched everywhere. There's no more guns. Him and this kid were just waiting to get the last of the guns out. We found them down near the wall. They probably would have been gone in a few more minutes, and we never would have known."

"He's a damn liar." It was Zach's voice now, and to Mule it sounded shaky, as if Zach were not in control of himself. He wasn't.

Zach and Little Raven were standing before Aaron, who was seated behind his desk. Zach felt weak from the blow to his head, and he was certain he must have been kicked a time or two, for he felt terrible. He was also afraid for Little Raven, who stood unflinchingly beside him. But he could see from his tight clenched jaw that he was more shaken than he would admit.

"How do you explain the Indian?" Aaron questioned.

"Curious," Zach replied. "He just wanted to see inside the fort."

199

"Christ, you expect me to believe that, Zach? No Indians are allowed in the fort after the sun goes down. If he slipped past my guards, he had to have help from inside. Were you smuggling those guns out? How many?"

"Neither one of us are guilty."

"You defend him, too?"

"He's innocent. Caleb and his men are the ones you want."

"Zach, for God's sake, don't take me for a fool. Caleb had no contact with the Indians. Obviously, from your defense of him, you do."

"You'd be a fool if that's what you believe."

There was a long moment of silence, then Mule had to bend closer to the window to hear. But what he heard was something he wished he hadn't.

"Take them both to one of the storage rooms. Lock them up," Aaron ordered.

"This is a hanging offense," Caleb reminded.

"I don't need to be told my duty, Caleb," Aaron said coldly. "Lock them up, and I'll make the decisions on where and how the penalties will be carried out."

"All right." Caleb sounded satisfied. He knew Aaron had little choice. He would be forced to carry out orders that had come from Washington some time before, and Mule knew for certain Caleb would be there to remind him.

Mule stood up and walked to the edge of the porch as the door opened. Zach and Little Raven were pushed out ahead of Caleb and one of his men. Zach saw Mule but said nothing. Mule just nodded his head. But it didn't go unnoticed by Caleb, who stopped beside Mule. The two watched Little Raven and Zach being shoved across the compound to be locked in a storage room.

"Don't get any wise ideas of busting him out of there, Mule," Caleb said softly. "Me and my boys will be watching close—real close. And I have a feeling Aaron will be watching pretty close, too. This time he made a mistake he's going to pay for, and if you get in my way"—he turned to look at Mule and

200

smiled—"maybe you'll pay, too."

Mule was so angry he could have killed Caleb where he stood, and Caleb knew it as he laughed softly and walked away.

Mule thought about trying to talk to Aaron but decided against it. Knowing how Aaron felt about Indians was bad enough, but finding them with the ability to slip in and out of his supposedly well-guarded fort would find him in a less than reasonable mood.

Mule's mind raced. It would do no more good to try and ask Zach why it had happened. It had happened, and now he had to find a way to do somehting about it.

"Mule, you better get your head to working, or sure as hell you're gonna see Zach and Little Raven hangin' and Caleb laughing," he said to himself.

He struggled for an idea, letting his eyes roam around the inside of the fort. There had to be a way . . . some way. Then he saw the sudden glow of a lamp being lit in Tara's quarters.

Before he could put any form to a plan or even figure out if Tara would consent to help, he was walking across the compound toward her quarters. He walked up on the porch and knocked.

Chapter 18

Tara's sleep had been intermittent, for she had awakened at every sound. Finally she gave up the effort and rose and dressed. She lit a lamp and carried it through the darkened quarters to the living room. She had found a great deal of her brother's clothing in need of mending, so she set about working on it. She was so surprised by the knock on the door that it was repeated before she had the presence of mind to answer it.

She opened it only a crack, enough to identify who stood on the other side of it. Then she opened it wider.

"Mule! Whatever are you doing here? It's after four in the morning."

"Tara, let me in, girl. I've got something to tell you, and I need some help."

"Of course." As he passed her, she questioned deeper, "What kind of help do you need from me?" He turned to face her as she closed and locked the door again.

"Well, it ain't exactly me that needs help."

"Not you? Then who? Mule, you're talking in riddles."

"Simmer down, girl, and I'll tell you." He hesitated for a moment, then spoke again. "It's Zach that needs help."

"Zach? What kind of help?"

"Right about now they're tossing him into one of the supply

rooms and locking him up."

"What's he done?"

"Nothing."

"Mule, Aaron wouldn't lock up someone who's done nothing."

"He would if there was a lot of things drummed up against him by a snake."

"Mule, we'd get a lot further if you would just explain to me what's happened."

Mule made a sharp, exasperated sound and tried to gather the story together as much from the beginning as he could.

Tara made no effort to interrupt until Mule had finished the story and repeated the words that had been spoken in Aaron's office.

"Mule . . . could he be guilty?" she said softly.

"Hell no, girl, you don't know a whole lot of facts, and you've been listening too long to one-sided stories. Now you listen. Zach's been tracing whoever's been bringing in guns and whiskey for well over a year. He's scared to death there's gonna be something exploding out here that's going to cost a lot of lives. Maybe you ought to know two sides of things."

"So he's locked up, Mule. What do you expect me to do about it?"

"I'll tell you, Tara, I got a lot of trust that you're a smart girl who has sense enough to know truth when she hears it. I want you to go to talk to Zach. . . . Then, I want you to help me bust him loose."

"Break him from jail! Mule, you're insane. I could never do that!"

"Even if a lot of lives, including many at this fort, were at stake?"

"Mule . . . I wouldn't know what to do or how to do it."

"I'm not sure how to do it, but I can't go talk to him because they got sixteen sets of eyes on me. I can't make a move to help him. All I'm asking is that you go talk to him. If there's a way out, he can think of it."

Tara was quite sure Zach would think a whole lot of other things about her visit as well.

"I don't know, Mule. . . ." she hesitated.

"There isn't anyone else at this fort that can help him. In a week or so, they'll hang him."

"Hang him!"

"Yep. Washington's new law. Anyone bringing in guns or whiskey for the Indians gets caught, he gets hung."

Tara sank down into a chair. Zach had been nothing but a thorn in her life. He had taken advantage of her at every turn. All she need do was nothing, and she would be free of his presence, his touch. . . . But that thought conjured up other more poignant images. She could see him vividly before her, the quick teasing smile and the glow of humor in his blue eyes. She could feel the touch of his flesh against hers and taste the hard mouth that had softened so fleetingly against hers. All these were reasons she should free herself from him. But could she free herself at the expense of his life?

"Tara, girl . . ."

"Let me think, Mule!"

"Then you'll help me?"

"I don't know what I can do, but the least I can do is talk to him and carry any messages you might have."

"Well, I'll put my head to it and see what I can get up."

"All right, Mule. I'll go see him just as soon as I can. Come back here tomorrow afternoon."

"You won't regret it, Tara girl. You're doing the right thing. When this all comes to a head and Zach proves who's really guilty, you'll see. He'll be grateful and you'll be glad you did it."

"I have my serious doubts about his gratitude, just as I have some serious doubts about his guilt. What I do, if anything, I do for you, Mule."

"I'll see you tomorrow then. Maybe the two of us can come up with something."

She nodded and Mule left quietly, leaving her caught in

thoughts that might have surprised everyone at the fort, even Zach.

By the time the fort was stirring to life, Tara was already dressed and walking across the compound toward Aaron's office.

The young corporal who was Aaron's clerk rose to his feet with a broad smile when Tara walked into the office.

"Good morning, Miss Montgomery."

"Good morning, Corporal. Is Aaron here?"

"Yes, ma'am, he's still in his quarters."

"I'd like to see him, if I may."

"Yes, ma'am. I'll tell him you're here."

He went into Aaron's quarters, returning in less than fifteen minutes with the commander behind him.

"Good morning, Tara," Aaron smiled. "What are you doing up and about so early?"

"Well, I've been hearing there was some excitement last night."

"Excitement?"

"Well, everyone's whispering," she smiled as if she were pleased, "about how you captured Zach passing guns out of the fort."

"And that pleases you?" he said suspiciously.

"Zachary Hale has taken advantage of me for the last time. I'm terribly embarrassed by my naiveté and my ignorance of the way of life out here."

"I suppose it's just a lesson you had to learn, Tara," Aaron said smugly. Tara could have struck him.

"Oh, Aaron, please be a dear and let me see him."

"See him! Now, Tara, that's impossible."

"Just for a few minutes. You don't know how good it will feel to be able to tell him face to face what a scoundrel I think he is. Aaron, all you need to do is give me a pass. I promise once I tell him just what I think of him, I'll leave. A few minutes, Aaron, please."

She was the sweet, innocent eastern girl again, her eyes wide

205

with excitement and no obvious knowledge of what was going on. She was also captivating, and Aaron was unprepared for the effect she had on him and the very interested young corporal.

"All right, for a few minutes. I'll go with you."

"No, Aaron, please, just give me a pass. I wouldn't want to be embarrassed. I'm sure there are plenty of guards to protect me. Besides, I know you're too busy to be escorting me all around. I'll see him for just a few minutes, I promise."

Aaron sighed. He couldn't find a legitimate excuse to stop her from paying Zach a visit. It was safe, he had no doubt of that, and Tara deserved the moment to express her disgust.

"All right, a few minutes." He sat down at his desk and wrote out a pass, which Tara nearly snatched from his hand. She had to control her enthusiasm. She reached her hand out slowly, breathing a sigh of relief when he placed the pass in it.

Zach sat in silence, nursing a headache and a brilliant anger at his own stupidity for falling so neatly into Caleb's trap.

Little Raven was probably even more miserable than Zach, blaming himself for disregarding his brother's warning words and thus placing Zach and all of his tribe in jeopardy. He had not spoken, nor had he tried to disturb his brother who seemed to be in deep thought, but he was alert, hoping Zach would have a word that would offer some solace for his guilt.

Truthfully, Zach was more worried about Little Raven than he was about himself. He was plagued by the thought that even though he knew who was bringing the guns, he would never be able to prove it unless he was free.

He was pretty sure Caleb would move soon, probably before anything was done about him and Little Raven, and all Zach would be able to do would be to watch him go.

When they were thrown into the storage room, Zach had tried every way possible to find one vulnerable spot, one chance for escape. But there was none. They comfortably sat across from each other in the small eight-by-eight room on huge sacks of grain. The room had one barred and heavily guarded door and one window with heavy wooden shutters that were also closed and, he accurately presumed, barred from the outside. Thin rays of light came through the shuttered window. There was very little chance for escape.

"I'm sorry, Windwalker," Little Raven said. "If it were not for my ignorance, you would not be here."

"Forget it, Little Raven. I have a feeling, somewhere along the line, Caleb and Aaron and a few others here would have found a way to get me into this spot."

"He will take the rest of the guns out soon, won't he?"

"You can bet your life on that."

"Windwalker, when—"

"When are they going to hang us?" Zach laughed gruffly. "Probably as soon as Caleb can get up some kind of a trial. He's a very fair man. We are . . . not of his race, so he'll hurry it up a bit."

"It is a terrible way to die, my brother," Little Raven said weakly. Zach sensed his fear of dying in a way that left little to pride and honor. He felt a bit like that himself, but because Little Raven needed his courage, too, he smiled.

"Maybe the gods do not mean for us to die, little brother. We must have more trust than that."

"I have trust in the gods," Little Raven grinned, "but not as much in the whites here at the fort."

Zach chuckled and rose to walk to the window. He hated confinement. He could feel his mind and body cry out against it, screaming at him to pound on the barrier between him and the free air and sunlight. He turned away from it before it got beyond his ability to control. He was about to say some encouraging words to Little Raven when he heard the key turn and the bolt of the door slide away. He expected to see anyone except Tara Montgomery.

To him she looked like a golden vision, and he found himself momentarily speechless.

If Zach was caught unprepared, Little Raven was absolutely

astounded. He sat immobile, his dark eyes absorbing the girl that stood framed in the doorway. He had never seen a woman wiht skin like ivory and hair the color of the sun. Besides that, he had no idea who she might be or why she had come there. His eyes snapped to his brother, and he knew at once that Windwalker did know her. He had never seen his brother react in such a way.

Zach moved from the window and took a few steps toward Tara. "What—"

"Hello, Zach," Tara interrupted. "Looks like you've got a small problem."

"Is that what you came here for, Tara? To gloat a little?"

"Why not?" Tara taunted for the benefit of the guard who was still within hearing distance. She stepped inside and closed the door between them. "Zach, Mule sent me to talk to you," she whispered quickly.

"Just what kind of fool does Aaron think I am?"

"What?"

"Am I supposed to confide in you or something? Maybe tell you how guilty I am and how I sent those rifles off to my 'red brothers'?"

"Don't be a fool!" Tara snapped.

"I'm not, don't forget that."

"You are so arrogant you'd hang before you'd believe me?"

Little Raven watched the exchange between the two and sensed an undercurrent he couldn't understand. Why should Windwalker be so cruel and cold to a woman as beautiful as this one? And she had said Mule had sent her. Mule would be the one person who would help them, but Windwalker would not listen. He rose slowly to his feet.

"Mule would help us, brother," he said quietly, his eyes on the golden-haired woman. Tara turned her eyes to him and he was stricken with a sensation quite new to him. She smiled, and Little Raven could not help but return it.

"So at least your friend is wise enough to hear the truth," Tara said as pleasantly as she could for Little Raven's sake.

208

"This is my brother, Little Raven." Zach's voice still held a chilly residue.

"Your brother?"

"We are fortunate enough to have the same father."

"Hello, Little Raven." Tara smiled at Little Raven, who again smiled back.

"You have come from Mule to help us?"

"Forget it, Little Raven," Zach said firmly. "Just what do you think she could do?"

Tara had reached the end of her patience with Zach. She walked to Little Raven, turning her back to Zach. "Despite your aggravating and insulting brother, I have come from Mule, and I have come to help if I can. Not because I believe in a man as insufferable and nasty as he is, but because Mule has asked me to. Now if he doesn't have the sense to listen to me, maybe you do."

Little Raven was astounded at this. No one had ever spoken to or about his brother in such a manner. If a man had spoken so, he would most likely be walking close to death. He was shaken by this strange new thing.

"Mule has sent you?" he asked in an uncertain voice.

"Yes. We need to make plans if we're going to get you out of here. Mule has no ideas and neither do I, but he can't come in so he asked me"—she turned to glare at Zach—"to come in and see if you had any 'useful' ideas."

If it had not been for Little Raven, Zach would not have given credence to anything she said, but if there was one remote chance that she could help them get free, he would have to take it.

"Just what does Mule have in mind?"

"I don't know. Nothing as far as I know."

"We'll need blankets and food."

"I'll tell Mule."

"Tell him to take the supplies out of the fort and put the cache in a safe place if he can."

"All right."

209

"Enough supplies for several days," Zach said firmly. Little Raven cast a surprised look in his direction but said nothing. Windwalker would know already that they could travel to the village on very little. If he wanted extra supplies, he must feel he needed them. He just wondered how Mule would get the supplies outside the walls, and if he did, how he and Windwalker would get to them.

Zach walked to Tara and stood close enough that she was forced to look up at him. "So you would help us get out of here," he said softly. "Do you realize just how dangerous that is? You could find yourself in a lot of trouble. Aren't you afraid?"

"I—I'm afraid they will hang someone who is innocent."

"Are you sure of our innocence?"

"Mule believes so."

"And what do you believe?"

"I don't know." Her voice was almost a whisper as she fought the desire to move into his arms. He was in the worst possible position, yet she had the insane feeling that she would be safe there.

"You don't know, and yet this is the second time in the past few days you've gone out on a limb to help me."

"I—I would do the same for anyone in danger." She saw the half smile twitch his lips and the echo of the derisive humor light his eyes. "Don't read any more into what I'm doing than sympathy for your situation," she said quickly. "Your brother is quite young to die beside you for crimes I'm more than certain are yours alone."

"You scratch deep, little cat. Maybe one day we can finish this argument on a more equal basis. For now, I want you to know, if not for me at least for Little Raven, that I'm grateful for your help. I'm just not sure you understand the price you might pay for it."

"What can they do to me? Hang me in your place?"

"There are punishments worse than hanging, Tara, believe me."

She wasn't sure of what he meant, and she was finding his

proximity disturbing. It would be better for her peace of mind when Zachary Hale was gone from the fort.

"I will go and tell Mule what you said for him to do, but that does not make your freedom any closer. What will we do next?"

Zach was amused at her unconscious reference to them as "we." "I'm thinking," he said dryly, "we have a couple of days at least."

"What makes you believe that?"

"Aaron is going to be very careful about what he does. He doesn't want to start an uprising. Most likely he'll give us a trial to ease his conscience. Then he'll hang us and have the mistaken idea that he's solved all his problems."

"And he hasn't?"

"Tara, do one thing for me, will you?"

"What?" she replied, surprised that Zach would ask her for any kind of a favor.

"Keep an eye on Caleb and his wagons. Come and tell me if he's making plans to leave the fort, and if he plans on taking wagons and how many."

"You're still accusing Caleb?"

"Because he's guilty as hell, and I'm not going to let him get away with it."

She looked up at Zach in disbelief. He was imprisoned, due to be hanged, and he talked about his plans as if these two facts were inconsequential.

"Will you do that?"

"Yes." Again she was surprised, this time at herself.

Before she could speak again, the guard swung the door open, making it clear that any more privacy was gone. Without a word, Tara turned away from Zach and left.

Tara found Mule seated on the porch in front of her quarters, casually whittling on a stick. She started up the steps. "Do you want to come in, Mule?"

"Better not, girl. Aaron's suspicious of everything."

211

Tara repeated Zach's request, and Mule nodded in silence. Then he spoke softly so his voice wouldn't carry. "Leave your window open tonight. I'll come around midnight or so."

Tara nodded, went inside, and closed the door, while Mule continued to whittle as if it were his only interest at the moment.

An hour or so later he went to the stable and saddled his horse. Then he packed food and blankets on his packhorse. He mounted and rode toward the front gate.

"Hey, Mule, where you going?" one sentry inquired. Mule's comings and goings were rarely questioned. They were used to his restlessness.

"I brung some things from back east for a trapper friend. I'm going to take 'em out. I should be back tomorrow."

The sentries had no orders that concerned Mule, and Mule chuckled at Aaron's oversight.

After he left the fort he rode far enough away that he could make camp and no one from the fort would spot him. There he waited until the sun began to set and the stars began to sparkle in the night sky.

Mule had an acute sense of time. It was within minutes of midnight when he made his way over the wall and found Tara's open window. He tapped once and Tara was there. Mule realized she must have been right by the window waiting and that she had had enough sense not to have any light.

"Mule?" she whispered.

"Yes, I can't get back into the fort before tomorrow. Tell me what else Zach said."

"Nothing much." She continued to tell him the rest of what Zach had said, leaving out his curious question to her about why she was doing what she was doing. She had no answers for it that she would admit even to herself.

"Do you think he has some plan, Mule?"

"Reckon he's got something in mind, but I sure as hell can't see what. It's gonna be a sticky affair, and I hope he can pull something off."

212

"How can he do anything if he's unarmed?"

"Don't count on him being unarmed."

"They took his gun."

"Don't make no neverminds; he's slick as greased lightning. Just hang on, girl. He's got something in mind, and in the next few days we'll find out," Mule replied. "I got to get along before someone hears us. Don't worry. We'll get them out."

Before Tara could reply, Mule was gone and she was aggravated again that he would believe her so worried about Zach. The man had been nothing but a problem, yet she felt sorry for his brother, who seemed to be totally shaken and out of his element in the close quarters of the supply room. "Oh, well," she sighed. She had done her best. The rest was up to Zach and Mule. She need only visit him one more time to end everything between them. She curled up on her bed and tried to sleep.

In the dark supply room Zach paced the floor in a slow, measured tread. In his mind he knew every inch of the room. Little Raven sat immobile and wondered wondered what was going through his brother's mind. To him there seemed no avenue of escape.

That he was terrified of the thought of being hanged was something he kept to himself. He would not shame himself or his brother by being like a weeping woman.

He thought of the sun-haired woman and realized his brother was a different man when he spoke to her, even though Zach denied that there could ever be anything between them. Still, Little Raven had read much more in her eyes when she looked at Windwalker than she had realized.

The next day dawned bright and warm, and by mid-afternoon Mule returned. Obvious questions about the packs he had taken out were answered by his tale that he had traded

213

material and horses. No one seemed truly interested or suspicious. Too much excitement revolved around Zach and Little Raven's capture to give much attention to Mule, which pleased him greatly.

Mule was on his way to loiter in Tara's general vicinity when he saw the huge front gates of the fort being opened. Then, from around the corner of the stables, five wagons made their slow, lumbering way to the gates.

Tara opened her door to walk out on the porch. Caleb rode beside the first wagon, and as Tara walked down off her porch toward the center of the compound, he saw her and waved. He rode to her side.

"I'm going to take the last of the supplies out to some of the homesteaders and should be back in about a week, probably in time for the hanging."

She felt a vague annoyance at his confidence. To her surprise she found herself wishing Zach's escape plans, whatever they might be, would thwart Caleb's arrogance a little.

Tara remembered Zach's concern about Caleb leaving, but she thought that a few wagons everyone knew carried only supplies shouldn't have an effect on his escape. She spotted Mule and walked to him. They stood in the center of the compound with the other curious onlookers, watching the wagons leave.

"You can get to Zach again?" Mule whispered.

"I'm sure there won't be any problems. The guards know Aaron has let me in. I just won't mention it to Aaron again."

"Tell him the supplies are where he can get to them. I found Little Raven's horse. If he does get away, tell him I'll meet him in a week's time down by Deep Valley. He'll know."

"Do you really think he'll manage to get out of here, Mule?"

"When you tell him Caleb's left with those wagons, he'll find a way, believe me. Only, right at this minute, I sure as hell don't see how he's gonna do it."

Chapter 19

Tara was quick to notice that Zach and Little Raven's meals were carried to them from the mess hall by a young trooper. The supper meal would be the same, and most likely the only way Tara would be able to find out what Zach's plans were. She knew the fort buzzed with all kind of stories, some in favor of Zach and some against, but almost all were tinged with the fear of an Indian uprising.

If Zach were to get away, it would have to be tonight, for the rumors were even stronger that the next day Aaron planned to bring Zach and Little Raven before a panel made up of the officers. Tara knew exactly how they felt about Zach being so friendly to her. Zach was a threat that everyone at the fort seemed to want to be rid of. But . . . hanging . . . The thought was too terrible to contemplate.

Tara carried the tray of food with both hands. It was a large tray made of wood and covered with a blue checkered cloth. The guard outside the door lifted the cloth to check the contents of the tray and make sure there were no weapons.

Satisfied, he unbolted the door and let her inside, then pulled the door shut. Zach turned from the window and Little Raven rose abruptly to his feet. This was the first time Tara had brought them food and both were certain there was more to it than just the fact that it was dinner time.

"Tara?" Zach questioned.

"Mule has come back. He said to tell you he's put the supplies where Little Raven's horse is. He also said to tell you he will meet you in a week at Deep Valley. He said you would know."

"What of Caleb?"

"He's gone."

"With or without wagons?" Zach asked, his voice cold, as if he already knew the answer.

"Five wagons filled with supplies, I might add, and no guns."

"How do you know that?"

"I'm the scatterbrained little eastern girl. Nobody minds if I look around," Tara replied, the chill in her voice matching his. "Or if I ask questions. I asked some of the men who loaded the wagons. They weren't Caleb's men, and they didn't hesitate to tell me. Surely if there were rifles there, they would have told someone, wouldn't they?"

"Don't kid yourself, Tara, there were guns in those wagons, and I'm kicking myself for not figuring out where they were before this. I was searching through the wagons."

"So?"

"So I didn't rip up any floorboards to see if they could be stowed under them, which is precisely where they are. How long have they been gone?"

"Several hours."

"Then we have to get out of here tonight."

Tara's heart began to race. What was he planning? she thought first. The second thought, coming uninvited, was that either he could be killed in the escape attempt, or he could succeed and she might never see him again. It was an unwelcome thought.

"Even if you do get free, which I doubt, there is no way to find him now."

Zach grinned, "I'm an Indian, remember? A snake can't crawl across a rock and keep itself from being followed by me

216

and Little Raven. We have tracked tougher quarry than Caleb and his wagons."

"Your single-track mind is going to get you killed!" Tara said sharply.

"My single-track mind is going to keep a lot of others from getting killed," he snapped in response. Little Raven was totally overpowered with the uncharacteristic attitude of his brother. Tara had done nothing but help them, yet he seemed to turn on her at every opportunity.

"Why are you carrying food to us this time of night? I expected young Simms to come."

Tara flushed, not wanting to tell him that she had teased Simms into letting her do it. It would be like Zach to believe she had motives other than to see he had eaten.

"He—he was tied up with something else, so I said I would bring it for him."

"Besides," Zach grinned, "you wanted to satisfy your curiosity about how we're going to get out of here."

"Zach, there is a lot of distance between here and the front gate. Even if you make that, how will you get away without horses? This is foolhardy. You'll get killed before you get twenty feet."

"Not a bad risk," he chuckled, "since I'm sure if I stay put, I'm going to get killed. Why not take the chance and run?"

"Because you can't make it. Let me go to Aaron again! Let me beg him. . . ."

"No! You don't beg him for anything!" Zach said, his eyes darkened like thunder clouds and his mouth grim. He was standing several feet away from her. "Come over here, Tara." He lowered his voice so the guard outside would not hear him.

Every instinct told Tara this was a very dangerous thing to do, and from the corner of her eye she could see the puzzled look on Little Raven's face. She walked to stand inches from him. He didn't move but his gaze seemed to pierce her.

"What?" she questioned.

"I want you to understand something."

217

She drew her brows together in a frown, not being able to associate his words with the situation they were in.

"Sometimes," he said gently, "people have to do things they don't really want to do, because circumstances force some kind of action. In this case, I'm afraid I'm in that position, and I want you to know that this is beyond my control."

Now she was really puzzled. "Zach, you're talking in riddles."

"Maybe now I am, but I'll make myself real clear pretty quick. Now is the only chance Little Raven and I may have—and you're our opportunity."

"You're asking me to help you escape? You must be truly mad! Do you think I could live in this fort for however long David must be here if I did that? My brother would never forgive me—and neither would these people. I can't! I won't!"

"I didn't ask you to do anything," his smile was grim. "I'm just letting you know what's going to happen." He seemed to casually reach his arm up to brush his hand through his hair, but instead it dipped to reach for the knife he carried hidden. The sheath seemed like only a leather thong about his neck, but the flat slender holder for the knife hung between his shoulder blades. It flashed in the slight light as he withdrew it while Tara gasped and stepped back. She was quick, but not quick enough. Zach caught her to him roughly, pinning her arms against him. He held the blade before her, and the face she looked up into now was completely savage. She had no idea that he was bluffing or that Little Raven was as shocked as she was.

"You can't mean this! You'll never get away with it!" Tara choked.

"Be quiet, Tara," Zach snapped. "Little Raven, call that guard in. Be ready to relieve him of his gun as soon as he sees this knife. Move quick. Tell him something happened to Tara."

Little Raven wasted no words, moving rapidly to the door. "Guard! Guard! Come quick. The lady is very sick."

Fate was kind to Little Raven and Zach, for the guard was

218

inexperienced and certainly not thinking for a moment that the two prisoners would be armed and planning an escape. He set his rifle aside and unlocked the door. He was a step or two inside before he caught the full meaning of the action being played out before him.

"What—?" he began. But Zach's voice stopped him.

"Be very quiet and stand very still if you don't want something to happen to her. You understand?" Zach's voice was threatening and low. The young trooper swallowed convulsively and nodded.

"Get his gun, Little Raven, then get that rifle."

Little Raven nodded and returned in seconds with the rifle, then he slid the trooper's gun from its holster.

"Put the pistol in my belt." Zach snapped the order and Little Raven obeyed quickly. Then he stood next to Zach, not quite sure of what the next move would be. Things were moving rapidly.

"What's your name?" Zach spoke to the guard in a voice so full of command that the trooper never hesitated to reply.

"Murphy," he spoke in a voice that was being held in control. His eyes were on Tara, who seemed to him to be frightened speechless.

"Well, Murphy, I have a little job for you."

"Let the lady go, and I'll do anything you want."

"You'll do what I want anyway." Zach smiled, but the smile wasn't pleasant. To Murphy it looked deadly.

"What do you want? You'll never get out of this fort."

"You don't need to worry about that. What you do need to do is get to Aaron's office and tell him to come over here. And Murphy, be sure you caution him very carefully to come alone . . . or else. There'd better be just you and him when you come through that door."

Murphy nodded and backed away from the cell. There was a long silence. Only the labored breathing of the three within could be heard.

Zach could not read Tara's thoughts. He was sure she was

219

both terrified and angry. What he didn't know was that she had slipped beyond fear. She trembled in the embrace of his hard-muscled arm, but she didn't tremble from fear. Something deep within told her Zach was counting on her reaction being fear, so she remained silent. He would let her go, she was confident of that. He wouldn't hurt her, but she knew Zach was counting on Aaron not knowing that, not trusting that.

All she would need to do would be to fight back when Aaron came. She could twist from his arms and prove what she knew—that he really wouldn't hurt her.

The thud of running feet was heard, and in a few minutes Aaron and Murphy reappeared in the doorway.

"Zach, you can't get away with this. We'll hunt you down."

"You really think you stand a chance of doing that with me, Aaron? Out there." Zach laughed, "I doubt it and so do you."

"I'll never let you out of this fort."

"Then I guess the lady isn't important to anyone here. Will you explain to her brother what happened? That your stupid pride was paid for by his sister?"

Aaron gulped back the words he wanted to say. "What do you want, Zach?"

"Send Murphy over to the stable and saddle two horses. Bring them to the front gate. Then come back here and tell us it's done."

"And then?"

"And then Little Raven and I will be walked safely across the compound by you . . . and the lady. One cross move by anyone—and I mean anyone—and the two of you will be the first down."

"All right. . . . Murphy, you heard what he said. Get moving and make it fast. The sooner we get them out of here and Tara's safe, the sooner we can get on their trail and hunt them down like the animals they are."

Zach and Aaron gazed at each other levelly. Zach knew there was no way to get through to Aaron that he was doing what needed to be done to save him and his command.

"Aaron, I'm sorry," Tara said. "I didn't think it was possible that either of them would be armed. I was just bringing their supper."

"It's all right, Tara. My mistake. I should have known. This will be over in a few minutes and you'll be safe. Don't be frightened; he won't hurt you while he needs you."

Tara felt Zach's arm tighten about her. She was molded against the hard length of his body and the knife was inches away. She had less reaction to it than to the tumultuous sensations that were sending unwanted reactions through her. It struck her violently that she was afraid for Zach and Little Raven more than for herself. One slip and they would be shot where they stood. There would be no trials then; it would all be over.

It seemed to all of them that Murphy was gone for hours, but it was less than twenty minutes when he returned, breathless from running.

"They're ready, sir. Two horses by the front gate. I told the guards to move back. They've got a clear way to the horses."

"Good work, Murphy." Zach smiled for the first time since the confrontation began. "Little Raven, get behind Aaron and keep that rifle on him. Let's get moving. Murphy, if you come out of here before we get to the gate, you'll have killed your commanding officer."

Murphy nodded and stood aside as the four began to leave the confines of the storage room, making their way outside.

The supply room in which Little Raven and Zach had been held was right next to Tara's quarters. They went out the door and started across the compound toward the front gate, feeling the eyes behind every window and door following them. Little Raven had never been more shaken in his life. Within minutes they would be free, and he vowed to himself he would never enter the white man's fort again, nor would he ever disregard anything his brother said to him. He prayed silently, to all the gods he knew, that they would make it.

They passed the flagpole and started toward the gate. The

221

two saddled horses stood just inside the gates that had been swung open so they could leave.

Zach was grimly silent as they moved forward.

"You let her go as soon as you get those horses, Zach," Aaron said coldly. "I'll see that you get a start."

Zach remained silent as they drew closer and closer to the two horses and the open doors of the fort that led to freedom.

It was a matter of minutes and he would be gone. He would be free . . . and he would be out of her life forever. Tara's heart beat wildly. If one trooper were to make a mistake and shoot, Zach and Little Raven could be dead in the same minutes.

But no one did. Zach had counted on the stories that had been spread about, for he knew everyone in the fort was certain these two bloodthirsty Indians would murder both their commanding officer and an innocent woman if they made any effort to stop them.

They reached the horses, and Zach studied the situation carefully. "Get your men off the walls, Aaron."

Aaron called out a sharp command and soon the walls were empty.

"Mount, Little Raven, and keep your rifle on him."

Little Raven was in the saddle in one swift move. Then Zach, drawing Tara with him, backed toward his horse. He knew for certain what he planned to do was the last thing on either Tara or Aaron's mind. The fact was he had no reason to carry out his plans—except that he wanted to and didn't want to read his own motives too closely. He drew Tara with him to his horse. Aaron took a step toward them, the first sense of alarm touching him.

"Don't move, Aaron," Zach ordered. "You don't want to end your days here in the dirt."

"No," Aaron grated. "I want to have the time to catch you and see you hang for this."

Zach mounted swiftly, thrusting the knife in his belt. Tara remained motionless, unprepared for what happened next.

"Aaron, don't follow me for one full day."

"And just why should I give you that much time?" Aaron started toward Zach, his heart pounding, for he had a suspicion of what Zach might do and he wanted to be close enough to stop him. But his move was not in time. Zach bent forward and scooped Tara up to the saddle in front of him.

"No!" Tara cried as she struggled to get free.

"Little Raven, ride!" Zach commanded. They spun their horses about.

"Zach, you damn fool!" Aaron shouted. "Let her go! You'll never get away with kidnapping a white woman!"

A safe distance away, Zach stopped and turned about. "Don't follow me for one full day! If you do, you'll find her on the trail and you'll be responsible for what's done."

"I'm going to get you, Zach."

"One full day! Do you hear me?"

Tara was struggling but it was useless. The arm about her felt like steel, and she was pinned with her back to him so she could not do him any harm. The horse was made nervous by her thrashing and was prancing about, but Zach retained control.

"I hear you. But after that, I want you to promise me her safety."

"She'll be safe."

This was all Aaron needed to hear. Zach turned his horse about and soon the three riders were no more than a cloud of dust in the distance.

Aaron knew quite well that one day's wait with a man as competent as Zach and there might as well be a thousand miles between them. Zach could vanish without a trace in this wilderness. But he had threatened to leave Tara on the trail for him to find should he start before a day's wait, and Aaron was scared of what Zach might do to her before he left her there.

He turned and walked back into the fort, and was soon surrounded by angry soldiers and even more frightened and angry civilians. It took him some time to calm them down and explain what had happened.

223

"We've got to go after them now," Murphy said quickly. "I'll saddle up a detail, and we can be on their trail in no time."

"I'm afraid we can't do that, Murphy," Aaron said.

"Can't, sir? Why?"

"We have to give him a full day. He'll see our dust if we start trailing him before that. If he does, he'll kill Tara or maybe worse. He said if he saw any sign of us for a day, he'd leave her behind—and we'd be responsible for the condition he left her in."

"Damned savage," one person muttered.

"Ought to have been strung up instead of jailed," another offered.

"But he seemed so different on the way out here," another traveler protested.

"Yes, he was always caring for us. I find it hard to believe he'd kill Miss Montgomery so brutally. He seemed to like her while we were traveling."

"Sure, liked her too much," one man snarled.

"He most likely had his eye on that poor girl right from the start. That poor girl is as good as dead this minute, so I say we go out after him right now."

Aaron turned on him angrily. "And if he sees us coming and does her any harm, do you want to take the responsibility for it?"

This brought silence, and Aaron ordered everyone back to his own quarters. Then he called his officers aside.

"We can't draw all the force away from this fort. If the word got out, there could very well be a massacre here. I want one detail to pack light and get ready to travel. We'll leave the fort around midnight. That way, if Zach is looking back over his shoulder, he won't think we're moving."

"Major, do you think he'll do her any harm?"

"I—I don't know," Aaron said quietly. "We'll just have to pray that he doesn't think he needs to. Maybe he'll just let her go when he feels safe. I've known Zach a few years, and even if he's part Indian, I've never known him to attempt to harm

224

any white woman. He's free. . . . Maybe that will be enough."

"If he lets her go," Murphy asked, "just what will he do? Leave her on foot?"

"Hell no, he'll more than likely drop her at one of the homesteads in the territory or with a trader coming this way. Speaking of traders, where's Mule? One of you go get him. I'm going to need his help."

One trooper left the group immediately and loped over to the stable. He went inside, only to come out in a few minutes and trot back to Aaron.

"Mule's gone."

"Gone? Gone where? When?"

"Stable boy says he lit out just a couple of minutes before Zach and that Indian boy got away."

"Lit out? You mean he damn well knew what was going to happen? He's a friend of Zach's, and he's going to meet him. I wouldn't be surprised to find he was the one that slipped that knife to Zach."

"I could swear he never went near that supply room the whole time those two were locked up in there," Murphy said in a perplexed voice.

"Well, he must have had a way. Damn! After Zach, Mule was the best guide around. If anyone could have caught up with them or tracked them, it would have been Mule."

"Maybe that's why Mule left," Murphy offered. "Maybe he didn't want to be the one to have to track Zach down."

"Well, with or without him, we're going to track Zach down," Aaron stated firmly. "And if he's harmed one hair on Tara's head, I'll make sure it's the last trouble he ever causes. Him with his guns and his lies and his 'worries about his people.' If we don't stop him now, he's going to hand us a real uprising. Get everything together. At midnight we leave."

The men watched a very angry Aaron walk back to his office. He went inside and slammed the door with a solid crack. Aaron walked to his desk and opened the top drawer, removing a half-full bottle of whiskey and a glass. He poured a hefty

225

drink and threw it down his throat with a violent gesture. But Aaron drank only one drink, solely because of anger. He was a strong man who did not depend on whiskey for courage. He corked the bottle and put it back into the drawer. Then he walked to a huge map that was pinned on the wall.

At their very best, maps were uncertain things. This territory was just as uncertain. White men knew very little of it, and Indians knew too much. He realized what he was up against. Finding Zach would be like finding a ghost, and he was trying to fight the realization that they might never see Tara again. He thought of how he might have to explain to David just why he'd been so careless as to let Zach get away and take Tara with him. His condemnation would not be any more severe than Aaron's own condemnation of himself. He should have known, when Zach seemed so calm and self-assured, that he had some plan of escape in his mind. But he had never dreamed that Zach would take Tara. Zach was wild and had his own way of doing things, but he had always been trusted by the men and respected by them. To take a white woman had broken every bond that might have existed between Zach and the white world. From now on he was Indian and Aaron meant to track him down, to find the guns that were a threat to the fort and the white settlers, and to get Tara back.

He studied the maps carefully and tried to think of the most feasible ways that Zach might go. He tried to cover every possibility, but deep inside was the nagging fear that his efforts wouldn't amount to much. He needed someone like Mule, someone who knew every canyon and valley. But Mule was on Zach's side, and that he couldn't understand. Caleb was due back in a few days. He would leave a message for him to catch up with them. Caleb didn't know the territory as well as Mule, but he and his men knew it better than Aaron. With their help he just might make Zach's run for freedom a very short one.

Aaron sat in his office and contemplated strategies until midnight. Then the expected knock came, and he rose to go out and begin the search.

Chapter 20

Tara struggled and fought until she was exhausted, but she might have been a child in his iron hold. Now she sat rigidly, trying to keep her tiring body from resting against his.

They rode in silence now, because Tara had exhausted her repertoire of anger as well. Little Raven was staggered by the extent of what they had done, but his loyalty to Zach could not be shaken even by the enormity of their situation that was, as far as he was concerned, the worst he'd ever been in.

They had made their way rapidly to the place where Mule had stored the supplies. Little Raven's horse was there as well. At first he wanted to give it to Tara so she could ride in more comfort, but Zach refused to let him do this, ordering Little Raven to pack the supplies on his horse.

It took Little Raven very little time to do as Zach had said. In a short while they were again on their way, leading the horse behind them.

The moon was already just above the horizon, but Zach showed no sign of planning to stop. Both men had ridden hard, enduring miles many times. They knew that to keep from getting caught they had to put a great deal of distance between themselves and their pursuers. They also had to do as much as they could to cover the trail they left behind and to make following them as difficult as possible.

Tara felt as if every bone were bruised and every muscle stretched beyond endurance. But she refused to give Zach the satisfaction of her complaining.

They reached a shallow stream, only a foot or so deep but wide. Zach stopped just for a moment, turning to look at Little Raven.

"You will go upstream and I will go down. When they reach here they will have to decide which way to go. They may split up. Take them for a long run, little brother, then loosen them. Meet me and Mule at Deep Valley."

"Do not worry." Little Raven laughed for the first time. "They will chase shadows all through the hills. I will meet you in Deep Valley. It should take no more than two days."

"It will take me longer, but you and Mule stay put."

The question was immediately on Little Raven's lips. "And you, brother, why will it take you so long?"

"I'm trying to find Caleb and those guns. By now he has unloaded the wagons and has the guns on packhorses. He's clever, but I have to find him or no one will ever know the truth. Go, Little Raven. I'll meet you as soon as I can. Leave the supplies with me. I will need them more than you will."

Little Raven passed the reins of the packhorse to Zach, who took them and urged his horse into the stream. Little Raven turned in the opposite direction and made his way upstream.

Tara was hungry, tired, angry, and determined not to show Zach one moment of weakness. To her they seemed to go on and on and on, as if this nightmare would never end. Zach still offered no excuses or explanations for the cruel and ungrateful way he had rewarded her for being so kind to him.

The moon was high and Zach knew it was nearing midnight. He also knew Aaron was in his trail by now. He could feel the exhaustion in Tara's body, along with the pride that held her erect and uncomplaining before him. He knew he would have to stop before long, for despite her pride, Tara was close to collapsing.

He found what he was looking for—a place where there were rock formations on three sides of a narrow valley. He could

228

watch from a ledge that gave some height and still afforded Tara a comfortable place to rest.

He drew the horses to a halt and slid off, reaching up just in time to catch Tara as she nearly tumbled to the ground. Tara felt faint for a moment, her head spinning from the weariness. But when Zach caught her to him, all her anger came back like a thunderbolt. She pushed his hands away and stood erect.

"Don't touch me, you damned ungrateful savage! Don't ever touch me!"

"Tara, you're tired. I can't build a fire because it might be seen. But you need to rest and to eat. I'll get you a blanket, and you can get a little rest before we have to move."

"How generous of you," Tara snapped. "You tear me away from my home, drag me into the wilderness like an animal, and then you're suddenly concerned for my safety? You'll forgive me if I don't quite believe anything you say anymore."

Zach was much too tired to argue with what she said, and at the same time he wasn't quite able to face the true reason he had taken her. Escape would have been just as easy if he had left her at the gates of the fort. The guilt only made his reaction one of irritated anger. He went to the packhorse and removed a blanket and saddlebags containing dried corn and jerky. To these he added a canteen of water. Then he went to her side and dropped the things at her feet.

"Eat," he commanded hoarsely, "then get a little sleep. We'll be moving again before dawn. And, Tara," he added, "don't try anything foolish. You're in a wilderness you don't understand. If you try to run from me, you'll only succeed in doing one of two things: getting lost and dying out here, or getting found by renegades. I assure you the second will be worse than the first."

He turned from her before she could answer. Taking the horses to water first, he then hobbled them so they wouldn't drift away. He knew staying here too long was dangerous. Tara would never know he had stopped only because she needed the rest. His self-discipline would have let him ride for hours longer.

Tara wanted to cry as she watched his broad back when he moved away from her. She was frightened and sagged to the ground. Her hunger was too much for her pride, so she ate some of the jerky, then spread the blanket to sit on it. But exhaustion quickly claimed her, and she sank back on the blanket and closed her eyes. In minutes she was asleep.

The sun had not risen, but a gray misty dawn was beginning to form. Zach moved like a shadow from his position of concealment. He went to Tara's side and knelt beside her. She lay on her back, one arm curved above her head and the other resting across her waist. Her hair had come loose from the pins that had held it in a chignon at the nape of her neck. Now it spread about her in burnished profusion. Her skin had taken on a golden tan since she had left the East, and he had to resolutely control the urge to touch her. Her thick lashes lay against rose-tinted cheeks, and her lips were parted slightly as she breathed gently in relaxed sleep. His eyes skimmed down the soft curves of her body, the memory of its silken touch still vivid in his mind. He would have given anything to lie down beside her, gather her into his arms, and make love to her until he was exhausted. He almost hated to waken her, but he had gathered everything and packed it on the horse, and it was time for them to move on.

He had slipped from the camp for over two hours while she slept, retracing their trail and making sure all evidence of their passing had been wiped away. Another day of travel would find them beyond Aaron's reach.

He reached to take hold of her shoulder and gave her a gentle shake. Tara's eyes fluttered open and she drifted up from sleep. To her, Zach wavered in a white misty haze. He was like something that had stepped from a dream. Reality had not found her yet.

"Zach," she whispered. Her eyes were misty and her tremulous mouth was so inviting that Zach could no more resist than he could have flown. On his knees beside her, it took little effort to slide an arm about her waist and draw her up into his arms. She breathed his name once again as he

230

claimed her mouth with his. It was as inevitable as breathing the air about them. Neither could escape the unnamed thing that drew them to each other with a force they were helpless to battle. He drank deeply of the sweet, soft taste of her as if he could devour her, and her lips parted to accept his with the same urgency.

Only when she was breathless, when his arms pulled her to him until she felt as if she would be crushed, did the reality of her situation explode within her senses. She gave a choked sob, pushing against him so hard and so suddenly that he released her. As the dawn broke he could see the distrust and a new kind of fear in her eyes as she moved away from him. He had no way of knowing that the fear was of her own weakness. She had wanted him, had come alive with the flame that only Zach could ignite, but he was one who took and betrayed, and she could not allow him to destroy her will again.

She sat with her back to the rough rock wall and he remained on his knees a foot or so away from her, yet both could feel the gulf between them growing wider and wider.

"If you want to prove the fact that I'm helpless in this wilderness, I won't deny it," she said angrily. "But don't expect me to fall into your arms like a little girl afraid of the unknown. I will not be a pawn for you to play with, get that straight. If that's your plan, then leave me here now, because I'll never let you use me again."

"This is not what I planned to have happen, it just did." Slowly Zach rose. "It's time for us to get moving."

"Where? Where am I going? Why do you want to do this to me? My God, Zach, explain to me why you're doing this when all I've ever done is try to help you." She was close to tears, and he could see the battle she fought to keep them under control.

Zach tossed the blanket down and went to her. Her eyes widened as he towered over her, his eyes like chips of blue ice. He reached out without a word and pulled her against him, holding her so tight she could do nothing but look up at him.

"Somewhere out there a ruthless man is taking guns to a group of hotheaded young warriors. He's doing his best to stir

231

up a group that will attack and destroy the fort. If I can't find him before he does this, that fort will go up in flames. I couldn't leave you there. If I failed to catch up with him, I couldn't come back and find you dead at the hands of people I love as much as . . . Whether you believe it or not, what I did I did for your own good."

"But you can't find him!"

"I have to," he said grimly. "And you'll have to stay with me. You have no choice."

"Why should I believe you? Why shouldn't I believe that you deliberately dragged me away just to be vicious?"

"Don't be a fool, Tara. You can say all kinds of words to deny it. But both of us know that I didn't need to drag you here to prove that we already share something. Do you remember that night in your quarters?" She struggled and his arms tightened. His voice grew deep and resonant. "You wanted to surrender to me."

"No!"

"Yes, to this savage! To this man that would have destroyed your reputation." He held her now with one arm and gripped her chin in his other hand to force her to look up at him. "Such a sweet lie, Tara, but maybe one day I will get you to admit the truth to yourself. Until then I can keep you from getting killed by the white 'gentleman' who would sell you to get what he wants."

"You'd like me to believe whatever you say and do, but I'm not going to be so stupid."

Zach chuckled at her stubbornness, but he could feel the tremors in her body and could see the elusive fear in her eyes.

"Shall I prove to you," he said softly, "that you wanted me as much as I did you?" His lips brushed her cheek and the length of his body pressed intimately to hers, shattering her cold reserve. "Shall I prove that you lie as much to yourself as to me?"

"Don't, Zach, let me go," she half whispered, half gasped.

"Not yet," he whispered. "Not this time." He held her immobile, the hand on her chin slipping to the back of her head and tangling in her hair, drawing her head back so that her mouth was raised to his, already parted in a rebellious gasp. His open mouth slanted across hers, his tongue delving deep to taste fully a well-remembered sweetness.

An uncoiling ball of heat expanded within her and exploded through her limbs, making her legs go weak as she clung to him. Despite the agony of her thoughts, her body responded to the memory of past pleasure. It caught fire, sending the blood coursing through her veins and her heart pounding a rapid tattoo.

His kisses continued down her throat to the curve of her neck. Her eyes closed, she could only feel as his hands deftly opened buttons and slid her dress and chemise aside, baring her high, firm breasts. He cupped them in his hands, feeling the perfection of her silken skin and passion hardened nipples one after the other. Then he bent to enclose one in his mouth and tug gently. The rising sun touched her skin with warmth, but no heat could compare to the intense heat he was arousing within her. His hands created sensations that forced a small inarticulate sound of pleasure from deep in her throat. She writhed against him, arching her body to meet his more fully. Their breathing was erratic now, and she gave no heed to the fact that her dress was being slipped down over her hips. He absorbed her golden loveliness, letting his eyes move over her slowly, as if memorizing every line and curve.

Tara was consumed with a hunger for him that left her beyond any control she might have had. A slow throbbing ache began in the center of her, drugging her to all but the delicious sensations his lips and hands could create within her.

Zach worked free of his clothes as rapidly as he could, tossing them aside. Then he drew her body against his hard, heated one. She could feel the frantic hammering of his heart against hers, matching almost beat for beat. Slowly he drew her down beside him on the blanket. In a misty haze of ecstatic pleasure, she opened her eyes to look up into his deep blue gaze. She was overpowered by the gradually growing core of heat within her, but powerless to deny it. His hands moved over her slowly, drawing up her thighs and across her belly in slow teasing strokes while his mouth continued to play havoc with her senses, moving from her mouth to her breast, and then to glaze her skin with soft licks and nips that set her on fire.

Now his hands moved ever closer to the throbbing moist core of her, and she could have screamed out her pleasure as his fingers gently separated the protecting lips and began a slow but firm probing caress that nearly drove her mindless.

She wanted more . . . no, she needed more. Her body arched against him, demanding all. Her hands slipped over his hard-muscled body, caressing one moment, kneading roughly the next, each time seeking more and more intimate knowledge of his bronzed and masculine physique.

As if she could restrain them no longer, her hands found the throbbing shaft, caressing, slowly drawing him to her until he touched the core where only seconds before his hands had been.

Very slowly he pushed forward, not far enough to enter but far enough to torment Tara and draw a ragged groan of protest from her. She felt as if she would lose her mind if he did not complete the promised pleasure, but he still moved with mind-draining slowness until she whimpered aloud. "Zach," she gasped as she tried to arch her body up to enclose him.

"I want you, Tara," he whispered against her throat. "But it must be that you want me, too. I want to hear you say it."

"I do," she groaned softly. "Make love to me, Zach. I want you."

In a sudden move that made the soft cry one of surprise and pleasure, he filled her. Then he began to move slowly, slowly, lifting them both higher and higher.

Like the petals of a rose opening to the morning sun, the ecstasy within her began to unfold. It grew and grew until the flames licked her body into wild life. She was on fire with the joy of his hard strength deep inside her, penetrating until she felt abandoned and totally lost to all but the deep sure strokes, wanting them to never stop.

234

Now he knew only the need of completion. Her slim legs wrapped around his waist while her hands drew him closer and closer. Now they moved in unison, caught in a rhythm that set their blood pounding in fury. When he knew she was nearing the brink, he rose on his elbows. He wanted to see her face when the climax struck.

He watched with deep pleasure as her eyes widened and her parted lips were breathlessly panting, and he knew a brilliant pleasure himself as he watched the orgasm burst within her, one contraction following another in brilliant waves. Only then did he speed his stroke, thrusting deeply and rapidly until he could feel his seed burst and flood deeply within her. They collapsed into each other's arms, gasping and trembling, holding each other as a spiraling world began to slow from its dizzy speed. With the slowing of her racing heart came the intrusion of reality. Zach held her close, knowing the working of her mental process as well now as he knew the intimate working of her body. He knew the passion would soon be replaced by recriminations, yet he couldn't let her go. He wanted to say or do something that would make her understand what had happened had been right and wonderful, that there should be no self-recriminations and no more lies between them. Her head was nestled in the curve of his shoulder, and her body lay pressed intimately to his. Before he could say anything, he felt the heat of the tears she shed in silence against his skin. Each teardrop burnt against his flesh as the truth burst into his senses. He had forced her again to respond physically. But not for a moment had he reached the inner woman who was Tara. First he denied it. Who cared if she were outraged because a "savage" had taken her so easily? Why should it now matter to him? She would remain with him as long as he felt it necessary, and when the time came, he would let her go without regret. He had things to do that were more important than her obvious hatred. Yet a part of him bled from the wound of her hatred, a part of him he denied vehemently. There were hundreds of other women to be had, and when this was done, he would find another willing one to replace her.

He moved from her side, sitting up to look down into her wide green eyes filled with tears. He felt the sting of them like a physical blow, even though she made no move and remained silent.

"Get dressed," he said. "We must move. We have a lot of ground to cover before we rest again." He rose and began to dress himself, now doing his best to keep his eyes from meeting hers again. The hurt in her eyes was more than he could face at the moment.

"Of course." Her voice was soft, but he sensed more than heard that the softness covered an iron control and a fury so deep she couldn't articulate it. "You've proven your point, at least for one day. How many days and nights will it be before you are satisfied and let me go? How long must I tolerate your brutal use of me before you're finished?"

Again the words were like arrows. His kitten had sharp claws, and she knew how to draw blood. He had no intention of letting her know he was in the least vulnerable to her barbs. He had a feeling that if he gave her the ammunition of knowing the effect she had on him, she would not hesitate to deliver a mortal wound.

"You'll be with me for a long time, so it will do no good to fight anymore."

"Damn you," she breathed, her voice growing even softer. "I hate you."

"Words," he stated firmly.

"No! Not words," she replied as she reached for her discarded dress and slipped it on. Zach watched it skim down over her body and was totally shaken by the urge to tear it from her, throw her to the ground, and possess her until she admitted the truth—that the desire was not of her body alone, but of her mind, her spirit, and her heart as well.

"Do not say things that I can prove so easily are lies," he smiled defensively. "Or would you like me to prove to you again that you will belong to me when and where I choose?"

"I hate you, Zach, and if I can find a way to avenge myself, I will. Remember that one day you will be too confident, too arrogant, and I will make you pay for what you have taken from me."

"What have I *taken* that you did not share, did not, in the end, give willingly?"

"Maybe you've touched my body and taught it to respond to you. But I will teach it just as easily to forget. One day I will be free of you . . . and I will forget you if it takes my last breath."

She turned her back to him and knelt to pick up the blanket, then rolled it and attached it to the packhorse. She was aware of his eyes on her, but she refused to acknowledge his gaze. She never saw the puzzled look nor the momentarily gentle one. Then he turned and walked to the horses to finish packing. He led both horses toward her. Wordlessly, she handed him the blanket and just as silently he put it with the rest of the pack. Then, in a swift, graceful move, he swung up on the horse, kicked his foot free of the stirrup, and extended his hand to her.

"Will you ride in front or behind me?" There was a tug of challenging amusement on his lips, and she grit her teeth.

"One place is as bad as the other," she said frigidly. She put her hand in his and her foot in the stirrup, and he lifted her easily to a seat before him.

Without another word, he kicked the horse into an easy rolling motion. Tara didn't want to lean against him, but she had very little choice. The motion of the horse made it impossible for her to ride in a rigid position.

She did not see the return of the amused half smile as she relaxed against him. Nor did she know the feelings that tore through him as he recalled her vow to remember and to seek revenge. There was a long time, he reminded himself, between now and the day he would freely let her go. In that time a whole lot of things could happen and even more things could change. For now she was here, her body warm in the curve of his arm, and he would have to be satisfied with that . . . for now.

237

Chapter 21

Little Raven was enjoying himself. His sense of outrageous humor was always predominant with him, and leading Aaron's men around in circles was just his brand of fun.

Aaron and his men had left the fort before midnight, hoping Zach had not left someone to watch. Still, it was just becoming a hazy dawn when they reached the stream. He was pretty sure Zach, Little Raven, and Tara had not crossed, but he was unsure as to whether they had gone upstream or down. In the misty half-light it was difficult to see tracks, and he cursed under his breath as they searched about for a trace of the escapees' direction.

It took several minutes before one trooper came back to Aaron's side.

"There's two sets of tracks, sir. They've split up, going both upstream and down. Which way do we go?"

"How many?"

"If I was to take a guess, I'd say one went upstream and two horses went down. But one could be supplies. He could have taken the lady in either direction."

"Scott, you take three men and go upstream. I'll take Labus, Brady, and McNight and go down."

"Yes, sir." Scott wheeled his horse around.

"Scott? What do you have in the way of provisions?"

238

"Three or four days, sir."

"We'll meet back here in four days. Good luck."

"Yes, sir, thank you. Let's hope one of us finds that red devil before—"

"Get going, Scott," Aaron broke in gruffly. He sat on his horse for several minutes, watching Scott and the other three disappear. He still couldn't believe Zach had done what he had. Aaron had always given Zach the benefit of the doubt because of the immense respect he held for him, but that was slowly disintegrating.

Slowly he turned his horse and the three troopers followed him in silence. As he rode downstream, his eyes scanned both banks of the stream, watching for the place where the riders he followed had exited the water. He only hoped the trail he followed was that of Zach and Tara, not of his brother, Little Raven. Aaron also knew it would only be a day or two before Zach was beyond capture. Zach knew this land like the back of his hand, while Aaron was always the reluctant visitor.

There was a magic in this land and it called to Aaron. But with the magic was the bitterness of the loss of his family at the hands of rebellious Indians. This was an area where he could not keep his thoughts logical. He hated all Indians for what had happened to him and could hardly look at one without thinking of his parents and the small homestead they had once had.

He denied that fact as completely as he did that he was still uncertain about Zach's guilt. It angered him that he couldn't hate Zach as much as he wanted to. If he found Zach with Tara, he would put an end to all the problems.

He worried about Tara and her safety with Zach. She would be helpless here in an alien land filled with unnameable terrors for women. The thought of her helpless and frightened broiled within him.

They had ridden some distance upstream when one of his men called his attention to a trampled area on the bank where horses had left the stream.

"Here, sir! They left the stream here."

Aaron looked at the tracks, then off into the distance, completely sure this would be the last ground signs they would see unless Tara had been clever enough to leave some trail behind without Zach's knowledge—and that was a remote chance.

"Let's go." Aaron spurred his horse forward. They left the stream bed but had to travel very slowly, their eyes glued to the ground ahead, searching for the elusive sign that someone had passed here before them.

Little Raven squatted on the edge of the overhang and chuckled to himself as he watched the three riders approaching in the distance. His horse was well hidden and it amused him to watch the troopers move in slow circles, hunting in vain for a trail to follow.

He had been playing the game all night and most of the day, and now the sun was lowering toward the horizon. He would allow them to pass him, then he would finish the game by circling behind them and riding in a different direction than he had led them. It would take him yet another day to get to Deep Valley and Mule.

He was immobile, blending with the wilderness about him. The unsuspecting soldiers passed within fifty feet of him without any idea that he was there.

When Little Raven was sure they were gone, he returned to where he had hidden his horse, leapt into the saddle, and rode toward his meeting with Mule. The worry still lingered in the back of his mind that Mule was another who was going to be puzzled by the kidnapping of Tara. Mule would be surprised and most likely very angry. He smiled to himself. Mule was not one to hold his tongue with anyone, including Zach.

Little Raven made camp that night without a fire. He ate a handful of dried corn, drank some water, and cared for his horse. Then he rolled in his blanket and slept a carefree, peaceful sleep.

By dawn he was already up and riding on. He rested a while

240

when the sun was high, then rode on without taking time to eat. He was sure by nightfall he would be with Mule, in time for the evening meal.

Mule had learned infinite patience a long time ago. Now he knelt by a low burning fire and prodded it with a stick. The rabbit roasting, impaled on another stick, sent up a heady aroma. His thoughts were on Zach. He loved Zach like a son and knew some of the bitter things his friend had fought for a long time. Zach still wanted to keep peace between both his white and his Indian people, despite his own anger at wrongs done on both sides.

At least Zach and Little Raven would be free of the fort, its prison, and its sentence. He would have to remember to thank Tara for all she had done to help in the escape.

He sighed, gave the fire another poke, and was about to retrieve the cooked rabbit and begin to eat, when he grew suddenly still, his body tense and his senses alert. After a few minutes, he smiled.

"If you're hungry, c'mon and eat. This rabbit's near done." His voice rose just enough to carry to the shadows beyond the fire, where he knew either Zach or Little Raven stood.

It was Little Raven who walked smiling in the circle of firelight. He dropped down cross-legged across the fire from Mule.

"'Bout time you got here," Mule complained.

"Mule, I've been watching you for a long time. If I were a warrior wanting to take your scalp, you would be dead," Little Raven bragged cockily.

"The hell ya say, boy. Ya got here two minutes before I gave ya an invite to eat. Iffen you'd been a randy buck on the prowl, I woulda been behind ya and taken your hair before ya could think twice."

"You knew when I came?"

"How do ya think I've kept my hair this long?" Mule broke the rabbit in two pieces and handed half to Little Raven.

241

"Where's that brother of yours?"

"We had to separate, Aaron had men following." Little Raven went on to explain everything—everything but Tara's presence. "So I have just gotten here a little before him."

Mule's eyes squinted across the fire at Little Raven, whose gaze studiously avoided his. It took Mule the flash of a second to accept the fact that there were important things Little Raven wasn't saying.

"Have any trouble getting away?"

"No," came the noncommittal reply.

"No trouble findin' the supplies?"

"No."

"Then what in tarnation are you hangin' onto, boy? Let's have it. There's somethin' I don't know and I've got a feeling that I should, and I bet I'm not going to like it."

Little Raven was silent as he gave his concentration to the piece of rabbit he was eating.

"You better come out with it, Little Raven. They ain't no secrets twixt us. If there's somethin' I should know, then you better spit it out."

Little Raven was uncertain. He loved and trusted Mule, but he was worried about his reaction to Zach's taking Tara. After all, Mule was still a white man, and friend or not, he might just draw the line at this.

"Mule, it is better we wait for my brother. It is for him to explain what he has done, for I do not understand his reasons either."

That Little Raven was growing steadily more uncomfortable alarmed Mule.

"Now boy," he said softly, "I've been mixed up in this from the beginning. I have a business to know what's going on. Zach ain't here and I ain't waitin'. Now you tell me just what's wrong."

"I'm not sure anything's wrong."

"Don't pussyfoot around playin' with me!" Mule growled. "What's goin' on with Zach?"

"Mule," Little Raven began hesitantly, "when we left the

242

fort, my brother took the red-haired woman . . . Tara, he took her with him."

"He did what!" Mule exploded. "What in the Sam hell was he tryin' to prove? They might give up followin' him, but they shore won't quit comin' after her. How dad-blamed stupid can that boy be! What's he tryin' to prove? Besides all that, why does he want to do a thing like that to a girl like her? She ain't been nothin' but good to him. He owes her a debt and that's a hell of a way of repayin' it!"

"Mule"—Little Raven was uncomfortable with Mule's anger because he knew it was more than justified—"I feel there is something strong between my brother and this white girl. Maybe even stronger than he knows."

"You mean he wants this one as his woman?"

"I'm not sure he understands what he wants. It seems he can't hold her . . . and he can't let her go. It is a strange thing."

Mule was silent for several minutes. "He shore as hell is playin' with fire. If they find him, they'll string him up for shore."

"They won't find him," Little Raven said confidently.

"Will he be here soon?"

"No, not too soon, I think."

"Why?"

"He's tracking the wagons Caleb left with. He wants to find out if he can trace the guns through."

"You mean he's dragging that girl all over creation! Hell's fire, this goes from bad to worse."

"She's safe with him, Mule. He would not let harm come to her." Little Raven came quickly to Zach's defense.

"Shore," Mule said gently, "safe *with* him, but I wonder if she's safe *from* him."

"Zach would not hurt her," Little Raven retorted angrily. "He is not a man with so little honor that he would war with women."

"Then why didn't he leave her at the fort where she belonged?"

Little Raven had no reply for this because he could not give

243

an acceptable answer to himself. He remained silent.

"When I get my hands on him, he's gonna have a hell of a lot of questions to answer, you can bet on that," Mule muttered.

By the time they rolled in their blankets and slept, Mule was still mumbling under his breath, and Little Raven was still caught between loyalty and the fear that Zach had made a very drastic mistake.

Zach and Tara traveled the morning in a silence that frayed the nerves of both. Tara was well aware that Zach was concentrating on the trail he seemed to be following, and she was angrily certain she was not given one thought. She was uncomfortable, trying for hours to restrain her body from seeking the comfort of his to rest against the security of his arm to hold her.

But Zach was more than aware of everything about her, from the scent of her hair that, lifted by the breeze, brushed occasionally against his face, to the cream-colored skin his unobstructed downward view gave him. He could feel her rigid body and knew she was physically paying the price for her stubbornness.

When the sun was high, Zach could see the beads of perspiration on her skin. He knew from her tight lips and heavy lidded eyes that she was tired. Though he secretly admired her control, he could have shaken her for being too obstinate to even ask for a drink of water.

Accustomed to long rides with little sustenance, he had to try to remember she must be thirsty and hungry. He drew the horse to a stop, slid easily to the ground, then reached up to span her slim waist with his hands. She felt so tiny and fragile in his hands, but she was grimly silent as he stood her before him.

"Take some water from the canteen and cool yourself. We will reach water again by tonight, so it can be spared."

Tara was grateful for this. She took the canteen and poured

244

small amounts of water in her hand, splashing it on her face. Zach loosened the saddle girths to let the horses rest. He carried some dried meat to her, handing it to her in silence. He knew she was in the mood to accept no conversation from him. She refused the food with a silent shake of her head, walked a short distance away from him, and dropped to the ground beneath the shade of a small tree.

He chewed his lip thoughtfully. Was she just being tenacious? He had no time to waste in proving how foolish she was acting. If she was determined to make herself sick, he was just as determined not to. He walked to her and squatted down beside her, extending the meat. "Eat!" he commanded. "You will need all the strength you have to travel. If you make yourself weak and sick"—he mentally crossed his fingers so that she would believe him—"I will be forced to leave you here."

The eyes that lifted to him were brilliant green and filled with a contempt and anger whose effect on him was surprising. He had been hurt many times, but this time stung deep.

Tara reached out and snatched the food from his hand. "You would, wouldn't you?" she said scathingly. "Being what you are, that is the way you would deal with me if I held you back."

"There are more important things than you or me."

"That is what you say. I will believe it only when I see for myself. I will eat, just to keep from giving you the satisfaction of making me suffer any more than I have."

"A little discomfort, a little inconvenience. You haven't been hurt," he scoffed. "Stop being a child."

He was rewarded by a glare that could have withered him, but he was satisfied. He would rather have her fighting than defeated, even if it was fighting him.

He sat beside her, chewing some dried meat and drinking. Tara chose to ignore him completely, so he gave himself over to trying to outguess Caleb and find a way to the guns before he could get them to their destination.

He knew every inch of this land, and a route formed in his

mind that was more than plausible. If he was right, Caleb had hidden the wagons somewhere, so he was looking for the track of packhorses. He still wasn't sure what he was going to do if he found them—except prove to one green-eyed girl he was right. The thought of an apology from her was more than interesting.

He stood up, bent down quickly, and drew her up from the ground and into the curve of his arm. She pushed against him, but he held her easily.

"Now, let's get something straight. We're riding together, and you're deliberately wearing yourself out riding stiff. Any more of that and I'll tie you across the packhorse—on your belly. Do you understand?"

"Yes," she spat furiously, "but maybe I'd choose the packhorse."

"So be it," he said calmly, then he swung her up into his arms and started toward the packhorse. Her eyes grew wide and her mouth oohed in total shock. He meant to do it! To tie her to a horse like a bundle of supplies!

"You—you can't!"

"Can't I? Just pay attention and see if I can't."

"No! Please . . . I . . ."

He stopped walking and looked into eyes filled with a combination of shock, rage, and a slight touch of fear. He wanted to kiss the look into passion with a sudden surge of desire so strong it left him weak. Her soft, vulnerable mouth was so close . . . so intoxicatingly close.

"You'll ride a little more comfortably and a little less like a stone. That way you won't be so tired. You will!" he demanded, making his voice rigidly controlled and trying to keep some kind of control over the senses that were going wild with her close proximity.

"Yes," she replied, fighting the tears that glistened in her eyes. She would obey him now, but she wouldn't let him see her cry over her temporary defeat.

He slowly let her feet touch the ground, reluctant to let her go. Her warm curves pressed against his side, playing havoc

246

with him as he responded totally against his will to remembered pleasure.

Tara was suddenly caught in the same web of past magic. She could feel the slow spread of warmth through her and fought wildly the almost overpowering urge to melt against him, pull his head down to hers, and feel the touch of his mouth on hers.

One moment, one breathless moment, they lost touch with all that tore them apart, and they could only feel the shimmery web that seemed to be drawing them closer and closer until their mouths hovered only inches apart.

But reality struck with the same force, and Tara pushed away from him with a small sound of disbelief.

He walked to the horses to relighten the saddles, fighting the knowledge that he wanted her so badly his whole body shook with the force of it.

He mounted and rode to where she stood with her back to him. She turned to look up at him, and now her eyes were guarded and cold. He extended his hand and kicked his foot free of the stirrup. Without a word, she put her hand in his and he lifted her up before him.

She was silently obedient and leaned against him, letting the strength of his arm make her relax. But in her obedient silence she defeated him much more effectively than if she had fought him further.

They rode slowly so Zach could watch for any sign. He had to really concentrate, because Tara's close proximity was more than distracting. But he found a perverse tormenting pleasure in having her close and soft in his arms.

But the afternoon waned with no sign of a trail. The sun hovered near the horizon by the time they stopped again. This time there were a few more trees, and the soft sound of rippling water intrigued Tara with the promise of a bath.

Zach unsaddled and cared for the horses, and as he moved around, Tara came to his side.

"Can we have a fire tonight?" she asked in a chilled voice.

"I will build a small one that leaves no smoke. We have the

shelter of the trees to keep the glow covered. Besides," he smiled, "Aaron is chasing his tail. He'll never find us. Not until I let him, and I don't intend to let him—not yet anyway."

"And what are we to eat?"

"I'll build the fire and go rustle up something we can cook."

"Like what?"

"Fish maybe," he replied. "If we're lucky."

He laid saddles, bridles, and blankets aside and cared for the horses. Then he turned back to Tara. "Stay by the fire. I'll be back in a few minutes." Before she could question him, he was already disappearing into the trees like a shadow.

Tara did stay by the fire, for all of five minutes. Then the sound of water drew her. She went to the stream and, in moments, shed her clothes and waded into the water. It felt good and she washed herself, using the soft sand of the bottom to rub her skin until it glowed, then rinsing. She washed her hair, feeling the dust and dirt and discomfort of the past two days drain away.

The water felt good, but she didn't want to be caught where she was by Zach. It was a difficult situation already, and she didn't want to make it worse. She rose from her kneeling position, turned, then stood motionless. Zach stood on the bank, as motionless as she.

Zach had been lucky and had speared a fish within minutes of leaving Tara. He brought it back to the fire quickly, realizing how hungry she must be.

When he didn't find her by the fire, he became alarmed, rushing to the horses to see if she had given such a stupid idea as running away any thought. But they were still quiet and content. Only then did he walk toward the stream.

He stood, too struck by the vision before him to move or, for that matter, to even breathe. She knelt with her back to him and slowly lifted water in her cupped hands to let it roll down her skin. Beads of water glistened in silver rivulets down her slim, tawny body. The copper-red of her hair was kissed by the last rays of the sun, and the picture she made was one that

248

would never leave his mind.

She rose slowly and gracefully, her wet body gleaming in the dying light. Then she turned, and the effect she created knocked the breath from him.

There was a tawny gold glow about her and a hazy, misty look in her eyes. He wanted her, but for the life of him he couldn't move. He couldn't force her to respond again. He couldn't make her body obey its needs if he couldn't make her give more than just that.

Tara had never felt what she was feeling at this moment. It took a concentrated effort to curb her disobedient body into not answering what she saw in his eyes, into not heeding the call every instinct demanded.

She looked so vulnerable and helpless, and this is what defeated Zach. If she had grown defiant, even if she had said one word of anger, he might have forgotten good intentions. But he didn't want her to hate him any more than she did.

"Come back to the fire," he said gently. "There's food."

He walked away and Tara was uncertain if she was pleased . . . or disappointed.

Chapter 22

Tara put her clothes on rapidly, leaving her hair to fall about her in still-damp tendrils she intended to dry by the fire. When she went back to their camp, Zach was already kneeling by the fire and something smelled very good. He had placed two flat rocks in the low fire and they had become extremely hot. On this he had placed a shallow pan Mule had packed, and within it fillets of fish were sizzling. A pot of coffee bubbled on another rock.

He had spread a blanket not too far from the fire and Tara sat down, pulling up her knees to hug them with her arms and gaze at him meditatively.

He knelt on one knee, his dark head bent toward the fire. The bronze of his skin was enhanced by the fire's glow, defining his features. His jaw was firm and a thick strand of hair drooped over his forehead. His body seemed controlled by powerful condensed strength as he bent to test the fish. And her ability to understand him was as impenetrable as he was. The rage she had carried from the time he had taken her from the fort seemed useless against him. He was impervious to her discomfort at one minute and making her supper the next. He insisted she ride comfortably with him and showed absolutely no concern that he was dragging her all over the wilderness with him in search of something she still found hard to believe.

He maneuvered a piece of fish onto a tin plate, handing it and a cup of coffee to her. Then he did the same for himself, finding a seat across the fire from her and sitting cross-legged before it.

In the glow of the firelight, his eyes were like blue crystal, alarmingly aware of everything about her. She could actually feel them skim over her.

"How long are you going to keep up with this miserable trek?" she demanded.

"Until I find what I want," he replied, unconcerned. His mind seemed to be on eating, and she was again filled with the supreme urge to slap the half smile from his lips.

"Zach, take me back, or let me go somewhere near the fort. I can only hold you back."

"You won't slow me down." His smile grew a little. "Besides, I have a point to prove and I want you along when I do."

She gave an exasperated sigh and concentrated on finishing her food. When she did return her gaze to him, she found him intently watching her with a look she couldn't read. Her eyes must have asked the question.

"I was thinking of what I would call you if you were one of my father's people."

"Well, I'm not, and I don't care to know what you would call me." She finished her food and set the plate aside. "So, what would you call me?" she asked again, agitated at his quick smile.

"I've been giving it a lot of thought. You are all sun-colored and brilliant, like the season before winter, yet you are soft and delicate like the wild dove. I think I would call you Autumn Dove." He nodded. "Yes, Autumn Dove fits you well."

"Autumn Dove," she repeated. "It's a beautiful name."

"As I said," he spoke softly, "the name fits you."

She looked at him, realizing the puzzle of Zachary Hale was growing even more difficult to understand. "And Windwalker fits you as well. You move like the wind and never leave

251

answers or any part of yourself behind."

"I have left too many pieces of myself in too many places. The white world has a way of chipping off pieces if one isn't careful."

"Do you think the people of your father's village would be any different to me?"

"Of course they would," he replied at once. "You listen to people who see nothing in my father's people than ones to push and to steal from."

"You're always so certain of everything. But I have a feeling it wouldn't be like you think."

"One day I'll take you there," he said firmly. "And you'll find out what the difference is."

"Or you will."

"You are much too stubborn, Autumn Dove." He eased his words with a renewed smile.

"Of course you're not stubborn," she countered. "You just force people to do what you want whether they like it or not."

"I told you what I'm doing is for your own good. The guns your friend has brought will be combined with whiskey. How long do you think it will take young men like my brother, Little Raven, to fall beneath the force of the whiskey and allow Caleb, and I'm sure Tall Bull, to push them into doing something foolish? Then your commander need only wipe my village out and all threat will be gone—and so will a lot of innocent people."

"Zach, what does Caleb have to gain from all this? Surely he has little chance of gaining anything."

"You mean he has less to gain than I do?"

"If the white fort was gone, you and your father's people would have their land back, and it could be years before another fort was built or more whites came."

"For how long? Do you think I'm stupid, Tara? I've been east. I know how outnumbered we are. I'd rather see peace than an eventual slaughter of my people."

"But you still don't know what Caleb has to gain—or even if

252

he's guilty."

"I don't know what he has to gain, but I have no doubt about his guilt. Would you like me to tell you what plans he probably has for you?"

"Me?" she questioned. "What plans could he possibly have for me? I was safe at the fort."

"Were you really?" he laughed. "You are still a child if you believe that."

He seemed to be beside her suddenly, kneeling next to her and catching her face between his hands. "Tara, you were not safe at the fort; In fact, the only safe place for you is here."

She caught her breath, stirred by his proximity and the intensity of her body's reaction, even though her mind resisted.

"Let me tell you something, sweet Tara," he grated. "Caleb would sell you to any one of the braves that offered him whatever it is he wants. Of course, he'd collect the sale price after he enjoyed your charms before the others."

"Others," she rasped weakly.

"Oh, there would be others. You're something very rare and beautiful, not a sight seen often out here. I guarantee you there would be lots of others." He released her but remained much too close for her to regain her equilibrium. "I said you're safe here, and I'll see you're returned—maybe by Mule."

"Mule! He knew you were going to kidnap me?" She was astounded.

"No, he doesn't know yet. But when we get back to him, he'll probably raise cain about it." Zach stood up. Gazing at a vulnerable-looking Tara tried his control. "Get some sleep, Tara. We have to move very early in the morning." He said the words harshly, so she wouldn't be able to read, in his face, the power she had over him. He had told himself enough lies, saying that he had only taken her for her own protection. He didn't want to admit it was any more than that.

But Tara was aware of a potent new element that had leapt between them, even though she had no name for it. Zach

253

moved back to the fire, took up his rifle, stepped out of the ring of light, and disappeared.

Tara lay down on her blanket slowly. She was overcome with question after question. The only thing in her mind that was a certainty was that she was shocked at the fact she felt safe. It was her last thought before she slept.

Zach sat in the shadows and watched Tara as she slept close to the fire. He saw the spill of her burnished hair against the dark blanket. He was powerless to fight the memories of the scent of her copper-red hair and the feel of the smooth texture of her skin beneath his touch. Damnit! Why did she have the ability to strum his senses with ghost-like fingers? Why did he allow such a thing? He had had many women prettier and more seductive than her. He tried to conjure one up in his memory and grew even angrier when he couldn't.

He neatly dodged any mental questions about why he had done what he had. He had been doing it since the time he had left the fort with her. If his calculations were anywhere near right, he should cross Caleb's trail sometime in the next day or day and a half. Once he found out what direction Caleb was moving in, he could put Tara safely in Mule's hands, take Little Raven with him, and put a stop to Banning once and for all . . . one way or the other.

It wasn't even dawn when Zach shook her awake. She opened her eyes slowly. Drugged with sleep, she was more than inviting. But he was determined not to allow her to get behind his guard again.

"The Autumn Dove does not sleep so late," he smiled. "She's about her business by now, as we have to be."

"It's hardly day," she groaned as she sat up. Zach had to turn his back to her to keep from gathering her up in his arms and making love to her as all his senses cried out to do.

"It's late. Come on, get moving. The supplies are all packed and my horse is saddled. I want to get going, so get up."

She knew better than to argue with that firm, cold voice and rigid back. He was the captor again, and there was no way anything she said was going to do any more than make him force her to do what he had already commanded. She was not going to put herself in the position of being forced to obey his will.

The first gray streaks bordered the horizon by the time Zach swung up on his horse and reached to lift her before him. They moved on wordlessly.

Tara was fascinated that Zach actually felt he could find some kind of trail in the immensity of this wilderness. To her, it was like finding that proverbial needle in a haystack. Yet, she felt self-assurance in every move of his body, every glance of his eye.

For her own peace of mind, there was much too much she noticed about him: the strength of the large hand that held the reins, the hard muscle of the arm that held her close, and even more the lithe body that pressed against her so intimately.

Questions were answered with one-syllable answers, very pointed and direct, until she gave up trying to get any information from him and remained silent. She had no idea of the difficulty Zach had concentrating on finding the trail he sought at the same time he was trying to keep his mind off the effect she was having on him. By the time the sun was directly above them, both were grateful to stop and get away from each other.

As they continued to move on later, Tara's nerves were being stretched to the limit and Zach was not in any better emotional condition. It was frazzled nerves and a physical need that eventually erupted into a battle.

By the time Zach had made the evening fire, he was doing his best to keep his eyes from her to restrain the desire that gnawed at him.

Tara sat down by the fire, exhausted but trying to work the tangles from her hair with her fingers. Zach returned to the fire a short while later with a cleaned and gutted rabbit, which he impaled on a stick and braced over the fire. Annoyed at the vision she made as she leisurely ran her fingers through her hair and more annoyed at his desire to do the same, Zach snapped peevishly.

"There's more to be done than to preen yourself like a peacock."

"I didn't ask to be dragged out here, and I'm not about to help you."

"If you want to eat, you help," he snarled. He had no intention of letting her go hungry, but her stubborn resistance angered him.

"Then keep your food!" she said through gritted teeth. "What's one more discomfort? If you think I'm going to serve you like a slave after you've dragged me halfway across this"— she waved her arms to include all about—"wilderness, then you're crazy. I'd rather starve."

"So starve," he said frigidly. "Only a stupid, obstinate female would deprive herself of food to prove a point."

"And only an arrogant, self-opinionated, and very hateful man would be as uncaring and heartless as you are," she retorted coldly.

"What I'm doing has to be done," he replied as he took his blanket near the fire and spread it out, "because you have an open heart for any scoundrel who acts like a gentleman. . . ."

"Oh, you are a—a damn savage! Just as they say you are. Yes, Caleb was a gentleman. He certainly never tried to drag me halfway across the godforsaken nothing."

"Of course not," Zach grinned now, pleased he had pricked her anger. Having her at war with him was much easier to handle. "He would have just let you follow your own naive little mind right into his bed."

"Are you accusing me of permitting any man to have me just because he has good manners?" she nearly shrieked. "God, you really are a beast!"

Zach bent forward to turn the rabbit on the makeshift spit. The scent of it wafted on the breeze, causing Tara's mouth to water. Zach knew her hunger must be as great as his, but he also realized her own stubbornness was going to prevent her from sharing the food.

"I didn't say that, Tara," he chuckled. "But I'm pretty sure Caleb was hoping along that line."

"Well, I'm nobody's plaything. I've not really had a choice in our situation, now, have I?" she asked bitterly.

His quick dark look gave her some pleasure, which his answer quickly drained away.

"Are you trying to tell me I'm all to blame, that I forced you?"

"Well, didn't you?" she protested too quickly. She regretted the words as soon as she said them, because she saw the look of challenge that leapt into his eyes.

He laughed softly in disbelief. "Your memory is much shorter than mine if you intend to cry rape at this late date."

"Your memory is as obnoxious as you are!" Tara's fury was getting the better of her good sense. She wanted to strike out at him and only succeeded in tossing a gauntlet in his face.

"So you find it so difficult to spend any time with such an uncivilized man?" he asked softly. "The genteel lady can't lower herself to admit true feelings."

"I have no true feelings concerning you except a fervent desire that Aaron is closer than you think and catches you!"

"Aaron doesn't stand a snowball's chance in hell of doing that." Zach was aggravatingly calm. Tara was about to answer when he stood and started around the fire toward her. "But no matter where he is, he won't be coming to interfere in you proving a point."

"A—a point?" she stammered as he towered over her. Her realization that she had pushed him one step too far was bursting into her consciousness. She moved back on the blanket a little, but he dropped to his knees beside her. Now a fluttering panic gripped her. She wanted to run, with no place to run to, yet she didn't want to retreat before him, because she knew he was trying to force her to do just that.

257

She held herself rigid and their eyes met in silent combat, a combat from which neither intended to retreat. She raised one hand slightly, almost as if she intended to push him away. He caught it in his and lifted it to his lips. She inhaled raggedly, struggling for defense as he pressed his lips gently to the palm, then touched it lightly with his tongue, making small circular movements that sent shivers up her arm. He watched in satisfaction as her eyes widened and her lips parted as if her breathing were difficult to control. He could feel his own pulses pounding wildly to match the racing of her own, which he could almost taste as he pressed his lips gently against her wrist.

He wanted her to plead, to fight against him so that he could have the last bitter word, but he was captivated by the brilliant flame that seemed to suddenly ignite behind the emerald eyes. If he wanted to let her go now, he couldn't. It was as if he had suddenly fallen into a swift moving current against which he couldn't battle.

Tara was futilely reaching for some kind of resistance, but she couldn't find anything solid in a world suddenly gone topsy-turvy.

Her palms were pressed flat against his chest now as he reached down to grip her waist and lift her to her knees to face him. He found himself catching the length of her hair in his hands to draw her head back and lift her mouth to meet his. He kissed her gently at first, slowly drawing her deeper and deeper into the kiss. His hot probing tongue entered her mouth and teased at her, and Tara felt as if she were drowning. It seemed too natural to return the intimate caress.

He marveled that she seemed such a perfect fit as his hands moved down her back to mold her wonderfully pliant body against his. She seemed to melt and flow around him, swaying with him as they blended together.

Then slowly, as if each could answer only the primitive need, their hands reached to help the other remove their clothes. With only the glow of the fire to illuminate them, they touched and caressed. Her body was like gold fire beneath his hands, and she ran her hands over the lean rippling muscles, both entranced, gazing hypnotically into each other's eyes.

Then he gave a low groaning growl and swept her down to the blanket with him. He was kissing her temples, her neck and shoulders, with tender nipping kisses, and their bodies surged together wildly, seeking the joining that would ease the flames that seared them.

It grew like mounting volcanic pressure, and Tara arched to him, wanting, needing. Zach braced a hand on each side of her and supported his weight as he moved to fit himself within her, finding her moist and ready. He remained braced so, looking deeply into her brilliant eyes as he began to move. He felt her long slim legs twine about his hips. Watching her, knowing she was finding the same miracle as he was, he clung to this fascination. Her body beneath his was molten gold, and her hair spilled about her in a brilliance that reflected the firelight. Her eyes were closed and her head was thrown back as she arched again and again to meet his powerful thrusts. He was straining to hold back his completion, watching to make sure she found hers first.

She gasped and cried out his name, clinging to his rigid arms as one wave of fulfilling orgasm after another rippled through her. Her whole body was alive with it, undulating wildly, and now he joined her, moving in a rough straining rhythm until his body gave several long, convulsive shudders.

They were gasping for ragged breath and clinging to each other now, as the spiral down was just as convulsive as the spiral up had been.

He didn't want to crush her with his weight, so he lay on his side and held her close to him, letting his hands gently caress the still-trembling softness of her body.

Tara found herself curled against him, her head nestled on his shoulder. She felt as if she were floating back to reality, a reality she couldn't face. All her strong words and disclaimers had been for nothing. There was a wide chasm between what all

259

her rational ideas were and what her wayward body had demanded. She could feel the tears of frustration, and the last thing she wanted was to have him see her cry.

But Zach felt the touch of tears and was sure her hatred for him had grown because he had forced her to respond. He had known her body better than she did, but was that enough?

Had he been right in what he had said? Did she feel the blood he carried in his veins was tainted by something that she couldn't handle? It was amazing how much the thought hurt. Yes, it hurt, but he had to give her a way out if she chose to take it. He would give her back her anger and let it be her defense as long as she felt she needed it. He only hoped one day she wouldn't.

"You see," he laughed softly, "it's not too hard to admit what you feel, and maybe being with an 'uncivilized man' is just what you want. At least it feels that way."

Tara jerked into a sitting position as if she had been stung. Her eyes shot brilliant green sparks and her jaw was clenched.

"That was all it was to you, wasn't it? A chance to prove something. Well, I guess you succeeded . . . this time. But I swear to you, Zachary Hale—or maybe I should call you Windwalker; the savage name fits you better—there will never be another time. Never!"

She grabbed the edge of the blanket and pulled it around her. Zach rose and dressed silently. He tried to ignore the strange ache that began somewhere in the center of him and spread like a cold liquid throughout him. He had done just what he should have done. Why then, he thought miserably as he rolled in his blanket, did he feel like hell?

Chapter 23

Aaron had never been more disgusted in his life. It was as if Zach had vanished into thin air. He was forced to turn back and meet his men at the stream to see if they had had any better luck. They hadn't. Little Raven had been an elusive will-o'-the-wisp, having vanished as effectively as Zach had.

"We have to go back to the fort and get enough supplies to go out again," Aaron stated.

"Sir?" one sergeant spoke in a gruff voice. "If we can't find their trail now, how are we going to find it later?"

Aaron turned an angry yet understanding gaze at him. "Would you like to explain to her brother what happened and that we couldn't find her?"

"No, sir." The reply was subdued, as every man's mind jumped to David and how he was going to take the news. Some were quieter than others, because they knew what David had thought to be his secret and they weren't sure how he would react to the Indians now, once he found his sister had been stolen.

"Then let's get back to the fort. I wouldn't be surprised if, with my luck, Lieutenant Montgomery would be back by now and I'll have to explain this."

They rode the distance to the fort in silence, broken only by the jingle of harnesses and the rattle of equipment. Men refused to look at each other for fear questions might have to be answered.

Aaron rode in glum silence. He had a premonitional feeling that there was an even bigger problem brewing and Zach was near the center of it. Strangely, he was almost certain Zach wouldn't hurt Tara, but he couldn't figure out why he had taken her. She could only be a hindrance considering the speed he could travel alone.

Aaron knew none of the whites at the fort would be welcome in Waiting Wolf's village, but if worse came to worse, he would send someone—maybe David—to find out if Zach had brought Tara there, even though he was reasonably sure Zach wouldn't bring his father any problems. That thought irritated him. Why was he so sure Zach was such a sterling character? He hated all Indians. Yet he couldn't push the aggravating thought from his mind that Zach had a motive he had not seen . . . and might never see.

To David's immense satisfaction, Colonel Chivington gave him the dispatches that freed him to leave Denver and return to the fort. He had no intention of letting Chivington know that he would travel with Long . . . and that he would be stopping first at Long's cabin to meet his wife and children, then at Black Kettle's village to see the woman he loved.

He knew for certain this forbidden love could destroy his family and his career. Yet, he couldn't surrender her and he couldn't hold her. He tried to push the questions from his mind but they remained. Funny, he thought, but Tara leapt to his mind. As close as they had always been, he had the strangest idea that if he could talk to her, she might just understand.

David walked across the dirt street to the saloon to meet Long. As he reached the other side, he stopped and looked up the street to where a large group of men, led by John Chivington, was leaving the town.

"Looks like he's gathered a small army," David muttered to

262

himself. "He's headed for trouble one of these days."

He entered the saloon and found Long seated in the corner, nursing a drink. David slid into a chair opposite him.

"Sounds like a big ruckus out there," Long said.

"Colonel Chivington," David grinned. "He and his hand-picked army are playing soldier again,"

"He's not exactly funny, David. I want to get home. My cabin's kind of isolated, and my wife and kids are alone. He's the kind of man could find a lot of fun in that. Winter Snow is a brave woman and she would fight for our children. Chivington is just the type to have a little fun with that, too."

"Then let's get going. I can be ready in an hour, and we'll head straight for your place, then stop by Black Kettle's village on the way to the fort."

Long nodded, and with a surprising quickness for his huge form, he stood to toss down the last of his drink. "Sounds good to me. I'll meet you at the stable."

It was just over two hours later that David and Long left Denver, each with a well-loaded packhorse in tow. It would take them two days of rugged travel to reach Long's cabin. Both men had adapted long ago to the strenuous physical energy moving from one place to another took. They didn't talk much nor did they rest much, except to give their horses a chance at very short intervals. They would dismount and walk for a while. The midday meal was eaten while on the move, and they didn't make the last stop until it was long after dark.

They sat close to the fire to eat, secured their horses carefully, then rolled in their blankets and slept.

At dawn, both were up and making swift preparations to leave. There were several more hours of travel, and the sun was dropping low when Long pulled his horse to a stop and sat motionless. Then he smiled as David turned a curious gaze to him.

"Something wrong?" David questioned.

"Nope," Long chuckled. "I think we're being snuck up on."

"By whom?" David's brows drew together in worry.

"I'd say," Long spoke softly, "it would be Blue Hawk. He's been trying to catch me unaware every time I come home. He's gettin' good at it, too. I'll bet he's been with us for nigh onto an hour before I picked him up. I must be getting old. He'll get a laugh out of this."

"How long are you going to let him get away with it?" David grinned.

"Well, I think he's showing off in front of his kid brother. I don't want him to lose face, so I'll play along for a while."

David got the warm feeling that Long got along very well with his sons. It was a feeling that gave him a lot to think about. A man could be happy out here with a woman like Small Fawn. If it weren't for the love he felt for his family, he wouldn't have given the situation a second thought. But he had a lot to be grateful for from his parents, and he just couldn't turn his back on them. Besides that, his sister Tara was a lady, and he couldn't see her being sisterly to a woman from a culture so radically different from her own. But the thought of it teased his mind with hopefulness. Maybe someday he'd find a way out of his dilemma.

They rode into a stand of trees and Long bent slightly toward David. "You can expect to be attacked by a wild kid sometime soon. They'll be yelping their heads off, and I wouldn't want you grabbin' for a gun thinkin' you was gonna get scalped."

"Don't worry, I'll fall in my tracks like a good white soldier," David laughed.

The words were barely out of David's mouth when two ponies broke from the trees. Shrill yelps broke the air as David and Long spun about in well-portrayed surprise.

When the two reached David and Long, their young faces were bright with wide smiles. The oldest, and obvious leader of the attack, was a sturdy young boy David would have guessed was nearing twelve. The second couldn't be more than ten, and his dark eyes moved from brother to father as if this were his entire world and one he was more than happy with.

The older boy sat very erect, a kind of pride in his face that stimulated a twinge of admiration in David. He had Long's height and build and the deep slate-gray of his eyes. Yet the high cheekbones and tawny skin, coupled with midnight black hair, spoke of his Indian blood.

The second boy was slighter in build, with fine-drawn features that promised to turn to extreme handsomeness.

"I have followed you since midday, my father," the oldest spoke first.

"Have ya, now? Well, I don't recollect hearin' a sound, did you, David?"

"Nope, nothing," David agreed readily.

"You're getting pretty good," Long added. David could see the boy swell with pride. Obviously his father was the ultimate word in anything.

"David, these are my boys, Blue Hawk and Small Otter. Boys, this is a good friend of mine, David Montgomery."

Both sets of eyes assessed David, who found himself, with some surprise, hoping he passed the obvious inspection.

"I am Blue Hawk," the oldest said, "and I am pleased to meet my father's friends."

"And I am Small Otter," the youngest added. "You are in the white man's army?"

"Small Otter," Long said gently, "one does not ask such questions of friends. It is for them to offer words of themselves first."

"I am sorry, my father," Small Otter's head dropped. "I am pleased to meet my father's friends."

"As I am pleased to meet the strong sons of my friend," David replied. He didn't see Long's quick glance of surprise.

David found himself deeply curious about the mother of such sons.

"Your mother is well, Blue Hawk?" Long questioned.

"Yes, Father. I have seen to her care as you told me. There is plenty of food and wood for the stove, and I have guarded the house carefully."

265

Again David found himself believing exactly what Blue Hawk said. Long had trained his sons well. They would be responsible men as time went on. It was only then that David thought of what kind of future their mixed blood would give them. He knew Long and was anxious now to meet his wife. Maybe they had some answers to his questions.

"Well, let's get home, boys. I've got a lot of things here in these packs, some of which belong to you. So I guess we'd better get crackin' if we want to be home before night."

Long kicked his horse into motion as did David. The two boys silently fell in behind them.

They had traveled so for about twenty minutes when the trees thinned and David could see a small clearing in which stood a rough-cut cabin. Smoke spiraled up from the chimney. Long increased the horse's gait and David could feel his excitement in returning to a place he so obviously loved.

They drew their horses to a halt in the front yard, and as they dismounted the door was flung open.

Long gave a deep throaty laugh as he caught a flying bundle of woman up in his arms and crushed her to him. He spun her around and their laughter mingled. David caught the look of satisfied pleasure in the eyes of Blue Hawk and Small Otter and realized that the relationship between Long and his wife was always like this.

When Long stood his wife down beside him, she seemed almost tiny beside his huge frame. Her eyes moved to David, then quickly back to Long. With his arm still around her, moving her with him, Long stopped by David who was just dismounting.

"David, I want you to meet my wife, Winter Snow. Winter Snow, this is David Montgomery, a very good friend of mine."

She smiled shyly and nodded toward David. "You are welcome to our home."

"Thank you, Winter Snow. I have met your sons. You must be quite proud of them."

"They walk in the footsteps of their father, and of him I am

266

very proud," Winter Snow said softly. "If you will come in, there is food and drink inside."

Without questions, Blue Hawk and Small Otter slid from their ponies and went to Long's and David's to lead them away.

"Unpack the horses and bring the packs inside," Long called after them as they walked toward the small barn.

The three walked into the cabin. There was one large room, with a fireplace on the far wall and a door opening off of each side wall, and three other rooms, very comfortable with rough-hewn furniture obviously made by Long and colorful blankets and objects that spoke of Winter Snow's presence.

She immediately set about preparing whatever it was that smelled so enticing in the simmering kettle that hung near the fire.

The two boys entered, lugging the two packs with difficulty. Long made no move to help them but waited patiently until they dropped the bundles near his feet.

That both boys were breathlessly expectant was obvious, but they were silent as Long began to unbundle the packs. David smiled at the combination of the glitter in the boy's eyes and the patience with which they tried to suppress their excitement.

Long finally got them open and reached inside to withdraw a long slender object wrapped in a piece of blanket. This he handed to Blue Hawk, who took it with a quick smile. For a moment he just held it. Then, slowly, he unwrapped the piece of blanket to expose a rifle. His eyes widened first in shock, then turned to his father with a look David could only describe as a combination of awe and worship.

"This is for me?" he whispered.

"You are no longer a child," Long stated firmly. "And it will be up to you to protect our home should I be away and anything happen. I expect you will learn to handle it safely and be the man here when I cannot be present."

"I will, Father," Blue Hawk breathed. Now his hands caressed the gun. "When will you teach me?"

"Tomorrow," Long replied as he again reached into the pack to withdraw a new bundle. This one he handed to the younger boy, who unwrapped it with the same contained excitement. There were two things inside. One was a beautiful knife with a wood handle carved with pictures of birds, the other a long slim flute made of the same carved wood.

The boy smiled and his eyes lifted to Long, who nodded. There were unsaid words both child and man understood. David felt as if Long had said something to Small Otter that had meant a great deal to him.

Winter Snow had sat beside Long's chair in silence all the while, occasionally looking up at Long, then back to her sons.

Obviously there were things in the packs for Winter Snow, and just as obviously Long had no intention of giving them to her in front of anyone.

When they finished a late supper, Long sent his sons to fetch blankets to lay before the fire.

"Blue Hawk and Small Otter will sleep here," Long said to David.

"No, I will not put the boys from their beds for me. I'll sleep here," David protested.

"You will insult my sons if you do such a thing," Long replied. "Their mother has given them a whole lot of her ways. If they do not show you all the hospitality they can, she would be most upset with them and they would be very shamed as well, so you might just as well not fight it unless you want two nervous kids on your hands."

"All right," David laughed.

"Besides," Long added, "they enjoy sleeping out here. The fire stays warm, and they can be up and out to try out their new possessions before I am."

"All right," David surrendered, and went to the bedroom. Before long the house was silent, and David slept more comfortably than he had for a long time.

*　　*　　*

268

David relaxed within an atmosphere of unspoken affections. Blue Hawk and Small Otter were Long's shadow. Blue Hawk took well to the handling of the rifle. With wide intent eyes he hung on Long's instructions until he could snap a leaf from a tree at thirty yards.

After a day or two David noticed the difference between the boys. Obviously Blue Hawk had his father's adventurous nature. He loved to hunt and to ride. Small Otter was the quieter and gentler of the two, most obviously his mother's reflection. Yet the two boys made an agreeable combination. Small Otter would go with his brother to hunt, and Blue Hawk would sit beneath the shade of a tree and listen as his younger brother searched out notes on his flute.

Winter Snow was very quiet, and occasionally David would be the beneficiary of a quick smile or a little extra food on his plate. He never heard her, in the few days he stayed, raise her voice to her sons and he knew Long's hand was there. They cared for David's horse and equipment, and when he offered a trifling reward they looked almost insulted, shook their dark heads, and went on with their work.

That David's curiosity was mounting every day was clear to Long, and after supper one night, he invited his friend to walk with him to a nearby stream.

The night was especially pretty and the air warm and scented. David could not help but think of Small Fawn on such a night.

They walked in silence for a while, then Long spoke, "David, I think you've been a little curious about Winter Snow and my boys."

"I have no right to pry into your personal life, Long. If it looks that way, I'm sorry. Do you want me to go?"

"No. Most men would have been askin' by now. I guess that's why I stay away from them. You're kind of different and Winter Snow likes you, not to mention my boys who refer to you as the white Indian. Quite a compliment if you know them. It just means you were born with white skin but you have an

Indian heart."

"I'm pleased they like me."

"David, it's not easy to get away from your own world and still not fit in anyone else's."

"You've done it. Pretty successfully, I'd say, from what I've seen."

"I'm one of the few lucky ones who understands both sides. Who knows both sides are wrong sometimes. I'll tell you a story." Long paused, reflecting back in time. He scooped up a handful of pebbles and tossed them one at a time in the stream, then he began to talk again. "I ran away from some pretty ugly things in my past. Out here I found a lot of peace just being alone. I trapped away from everyone. Oh, I went to the fort a time or two and to Denver for supplies, but most times I kept to myself. I got along well with the Indians. They respected my privacy, and now and again I spent time with them.

"One day I was on my way home from Denver when I ran across this kind of a deep woody place. I was going to skirt it when I heard some sounds. Then I noticed three or four horses saddled and standin'. Well, I got curious and went in easy like." He again became silent for several minutes, and David could feel an anger still hard to control. "There were three or four of the army's brave warriors, and they had this pretty young Indian girl and were having quite a time with her. They'd obviously had her for quite a while. Her clothes were torn off, and she was crying and begging. But, you see, she could only speak Cheyenne, and they didn't understand that and they didn't want to. They'd hurt her pretty bad, takin' turns on her and they were far from finished," Long sighed. "Anyway, I got a rifle on 'em and scared the hell out of them. But I'll never forget what one said. He said, 'What the hell do you care? You might as well take a turn yourself. She's only a dirty Indian, and she's like an animal. After a while she'll learn to like it. C'mon, take a turn or two.' I looked into her eyes and saw a terror I never hope to see again. I shot him, and I shot the others, too. I got rid of their bodies, took their equipment, and run their horses off. But that didn't end it. She was in such a state that I had to nurse her most of a week. When she came out of it, she said I should have let her die, for no warrior in her tribe would have her and she had no life left to live. I took her home and for most of a year she was like a shadow, workin', sleeping, and wanting to die. But for me it was different. I'd never met a woman as gentle and sweet as she was. I fell in love with her, but she wouldn't believe that. She thought I was being kind. It took me another six months to convince her that just wasn't so. Then the worst came—when I tried to love her and she couldn't. Then I was sure she was going to do what some of them have done, will herself to die. I argued, battled, and tried everything in the book from begging to threatening. I never thought of what happened."

"What?"

"I got sick," Long laughed.

"You what?"

"I got sick, near to dying. I think that's what made her understand what there was between us. Besides, I don't know to this day what I said when I was out of my head. Anyway, I'd been on my feet for a week or so, feelin' pretty good, and that night she came to me. I guess that's about the closest to heaven I'm ever gonna get. Anyway, she's given me two of the greatest sons a man could have and been a wife any man would die to have. I'm happy, but unless you're ready to cut off all the past you have, then don't try it. Because there isn't any other world you can stand in. Not hers, not yours, nobody's, because neither side understands. Maybe one day they will. I hope, at least, by the time my boys are grown. But I'm teaching them to walk alone."

"I don't have the answers, Long. I'm grateful you told me this, but I still want Small Fawn. I just don't know if I'm man enough to do what you've done. I have parents and a sister that I love, too. I don't know if I can break that apart. I have a career I worked hard to get. I have to understand me first, I guess, before I can try to understand what you already know."

271

"Just remember it's a one-time decision. You can't go back. Make sure, David, because you'll end up hating her if you make a mistake now."

"Long, I want to go see her. I guess I better leave in the morning. It's time she and I had a serious talk."

"What about what other whites do?" Long questioned gently. "Keep her out here in the wilderness, see her when you can, and when it's time to leave, go and forget about her."

"Maybe," David said softly, "if I didn't love her I could, but I do. I'd rather leave her now than hurt her like that."

"I thought you might say that," Long smiled. "I'll ride as far as Black Kettle's village with you. I haven't seen the old bear in a long time."

"I'll leave in the morning."

Long nodded and they walked back to the cabin together. David lay awake a long time that night, seeking answers that never came.

Chapter 24

David and Long planned to ride from the cabin just after daybreak, to the obvious disappointment of both boys. Long stood on the porch with Blue Hawk, one hand on the boy's shoulder.

"Blue Hawk, listen to me. We have talked before of protection and I've told you all the things to do. I want you not only to be very close to the house and your mother, but to protect yourself as well. Watch carefully for intruders." The boy nodded, "I should be back in a little over two days. I will not stay long. I have been away too much and want to be here with you."

"I shall be very careful," Blue Hawk said.

Long kissed Winter Snow soundly, and the three watched them ride away.

The two rode without speaking. Long felt he had given his friend quite enough to think about, and in truth, David was just as glad for the silence. His mind was like a tangled ball of twine. Just when he thought he had a clear strand of thought it led to a knot he couldn't untangle.

He wanted Small Fawn. He wanted to live in the broad and beautiful country and raise the kind of sons Long had. Yet he loved his parents and his sister completely and knew they would never be able to understand. It all led to the same dead

273

end, and to the same desire to see and hold Small Fawn again.

That night they slept early. It was only four in the morning and still dark when they rose and started on their way again.

Noon found them only a mile or so from big Sandy Creek, along the banks of which they would find the village they sought.

As they broke from a stand of trees and started across a wildflower-strewn meadow, Long suddenly drew his horse to a halt. David looked at him in surprise, then turned to let his eyes follow Long's. He sucked in his breath first in surprise then in cold fear. He could feel the sweat pop out on his brow, and his horse sensed his sudden tension and skittered sideways.

"Long?"

"It's Black Kettle's village," Long said, definitely confirming David's worst fears. Several spirals of gray-black smoke rose to the sky. Spirals too dark and too big to be campfires.

There was no need for either to say anymore. They spurred their horses ahead, and when the village came in sight, David uttered a groan of disbelief. Remnants of tepees still smoldered and bodies lay strewn about the village, all unarmed and all proving they had been unprepared for what had happened.

Slowly they moved through the village, finding no sign of life. David looked at every person, afraid each time he would see Small Fawn cold and still on the ground before him. But she was not among the dead they found, and in a few minutes Long found a trail that led away from the village toward the forest.

"A few of them left this way," Long said grimly. "I would say very few, and they were taking wounded with them. There are spots of blood here and there."

"How many would you say, Long?"

"Can't be more than five or six. Chances are they're women and they're trying to hide their tracks."

"If there's only a few women and most of the dead back there are woman and kids, then where are the men?"

"I would say a hunting party left and they were attacked while the men were gone. They haven't returned yet or they would be caring for the dead. Some bastard . . ." Long paused, but David finished the thought.

"Chivington. I'll bet my life on it. Where do you think he's gone?"

"We have to find the trail. He might have circled back and gone to my place."

"Long, you get back to your place fast. I'll follow this trail and see if anyone is still alive. I'll see to the dead, too. You come back when your family's safe."

David was used to giving quick orders. But in this case Long was too afraid for his family to consider arguing.

"The men, if they've gone hunting, will most likely be back by nightfall. I'll get back as fast as I can. David?"

"What?"

"Be careful, and . . . I hope you find Small Fawn alive and well."

"Yeah," David said bleakly, "so do I. If this is Chivington's work, then he's got to pay for it," David said bitterly.

"Where?" Long questioned quietly. "In the white man's court? Forget it, David. Just hope you find her. I'll see you as soon as I can get back."

"Good luck, Long."

They separated, Long riding as fast as his horse could go and praying just as hard. David rode slowly, watching the trail that led into the woods. Step by step he moved forward. Now and again he saw patches of crushed grass where someone had rested. Occasionally he saw a drop or two of blood, and he knew someone had been hurt bad but was still driven by fear. The woods grew thicker, and he dismounted and tied his horse. Then slowly he moved forward on foot.

He paused for a moment to look around him. The trees shielded the forest floor from the sun and it was getting difficult to see the trail he was following.

"David?" The voice was whisper soft, but his heart leapt

275

with the recognition of it. He spun around. She stood behind a tree, her eyes wide with fear and her face tear-streaked. He reached her in a few long strides as she stepped from behind the tree. He caught her to him, so relieved that he could only repeat her name over and over as he rocked her in his arms.

After he could bring his relief into control, he held her a little way from him. "Small Fawn, are you hurt? Can you tell me what happened?"

"I do not know who it was."

"White men?"

"Yes."

"Where were your warriors?"

"Gone to hunt. A herd of buffalo is nearby. They left at dawn, only short hours before . . ."

"I'm so glad to see you safe," he breathed as he again enclosed her in an embrace. She clung to him with a kind of desperation that came from both fear and pain. "How many are with you?"

"My sister, Star, she is badly hurt, and three other women and four children. I did my best to get them to some safety, but I did not know where to go."

"You are very brave, Small Fawn, and I'm proud of you. Where are they?"

She led him to a shallow ravine where the small cluster of women and children huddled together. Beneath a tree, on a blanket, lay a slim and too-silent girl.

David went to her side quickly and knelt beside her. A low moaning whisper flowed through the survivors. Small Fawn was quick to go to them and comfort them, explaining that David was not one of the ones to do a thing such as this. They were quiet but still frightened.

The girl on the blanket looked to David to be nearing death. She lay very still, breathing shallowly. He raised the edge of the blanket that covered her and saw the wound low on her left side. She had bled a great deal. If she was alive, David wasn't sure it was going to be for long.

276

He rose again and stood close, looking down into Small Fawn's tear-filled eyes. She was slim and very small-boned. Her almond eyes were agate-black, as was her long thick hair. Her face was finely chiseled and delicate, with a wide mouth and straight nose. She was exceptionally beautiful, and the girl who lay on the blanket below them was an almost exact copy, for they had been born only minutes apart, Small Fawn being the eldest by less than ten minutes.

"She cannot die, David," Small Fawn said brokenly. "If she does, a part of me will die as well."

"I don't know what I can do, Small Fawn. Have you cleaned the wound well?"

"Yes, but still she sinks."

"Did you take out the bullet?"

"No, I have nothing to do so with, and I was afraid to build a fire or to return to the village for something to work with."

"Well, build a fire now and I will do what I can."

She started to turn away, and he reached to take hold of her arm and draw her to him.

"I love you, Small Fawn, and I am grateful to both my God and to yours that they have kept you safe so that I could tell you so again."

"And I have prayed so for you," she tried to smile. "Oh, David."

"I know," he whispered as he held her. "But you and I will see this thing pass, Small Fawn. One day we will be happy together. I promise you." He kissed her very gently, sensing the terrible shock she had just suffered and the fact that she needed his strength now as she never had before. "Now go and have the women help you get a fire lit. The children need to be fed and cared for before dark. You care for them and I will care for Star. Get some water from the canteen on my horse and get it hot."

She nodded. David knew all of them needed some activity to get them moving and take their minds off the tragedy that they had lived through. He also knew he and Long would have to bury the bodies before they attracted all kinds of predators.

Everyone moved sluggishly in response, but David was satisfied that they moved at all after what they had been through.

The fire hot and the water ready, David finally knelt beside Star and prayed he could save her life.

Long rode with anger and fear lending him strength. He had never pushed a horse beyond endurance before, but this was one time he cared for nothing. If he found the same scene before him that he had left behind, then he cared for nothing else at all. His life would effectively be over. All he could have left would be revenge.

Blue Hawk oiled and polished the rifle that lay across his knees. He smiled again as he thought of his father, the giant of a man who made his life. Again he felt the pride that his father had left him in trust of everything, including his gentle mother. He could not envision anyone in his world who would want to hurt his mother. She was always warm and quick to smile, and she did so much for him.

He thought also of his little brother, so much like his mother that sometimes he couldn't believe it.

He slipped the shells into the rifle, and his mother turned from the fireplace and her cooking to look at him.

"Why do you put the bullets in your rifle, Blue Hawk?"

"Because I will go and care for the horses and I must be armed. Father says this must be."

She nodded. Contradicting Long's words when they concerned their safety or his teaching of his sons was something she had never done. She knew Blue Hawk was at a fragile age when honor and pride meant a great deal. She would not damage either of these, for no one knew better than she how he would need them as he grew up in a world that was

278

changing rapidly.

Blue Hawk left the cabin, pausing for a moment by his brother who sat on the edge of the porch breathing soft notes from his flute.

Blue Hawk couldn't understand why, when he blew into it, it squawked gratingly, but when Small Otter did the same the sounds were very pleasant to the ear. Small Otter said it was because he didn't hear the sounds in his head first, but Blue Hawk couldn't understand that, so he simply let his younger brother be the one to make the music.

Small Otter looked up at Blue Hawk, pausing in mid-note.

"Come and help me feed the horses, and I will let you try my rifle again after supper."

Small Otter nodded, slid the flute in the waistband of his pants, and followed Blue Hawk to the barn. Inside the barn was dim and Blue Hawk stood his rifle in the corner. He and Small Otter picked up a pitchfork and began to lift the hay into the horse's stalls. So engrossed were the boys in their work and the moving about of the horses that they didn't hear the riders who entered the yard.

John Chivington sat on his horse, leading a group of men drunk on the blood and killing they had just left behind. Reason had long been replaced by a kind of insanity, which no longer knew the difference between right or wrong.

"Whose cabin is this?" Chivington demanded.

"Belongs to a man named Longstreet. He ain't no one to tangle with."

"Does he knew it isn't safe out here for a white man?"

"Longstreet gets along with the Indians," another offered. "Fact is, he gets along with most everybody if they just leave him be."

"Gets along with the Indians," Chivington snarled. "You mean he's a slimy Indian lover?"

No one answered. But at that moment the door opened and Winter Snow stepped out on the porch. She froze as dozens of cold eyes seemed to pin her to the door.

279

"A squaw," Chivington breathed in a sneering voice. "A dirty little Indian squaw. Well, maybe Mr. Longstreet needs to be taught a little lesson about takin' in squaws. Go and get her," he ordered.

Winter Snow turned, pushed the door open, and ran inside, but before she could slide the bolt across the door, it was slammed open by two leering men who grabbed her and dragged her back out onto the porch.

Old memories of old terrors made her so frightened she could barely stand. She had been victim to such callous, heartless men before. She saw the intent in their eyes and knew she could never survive it again. Her mouth was dry, and sheer terror made her eyes wide and wild like a doe hunted down for the kill.

"We're going to teach your husband a little lesson about consorting with filth like you." Chivington smiled a deadly smile. "After you boys finish having your fun with her, then burn the house down."

The one man in the group who knew Long licked his dry lips. "Colonel, I just wouldn't hurt her. Long ain't one to be fooled with. He'll take this bad and he'll go on a killin' spree."

"You all afraid of one man?" Chivington snapped at them. "Go on about your business, boys. She's a pretty one; ought to be worth some fun."

The two who held Winter Snow began to pull her back into the house. But before they could cross the threshold, a bullet ricocheted off the wood frame, sending splinters flying and the two men cursing. They all spun about to see Blue Hawk and Small Otter in the doorway of the barn. Blue Hawk had his rifle to his shoulder and was aiming carefully.

"Let my mother go!" he called out.

"Well, well," Chivington smiled, "a couple of little breeds as well. This is even better. We'll teach the white man not to breed with animals and make more breeds. Take her in, boys. We'll take care of these two little half-breed lice."

Again they jerked Winter Snow about and again the rifle

280

barked, and this time it was so close that the realization finally hit them that Blue Hawk was hitting exactly what he was aiming at. Now Chivington was angry and his murderous intent was on two small boys.

Blue Hawk licked his dry lips and prayed to all the gods he had ever heard of that no one would know just how scared he was. He had never even killed an animal, much less a man. He didn't even know if he would be brave enough or capable enough to do it if the need came. He only knew that at this moment the life of his mother and his brother and the trust of his father were in his two small shaking hands.

"Well, boy, you can't take us all, you and that rifle. So you better put it up before someone gets killed, because if you shoot one of my men," Chivington lowered his voice to a deadly sound, "I'll take you and hang you, and your mama can watch. Then I'll hang that little nit beside you. So come on, boy, give it up before you get hurt."

"You let my mother go and get off of my father's land, or I will kill you," Blue Hawk said as firmly as his voice could sound.

"We better put a stop to this right now." Chivington's voice had grown hard. "Get out your guns, boys. Looks like we have to kill a couple little vermin before you can get on with your fun."

Blue Hawk knew he wouldn't stand a chance with all the men facing him, but he could not find it in him to break faith with his father. Resolutely he stood his ground, hoping to kill at least the leader before they killed him.

But the guns never cleared their holsters, because a voice colder and harder than any of them had heard before broke the strain.

"One of you gets his gun out better be ready to die for it." They froze. "Let go of my wife, you filthy scum, before my finger gets itchy." They let Winter Snow go and she ran to her sons, "Now," the voice was level and sent a chill through every man, "just which one of you wants to be first to die?"

281

There was no sign of Long, but Blue Hawk and Small Otter smiled and none of the men doubted Long's voice for a minute.

Their only hope, even though they didn't know it, was that Long knew David would be needing his help and he wanted these men gone as quickly as possible.

"You aren't going to be able to kill us all," Chivington called out.

"Right," Long answered, "but I sure as hell can get you first and that will make me feel pretty good."

"I'm an official of the United States Army!"

"The hell you are! You're a self-made vigilante preying on women and kids, and you make me want to puke. Now clear out of here and make it fast, before I forget how charitable I am. You better be grateful you didn't hurt none of mine or I wouldn't be so easy. Now get!"

The cowardice of all the men behind Chivington made the colonel furious. He would have called Long's bluff and, despite the loss of a few men, he would have taken Long. Then he would have satisfied his blood lust by hanging his sons and destroying his wife and his home to teach him his power. But the men wheeled about and left, and Chivington could do little but follow them.

By the time Long reached Winter Snow, she was weak and shaking. He held her as he watched Blue Hawk and Small Otter approach. That Blue Hawk was still shaken was obvious. But Long smiled and reached to lay his hand on Blue Hawk's shoulder, his oldest son still amazed by the whole thing. "Father, why did they want to hurt our mother? They said they would hang Small Otter and me. Why, Father, why?"

"These things are hard to try to explain to you, Blue Hawk."

"These whites are evil," Blue Hawk stated firmly.

"Not all of them. What of David?"

Blue Hawk was confused. Long knelt before him. "Look, Son, there is good in both white and Indian, just as there is bad in both. You must learn to judge each man by his heart and not by the color of his skin. These men were bad and have hurt your mother's people just as some of your mother's people are bad and have done hurt. It is the way things are."

"But you have told me it is wrong to kill a man, and yet I would have done so. Was I wrong?"

"No. If a snake had threatened to strike at your mother or brother, what would you do?"

"Kill it!"

"Then, in this case, it would have been the same. Do not think on it again, Blue Hawk."

Blue Hawk nodded, but Long was afraid this was going to stick with him for a long time.

"Gather some things together," Long ordered crisply. "We must go and help others who have crossed the path of these same men and were not as fortunate."

They obeyed him and soon they were riding away from the cabin.

Long had no trouble finding David. It was a silent camp, and when everyone was settled, Long took David aside to find out about the events that had happened while he was gone and to explain to his friend the affair he had run across.

"I don't know if Star will live," David said miserably.

"I think it would be wise to make a travois and carry her to the fort."

"With Aaron? Feeling like he does?"

"At least there is a doctor there, and Aaron can't be so ignorant as to let a young girl die because he is too prejudiced to help."

"I'm not too sure."

"Well, we've got to decide. I think it best I help you get ready. Then I'll go hunt down that hunting party and explain what has happened to their village. At least I can try to make them understand those at the fort are not to blame."

"I suppose you're right. But walking into Aaron's hands with this group is going to be some affair."

"We can't let them die, David."

"No, of course we can't. Do you want me to take your

283

boys, too?"

"I think I will take Blue Hawk with me. I feel he needs to talk. He received one hell of a shock when he realized he was actually going to kill someone. He needs to get it out of his system."

"Okay, Long. I'll build the travois tomorrow and we'll head for the fort. Maybe between us we can keep another massacre from happening."

"Yeah . . . maybe."

Chapter 25

David and Long made a makeshift travois and they gently lifted a still-unconscious Star to lay her upon it. It would be a very difficult trip for them all. Long had thought to bring along all the rest of the horses he had. Still, it was not enough for everyone to ride, so they would move slowly and alternate, making sure the weaker children rode the most.

They started toward the fort. Long and Blue Hawk watched them ride away, then the two of them rode back toward the village where they hoped to be able to trace the hunting party without much trouble. What worried Long was what was going to happen when the men rode to the fort after their women and children. Long would have to convince them not to make it look like a war party.

David moved at a snail's pace. He kept one eye on the wounded girl and the other on the rest of the tiring group.

Small Fawn watched David closely, knowing the thought of taking them to the fort was upsetting him. They stopped to rest often and night was upon them before they had traveled far.

He made everyone as comfortable for the night as he could, checking carefully to see if Star were growing weaker. Small Fawn knelt beside her sister, her worry obvious to David who knelt beside her.

"She seems to be resting easier, Small Fawn," he reassured

her with more optimism than he felt.

"I feel as if I should do so much more, yet I am helpless to do anything."

"There is nothing else, Small Fawn, and you need rest too. Come to my blanket and sleep. I'll stay and watch."

"But—"

"No buts, you're exhausted and we have a long trip ahead of us yet. Now get some sleep."

She rose reluctantly and went to his blanket to lie down. She was asleep in minutes.

David remained vigilant through most of the night until one of the other women came to him.

"I will watch now," she said firmly. "If you are to guide us tomorrow, you must have some sleep tonight. Go. I will take care of her."

David was grateful. Everything had happened so fast he had not shared one moment alone with Small Fawn. Even to be beside her for the balance of the night would be enough. They needed time to talk, but this certainly wasn't it. He walked slowly to his blanket and looked down on her. Would it ever be possible for them to share a life together? He stood for a moment, thinking about Long and his family . . . and what he truly wanted.

After a while he lay down beside her and gently pulled her into his arms. Exhaustion held her and she curled into his warmth. After a while he, too, slept.

Aaron had sent out two more patrols but they had come back with as little success as he had. The dawn had seen yet another patrol leave. He wouldn't give up; he couldn't do that and face David to tell him he had given up the search for his sister and left her in the hands of . . . He thought of Zach with renewed anger, and of Tara with renewed fear. He wondered just where the most logical place would be, in Zach's mind, to find a hiding place. He also tried not to face what might be happening to Tara

286

now . . . and what the repercussions were going to be.

Zach had wakened habitually before the first light of dawn. He was surprised to find Tara dressed and seated not too far away from him. It was obvious she had been watching him. It was just as obvious that a barrier had been raised between them that was higher and stronger than anything before. There was silence as he rose and finished making preparations to travel, and he wasn't too sure how to break it.

"Tara, if we don't run across Caleb's trail by midday, this will be over for you. You'll have won without even knowing what it has cost a lot of people."

Tara felt shaky, never quite sure if what he had said about Caleb had been true. Surely if he thought it were so, he wouldn't give up so easily. No, he had some devious plan up his sleeve.

"I don't care if you pretend to trail Caleb forever. All I want is to get back to the fort and find my brother."

He was going to explain again but realized she wasn't listening. "I'll make it easy for you. If I can't get to Caleb's trail by midday, he'll be out of my reach. I'll take you straight to Mule. He's waiting for me. He can take you straight back to the fort. Little Raven and I will keep on Caleb's trail and hope to God we can do something to keep a massacre from happening."

"If you wanted Caleb so badly, you never would have bothered taking me with you. You can travel a lot faster alone. This was just some kind of game of yours. I guess it was some way to hit back for all the times you have been hit. I'm sorry for all the hurts, Zach," she added softly. "But all your hitting out at me isn't going to make it any better."

"You really believe that?"

"Yes, I do."

"Then there's not too much more to say. You still lie to yourself and there's not much I can do about that, either. Come on, let's go."

287

"You're taking me to Mule now?" she asked hopefully.

"No, I'm still tracking until midday."

She clenched her teeth and turned from him. He mounted and rode up beside her. Reluctantly she took his hand and again they were on their way.

Again they rode in strained silence, Tara clinging to her doubts and Zach clinging to his determination. The sun climbed higher and higher, and they rode for what Tara felt would be an endless journey.

Suddenly Zach reined to a halt. It was so sudden that Tara swiveled her head around to look up at him. His eyes were some distance ahead and a half smile of satisfaction touched his mouth. She turned to follow his gaze but saw nothing out of the ordinary.

"What is it? What do you see?"

"Something you obviously don't see yet, but you will."

"What is it?"

"Wagons," he answered shortly.

"Where? I don't see wagons."

"But you do see a thicket, some trees, tangled brush?"

"Yes."

"And behind them are wagons. The very same wagons Caleb took from the fort."

"This is ridiculous! Why would he leave the wagons there?"

"Because, my sweet innocent, it's much easier to move rifles by packhorses to the places he has to take them. He had to leave the fort with wagons, so he took them this far and then left them to pick up after he takes care of the guns."

"I still don't see wagons."

"I don't think you want to. Admitting you're wrong won't be easy for someone as obstinate as you." He kicked his horse into motion, and as they drove closer to the thicket, he moved slower and slower until he assured himself there was nobody about. Obviously Caleb thought the wagons were hidden safely and that Zach was going to be in no position to find them.

They were there! And Tara could not believe her eyes. They

were there as he had said they would be. Zach and Tara walked around each wagon and Tara had no trouble recognizing them.

Zach also covered ground carefully, finding where the packhorses had been loaded and the trail they were using. There was no place in this territory that Zach had not traveled and very few trails whose destination he did not know. He could not pinpoint exactly where Caleb might be meeting whoever was getting the guns, but he had a reasonable idea of places where it could occur. He walked back to Tara, who was still overcome with the truth that the wagons were truly here. She hated to look into Zach's eyes and see the satisfaction there. She heard him move about, then he was again mounted and waiting beside her.

"Where are we going now?"

"To meet Mule. I have to leave you some place safe while I try to stop this trade."

"But you'll lose their trail if you take the time to take me to Mule," she said quickly, surprised that she was reluctant to be separated from him even if it was to promised safety.

"Mule is meeting us at Deep Valley. That's not far from here. I'll be able to take you there and collect Little Raven. We'll finish up finding out where those guns are. With any luck, we might just put an end to it this time."

"And how long am I supposed to stay there? Look at me, Zach. I need clean clothes and a hot bath. I want to wash my hair. For God's sake, I can't go on like this!"

"You'll be all right with Mule. There's water. You can bathe and wash your hair."

"Why can't Mule just take me back?"

"Because I want you there," he stated firmly. "Now, are you riding with me or would you rather be dragged at the end of a rope?"

She recognized the same look in his eyes as she had when he threatened to tie her to the pack horse. It looked wicked enough for her to swallow the words on her lips. She had no way of knowing Zach was just as frustrated and without

289

answers. He could easily let her go and Mule would take her back. He used the threat of the fort being attacked, but the whispering voice in the back of his mind annoyed him with the thought that once he let her go, he would never get her back.

He held out his hand to her and she took it. Her cheeks were pink with her anger and her lips pressed tightly together. But he ignored her anger, satisfied with holding her for now.

The time seemed too short for him when he sighted the entrance to Deep Valley. He rode into it, knowing most likely he had been spotted by now. Neither Little Raven nor Mule would be taken by surprise. He had to prepare himself because he knew Mule would be asking angry questions, and he had no answers he knew Mule would accept or understand.

He was right, and he smiled when he heard a soft whistling call. He reined up and in a few minutes Little Raven stepped out onto the trail.

"The trail is clear behind you." Little Raven spoke to Zach, but the smile in his eyes was for Tara. "You are well?" he questioned.

"Did you think she wouldn't be?" Zach snapped. Little Raven's eyes returned to his brother's, filled with surprise. Zach regretted his words but couldn't recall them. "Where's Mule?"

"Our camp is a short distance from here. Just around the bend in the valley wall," Little Raven replied.

"Is there food? We're both hungry."

"Yes."

"Good. I'll meet you back there." Zach spurred his horse forward and Little Raven watched after him with puzzled eyes.

By the time Tara and Zach rode into the camp, Mule also knew they were there. He had been squatting by the fire, in the process of preparing food. He rose slowly, watching Zach bring his horse to a stop and slide Tara gently to the ground before he dismounted.

Mule's astute gaze assessed Tara carefully. She seemed to be fine and he was relieved. Of course, he hadn't expected Zach to do her any physical harm, but he had half expected a frightened, tearful woman. There'd been a drastic change and Mule knew for certain who was responsible for that. He meant to have a few harsh words with Zach at the first opportunity. At the moment he was worried about how upset Tara was with him.

Tara walked toward him and he smiled a little hesitantly. "You're lookin' fit, girl."

"I'm fine, Mule. A little shaken and puzzled by all this, but really, I'm fine."

"Zach," Mule nodded toward Zach, who knew beyond a doubt Mule was not too happy with him.

Zach dismounted without response. There would be time to talk to Mule when they had an opportunity to be alone.

Little Raven arrived a few minutes behind them and Zach immediately took him aside. Mule watched their quiet conversation and wondered about it, but Tara paid little attention.

Mule sat down near the fire beside Tara. "You really okay, girl?" he asked gently.

"Yes," Tara answered. "Mule, what does Zach think this will gain him? If the whites at the fort hated him before, this kind of thing can only make it worse."

"I know you did all you could for him 'cause I asked you to. I'm gettin' to regret that. I never thought this would happen."

"But it has no point, Mule. He could have moved faster and safer without me. It just isn't logical."

"Wal, maybe it ain't . . . then again, maybe it is."

"I don't understand."

Before Mule could confide his suspicions to Tara, Zach came and sat down across the fire from them. To Tara his expression was closed and one she couldn't understand. But to Mule, who had known him since childhood, a lot of questions found answers. Answers he planned to keep to himself for a time or at least until he was a lot surer of them.

"Where'd Little Raven run off to?" Mule questioned Zach.

"He's gone to check on a couple of things for me. He'll only be gone a day or so."

"What's your plans now?"

Zach's eyes moved to Tara, who was listening for his answer.

"I have to leave in the morning. I'll find where this transfer is taking place. If I know who is involved, I can take the words to my father. Between us, we can see that those rifles are never used for anything but peaceful purposes. If we can control their use, then Caleb will be helpless. I have to know who all involved are."

"It would serve Caleb right if those guns found some good instead of what he plans," Mule added.

"I still can't believe this is Caleb's purpose," Tara protested. "He is a trader, that is how he lives. Is it wrong to trade guns for other things?"

"It's wrong if he expects people to kill and be killed by them," Zach replied.

"But you're not sure of that."

"What does it take to convince you?" Zach's anger was swift and cold, and Mule was speechless in the face of something he had not seen before. "You want to see the fort burnt to the ground, your brother and all his friends dead, and my father and his people shoulder the blame before you'll turn your trusting little girl's eyes on him and see him for what he really is? Do you want your brother's blood on your hands before you can look at your fancy gentleman and realize he would even shed your blood if it pleased him? Where will your ignorance carry you?"

Tara was tired and tears she tried to contain sprang to her eyes, but matching anger sprang just as rapidly to her defense.

"Obviously my ignorance of people and my trust in them has dragged me through the wilderness like a packhorse, with no care for me in any way. I should never have been so ignorant and trusting as to think you have one ounce of feeling for anyone else but yourself and whatever it is you want. Believe me, I've learned. You'll never find me so trusting

292

again. Trusting you, you damn savage, has brought nothing but misery."

She spun away from the fire and ran into the comforting darkness. Zach wanted to follow her—he even stood up—his emotions were more than easy for Mule to read. But Zach was sure it was better for Tara to never know the depth of feelings he could not handle himself. Slowly he sat back down, trying to control a surprising hurt and to keep Mule from knowing. Zach turned his gaze to Mule.

"'Pears to me," Mule said casually, "that ignorance must be catching."

"I'm too tired for puzzles, Mule. What's that supposed to mean?"

"Means you shore must have caught yourself a good dose of it."

"If you're talking about Tara, I took her from the fort for her own good," Zach protested, but his eyes reverted to the stick he held in his hand as he studiously poked the fire into new life.

"Her own good," Mule repeated. "You mean she's been treated good and been more comfortable with you, and her reputation with the ladies at the fort is in real good shape?"

"If I don't stop what's happening, they are sure to hit the fort. There's enough warriors to wipe the fort out. You remember how easy it was for Little Raven to get in and out. How many other young braves would do the same, and how many do you think it would take one dark night to get the gates open from the inside? If she was there, Mule . . ."

"If she was there, you wouldn't be able to protect her."

"No."

"And the only reason you took her with you was to keep her safe. This is kinda new, Zach. I ain't ever seen you lie to yourself, and you sure as hell ain't never lied to me before."

"Stop it, Mule."

"I think you're scared for the first time in your life."

"Scared of what?"

293

"Scared of lettin' somebody close again, scared of seeing something in her eyes you've seen before."

"It's there, Mule. To her I'm a half-breed savage. You just heard her say so. You don't think our little eastern lady is going to look at me any other way, do you? No, Mule, it's better this way."

"You're in love with the girl, Zach boy," Mule said softly. "And you're makin' the fool mistake of makin' up her mind for her. Cause she called you a name or two. But she was mad. Back at the fort, though, it was her come through for you every time."

"It's no good for me to think things like that, Mule. Tara's not for me. She doesn't see . . . No, it's best that we keep it the way it is."

"You just ain't gonna give her a fair chance, are you? She's different from you and she don't know or understand our ways. But that don't mean she's not a sweet, loving woman who'd not really be lookin' at what you are but who you are. I wonder if you ever understood your ma, either. She was an eastern lady. Your pa was more to her than anything." Mule narrowed his eyes at Zach and smiled a thin-lipped smile. "Zach boy, you ain't just a little bit jealous too, are you?"

"Don't be a fool, Mule. Caleb is going to end up too busy running," Zach said, the irritation deep in his voice that Mule had struck a sensitive point. "I'm going to catch him with this one, and he'll be a toss-up between the soldiers at the fort and my father's village, not to mention the warriors he's made such fancy promises to."

"So that's going to take care of Caleb, all right. Now what about that girl?"

"You're going to take her back to the fort in a few days."

"A few days?"

"By that time I should have Caleb cornered."

"And you'll walk away just like that? Can you do it, Zach?" Mule asked quietly.

"Are we back to that again? I'm not my father, Mule, and

294

she's not like my mother! She's the kind that needs . . . I'm not sure what she needs, but she's made it pretty clear it isn't me."

"Oh? You asked her?"

"Hell no. I didn't have to ask her." Zach's voice was sharp with disgust. He stood up and his eyes were blue ice. "And you stay out of this. She's going back when it's safe and that ends that." He threw down the stick and stalked away. For a few minutes Mule gazed after him. Then his frown turned into a smile. He wondered just how easy it was going to be for Zach to walk away this time.

Zach moved away from the fire, making sure it was in the opposite direction from the one Tara had taken. After Mule's nudge to his rigid control, he didn't need Tara to awaken his senses again. One battle at a time was enough to handle and he was fighting his own self hard enough.

He stood with his back to the rough stone of the valley wall and looked up at the brilliant stars in a black sky.

Until he had met Tara Montgomery, his life had been his own. He had known what he was and had been able to live with it. He had also known he had been just in what he was doing. She had made herself a part of his life somehow and he couldn't push her out of it. She had done what no other woman had ever been able to do, and now she would walk out of it and leave him with a scar he wasn't too sure would heal. He could not let Mule or anyone else see how vulnerable he was, and he couldn't let Tara see it, either. She had the opportunity to hurt and he wasn't going to let her use it.

He could not lie to himself now. He knew he had taken Tara with him for a much deeper reason than he had admitted to Mule.

He couldn't hold her, and he couldn't let her go. He wanted her and he knew she didn't want him. Oh yes, he could awaken her body, but he couldn't awaken her mind and her heart. When she looked at him she didn't see the man, she saw the mixture of tainted blood. She saw a man that didn't belong in either world, especially hers.

Maybe in some angry way, he had wanted to hurt her, too. He had wanted her to taste what he had tasted so often.

Now he tasted the most bitter thing of all. She had stood beneath all he had done and been more of a woman than he had ever had. He had struck brutally every time she had shown kindness. She had been flame and passion in his arms, and from the battle she had come out the victor.

But he would not love her! He could not! It would be the ultimate rejection. He could almost hear her laughter if he professed that he didn't want to return her to the fort; that he wanted to take her, first to his father's people, then to someplace where they would not have to make the choice between Indian and white.

No, he could not tell her. He must finish what had to be done. He must find the answers to all his questions about Caleb and what he had to gain from this, and he must make sure there was no battle between his father's people and the whites at the fort. And after all that, he must give up all thoughts of Tara Montgomery.

But could he? She was here, and his desire for her was so strong he could hardly control it. Was it wrong to taste once again, even if he knew it would be for the last time?

Chapter 26

Tara had stood far enough away from the fire to still hear the murmur of voices but not to define the words. She didn't care. She didn't want to hear any more of anything Zach had to say.

No matter what her feelings were, she knew whatever existed between her and Zach, as far as he was concerned, was just the lustful use of her body and some kind of vengeance against all whites.

She felt sorry for all that must have happened to him to twist him so badly. But she had been stung by it one time too often. Soon she would be returned to the fort and hopefully reunited with her brother. Maybe, with his help, she could erase from her mind the days spent in the wilderness with a coldhearted, uncaring savage. Maybe, in time, they could leave this place and she could put behind her the memory of Zach's deception, of his gentle touch, and of the sweet words that were all part of the game he seemed to enjoy playing with her. It nearly crushed her to face the fact that he had the ability to set her afire. His hatred of Caleb and of all things white was an obsession that drove him to the things he did, and she was just another tool for an opportunist who would use whatever means were at his disposal to have his own way. Hadn't he done so with her? She could still hear the taunt of his voice that destroyed any beauty his touch might have had, could still hear him challenging the defenseless white woman with the fact that his savagery was a power over her.

If he could just forget what others said, if he could stop being hurt by it and let the man in him overcome his own bad memories, maybe he could find some peace and some happiness. She wondered about the woman who might one day make him realize he was not just mixed blood, but a man to love and to be loved.

She sighed, It would never be her. It could never be her. Maybe they had walked down the wrong road too long to turn back now and try to find a meeting ground. She closed her eyes for a moment, remembering the touch of his mouth on hers and the wild response of her body when they were together. It was as if he wove threads of magic about her, rendering her powerless to control her body's need for his.

A soft breeze brushed her skin and she lifted her face to its touch. It was an extraordinarily beautiful night. The prairie grass felt silken against her ankles and even the night sounds were full of a strange, enchanting melody.

Then suddenly she grew still. Without turning around, she sensed his presence. She almost panicked, then reached for self-control.

He'd been watching her for several minutes, feeling her enjoyment of the night, sensing her attraction for this place. She was completely unaware of him, for he had approached with customary quietness. He was glad she didn't know he was there, taking these forbidden moments to impress the memory of her on his mind, for memories would be all he had left.

The moon glazed her skin and made it a glimmering gold, and her hair sparkled almost white in its pale light. He watched her lift her head and close her eyes as if she were savoring the breeze. He heard the deep discontented sigh and was stung again by the uselessness of his wanting her when he could hear her unhappiness at being here. A slow dull ache tore at him, leaving his emotions bloody and retreating from any further hurt. He could not keep her, but he could make her body respond one more time even if she hated him forever. At least he would have that much of her with him always.

He took one more step toward her and knew, from the sudden rigidity of her body, that she not only sensed a presence but knew instinctively who it was. She could deny him with words, but whether she would admit it or not, something volatile existed between them that she could not fight any more than he could.

He felt the desperateness of his desire and the battle it did with reason, but desire won.

His next step took him close behind her, close enough to touch her but he didn't, and she refused to turn around to face him.

"Leave me alone, Zach," she half whispered. "Haven't you done enough to me already? Must you hurt us both even more?"

Tara had coiled her hair and pinned it at the nape of her neck. Zach didn't speak but reached out and took the pin from her hair and let it fall to the curve of her waist.

They both remained silent in a battle of wills, both woven together with spiderweb bonds, unable to reach out toward it.

"You sound scared, Tara." His voice was teasing soft, but she could still hear the thread of challenge beneath the words. It was enough to make her turn to face him.

"No . . . not scared, Zach, but not foolish enough to believe it could ever mean anything to you, and I won't be victim again. You're the one who's afraid, and until you face your own ghosts and stop running, then don't try to put the blame on me."

This was a different Tara, not the girl who had retreated before him but a woman who now met his challenge with one of her own. For a moment it took him by surprise. But the surprise rapidly turned to a new kind of excitement. They stood only inches apart, and in the glow of pale moonlight, Tara could read the excitement mingled with a new touch of respect and a little confusion in his eyes.

299

"And what could it mean to you, Tara? Tell me that you are the courageous white woman who would flaunt her 'step beyond acceptance' to those in the white fort. Lie and say it would mean nothing to you when they rejected you. Tell me you would, or could, live that way. Tell me I didn't hear the words on your lips." He moved close enough that they were almost touching. "You use words you don't even believe to deny what you feel. We both know what can't exist between us . . . but we both also know what does."

Every rational thought she had protested, just as every sense she had responded to the same brilliant surge of desire he had the extraordinary power to ignite within her. She could do battle with words, with her mind, with her logic, but she could not fight the willful power of her own body and its response to him.

"You hear what you want to hear, just as you think and do what you want to do." She responded defensively. "Does it ever matter to you what anyone else feels but yourself? How do you think you know me so well when you've never questioned what I want or think or even feel?"

"I don't need to question. I know what you feel, and you would deny it with your thoughts. I've told you that before. What good does it do to ask, or to guess, when you won't even tell the truth to yourself."

"And it's enough for you, isn't it, Zach?" she said softly. "To live without committing yourself to anything and to expect others to live by your rules."

"Commit myself to what? Whose rules should I accept, those who hate me?"

She suddenly felt the hurt more vividly than before, but she could not reach toward him or she would be lost.

"You are commited to your father's people."

"I don't want senseless murder done."

"Then you are committed to your mother's people also, in a way."

"The only person who seems worried about that is you. Why

300

does it bother you where I stand? You've a white heart, Tara, and you'll always shy away from the fact that I don't."

"You thought this when you took me from the fort, Zach," she replied. "Why then did you bother? You could have just let me face the fate of any other whites."

"I told you it was for your protection. A defense against your own kind as much as mine."

Tara had moved a little away from Zach to lean against the rough stone that formed part of the valley barrier. Zach watched her, wishing she were not what she was, at the same time resisting the thought that it was remotely possible he and Tara could share anything but stolen moments. It would be so much better if he could just walk away from her as he had done so many others, and he cursed his inability to do so and for wanting her as he did.

He moved closer again, drawn almost against his will. He braced one hand against the rock and looked down into the moonlight reflected in her eyes.

"Your kind . . . my kind," Tara said softly. "Where is the difference, Zach?"

"I used to say that when I was a child, Tara. Where am I different? No one ever had the answer, but they clung to the difference. We are the same in all ways but one, and that difference is as large as a mountain." He didn't add that he felt the mountain too big for either of them to cross.

"And so it left you with faith in no one but yourself," Tara murmured softly. "How very lonely." The last words were added in almost an awed whisper, yet they ricocheted within Zach like the hollow clang of a tolling bell. He felt his own vulnerability and the reflex was instinctive. He didn't need her mock understanding, nor did he need her pity. There were only two things he needed: her anger, as a shield, and his possession of her one more time. Maybe then he could put her out of his life and his thoughts. . . . Maybe . . .

He raised his free arm to brace on the other side of her, effectively pinning her against the wall.

301

Their sudden awareness of each other was a time-stopping thing, for it seemed as if everything were held in a breathless silence. Even the night sounds seemed to be stilled. They stared at each other for a moment of suspended time.

She was mesmerized as slowly he bent his head and his mouth hovered unbearably close.

"No, Zach, no," she groaned as if to protect herself from something she feared. What was he doing to her? she thought wildly. Why could she not spit her anger back at him? Why did her body feel as though it were floating away from her, weightless and drifting, unable to regain solid ground?

Almost haltingly, Zach lowered his mouth to cover hers. The shock was so severe it shook them both. Then suddenly his mouth lost its hesitance and blazed with a raw and hungering need. Zach lifted his head and again they gazed at each other. The blue of his eyes deepened with the heat of passion that was gnawing at his heart. Anger had melted into passion, rage had turned to hunger. All battles were held at bay by the white heat of awakened desire.

When he released her lips, both were breathless.

"I'm sure you've know from the very beginning, from the first time we touched, that I went on wanting you. You've become a poison in my blood, and I've tried to stop whatever it is you do. I will not take you by force," he whispered against her hair. "You must tell me no."

Rage had become a raw hunger. And he kissed her again, a brutal kiss as his tongue forced her lips apart and thrust with overwhelming possession. She could not breathe, nor could her mind control her wayward body. It could not seem to concentrate on anything but the sensation that stormed her. She could not find the strength to fight. It was like being tossed into a current she couldn't battle. She was sure of nothing now except that her body raged with a fire she seemed helpless to extinguish. The kiss was angry, yet passionate and filled with tumultuous emotions. He was savage and thorough, seeking her will with destruction in mind.

He was too vital, too overpowering, and she could not think

clearly while his mouth played havoc with hers. Her body, first stiff and unyielding, seemed to suddenly disintegrate beneath the onslaught of passion.

Tara was held pinned against the length of his body and he kissed her savagely. She could feel the fevered pounding of her blood and her legs grew so weak she had to cling to him for support.

He seemed to sense the moment her body surrendered, but the battle continued. She struggled mentally to grasp her body's defenses, but after a while a soft whimpering sound told of her failure. She felt all protest slipping away, to be replaced by a wild and explosive warmth that seemed to uncoil within her.

Zach could only think of the miracle that seemed to occur when he held her. He knew her body yielded, but would Tara ever yield? Would she ever once come willingly to him? He could not let her go, yet he tasted some defeat as well as she. Again he would touch her senses, but would the maddeningly unpredictable Tara ever truly yield to him?

When she was in his arms like this, her mouth opening under his, her body arching to press closer to him, she drove every other rational thought from his mind. It was easy to lose sight of their battle and its causes when she filled his senses to capacity. He could do nothing more than take her and lift them both to the magical plain of forgetfulness, where they did not have differences, where only the brilliance of their blending was truth.

His hot mouth found the rapid pulse at the base of her throat, eliciting a sound from the depths of her, a sound of almost agony as he seared her flesh.

His hands moved over her body, releasing clothes and seeking soft warmth. They teased and aroused her senses until she trembled in his arms, desiring release from the fiery furnace. She whimpered against his flesh, craving more and more of this delicious and maddening desire.

Now he began to move slower, taking his time, playing with her, teasing her with hands and mouth until she was twisting and turning against him, her world filled now with nothing but him and the virulent pulsing need.

His teeth nipped her flesh, then he caressed with his tongue until she wanted to scream at the ecstatic torment.

Everything, every thought, every breath was completely mixed up. He drew her down to the soft sweet-scented grass and continued to torment her until she was trembling in primitive need. Gently he caressed her thighs, separating her legs. His lips gently stroked her flesh, seeking until they found the moist pulsing center of her sensual being, then his tongue was a hot piercing sword that sliced her soul and sent her senses screaming for release. He was fierce and possessive, and hands that wanted to push him away drew him closer. When she felt she could stand no more, when she stood on the edge of oblivion, the torment ceased—but only for a moment. Then the heat of flesh touched flesh as he melded their bodies together. She was beyond him, soaring in unrestrained passion, oblivious to all but him. But Zach wasn't going to hurry. This just might be the final time he could touch her, and he wanted the memory of it to be strong enough to carry him. He eased her frantic movements to slow smooth ones that matched his, trying to prolong the pleasure for both of them.

The spasms hit them simultaneously, making both dizzy, and wave after wave of heady completion consumed them. Enveloped in a haze of ecstasy, they could only hold each other, trembling and silent.

Her cheek against his bare shoulder, Zach could feel her tears, and the knowledge was so very bitter. Again he had conquered her body but again he had failed to reach the elusive Tara, and it hurt much more than he had ever bargained for. He moved to lie beside her, still holding her and knowing when he let her go this time, he would not be able to hold her again. She had defeated him with her passionate response and her tears in a way he had never been defeated before.

What would he read in her eyes when their gazes finally met? Ancient defenses rose in Zach, matching those that were silently being built by Tara. She could not let him have the satisfaction of knowing how she truly felt. He would only be smug and self-satisfied that he could tame her body at his will.

When their eyes finally met, bridges built by passion had been deliberately destroyed and one of them stood on each side of a raging river of misunderstanding.

Tara stood up, turning her head from him. He wanted to draw her back into his arms, to hold her and tell her . . . The thought brought a new surge of self-flagellation. She did not want to hear sweet words or comforting words from him. Tara felt as helplessly betrayed by her emotions, knowing that her body's subjugation was enough for him. If he would only say one word of love, of caring at all, maybe it would not be so hard, she thought miserably.

Words, desperately needed by both, were frozen to soundless pain. Tara stood to retrieve her dress and slip it over her head. She gathered the rest of her clothes, no longer caring about their condition.

Zach was watching her walk out of his life and could hardly control the desire to beg her to stay, to let him love her even if she didn't love him. But again the age-old bitterness prevailed. He could not beg because he knew he could break under her refusal. He couldn't stand to hear the cold disdain on her lips.

She stood, washed in golden moonlight, a vision he knew he would never forget. Finally she turned to him. Her voice was whisper soft, almost too soft to hear.

"Let me go, Zach, please, before you destroy me. . . .Let me go."

She ran back toward the campfire and Zach was left with the sharp taste of the ashes of their passion. He bent his knees and folded his arms across them, then rested his head on his arms. He was torn to shreds and had never felt so totally devastated in his life.

Tara returned to the fire, which now was only red embers. She was glad the fire was low, so that if Mule should waken, he would not see her tears. She rolled in her blankets, burying her face in the folds to allow the hot tears to flow. She muffled her choking sobs with the blanket.

But Mule wasn't asleep, and both Tara and Zach would have been surprised to know he was less upset over what was happening than they were. He knew they had reached the most difficult time, but Mule was sure he knew Zach better than Zach knew himself. He was having his first brush with love and found it hard to recognize. But Mule was sure one day he would, and when he did, Tara would never be allowed to get away from him.

"Iffen that boy don't tear himself apart, he's gonna wake up one day soon. When he does, I shore want to be around to see the fireworks." Satisfied with this thought, Mule rolled over and earnestly sought sleep.

Mule came awake long before dawn, when Zach knelt beside him and shook his shoulder slightly. He sat up silently. "What's wrong?" he questioned in a low whisper.

"Nothing. I have to go for a while," Zach whispered.

"I'll take Tara back to the fort tomorrow," Mule said in a half question, half statement.

"No. You stay here until I get back. Make sure she's all right but stay here. Do you understand?" Zach's voice was low and harsh.

"Shore I understand," Mule said peevishly. "I ain't six. Why you still keepin' her here?"

"Mule, do as I say. It's important. I have to know she's safe."

Mule could hardly make out Zach in the darkness. "Why?" he asked softly. For a long time Zach was silent, then his voice was even softer.

"Just take care of her, Mule," he said quietly.

He rose, and like a shadow he was gone, blending with the night. Again Mule smiled as he lay down and returned to a more comfortable sleep.

*   *   *

When Tara awoke it was to the sound of Mule moving about and preparing some breakfast. The sun was already warming the air, and she threw the blanket aside and sat up.

"Morning, Tara."

"Good morning, Mule," she answered him, but he was amused to see her eyes scan the area quickly and he knew who she sought.

"He ain't here. Rode out before dawn," Mule said, pretending to give all his attention to the food he was preparing and not noticing the flush on her cheeks.

"Rode out where?"

"Don't know. But if I was to guess, I'd say he has a pretty good idea where Caleb is meeting to trade the rifles. He wants to catch 'em at it and see who Caleb's tradin' 'em to."

"You really think Caleb's guilty too, don't you, Mule?"

"Shore do."

"Mule . . ."

Mule turned to Tara, "Come on over here and eat some vittles, girl. You and me can just sit down and have ourselves a nice long talk until Zach gets back. Yessir, I think you and me got a lot of things to say to each other."

Tara looked intently into Mule's kind, smiling eyes. Then she rose and walked toward the fire. She knelt down close to Mule and they smiled at each other.

Mule took a plate, put some food on it, and handed it to her. There was something expectant growing in Tara. Mule had answers about Zach that no one else seemed to have and right now, in her unsettled state of mind, answers to Zach's puzzling personality were what she needed most.

Tara returned to her blanket and Mule came to sit down beside her.

"Eat, girl. If I know Zach, it will be a couple of days until he gets back. We can do a whole lot of talkin'."

Tara nodded and ate obediently. Right now she wanted Mule's friendship more than she had ever wanted anything in her life.

Chapter 27

Long and Blue Hawk rode in silence for some time. Long knew his son was mentally searching for the answers to the questions that plagued him. It was hard to tell Blue Hawk that man had been searching for such answers for as long as he existed. Who could tell what it was that made men so different from each other or how you were to choose between what was right and what was wrong?

Blue Hawk was also still disturbed, not only by his close brush with the loss of his family and his own death, but also with the knowledge that the same murderous thing existed within him. He had come very close to killing a man and his young mind found this a fearful experience.

What bothered Long at all was the fact that his eldest son had always looked to him for answers and they might be reaching the time when Blue Hawk realized his father did not always have all the answers. Blue Hawk was stepping from boy to man and Long wanted to make the transition as easy as he possibly could.

"Something troubles your mind, Blue Hawk?" Long asked quietly. For a time Blue Hawk didn't answer, and Long waited patiently for him to find the words he struggled for.

"I—I was afraid, my father," Blue Hawk said in a half whisper.

"And you think that is something for which you should feel shame?"

"Is it not?" The dark questioning eyes snapped to his. "You are never afraid. Am I a coward?"

"I have been afraid many times in my life, Blue Hawk. A man who is not afraid of danger is a fool. You are not a coward, for even though you were afraid, you faced the danger anyway, to protect others. I am proud of your bravery. No, a coward would have run from the danger you faced."

Blue Hawk's eyes were filled with surprise and awe.

"This is true, Father, that you have been afraid?" Blue Hawk found this very hard to believe.

"So many times I can hardly count them," Long laughed softly. "Do you remember the time we tracked the grizzly?"

"Yes, he was wounded and you said we must kill him so he would not suffer."

"But he found us first."

"Yes."

"I was so terrified I couldn't even swallow my own spit. But I knew if he got me, he would get you too. I had to stand my ground—or lose you. You see, it has nothing to do with fear."

"But I wanted to kill."

"There's a lot of difference between wanting to kill and trying to protect. Wanting to kill for the sake of killing makes you an animal. Protecting, out of love, makes you a man."

Blue Hawk contemplated these words in a deep, thoughtful silence. "Then this white man was wrong, but it does not make all white men so."

"Now you have the idea. You just have to be careful that you look at a man carefully before you make decisions about him, no matter if he's white or red."

"When we find Black Kettle, he will be angry at all whites and try to fight them for what they have done."

"I have to explain who was the cause and why. Black Kettle has been friendly with those at the fort. He will listen and judge before he does anything."

Blue Hawk sighed, "I will be glad to go home and stay away from all the others."

"Amen," Long chuckled. "We must keep our eyes open for Black Kettle and his men. I don't want them getting back to the village before we find them. They should be told before they must face the shock."

Long could tell Blue Hawk was much relieved, and he left the boy to his own thoughts as he returned to his and to the matter of finding the hunting party.

But the day was waning rapidly by the time they did. Of course, Long knew he had been seen and recognized long before he had seen them, and that he only found them because they chose to let him.

They were met by three wary warriors, but Long and Blue Hawk knew the others were close enough to watch.

"I must speak with Black Kettle at once," Long informed them as soon as they questioned his presence.

They were silent, reading his face carefully. Only when they felt satisfied did they motion for him to follow.

Once they had joined the hunting group, Long sat before Black Kettle ready to explain to him what had occurred.

Black Kettle was not a large man, but the intense depth of his dark eyes made Long feel as if he were. It was lined with experience, harsh yet kind, strong yet open of mind.

"You seek me, Longstreet? Why is this?"

"I have words for you, Black Kettle. Words that will cause anger and pain. I ask you to listen before you allow yourself to feel."

Black Kettle's lips compressed as his eyes narrowed, and after a minute he nodded. There was not a sound from the men around him. Long felt the volatile silence, took a deep breath, and began to explain what had been found in his village. There was a low murmur among the men as Long ended, but they did not voice words. Long realized the respect they held for their leader. Despite the pain and uncertainty each man was feeling, he would not react until his leader commanded.

310

"This is not all you have to say to us," Black Kettle said coldly. "The terrible deed your people have done."

"Not my people, Black Kettle, only my race. And you are right. I have more to say." Long went on to explain what David and he had decided to do, and where the women and children were now.

"I know the soldier, David Montgomery," Black Kettle replied. "He has visited our village often."

"He urges you also to come to the fort and talk. Aaron, the man who commands the fort, he has no love for your people, but even so he would not have done this. Come, Black Kettle, so there will be no battle. Come and let us see if together we can put a stop to the one who is truly responsible."

Black Kettle was grim, but to Long's relief he nodded. The entire group moved, and Long was hoping that this was the right step; that when they came to the fort an all-out confrontation wouldn't result in a disaster.

David's nerves were taut from the slow pace they had to move because Star still remained unconscious and clinging to life. They seemed forced to rest more often than to move, and Small Fawn took every opportunity to kneel by her sister and minister what little help she could.

She was more and more frightened as they neared the fort, as were the other women. But David kept them moving on with the promise of a doctor, food, and safety until their men could come for them. He prayed he was right.

They had made camp for this last time before they would reach the fort. Everyone slept but David and Small Fawn.

David sat beneath a tree with his back to it, and Small Fawn sat between his legs and lay against his chest. He stroked her hair gently, and for these brief peaceful moments they tried to pretend their world was safe.

"Stop worrying, Small Fawn," David said gently. "You will be safe at the fort until Long can find your men. The doctor is

311

what Star needs right now."

"How long before we are there?"

"At the rate we must move, it will be tomorrow by midday unless a patrol were to find us sooner."

"How long do you think it will be before your friend can arrive with our warriors?"

"He can move much faster than we can, so I imagine it will not be many hours after we get there that Long will come."

Small Fawn turned in his arms and looked up into his face, "Oh, David, I'm so frightened."

David drew her up against him and held her close. "I know, Small Fawn, I know. But you just have to have faith in me this time. I swear I'm not going to let anything more happen to you or Star."

"I do trust you, David, as all in my village have learned to do. But your chief . . . it is known he has hatred for us."

"Maybe he does. Small Fawn, there is something in his past that has made him angry toward your people. Still, he wouldn't harm the women and children. He is not a brutal man. Can you understand the difference?"

She was struggling to do so, and David could see the battle against doubt and fear as it waged with the love and trust she had for him.

It had been a long time since they had been together. David, out of consideration for the shock she had suffered, had restrained his desire to engulf her in his arms and make love to her, waiting until she could forget her fear and concentrate on only how much he loved her.

"It is so hard for you, David. If you were to choose another woman, one of your own kind . . ."

His fingers stopped her words as they pressed gently against her lips.

"I want no other woman than you. I cannot set you free, for it would be separating myself into parts that cannot exist so. I love you. I have loved you, I think, from the moment we first met. Is it—is it that you would be free of me?"

312

"Oh, David, no! You are all that is good in my life."

He watched tears form in her eyes and regretted his words. He looked around the quiet night-shrouded camp quickly. Everyone slept, and they were far enough away from the group to be reasonably isolated. Again he looked down into her eyes, searching for any sign that he would upset her with the desire he was controlling with effort.

Placing his hands on each side of her face, he lifted her lips to his, telling her with the depth of his kiss that his need for her was a fire that raged through him. Their lips clung as he slid his arms about her, and in a blaze of happiness, he felt her cling to him, moving her body against his and holding him in her deepest embrace.

"I want you," he whispered against her silky hair. "God, how I want you."

Her eyes held his. "No more than I want you."

His heart leapt with the pleasure of their mutual desire, and Small Fawn rose to her knees. He watched as she began, with trembling fingers, to loosen her tunic. She let it drop and knelt before him, proud of what she saw in his eyes and the love written on his face. He reached toward her slowly, his hands brushing gently over one rounded rose-tipped breast, then continuing down her slender waist to rest on her hip for just a moment. Then, with a little pressure, he drew her again into his arms and his hungry mouth possessed hers. He felt the unleashed passion explode within him as her mouth opened under his and her hands gripped him. A soft murmured sound escaped her as he crushed her slender body against his and his hand moved restlessly, caressing her skin.

He drew her down to the soft grass beside him, then slowly, leisurely, as if the whole world had breathlessly stopped for them, he began a gentle and tender capture of Small Fawn. His hands traced seeking patterns across her skin; his warm questing lips followed and brought moaning gasps of delight from her. Her slender fingers, too, sought the feel of his lean muscled body. Eagerly and delightedly they touched, tasted,

313

enjoying the feelings and the sensuous pleasure they were experiencing, building their need for each other higher and higher.

Although he was more experienced than she, he was thrilled by the eagerness and obvious pleasure she found. There was no fear, no timid withdrawal. She met him need for need, touch for touch, until his mind reeled in a whirlpool of passion. Down, down, down they tumbled, into the oblivion of love, to a place where only they existed.

His lips traced gentle kisses along the curve of her throat. He felt her cool fingers touch his face, holding her against him. Her arms around his neck, she drew his mouth to hers again. The sound of their murmured sighs mingled. Her body, cool and soft to the touch of his hands, became warm and alive. She moved to meet his touch as his hands found the soft curves and valleys that made her moan softly in pleasure. The path his hands discovered his lips followed, until he felt her tremble with a need that was rising to match the one that almost consumed him. Quickly he moved away from her for the few minutes it took to discard his clothes. When he returned to her to pull her into his arms again, their bodies surged against each other, demanding and possessive.

His heart filled with joy when he felt the desire in her cause her to lose touch with reality and rise with him to the ultimate summit of ecstasy. There was no retreat, no holding away.

At the height of their passion, when nothing in the world existed but the beauty of the deep violet flame of their love, when her body writhed beneath him and her soft uncontrolled words of love urged him to possess her, when the need for fulfillment could be denied no longer, he lifted her hips to meet his thrusting body and pressed himself deep within her, catching her soft murmured cry with his mouth. Gently he moved her body to match the slow rhythm of his, murmuring her name as he felt her catch the rhythm, cling to him with silken legs, and begin to move with him.

Joyously, they surged together, blending, clinging, feeling

only the need to consume the other, to draw the other within, to hold forever the bright glowing love that rocketed them heavenward to burst among the stars and, like a flaming meteor, to skim the heavens in a blazing beauty that left them tumbling together, holding to each other, and knowing, with a deep and everlasting finality, that two were made one and nothing outside of death would ever separate them again.

He held her against him, cradling her body with gentle arms as he regained control, listening to her ragged breathing and feeling the trembling begin to ease. He had no words to tell her how he felt, of the joy that bubbled within him and of his deep pleasure in knowing that she felt the same.

It was a quiet, peaceful moment that needed no words to embellish it. He knew she had placed all her faith in him and he was warmed by this, but he had to suppress the one-minute tingle of fear that Aaron's reception at the fort would not be the friendliest. After a while, Small Fawn slept in his arms. David pulled a blanket over them both and he too sought sleep. The next morning he was awake early, but Small Fawn was already helping the women make preparations for travel. They moved again slowly, and as David had said, it was mid-afternoon when they sighted the fort. David could see a patrol leaving and riding in his direction.

Aaron was exhausted, as were the men who rode with him. They were returning to the fort after their third attempt to find some trace of where Zach had taken Tara.

As they approached the fort, two riders left it and rode to meet him. His instincts told him something had happened, and it wasn't something he was going to like. He reined in his horse and raised his hand for the men behind him to stop.

"Major Creighton." One of the men spoke almost before he had his horse at a full stop.

"What is it?"

"Lieutenant Montgomery is back, sir. I was told to ride out

and tell you he's brought a whole group of Indian women and kids with him. They been roughed up pretty bad and one of them's shot. Doc's lookin' at her now. Seems they were attacked by a bunch of whites . . . said they were soldiers."

"Whose village?" Aaron snapped.

"Black Kettle, sir."

"Damn! None of our men have been away from this fort except to search for Zach. They must have been scared and made a mistake. It seems easy for them to blame the military soon as anything goes wrong."

"It wasn't them so much as it was Lieutenant Montgomery. He's fired-up mad, and he says it was whites, too."

Aaron could hear the doubt in the soldier's words and knew it came from respect for David. He felt a touch of puzzled uncertainty.

"All right, let's get back to the fort and see what this is all about. Just what I needed, another handful of trouble."

They spurred their horses forward and fifteen minutes later rode through the gates of the fort. When Aaron dismounted before his quarters, David stood on the porch ready to meet him. David saluted and Aaron responded. "Come into my office, Lieutenant Montgomery," Aaron said as he moved past David. "We have a hell of a lot to talk about."

David was surprised by Aaron's brusqueness, but there was a lot he had to explain to the major, too, so he silently followed him inside.

Aaron left his office door open for David, who closed it after himself when he came in. He watched as Aaron took a bottle of whiskey from his top drawer and poured two liberal drinks. He slid one toward David who accepted it, a twitch in the back of his mind telling him something was very definitely wrong.

Both men drank in silence. Then David set his empty glass down. "Aaron, if you're angry about the Indians I brought back with me, I had no choice. It was the kind of situation that required a quick judgment and I made it. Long has gone for the men." He went on to explain all that had happened. "Wounded

316

as badly as Star was, I knew she needed help from our doctor."

"We'll discuss the Indians later. Right now we have another problem."

"Problem? What problem?"

"While you were gone, your sister arrived here from the East."

"Tara! What's she doing here? Did she come alone? I don't understand. My parents would never have . . ." He stopped as Aaron's face grew even grimmer. There was a hollow spot in the pit of his stomach and a premonition made his hands shake. "My parents?"

"I'm afraid it's bad news, David. They're both dead. Some kind of accident."

David's face was pale and he stood in an agony of silence, trying to fight the tears that had sprung to his eyes: Aaron silently poured another drink and David swallowed it, hardly knowing what he was doing. Then he sank weakly into a nearby chair.

"There's a lot of letters in your quarters and I'm sure the details are there. I only know what Tara has told us."

"Tara," David whispered. "God, I can't believe it. Where is she? I have to talk to her. It must have been terrible for her to go through that alone, then have to make this trip by herself. I'd better go see her. . . ." Again he was aware of Aaron's silent gaze.

"It's impossible. Tara's not here."

"Not here. Aaron, this is getting beyond my understanding. Suppose you tell me the whole story."

"You remember Zachary Hale?"

"Yes, I know him. He's been here a few times since I was stationed here. He's usually in his father's village. What about him?"

"Someone has been bringing in guns and trying to incite the Indians into an uprising."

"And you think it's Zach?"

"You don't?"

317

"I'd have to have proof. Zach always seemed to want peace out here."

"Let me explain what's been going on and then you tell me if you still have so many doubts." Aaron explained all that had happened from the moment Zach had arrived at the fort with the wagon train and Tara. When he told him of finding Little Raven and Zach with some guns and the subsequent arrest, David was already becoming suspicious.

He was prepared to hear of Zach's escape but he wasn't prepared to hear that Tara had been abducted and taken with him. When Aaron finished, David rose from his chair.

"We won't stop searching until we find them, David, that I promise you."

"I want to go with the next patrol," David said quietly.

"Of course."

David turned away. Then he turned to look back at Aaron. "What are we going to do for Black Kettle and his people? They'll need some help."

"I can't run a mission for these people, David. We don't have enough supplies for that."

"At least you can help these women and kids until their men come for them."

"I suppose," Aaron said reluctantly. "I can't just let them die. But what if their men cause a problem when they get here?"

"They won't."

"You guarantee that?"

"Yes, I will."

"Sounds like you know these people pretty well."

"I do. I've spent some time with them off and on. Come over to the doctor's with me and see what some of our white companions have done."

"No worse than they have done as well," Aaron said bitterly.

"Two wrongs don't make anything right. We can't just keep on killing each other. Somewhere it's got to stop. Will you come?"

Aaron sighed and stood up, reluctant to go but unable to justify not going. They walked across the compound to the doctor's quarters.

Dr. Morgan had treated Star and left her, in a hospital cot, under Small Fawn's care. He was seated at his desk when Aaron and David walked in.

"You have an Indian girl here?" Aaron asked bluntly.

"Yes."

"How is she?" David questioned.

"Holding her own. She's weak and has lost a lot of blood, but I think she's going to make it."

"Can I see her?" David replied.

"Sure, go on in."

Star and Small Fawn were close together, and as David and Aaron approached, Small Fawn looked up. She was frightened at Aaron's dark look but reassured by David's.

Aaron, holding his bitter hatred of the Indians as a shield, hardly looked at Small Fawn. His eyes were caught by the girl who lay silent and so fragile looking on the cot. He found his breath caught at the absolute beauty he had not expected.

He felt a wrenching jolt to his senses and a sudden unbidden anger at the man who could have done this. All Indians to him had been brutal savages. He had not been prepared to think of them any other way. But what he saw before him shattered his equilibrium, and Aaron found he could not drag his eyes from her beautiful and so-helpless form.

Chapter 28

Zach moved slowly but with a new kind of precision. He now had a reasonably good idea where the meeting place might be. He had covered many miles by midday and stopped for a while to make sure his horse would have no problems.

He had to keep a close watch to make sure there were no sentries and to make sure no one traveled forbidden trails. It made the going slow, but he was still on the right track.

He refused to let Tara walk into his mind, keeping rigid control. For now she was safe with Mule. What was going to happen later was something he wasn't sure of. Reasons were something he had no intention of looking straight in the eye. He was afraid of what he might see.

When it was nearing dusk, Zach was walking and leading his horse. He knew the meeting place must be near. If his memory was as good as he thought, there was a narrow valley just ahead. Protected on three sides by high rugged walls, it was the safest place of all.

After a while he secured his horse and began to move on foot. He found a rough ledge—one that gave him a good view of the valley—and in minutes his judgment was proven right. In the dying light he could see the flicker of campfires.

He was right, but he had to make sure that the rifles and Caleb were both in the same place. It wouldn't do him much good if he found the rifles and couldn't put the betrayers with them.

He returned to his horse, unsaddled him, and found a place of concealment. He would wait for day and the chance to finally put Caleb and the rifles together with whoever was coming from his father's village to collect them.

Zach hoped Little Raven was successful in the job he had sent him to do. If he was, it would give him time—and time was precious now.

After a struggle, Zach finally slept. But it only lasted a few short hours. He was up long before the dark night sky began to turn gray.

Again he returned to his vantage point and surveyed the camp below him. Men were moving about and he could clearly pick out the packs of rifles, but he saw no sign of Caleb. It might prove to be tedious, but he meant to wait, sure that Caleb would be coming soon.

Little Raven had ridden most of the night, pleased with the mission he was on. He carried out the first of Zach's requests as soon as he arrived. His parents were wakened with his entrance. Both rose immediately and the fire was stirred to life.

"You have been traveling long hours, Little Raven," his mother stated as she gazed intently at his face. "Is there some problem?"

"No, Mother, I came quickly because Windwalker has sent me. There is something he wants me to bring back to him."

"What is so important that you rode most of the night?"

"I will explain what he wants, but first I must take care of something else. Would you make some food for me, Mother? I must hurry. There is no time to waste."

He was halfway out the door as he spoke, and Singing Grass and Waiting Wolf exchanged a look of exasperated tolerance. Whatever errand Windwalker had sent Little Raven on would be done, so they knew patience was their only response.

Little Raven made his way to the tepees of friend after friend, all the young men he knew Tall Bull was trying to convince to follow him. He spoke the same words, made the same request, and urged with the same persistence until each gave the answer he wanted. Satisfied, he returned to his parents' tepee to sit cross-legged before their fire and eat. As usual, his appetite was enormous and it was some time before he finished.

"Now, my son," Waiting Wolf laughed, "do you think you have the strength to tell us just what it is that Windwalker requires of us?"

"It is a request for Mother." Both were again surprised, but they listened as Little Raven smiled and bent slightly toward his mother when he spoke the words Windwalker had told him to, plus a few of his own that he hoped his brother would understand the motives for one day.

"Windwalker sends for a dress."

"A dress?" Singing Grass repeated blankly. This was the last request she expected.

"A very special dress, Mother. One he gave to you to keep for him a long time ago. The dress in which his mother was married."

Waiting Wolf remembered the dress well, the memories lighting his eyes for a moment being brought under quick control. He loved Singing Grass now and would not let a ghost from the past injure that.

"He wants the wedding dress of his mother. Does he now choose a woman to marry?"

The direct question found Little Raven floundering for something that was not a direct lie. "He has a woman with him that he seeks the dress for. I am sure he will bring her here one day soon."

Singing Grass would have asked a million more questions but Little Raven gracefully evaded them by declaring he needed some sleep. He knew the questions would have to be answered but he hoped Windwalker would do it soon.

322

Little Raven slept for only an hour or two. The village was just beginning to start the new day when he left.

As Little Raven rode, the thought finally dawned upon him that Windwalker must have had a great deal of respect for his brother's position among the young warriors. Little Raven had asked them to wait seven days before again considering Tall Bull's words, and they had agreed. Little Raven was suddenly warmed with pleasure. One day he might be chief, and to know that the young warriors respected him enough to listen to the request filled him with enormous pride. This was exactly what Windwalker had planned on doing. Little Raven, knowing Windwalker was the eldest son, was ready to step aside and let his brother be chief. In a subtle way, Windwalker had told him that he was the one who would step aside for Little Raven. The intense love he had always felt for his brother grew to momentous depths. He rested his hand on the bundle that was tied to his saddle and his smile grew broader.

He traveled with the same mile-eating, methodical speed, hoping to reach Mule's camp at least by the next day's dawn.

Of course he would stop to eat and rest his horse, and he was grateful to his mother for the amount of food she had supplied. She knew he wouldn't want to stop long enough to hunt and cook his own.

He rested the horse only as long as was absolutely necessary. He wanted to get to the valley camp as fast as he possibly could. He wanted to see the look on Tara's face when he presented her with Windwalker's gift.

He turned his mind to the situation between Windwalker and Tara. He had never seen his brother so blinded by things that he could not react with careful thought. Little Raven liked Tara very much and wished whatever existed like a wall between her and his brother could be washed away. But at this moment they seemed to be at war with each other, and he couldn't supply answers that might change things. He thought also of Mule, who seemed amused by the whole thing. He decided, at the first opportunity, he would question Mule and hear his thoughts on the matter.

Both Tara and Mule were lying by the nearly dead fire when Little Raven rode into the valley. Mule, constantly alert, was on his feet, rifle in hand, when Little Raven approached. Tara sat up, sleepy-eyed and tousle-haired. Little Raven was quite taken by how pretty she was. If it had not involved his brother and, he thought in amusement, he were just a wee bit older, he would make any man fight to keep her. Again he couldn't believe that the thoughts in his brother's mind were not of keeping this beautiful white woman for his own.

Tara heard the approaching horse and her mind leapt instantly to the explosive hope that Zach had returned. She was still too unaware to analyze her reaction and the disappointment when she found it was Little Raven.

"Little Raven, where in tarnation have you been running off to? That brother of yours can hold more secrets than any ten men, and you ain't no better."

Little Raven laughed as he slid from his horse. Taking the bundle with him, he strode toward the fire.

"Windwalker sent me home to bring some things for Tara."

"For me?" Tara said in surprise. "Whatever could you get from your village for me?"

Mule had become silent, his narrowed eyes watching Little Raven walk to Tara. He had a sudden thought that the bundle Little Raven carried was going to mean more than Tara would realize. He moved closer as Little Raven handed the package to Tara.

She looked from one to the other: Little Raven, eyes aglitter with a pleased smile on his face, and Mule whose face had suddenly become closed and unreadable.

Tara sat back down on her blanket and began to untie the leather strips that held the bundle. When she unfolded the buckskin cover she gasped in surprise, then slowly lifted the dress. It was snow-white, the buckskin worked so soft it almost felt like velvet. The skirt, which would come to her ankles, was fringed, as were the sleeves. Fine and colorful beadwork

324

created intricate pictures on back and front. It was the most unusual and beautiful dress that Tara had ever seen. But it meant so much more to the two men who stood watching her pleased face.

Little Raven knew the purpose of such a dress when it was a gift. He did not question his brother's thoughts, even though he did not understand them. He would say nothing to Tara about the dress; any words were for his brother to say.

Mule, having lived among the Indians over thirty years, knew at once the ceremonial white wedding dress. He was at first startled. Zach could come up with one surprise after another. He watched Tara's admiring face as she lifted the dress from the cover and rose to hold it against her.

"Oh, how beautiful," she murmured as she brushed her hand gently over the soft buckskin.

"And you will be beautiful in it," Little Raven replied with a grin. "You will look like one of our own except for your red hair and those green eyes."

"I will braid my hair," Tara laughed softly. "And, for a little while, I will be sister to you, Little Raven. I am going to the stream to bathe and wash my hair. Oh, it will be glorious to feel clean again."

Tara laid the dress over her arm and walked rapidly away toward the small stream. Mule and Little Raven exchanged a look of silent wisdom.

"Sister, huh?" Mule grinned. Little Raven shrugged with the same devilish laughter in his eyes.

"I don't know Windwalker's thoughts. He only asked me to get a dress for Tara."

"And you're the one that chose the kind of dress to get?"

"If my brother's thoughts do not travel so, maybe to see how beautiful Tara will be in the dress might persuade him. Already I think he cares. Maybe he just does not know how much he cares." Little Raven's smile turned to a soft laugh. "She would be a pleasure to have as a sister."

"Oh, I think he cares all right, just like I think he's going to be all-fired mad at you for jumpin' the gun."

"Maybe at first, but after he sees just how beautiful she is, he might forget to be mad at me."

"You hope."

"I surely do," Little Raven chuckled.

"Little Raven, you red devil. One of these days your sense of humor is goin' to get you in a passel of trouble you won't be able to grin yourself out of. I just hope this ain't the time."

"Then you hope, as I do, that Windwalker's blind eyes will open and he'll see what he is in danger of losing?"

"There's a whole lot more of a problem with Zach than just seein'. He ain't blind. He's just about to lose her on purpose."

"I don't understand."

"Wal, sit a spell. I'm gonna do some explainin'."

Tara threw aside her soiled clothes and stepped into the stream. The water felt cool and refreshing. She took her time, enjoying the warmth of the sun and the silky feel of the water as she washed herself.

It felt so good to rid her hair of tangles and she ran her fingers through it carefully, feeling the clean strands whisper through her fingers. Then she separated her hair into two braids while it was still wet. Finally, she stood in the stream and let the warm breeze dry her skin, then she walked to the magnificent dress.

She remembered telling Zach she wanted to bathe and don clean clothes, but she had thought he had unfeelingly ignored her. The dress was beyond anything she had ever expected. The puzzle that was Zachary Hale remained unreadable.

She slipped the garment over her and let it fall, feeling the luxurious touch of it against her skin. She put the belt about her slim waist and tied the beaded leather thongs. She felt so different, as if she had stepped from one world to another.

Slowly she gathered her soiled clothes, promising to wash

them later. In the same bundle with the dress had been a pair of white moccasins beaded with the same intricate design. She slipped her feet into them, finding them a comfortable fit, which again made her a little surprised at Little Raven.

She started to walk back to the camp, unaware that several pairs of malicious, hungry eyes had been lasciviously watching her every move.

When Tara returned to the camp, both Mule and Little Raven were rendered nearly speechless with admiration. She pivoted shyly before them. "Isn't it the most beautiful dress you've ever seen?"

"It is not only the dress that is beautiful, Tara," Little Raven said smoothly. "You are even more so. With your hair like that, you look like one of us. You should truly have an Indian name. What do you think, Mule?"

"You shore are downright pretty, girl. Since you look like a white Indian, you oughta have two names. Maybe me and Little Raven can think up a pretty one."

Tara's cheeks flushed, but she smiled. "I have an Indian name." Both men looked at her now with puzzled expressions. "Zach gave me one." There was a delighted silence as both Little Raven and Mule tried to keep from looking smug and satisfied.

"And what did he call you?" Little Raven was the first to regain his curiosity.

"Autumn Dove," Tara answered hesitantly.

"Autumn Dove. How perfect it is for you with your red hair. I shall call you Autumn Dove from now on," Little Raven answered positively. Tara felt warmed by his sincere wish to be friendly and kind to her. Again she thought of Zach and wished he could be as generous with his feelings as Little Raven was. If Little Raven could accept her so easily, why could Zach not do the same?

Tara gave Mule a questioning look and he smiled. "He's right, Tara. The name sure fits you well."

"Thank you, Mule."

"You need one more thing, Tara," Little Raven said quickly.

"What?"

"Wait." He went to the supply pack he carried rolled at the back of his saddle. He unrolled the blanket and took a strip of beaded leather from it. Than he walked back to Tara and placed it around her forehead, tying it at the back of her head. He stood back to examine her again. He smiled and nodded, "Now you are one of us."

Tara felt a lump constricting her breath. Zach had told her she didn't belong, that she could never be a part of them because she was a "white heart." Her eyes grew moist with the memory of Zach's taunts.

"Do—do you think I can only be white, Little Raven . . . Mule? . . . Do you think I can learn and understand your ways? Some have said that it is impossible to think and feel both ways."

Both men were reasonably sure where those words had come from, and they were just as sure Tara was trying to belong, trying to understand and be part of the wild and untamed territory.

"It is not impossible. Look at Mule, look at so many others." Little Raven walked to stand closer to Tara. He took her hand in his and, to her surprise, pressed it against his chest. His face was serious and his eyes intent on her.

"I make you now my sister. I will be brother to you in all ways. I pledge my life to this."

Tara felt tears leap to her eyes and she was filled with delight. But before she could respond, a fierce and cold voice spoke from a short distance away, causing all three to spin about in surprise.

"Maybe you will die for your . . . sister, Little Raven."

Three men stood some distance away, two Indians and one white man. Their guns were directed toward Mule and Little Raven, and there was not a shadow of mercy in any of their eyes.

Tara took an involuntary step toward Little Raven, but a cold voice stopped her from any further movement.

"If you don't want to spill his blood right here, woman, then you had better not move again." Tara remained frozen.

"Standing Wolf, Running Fox," Little Raven said with a cold sneer. "Brave warriors," he spat angrily. "Why do you war on your own?"

The two Indians were angry. "Why do you and your half-breed brother protect those who harm us? We must drive the whites out and the guns the others bring will help us."

"It will not be so easy," Little Raven countered. The three exchanged glances. "The young warriors will not pick up any guns for seven days. This they have promised me. By this time, the plans of traitors will be dead."

"We should kill them here and now," the white man snarled.

"No," Standing Wolf said. "We will take them with us. What will be done with them will be decided when we meet." He motioned to Running Fox, "Tie them well, saddle their horses. They will be taken with us. They may be useful yet, especially the son of Waiting Wolf."

"He is also the brother to Windwalker," Running Fox inserted nervously. Little Raven was quite pleased to see the effect Windwalker's name had.

"And my brother will track you down and see that you die should you harm his brother . . . and his woman."

Little Raven could see both surprise and a new nervousness move through them.

"You are his woman?" Standing Wolf demanded. Tara could do little more than nod. Surely Mule and Little Raven knew what they were doing. She would not deliberately destroy any defense they had with the knowledge that Windwalker might come for his brother and his friend, Mule. But it was very doubtful if he would be led into a trap by a woman who had been nothing but a problem to him. "Woman or not," the white man snarled, "we can't leave any loose ends. We'll take them along with us and let the boss decide what to do with them."

There was no choice but to agree to this, because all of them knew if these three were to be left free, all their plans might be turned to dust. Little Raven knew the Indians too well. It was too dangerous to let him free . . . and they were afraid to kill him.

They also knew killing Mule would bring Windwalker's wrath down on them, and he was one who would trail them into eternity to exact revenge. They would let someone else do the deciding, and at the same time, someone else would take the blame for whatever was done.

"Tie them up," Standing Wolf repeated. The white man held his rifle on the three while Standing Wolf and Running Fox moved to tie them up. Their hands tied, their horses were brought and saddled. Careful to tie the men's hands behind them, they pushed each one up onto his saddle. Tara's hands were tied before her and she was forced to mount.

Her eyes caught Little Raven, who smiled and tried to reassure her with his gaze.

Each of the three took the reins of a captive's horse and they rode out of the valley. Neither Little Raven nor Mule had any idea how long it would be before Zach returned, and he was the only one who would know why they had been taken or how to find them.

Tara could only hold her thoughts on Zach and the silent prayer that he would come, that they could be freed, and that somehow she could convince him she had more than a "white heart."

Chapter 29

Zach had maintained a vigil without moving for several hours. His infinite patience had always been one of his strong points when he was tracking man or beast. He was almost certain Caleb would be joining the rifles as soon as he had made whatever connections he was making with whoever was responsible. Zach knew there had to be many others connected with the movement of guns and he wanted them all.

Zach used the time demanded by patience to allow his thoughts to dwell on Tara. He knew it was useless, but what was the harm in allowing his thoughts freedom when no one would know but him? He could vividly remember the taste and the scent of her, and he could almost feel the smooth texture of her skin beneath his fingers. Autumn Dove, he had called her, and the name fit her well. He felt a deep sorrow at the fact that he would have only memories and a name to remember.

He shifted only his eyes to scan the horizon. From his vantage point, he could see for a great distance in all directions. That was when he saw the dark specks on the horizon that he knew were approaching riders.

His nerves grew tense. Now some of the predators were gathering. In time he would know them, and when he did, he would find a way to destroy the guns. Once he did that, he would do what he could to bring the ones to justice that he could, but if he had to kill them, one at a time, he would do it. He would keep the peace no matter what the cost.

The riders were growing close, but he knew he had some time yet before they arrived in the camp. The men in the camp now, drifting about aimlessly, were not men of consequence. Zach wanted the ones behind them—the ones who paid them—and he wanted the answer to one question that haunted him. Who had something to gain by this?

He was hungry, so he went to his saddlebags and took some dried corn and pieces of dried meat. These he chewed on, occasionally sipping from his canteen of water. He watched the riders in the distance growing closer. Now he could make out that there were six of them. Maybe the gods had begun to smile on him and he would have all the ones involved in one swift move.

They would reach the camp just as the sun set and he was pleased to know he would at least be able to identify them.

He returned to where he could look down on the camp. The excitement within him began to grow as he watched the crest of the small grade that led to the valley. As soon as the riders appeared there he would know them. He waited. . . .

As he knew they would, the riders came over the rim of the hill. But he was not prepared to see Little Raven, Mule, and . . . It was Tara! He muttered an angry curse as he watched the six ride into the camp.

His eyes seemed unable to draw themselves from Tara. She was a very different Tara than the one he had left behind.

He had sent Little Raven to get a dress for Tara, but he had not expected to see her in his mother's wedding dress. The effect on him was so traumatic that, for a moment, he couldn't get his breath. His emotions were even more torn when he saw that Tara's hands were tied before her. He seethed in silent fury as one of the men gave her a rough shove, thrusting her against Little Raven who braced himself to keep her from falling.

332

Zach never questioned the blazing flow of white hot anger for what it was. Tara was his, and no man would touch her so and live to speak of it. He marked the man well in his mind and allowed the savage side of his nature to surface. That man would pay, and if he truly harmed Tara in any way, the payment would be beyond his belief.

There were too many of them for him to try and get the captives free now, but Zach watched through narrowed eyes.

Mule and Little Raven moved close to Tara on both sides. It was obvious to Zach that even with their hands tied, they meant to protect her as best they could. He felt the harsh prick of guilt. If he had not taken her, she would not have been subjected to this.

He watched as all three captives were untied, forced toward a rough lean-to, and handed plates of food.

Zach realized that if choices had to be made, he would have to get a lot closer before nightfall so he could know what was happening in the camp. It would be dangerous. At any moment he could be spotted by an alert guard. Practically inch by inch, he worked his way closer and closer. This was one time he wished the day would end quickly, and he was more than grateful to see the sun rim the horizon.

Campfires were lit, casting the rest of the valley into darkness. This, at least, gave Zach the chance to move close enough so that he could hear the inhabitants of the camp talking.

He had concentrated so long on approaching the camp without making a sound that he'd been able to put in the back of his mind the one unwelcome thought. When the others came—and he knew they would—he might be faced with a choice: Caleb and the rifles . . . or Tara and his brother and Mule. He knew he was weighing three lives against so many who would die because of the guns, yet they were three lives that meant the most to him.

He tried not to think of Tara at the mercy of men like these, but he couldn't erase so many vivid memories of Tara from his

333

mind. He cursed Caleb, fate, and finally himself for the position they were in.

He was within twenty-five feet of the campfire and within ten of the lean-to in which the captives sat. There was no chance for him to miss a word being said.

"The white woman," Standing Wolf said thoughtfully, "I am sure we will not return her to the fort."

"Why should we?" Running Fox laughed softly. "Those at the fort will die anyway. It would be stupid to waste her there when she could be more useful to us."

The other men laughed in agreement, and Zach gritted his teeth to keep control. With the one gun on his hip, a rifle, and one knife, he stood very little chance against the men who were there. He had counted carefully. Including the three that had brought Tara there were seven men, only two of whom were Indian.

One of the white men used a stick to prod the fire. He was a cold, unscrupulous man whose face wore his lack of humanity clearly.

"I'd still like to know what those three were doin' out there. That girl is no squaw, that's for sure," he said gruffly. "They had a camp made like they was waitin' for someone."

"Who the hell could they be waitin' for?" another white spoke.

"Windwalker," Standing Wolf said quietly.

"Just who's this Windwalker?" the first white asked sharply.

"He is the son of Waiting Wolf. He also has the blood of a white mother."

"A breed," came the sneering reply.

"He is not a man to take lightly," Standing Wolf said sharply. "I have seen his anger and I do not choose to feel it. I say we get rid of all three of them."

"We can't do that until the boss gets here. I don't think he wants to stir up anything until he's ready to have the fort hit."

334

"But," another man interjected, "we could find out just who they were waiting for, for certain, and when they expected him—or them. Leastwise we'd know if we could expect a surprise. Hell, they might have been waiting for an army patrol or something. That would stir up a passel of problems."

It was clear the two Indians would have preferred to leave the prisoners alone, but they were camped with an outnumbering amount of white men who could not be trusted not to kill with little provocation. They remained silent while one of the men walked to the lean-to.

Tara was frightened, but just having Little Raven and Mule close kept her courage up. They had sat together in silence for some time before she spoke.

"Little Raven, what do they want with us?" She kept her voice low so she would not attract undue attention.

"They are being careful," Little Raven responded.

"Careful . . . I don't understand."

Little Raven turned his head from those at the fire and looked at Tara. "Windwalker was right. There are men smuggling guns to our people. I am ashamed to say that I have known they were to come. Maybe if I had told him about Tall Bull, this could have been stopped. I don't know. I did not know how they were to get here. Now I am certain Windwalker was right about other things."

"Like what?"

"Like the white one at the fort."

"Caleb?"

"Yes. Somehow he is involved in this, but I don't think he is the chief of these men. There is someone else. No matter what happens to us, I pray Windwalker can put a stop to this before it is too late."

Mule, who had been silent up to now, spoke softly. "Wal, boy, if anyone kin do it, Zach can. I wish I knew where he was

335

right now. He's gonna be madder than all hell when he comes back and finds us gone. I hope he don't get mad enough that he forgets common sense."

Tara was praying for the same thing. Now that Caleb's name had been spoken by Little Raven, she realized that all along Zach had been telling her the truth. There was one more thing she had to know.

"Little Raven, Mule, one of you tell me the truth. If it is Caleb and he does come here, what will he do with me?"

Both men remained silent too long and Tara recalled the things Zach had told her. She trembled with a new kind of fear.

"You want the truth, girl?" Mule asked softly.

"Yes, Mule, I do."

"Then I'll tell it to you straight."

"Mule," Little Raven cautioned.

"She has a right to know, Little Raven," Mule replied. "He'll most likely . . . use you, share you with these men, then sell you to whomever pays him what he wants."

"God!" Tara gasped. "It is hard to believe a civilized man—"

"I warned you once about judging whether a man was civilized or not. Caleb Banning is worse than the bloodiest killer that ever crossed this land."

Before Tara could answer, a shadow crossed between them and the glow of the fire. All three looked up to see one of the men approach. He had drawn his guns so he would have no resistance.

"C'mere, girl. We wanna talk to you," he motioned with the gun. Tara felt terror fill her. She was afraid to go and just as afraid if she didn't, Little Raven and Mule would be made to pay for her resistance.

"Leave her alone," Mule snapped angrily.

"If you harm her, we will see that you suffer a great deal," Little Raven threatened.

"Now you got me scared to death, both of you. Old man, you stay put or I'll drop you, and boy, if you give me any trouble,

336

we'll take it out of her hide. You two understand?"

Both men glared at him with a cold anger that actually shook the man.

"We only want to talk to her. She'll be back in a while. Long as she answers our questions no one's going to hurt her."

Tara didn't want anything to happen to Little Raven or Mule. If it did, she would be left alone among these men. Little Raven and Mule were the source of courage that lifted her to her feet.

"Please," she said softly, "Mule, Little Raven, I'll be all right."

Both Mule and Little Raven felt helpless as Tara walked hesitantly toward the fire with the man.

Zach stiffened as he saw Tara moving toward the fire. In the glow of the flames she seemed a vision from one of his dreams. She stood erect and proud, and at that moment he wanted to hold her and kiss her with a fierce desperation. Her voice came to him, soft and filling him with tormenting memories of moments when she had called to him in passion. Moments he would not be able to have again.

Standing Wolf rose to his feet when Tara stopped beside him.

"White Woman, you will answer me," Standing Wolf snarled, trying to make his effect as fierce and terrifying for Tara as he could. But he underestimated Tara, who was not going to give him the satisfaction of breaking before him.

"I will not answer the questions of a man who deals in the deaths of others."

"You will tell me why you wait with Little Raven and his friend, and why you wear the wedding dress."

No one could have been more startled than Tara. For a second she lifted her hand to brush against the soft material. Then she became defiant. If this arrogant bastard wanted an answer, she would give him one to make his head spin. She lifted her

337

head and smiled proudly.

"I am here because I am the woman of Windwalker, and I wait in the valley for him to come for me. I will soon be his wife, and if you harm me or his friends, you will have many more problems than you ever bargained on."

The men around the campfire grew silent in the face of her proud defiance, but none were as shaken as Zach. This may have been a constant thought in the back of his mind, but his conscious mind had used every weapon to protect his heart's emotions from disaster. To hear her say these words shattered much of his protective shield. Tara would never know the effect this had on him. He gazed at her, realizing for the first time that he had stood on the brink of losing her forever because he had been so certain of her emotions that he had never spoken to her of his own. Now he was less than certain he would ever have the opportunity to do so. The only thing that was certain in his mind was that the sacrifice of the rifles and the loss of Caleb's capture, or any others with him, was a very small thing balanced against Tara's life. He knew now that she meant more to him than his own life. He would try to solve the problem of the rifles in the future. For now, he had to make sure Tara and his brother and Mule had a future. He moved stealthily away. He had to find some kind of a plan to get the three away, and right now that seemed a near impossibility.

Standing Wolf was amazed at the arrogance of this woman and too stubborn to admit that the threat of Windwalker's vengeance had disturbed him.

"Windwalker would not marry a white woman," he sneered. "His father made that mistake and Windwalker has paid for it. He does not belong to either Indian or white. He is an outcast."

"Maybe he belongs to both sides," Tara countered. "I have heard Windwalker speak with pride of both his mother and his father. You lie to make others believe Zach . . . Windwalker is less than he is. But he is more of a man than you will ever be!"

338

There was a collective gasp of shock at a woman saying such words to a man like Standing Wolf. But the sound had not died before Standing Wolf struck swiftly. The blow caught Tara's cheek and knocked her to the ground. For a minute Tara saw stars sparkle before her eyes and the forms about her wavered. Then she glared up at Standing Wolf. "This is a sample of your manhood, to beat a woman? This is what makes Windwalker different from you," she said in a cold whisper.

Both Little Raven and Mule had leapt to their feet when they saw Standing Wolf strike Tara, and Little Raven raced to her side before he could be stopped. He reached down and helped Tara to her feet. Now the entire camp was on their feet and several guns were pointed at Little Raven, who could only glare in intense hatred at Standing Wolf.

"Why do you not war with men who can fight you instead of attacking a woman who did nothing but speak the truth?"

Little Raven was caught in a deep and nearly violent rage, but Tara knew if he challenged too far, a coward like Standing Wolf would kill him. She pressed close to Little Raven.

"No, please, Little Raven." She was panic-stricken with the thought that Little Raven could be killed.

"Take her back and keep her quiet. I do not war with women, nor do I fight with boys."

Tara could feel the muscles in Little Raven's arm grow rigid.

"Give me a knife, Standing Wolf," Little Raven replied coldly. "and I will show you the difference between men and boys."

Standing Wolf had overstepped himself, but his pride would not let him back away. He was also shaken by the intense and murderous look in Little Raven's eyes. He had seen Windwalker in battle several times and it finally came to him that the brothers were much alike.

But this had gone far enough. One of the white men turned to Standing Wolf, "You ain't killing any of these three until the boss gets here. Now if you don't back off, we'll drop you right here. Is that clear?"

This was the opportunity for Standing Wolf to back down and still save face, and he took it.

"Take the woman back and be silent, Little Raven. I will give you your chance to die very soon. Now get her away from me. I cannot stand to look at her white face. She is worthless."

Little Raven would still have stood ready for battle had not Mule spoken from a short distance away. "Little Raven," he said quietly, "this ain't the time."

This was enough to bring Little Raven's rage under control. He drew Tara with him and the three of them went back to the lean-to.

Zach moved far enough away so that he could try and form a plan of action. If he could somehow arm Mule and Little Raven, at least the odds against him would be shortened. But how to do that seemed an impossible puzzle.

He had no idea when the others might come, but if their numbers swelled the camp, then he wouldn't stand a chance of either arming Mule and Little Raven or getting Tara safely out. He needed a diversion, but at this moment he could think of nothing. He worked his way to a high place where he could view the entire camp again and study the area carefully. He committed to memory every crevice and rock until he could have moved through the valley blindly.

The valley was shaped somewhat like an hourglass with one end closed. High, rough jutting rocks formed a barrier on three sides, so there was only one way in and out, and anyone coming in would have to pass through the narrow center section to get to the camp. Any amount of people approaching would warn the camp long before they could be reached. With enough guns, they could defend the valley forever if the need arose, and Zach was more than certain there were enough guns and ammunition in the valley to do just that.

Again he relied on patience. There was no way he could do

anything until the camp slept. As safe as they must feel, he was pretty certain one guard would remain awake. The wee hours of the morning were always the best time to move against any enemy.

He settled himself to wait, his body relaxed but his mind broiling with thoughts. He held Tara before him and took pleasure in the memories. He had to get her free. He had to tell her of the words he had heard her say and how foolish he had been to almost let her get away. First and most important, he had to tell her he loved her.

Chapter 30

David took off his hat and wiped the sweat from his brow with the crook of his arm. As he replaced the hat he spoke to Long, who rode on one side of him, and included the sergeant who rode on the other side.

"Christ, you'd think there'd be one sign of someone. It's like he vanished."

"David," Long said encouragingly, "Zach won't hurt your sister. If he took her, he must have had a reason we don't know or understand yet. But I'll lay my life on the fact that he won't hurt her."

"You're so sure about that?" David responded dryly.

"Yeah. I've known Zach a long time. He and I have hunted these hills many times and camped together. I can't put a reason to why he did what he did, but I know he won't hurt her. Just like I'm damn sure we won't find him 'til he's ready to be found."

"I've sent patrols in every direction but straight up," Davis complained. "He's about as easy to find as the wind."

"Maybe," Long laughed, "that's why he got the name Windwalker from his father."

"Aaron sent men to his father's village, but they swear they haven't seen a sign of him."

"Speaking of Aaron, have you noticed a difference in him

342

the past three days since I got back?"

"Yes . . . a little, but it's hard to say."

Long had arrived the day after David, and for several hours it had been touch and go between white and red. The Indians had decided to camp outside the fort walls until Star was able to travel. Still, the broiling anger beneath the surface of each brave threatened to burst out at any provocation. Aaron had kept a strict hold on his men, forbidding them, unless on patrol, to leave the fort or to fraternize in any way with the braves outside. He knew as well as anyone it would only take one incident to set off the powder keg.

"What do you see different, Sergeant?" David continued.

"I don't exactly know. He's . . . quieter, and he sure seems worried about the care Star is getting," Harrison answered hesitantly.

"He doesn't want anything to happen to her while she's in the fort. It might just light the fuse that sets everything off. But then I'm not sure it's just that," Long mused.

"The major sure ain't the same as he was a while back," Sergeant Harrison offered.

Both Long and David turned their attention to him. "What do the men think, Sergeant Harrison?" David inquired. Enlisted men were always a good barometer for the mental state of an officer.

"They think he's havin' a hard time between his duty, what he felt about the Indians before, and what he's startin' to think now. It's got him all mixed up."

"How?" David pressed.

"You know his folks were wiped out by the Indians some years back?"

"Yes."

"Well he was feelin' real safe thinkin' of them as vicious savages. Now, when his own kind have done the same, he's findin' it hard to swallow."

"I take it you don't feel the same toward the Indians as most do?" David inquired.

343

"Been out here nigh onto twenty years. I came up with one good answer. They're men just like the rest of us. They got a problem or two. It's a few makes it bad . . . on both sides."

David laughed. An age-old problem with no answers. He thought of Small Fawn back at the fort. He worried because she was the only Indian woman inside besides Star, who was still helpless and had no protection but him.

"Well, I'm hot, tired, and thirsty. We've been out since dawn. Let's head back." He knew he would have liked to press the search on but now he was torn between looking for Tara who Long assured him would not suffer at Zach's hands, and returning to Small Fawn, who might have problems in the fort.

They turned back, knowing that the search would continue the next day and the next, until David had exhausted any chance of finding Tara.

Aaron tipped his chair back and threw his pen aside in disgust. He couldn't concentrate and the reason, he tried not to admit, was he couldn't get Star to leave his thoughts. He had been to see about her condition at least three or four times since the day David had brought her to the fort. He had never seen anyone so delicate or so utterly helpless in his life. Worse, it made him feel helpless, which was something that had never happened to him before. He hated the Indians and was frustrated to find that he was somehow separating Star from all the others.

Reaching in his drawer, he withdrew the half-full bottle of whiskey, poured a drink, and returned the bottle to the drawer. He sipped thoughtfully, determined he would not walk across the compound to the hospital today. He had done so several times and realized his actions were causing some amount of whispering.

He gulped down the balance of the drink and tried to return to his paperwork, only to fail again. A half hour later he walked stiffly erect across the compound. Aaron came to the door of

344

the tack room. He would have to enter and cross it to get to the door of the doctor's quarters. But as he passed the inner door that led to the stables, he heard a soft cry of distress and a stifling noise. Sensing that someone was in trouble, he opened the door that led the the stable, beholding a sight that made fury bubble up in him.

Small Fawn had spent the days and nights as close to Star as she could. She had the doctor's permission to sleep in the cot next to her sister. When Star had wakened she had cared for her, fed her, bathed her, and remained close.

She was so pleased to see, on the third day, that Star found the strength to remain awake and be propped up with pillows. But she was thoroughly frightened by the fort's tall commander, who had come several times, ignored her, and spoken to no one, yet had stood and looked at Star for several minutes each time. She could not read the thoughts on his immobile face, but she knew of Aaron's hatred for the Indians and wondered if he were angered at their being there.

Whenever Aaron came, Small Fawn remained silent, her eyes downcast, terrified that Aaron would look at her and their eyes would meet and he would speak. It could only be cold and bitter words. She prayed each day that Star would soon be well enough to be moved. Small Fawn had never lived in such a state. Only when David was near did she feel any release from the fear, but he was gone often now in a futile search for his sister.

This morning she was awake very early, as was her usual way. She rose quickly and went to Star. Kneeling by her sister's cot, she was pleased to see Star was awake and her quick smile assured Small Fawn she was steadily improving.

"Would you like to try and stand today?" Small Fawn whispered.

"Yes," Star agreed. "It is better that I leave this bed as soon as possible."

"Our people wait outside the fort to take us with them as soon as you are ready to move."

"I will do my best today. We should do so now so I can gather my strength before the tall chief comes again."

"Does he frighten you, Star?"

"No. I—I feel . . . strange. He looks at me as if he expects something, and when he does not find it he seems uncertain, as if he's looking for the answer to something I am supposed to offer. It is a look I do not like, and he must know I do not trust him."

"He is not a dangerous or a dishonest man, Star. He has a hatred for our people that is more a misunderstanding."

"I wonder," Star said softly.

"What do you wonder?"

"If what I see in his eyes is not hatred, it's very close."

"Don't be so hard on him until you know him better. I feel you can trust him!"

"You want me to trust him just because you have a great trust in David. They are too different."

"David knows and understands us. He cares what happens to us and so will this chief, if you do not hide, Star, behind a woman filled with hate. Your heart is open and loving. You will not be hurt if you learn to trust again."

"Small Fawn, I must tell you this. If the white chief comes today, I will speak to him. I must hear him speak. I must know for myself what lies in his heart."

"I am glad you will agree to this at least."

"But just to speak to him, just to thank him for my care only."

"You worry me, Sister," Small Fawn said quietly.

"Do not worry. I am not a foolish girl. I will try not to anger a man who holds our life in his hands."

"You will have your way no matter what I say." Small Fawn smiled. "You always do. You have always been the stubborn one."

Small Fawn helped Star move cautiously until she sat on

346

the edge of the bed. She had grown thinner through her ordeal and her eyes were wide and deep, enhanced by her slightly hollowed cheeks. Her clothes had been cut away and now she was wrapped in a blanket.

"Oh, I wish I had some clothes. I feel ashamed to be seen like this . . . by anyone."

Small Fawn was afraid Aaron had had some drastic effect on Star, but there was little she could do except warn her sister that he was the last man to whom Star should display her distrust and anger.

"David has gotten clothes for me," Small Fawn said. "I keep them in a bundle near the horse David gave me in case of a problem. They are white woman's clothes, but at least they are better than a blanket. I will go and get a dress for you." Small Fawn rose to her feet. "Will you be all right or should I help you to lie down?"

"No, I have been lying long enough. You know it is not to my liking to be so still for so long."

"All right. I will return as quickly as I can."

Small Fawn left the hospital on silent feet. She crossed the empty doctor's office and moved through the tack room to enter the stable. She went directly to the pile of hay where she had secreted the things David had given her. She knelt in the hay, reaching into its depth to retrieve her bundle. So engrossed was Small Fawn in opening it that she was not aware she was not alone until a dark shadow fell over her. She looked up quickly and a terror choked her, rendering her unable to catch her breath.

"Well, well." His voice was soft and suggestive as he leered at her. "Now we got a nice little plaything here. What are you doin' all alone, little squaw? Lookin' for some company?"

"No," she half whispered. He towered over her, and there was no avenue of escape unless she passed him. "Please, I must go back. The doctor is expecting me to return."

"Yeah?" he chuckled. "I just don't think he cares what you're doing. We have time. . . ."

347

He moved closer. To Small Fawn he looked immense. He was tall and built like a scarecrow, with long legs and arms. His face was narrow and his eyes squinted as if he didn't want anyone to look too deeply into them. He reached down a huge hamlike hand and grasped her arm, dragging her up to him. She was nearly paralyzed with fear, but his intent was so obvious that she began to battle with what strength she had. It was a losing battle, and soon she was pushed back into the hay and he was fumbling for the bottom of her skirt. Her mind could only reason that no white man would believe her story. She had no defense, but she fully intended to battle to the limit of her strength. She cried out David's name as the man tore at her clothes. It was a voice as cold as ice that tore the man away from her.

"Trooper Gordon!" It was a harsh command that made the man curse and roll from her.

"Get your feet under you, soldier, before I shoot you in the ground like the stupid animal you are."

Gordon rose to his feet. To face his commanding officer in such a state of cold fury made him shake.

"Get back to your barracks. You're confined there until I can muster a court."

Gordon would have been wiser to obey Aaron at once; instead he made a grave mistake. Knowing Aaron's feelings for Indians, he counted on them for sympathetic understanding.

"She's only a dumb squaw, sir. Just another of them damn redskins that need killin'."

Gordon stopped suddenly, seeing something in Aaron's eyes that made him begin to sweat.

"I wonder how you would feel if she were your sister . . . or your mother? Get out of my sight before I lose my temper and use a horse whip on you as you deserve."

Before Aaron's anger, Gordon lost whatever courage he might have had. He slunk away, and Small Fawn and Aaron were left in the silence of the barn, staring at each other.

Small Fawn was filled with terror, but she had no way of

knowing Aaron was just as filled with uncertainty and a kind of mental shock at the look at his inner self that left all his past hatreds withering like dry autumn leaves.

"Are you all right? He didn't—"

"No . . . no," she whispered raggedly. "I am not hurt. I am grateful that you came when you did."

"What were you doing here?"

"I came to get some clothes for my sister."

"She's up?" His tone was one of surprise.

"Yes. Already she wants to stand and to move about."

"But she is too weak."

Small Fawn smiled hesitantly. "Star is too stubborn to admit a weakness. When we were children she . . ." Small Fawn hesitated and the smile died. Aaron, the white chief who hated her people, could not be interested in the childhood of her and Star.

But Aaron would have encouraged her words if he had not held himself in iron control. Aaron could see quickly that Small Fawn was very frightened of him. He stood between her and the door, and he was struck with the ugly thought that she felt no safer with him than she had with Gordon.

"Come." He resorted to a brisk order to hide his own tension. "Bring the dress and let's see to your sister. I'll go with you"—he hesitated—"just to make sure she is not damaging herself by moving about too quickly."

Small Fawn's head dipped in acknowledgment of his order, but she didn't move. Then he was made aware that she was waiting for him to move first. He turned and walked out, hearing her light tread behind him.

They crossed the tack room and entered the doctor's office, crossing it and entering the hospital. Aaron felt slightly ridiculous, as if he were a monarch with a subservient subject following. It shook his control and left him slightly angered and upset at the situation.

Aaron had seen Star in a helpless state several times. He knew her resemblance to her sister was remarkable, but he had never met her deep dark eyes until he and Small Fawn came close to her.

Star had been thinking of their situation also, and when she heard Aaron coming, she had no idea Small Fawn was with him.

Aaron stopped a foot or two from the bottom of the bed. Star's eyes raised to his and a soft gasp of shock came unexpectedly from her. Their eyes held for seconds and Aaron's brows drew together in a puzzled frown.

Small Fawn knelt before her sister and placed the dress in her lap. Still Star's gaze did not drop from Aaron's and a look he could not interpret filled her eyes.

"We can go out while you put on the dress," Small Fawn said.

"You need not bother, Sister," Star said, what defiance she could gather reflected in her voice. "I choose not to wear the clothes of those who have murdered our people."

Aaron had never felt such a flow of guilt, anger, denial, and uncertainty in his life. He'd been safe in his cocoon of hatred for the Indians for what they had done to him. He found it very difficult to handle a reversal of roles.

"My men and I are not responsible for what happened in your village," he stated firmly.

"That's the excuse of all white men. They butcher and murder, and each chief claims innocence. All whites are innocent, aren't they?"

"Star!" Small Fawn said quickly, shocked at words that might anger Aaron enough to cause a problem between the leader of the fort and the men outside.

"Why should I watch my words, Small Fawn?" Star replied. She had seen a flicker of guilt in Aaron's eyes, and she couldn't understand her terrible desire to hurt him in some way. He was a symbol of all the hurt and pain in her world, and she needed something to strike out at. "If he chooses, he will throw us from the fort anyway."

"You're being just a little unfair," Aaron protested. "You

350

don't know me. How can you say what I will do or how I feel?"

"All whites are alike," Star said quietly, but her voice was brittle and cold. Aaron was reminded of the many times he had made the same statement about Indians. A new kind of truth broke about him, and he was nearly speechless with the force of it as it rocked the foundations of his life, leaving cracks in the walls of his defenses. He found it impossible to cope with this strange truth, while he tried to deny what he read in her eyes. Another, much more volatile, emotion rendered him almost breathless. He couldn't handle this woman's scorn and anger. He wanted her to know him and to think of him differently than as just a "white" man. It was the first time he began to understand what Zach must have faced so many times, times when he had been guilty of the same hate and distrust he now saw in Star's eyes.

It was also the first time in Aaron Creighton's life that he felt the urge to run from some unnameable thing.

"I will send one of the men outside to your people who are camped there. Maybe they can get some clothes that will please you," he said, hearing the stiffness in his own voice and hating it. "In the meantime, you must rest, eat, and take care of yourself. If anything happens to you because of your own stubbornness, I don't want to be held to blame for it by those men out there who are itching for a fight. I'd like to keep peace around here, and contrary to what you believe, I don't murder the innocent."

He turned rigidly and walked away, sensing Star's dark eyes on him all the way to the door. Outside the door he stood very still, hardly able to understand a wayward body. He had begun to sweat, looking down with surprised eyes to find his hands were clenched into fists. He opened them with determined concentration and held them before him. They were shaking. He cursed under his breath and walked at what was frighteningly near a run, until he stood in the warm brilliant sun and breathed deeply.

Within the hospital room Small Fawn turned her eyes to

351

Star, noticing her sister watching Aaron until the door closed behind him.

"How could you speak such words of anger to him, Star? He has been kind to us. He has fed the men outside; he has made his medicine man guard your life carefully. It is terrible to reward kindness with hatred. Our parents would feel great shame at this."

"But is was he and his kind who have done these terrible things to us," Star replied, the anguish in her voice telling of the memories she held. "How can I smile and thank the men who have nearly destroyed us, who killed with laughter on their lips?"

"Star, we must understand. It is as David has explained so many times. There is not right on both sides and both sides are not wrong. Some of our people have killed with the same pleasure. Can we deny that? Don't you understand some battles cannot be won with arrows and guns? Some must be fought with trust and love."

"Small Fawn, you were there! You saw this terrible thing that my heart can never forget!"

"Yes, I was there, and I saw the men who did this," Small Fawn said softly. "But still my love for David is great, and I do not blame him for the things others of his people have done."

"I do not have your heart, Small Fawn," Star said softly. "I do not know if I can ever forget or forgive. Still I can hear the cries of the children and the sound of their guns."

"It is a terrible thing to remember. I, too, will never forget. Nor will I forgive the guilty ones . . . but only the guilty ones." Small Fawn looked into her sister's pain-haunted eyes. "We are alive, Star," she said softly, "and we must preserve our lives so we can teach the children ways of peace. Think in these words. You are exhausted; you must rest. I will leave this dress at the foot of your bed, and maybe . . . later you will choose to wear it and to begin to understand the spirit in which it was given. Sleep now and I will come later."

Star nodded and lay back on the bed. She found she really

was exhausted, but more mentally than physically. Small Fawn left and Star was alone with her thoughts.

She wanted to hate Aaron, but she was finding that she hated more the strange and unfathomable effect his green-eyed gaze had on her. She knew her anger at him had been some kind of self-defense, yet she found no reason for this. She looked at the dress and promised herself she would not take that one step toward Aaron and his people. For now, she could hold the pain and distrust close to her as a shield. If she took one step toward him . . . A new fear built that he might also take one, and this she was not prepared to handle. With grim determination, she forced Aaron from her mind, closed her eyes, and tried to find the relief of sleep.

Chapter 31

Aaron stood on the porch outside his quarters and enjoyed a cigar. Except for the guards who walked their posts and those by the closed gates of the fort, everyone else was asleep. He had found it nearly impossible to do the same.

Since David had insisted Small Fawn and Star use his empty quarters, they were even closer to Aaron than before. Aaron had questioned David about the wisdom of this, and David had said only that it was for their safety. Aaron was reasonably sure Small Fawn had told David about the attack on her. He was also more than sure there was much more between Small Fawn and David than either would say.

Dark accusing eyes had haunted Aaron from the time he and Star had talked. He was annoyed that she continued to come between him and the work he had to do. Although he hadn't seen Star since their confrontation the day before, he was well aware of her and Small Fawn's move, and the fact that she was no longer confined to bed. If he harbored some happiness at that fact, he did his best to ignore it.

He sighed deeply and tossed the stub of his cigar away. He knew sleep was beyond hope, but he could at least have a drink or two. Just as he stepped back into the shadows of the porch to reach for the handle of his door, he saw a movement near David's quarters. Hoping none of his men had gotten any ideas, he paused for a minute to watch closer. Again the movement came. Someone stood on the porch in front of David's door.

Aaron knew David slept in the barracks now, and he was more than certain someone had gotten wrong ideas. He moved along the porch silently, hugging the shadows. He passed in front of the cantina, and then the kitchen, moving to the corner shrouded in darkness. Still the figure was not just a dark form. One more step then, with a rapidly thudding heart, he knew who the form was. Star. She was standing with her back to him, looking toward the gate.

Star had jerked awake from a deep druglike sleep. Her flesh felt damp with sweat, and she knew she'd been having a nightmare, yet she couldn't recall it. She had sat up, uncomfortable within the enclosing walls of the fort. Across the bottom of her bed still lay the dress Small Fawn had brought her. She had refused to touch it, which had forced her to remain in bed, for she couldn't walk around among all these men wrapped in nothing but a blanket.

Small Fawn lay on the cot next to her, deep in sleep. But to Star the room seemed oppressive, as if she were imprisoned. She had to make a choice and she made it quickly. She rose quietly, picked up the dress, and slipped it on. The soft cotton felt strange next to her skin, but the dress fit reasonably well.

Barefooted, she walked silently to the door, opening it to peer out. There was no one in sight so she stepped out on the porch, pulling the door closed so it would not draw someone's attention. The air felt much cooler, and she reached up to lift the heavy weight of her long hair off her neck.

Even this small amount of movement left her feeling weak. She reached out and held onto the pole that supported the roof. Her eyes moved quickly toward the gate—the gate and freedom from her troublesome thoughts, freedom from the ominous presence of one man who could disrupt her life. Soon, she promised herself, soon I will be able to walk from this fort. Until then, I cannot let this man change my thoughts. I must remember what has been done to my people. I cannot forget.

I cannot. . . .

Suddenly she became aware of another presence. Fear held her immobile. Someone stood behind her, close behind her. Aaron could see her suddenly grow still and he knew she sensed him. He didn't want her terrified enough to cry out, so he spoke her name softly. "Star? Don't be frightened."

She turned to face him. "I'm not frightened of you," she said. In the moonlight she could see his eyes skim down the dress she wore and back to her face. "It is all I had to wear. I cannot be blamed if there were no clothes. I could not breathe in there it is so closed in."

"The dress looks beautiful on you." He said the words gallantly, from habit, but he realized suddenly that he meant them. She was so different, so beautiful in her own way.

Star, unused to gallant compliments, was suddenly uncertain. She turned away from him and looked toward the gate. Aaron moved to stand beside her.

"In a few more days I will be strong enough to travel. Small Fawn and I will leave then and go back to help rebuild our village."

"Maybe it will be possible for us to help you."

She turned just her head to look at him. "We need you to stay away from us, not to help. If the white man helps us any more, we might all die."

"Damnit, Star, my men are not responsible for this; I'm not responsible."

"As I told you, it is a story too often told and too often found to be lies."

"Is it lies, Star? Do you believe that, or is it just your way of not seeing all the truth?"

"All the truth? I don't understand your words."

"You're so caught in the hurt you feel you think it's impossible for anyone to feel the same. Well, others have felt pain before you. My parents came out here"—he inhaled deeply—"it seems like so long ago. They built a cabin and we had a fine life. We bothered no one. I was away, going to the

356

military academy," he laughed shortly. "Going to be the first general in the family. While I was gone, a group of braves decided to play war. They raided our farm, killed my parents, two brothers, and one sister. I've hated your people like you do mine. We're both right and, I guess, we're both wrong. What does it prove, Star. What does it prove?"

Star didn't want to face this kind of confusion. The only thing that had held her together since the attack had been her hate. Now Aaron was trying to take that from her.

If she was facing new realizations, so was Aaron. He was looking at her with a new awareness, through the eyes of a man instead of a soldier. The thought was most unwelcome. His hate was drowning in a pair of dark eyes and he couldn't seem to grasp it firmly again.

"I don't know what it proves, unless it is that your kind and mine do not mix, that we should stay away from each other."

"Listen," Aaron said hopefully. "They have a mission school somewhere down along the wagon train trail. You could go . . ."

"No! Why do you insist that your way is right? I will go home with my people. It is where I belong."

She turned away and reentered David's quarters, then closed the door softly. But he heard the crash of it closing between them. Why? He questioned himself in disbelief. Why should he care what happened to her at all? He walked back toward his own quarters, knowing he shouldn't care . . . and yet knowing somehow that he did.

The next day was oppressively hot. The air seemed thick and heavy. David walked up on the porch before Aaron's quarters and stepped inside. He saluted briskly and Aaron reciprocated.

"You haven't found a sign of your sister or the ones who've taken her?"

"No, sir, not a sign. It's a crazy ability the Indians have; they can seem to just vanish."

357

"You don't seem to be as upset as you were."

"I'm praying Long is right, that Zach doesn't mean to harm Tara, that he took her for some other reason."

"Like what?"

"I—I don't know. But Long and I feel it has something to do with those guns."

"Longstreet," Aaron said. "He's staying outside the fort with the Indians."

"And his wife and two sons."

"I didn't know he had a family."

"There's too many hard feelings for him to talk about it much. He's kind of anxious to get out of here."

"David, the girl . . . Star . . ."

"What about her?"

"She's recuperating rapidly."

"She's a strong woman, even though she isn't very big," David laughed. "She's a lot like Small Fawn. I remember when . . ." He stopped abruptly, knowing he'd already said too much.

"There's a great deal between you and this girl. I wondered why it was you that brought them in. How long has this been going on?"

"Quite some time," David admitted. "I'm in love with her." David was relieved the truth was finally out.

"There are some here at the fort who will not take to that too well."

"Does that mean you, Aaron?" David asked quietly. Aaron stood in thoughtful consideration of this.

"She's Indian and you're white. That's a world apart. If you have children, they'll be like Zachary Hale, half one world, half another, and belonging nowhere."

"Or belonging everywhere. Zach is a man I would love to see my sons grow into. And Long's boys, Aaron, you should meet them. They're fine boys."

"But the world they'll have to face will be full of problems."

"Every person's world is full of problems. I guess a man

358

faces them and a coward runs. I have a feeling Zach has always faced them . . . just as I think Long's sons will."

"What will your sister say about it?"

"I don't know," David replied honestly. "I hope that Tara will understand. She's all the family I have left. But I won't face that bridge until I get to it." David was becoming puzzled at the questions that seemed to be leading nowhere.

"Have you taken into consideration that a career you've worked for for years will not be worth a nickel?"

"I've given that a whole lot of thought, and every time I do, my career comes out second best."

"I find that hard to believe."

"Aaron, we've been friends a long time. What's all this leading to? If you're just worried about a friend making a mistake, I can understand. But I've got a feeling there's something much deeper."

Aaron wasn't sure, either. He had wanted answers when he wasn't even sure of the questions. He poured a drink for both him and David, carrying his to the window where he stood looking out over the compound.

"I've been in the Army since I was sixteen," Aaron said quietly. David remained silent, knowing Aaron was talking as much to himself as to David, and not really expecting an answer. "Since my family was killed I found it so easy to hate all Indians." He took a drink. "Hate is a kind of a thing that feeds on itself. You know, I always wanted to hate Zach because of his Indian blood and couldn't quite do it. Now I've seen my own kind do what they did to me." He swallowed the last of his drink and turned to David. "And now I don't know what I feel or what I believe."

In Aaron's voice David heard the confusion, but he still wasn't sure the commander had said all that was bothering him. He tried to take the safest route.

"If the Indians outside the fort are an annoyance, Aaron, I can make them camp some distance away. It will only be another two or three days before Star can travel, then they'll be gone."

"Yes, I know. Star told me last night."

David remained still, but he'd gotten an insight into what was really troubling Aaron—Star. He couldn't say anything to Aaron, but he certainly intended to talk to Small Fawn at his first opportunity.

Aaron contemplated his empty glass, then set it aside. "David, are you calling the search for Tara off?"

"No. I'll never call it off. I would hope if Zach needed her for protection, he'll at least find a way to send her back. But I won't call the search off until I find her."

"Patrols are out now?"

"Two."

"How is Small Fawn finding her treatment here?"

"It's not been too bad. Of course she doesn't go out much after . . . I guess I have you to thank for keeping her safe. She is very grateful, and so am I."

"Another one of my uncertainties," Aaron laughed, "—playing Sir Lancelot rescuing a damsel in distress. Did you know she was scared to death of me?"

"Yeah, I guess."

"Her sister is most certainly not—or at least she says she isn't. I didn't push it or she might have attacked."

Again David was silent, but a million questions buzzed through his mind. It was becoming clearer that Aaron wanted to know more about Star and couldn't ask.

"Small Fawn has always told me stories about Star and her stubborn will," he offered as a test of his supposition.

"She has?" Aaron prodded gently.

"Yes. I remember when Small Fawn said they were learning to ride and Star chose the wildest horse and was promptly thrown, again and again and again, until she got angry. It took her nearly three months but she eventually had the horse eating out of her hand and as docile as a lamb. She's a strong, determined woman."

Aaron would have listened to much more but they were

interrupted by a knock on the door.

"Come," Aaron called, aggravated at the interruption.

"Some of the braves outside want to have a powwow, sir."

"How many?"

"Three."

"Hold them at the gate. I'll be right there."

The sergeant left, and Aaron rose from behind his desk. "I hope there's no more trouble."

"May I accompany you, Aaron?"

"Sure, come on." Aaron took his hat from a peg behind the door, and with David a step behind him, they crossed the compound to the gates where three young braves stood waiting. When they drew closer David recognized all three: Spotted Fox, Buffalo Horn, and Running Deer. They were handsome and proud young warriors, and David felt linked to them in a subtle way.

Aaron and David stopped beside them, but it was David who spoke first. "Spotted Fox, Buffalo Horn, and Running Deer, it is good to see my brothers again."

Spotted Fox smiled. "Our brother does not need to hunt anymore. He has those to hunt and bring his food."

"Is my brother calling me lazy by any chance?"

"No," Spotted Fox said innocently. "Maybe you have just lost your ability and it shames you to admit it."

"Tomorrow morning?" David challenged. Aaron was just a little annoyed that he felt so excluded.

"There is something you want to talk to me about?"

"Yes. My father, Eagle's Feather, has sent us to see if Star and Small Fawn are prepared to travel yet."

"No," Aaron said firmly. "Our medicine man is still caring for her. It will be three more days."

Since David did not argue this point, Spotted Fox took the words to be truth. He nodded. "I shall tell my father. We will leave at sunrise on the third day. I will come for Star myself."

Again Aaron was annoyed, and this time it was the subtle suggestion that Spotted Fox meant more to Star than he was

361

saying. His thoughts were confirmed when David laughed softly. Spotted Fox grinned amiably.

"Spotted Fox, is it truly your father who worried about Star?" David inquired quickly.

"Of course all of us are worried," Spotted Fox said without a change of features, but his dark eyes danced mischievously. "Because Small Fawn has eyes only for a white eyes makes the rest of us worry for Star."

David chuckled but didn't answer. He could feel some kind of tension in Aaron, and he didn't want to prolong amenities.

"This is all you wanted to talk to us about?" Aaron's voice was rigidly military.

"No," Spotted Fox answered. "My father would speak to Star and Small Fawn."

"What about?"

"It is not for me to question my father's needs." Spotted Fox was taken aback by Aaron's question. "I bring you his words."

"But you have an idea what he wants to know?" David asked.

"Maybe," Spotted Fox said solemnly, "he wishes to ask of those who attacked our village. Maybe he would ask if their faces were clearly seen so that we can—"

"Do your father, Black Kettle, and the rest think that these women will possibly name some of us here in the fort, since they've been so close to us?" Aaron inquired.

Spotted Fox's eyes darkened, but his features remained immobile. "Some of the other women who were there, and some of the children, are confused and uncertain. Some of our braves have gone back and found others who escaped. All say the same words: white men . . . some soldiers. Star and Small Fawn may remember more."

"Even if they do, most likely they are far from here now. The winter will come in a few months, and you won't have time to go chasing off if you want to rebuild and have a winter food hunt. Tell your father you must leave these things in my hands. I will find word of the guilty one, and I will do my best to

362

see something's done about it."

There was no way that Aaron and David could avoid reading the doubt in Spotted Fox's eyes. "Maybe," Spotted Fox suggested softly, "you will not find them, either. White man's justice is slow. Am I to tell my brother that the men who killed his wife and newborn son are to go free until the white soldier finds them? Maybe . . . you will not find them at all." Spotted Fox's words were gently said, but Aaron could feel the damned force of bitterness and distrust behind them.

Davis was surprised at Aaron, who seemed to remain calm, his voice quite controlled. "Maybe," he repeated Spotted Fox's suggestive word with the same tone, "if someone would bring me word of who smuggles guns and whiskey out here, maybe I could put a stop to some of this violence. There could be guns for hunting, but at least they would be governed by the chiefs. Maybe then I could do something about the kind of thing that happened to your village."

"There are very few guns in our village. The men who did this would have done it even if there were more. They waited for the hunters to leave. Maybe, if you can bring these men to justice, maybe then we can talk."

Spotted Fox nodded slightly to David, and the three turned and walked away. Aaron and David stood for a moment in silence, watching them leave.

"Was that by any chance some kind of an ultimatum?" Aaron asked quietly, without turning to look at David.

"Sounded like it, didn't it? Of course Spotted Fox can't speak for the chiefs, but I'll sure bet their eyes are on us to see what we'll do about this. If we could find those guns and find the men behind the attack, we'd stand a hell of a good chance of having some peace out here."

Aaron turned to walk back to his quarters, with David beside him. "Do you and your friend Longstreet have some ideas?"

"You're still thinking about Zach?"

"Why not? He's half Indian. Maybe his sympathies got the best of him."

363

"You're reaching."

"I'm desperate. I don't want a battle here."

"These men are only a few."

"Don't underestimate my intelligence, David. I have a pretty good idea how long it would take to gather a whole lot more—maybe the ones who have all those rifles. Then what happens?"

"I'll go hunting with Spotted Fox in the morning and take Long with me. Who knows? We might be able to get some answers."

"This Spotted Fox, he's a pretty tough character."

"He's a well-trained, intelligent brave who just happens to be pretty angry about what happened to Star."

"Star is pretty important to him?" The question was asked casually, but Aaron could actually hear his heart pound as he waited for the answer.

"I guess she must be. Who knows? I haven't been to the village for a while. But he's a handsome devil and Star is really pretty, so it wouldn't be much of a surprise if he wanted her."

Aaron was quiet for the balance of the walk to his quarters, and David remained silent, too, his thoughts on Small Fawn.

"David, why don't you take Small Fawn out of the fort tonight? Take her to the chief and see what they want. Maybe we can find how the chiefs take what she says and if they plan to do anything about it."

"You think Spotted Fox was lying about the guns?"

"Do you?"

"Why should I? These men were angry enough to kill. Do you think they'd camp here and wait if they knew where those guns were or who attacked their camp?"

"David," Aaron said, suddenly aware of something David wasn't saying. "You and Long know who attacked their village, don't you?"

"Yes," David admitted, "we have a pretty good idea."

"Why didn't you tell them?"

"We don't want an uprising either. Long and I thought once

they were gone and in the process of rebuilding, you could do something about Chivington and his group, and maybe Long and I could help track down those guns."

"And make me look like a hero in their eyes so I can keep some peace."

David grinned. "It's not a half-bad idea—if we can get it to work."

"And what are you going to do if Zach is guilty and if your sister is never found?"

"Long is a man whose judgment I can trust. I have to stake Tara's life on it. I have to believe what Long says and pray Zach brings her back."

"That's a lot of faith in one man."

"Long's a pretty special man."

"Good enough," Aaron said pointedly, "to keep his loyalties in the right place?"

"I think you'd better see his boys. Then you'll see why Long doesn't want any more trouble out here either."

"Well, you take Small Fawn to the chief tonight. We'll both pray you're right."

"All right. And I'll bring Long in the morning and you two can have a talk. You might hear a lot of things you don't seem to understand."

"All right."

David was dismissed and left Aaron's quarters. He went straight to his own to tell Small Fawn that he was going to take her out of the fort after dinner. He explained about the talk at the gate, watching Star's face as he did. She did not seem to have a reaction to Small Fawn's being outside the gate. But her face was so still, her emotions so controlled, that David could hardly tell what she was thinking. He would question Small Fawn later, when they were alone.

The day seemed to drag. David was anxious to join Long and the Indians in their camp, and he knew Small Fawn was also. He wondered about Aaron's attitude, as well as his questions about Star and her relationship to Spotted Fox, but dismissed it all as wishful thinking. He wasn't sure Aaron would ever understand the Indians or be able to rid himself of his bitterness and distrust.

When darkness finally settled over the fort and the lights of the campfires could be seen clearly outside the fort, David walked back to his quarters and knocked.

Small Fawn was ready to leave, and as she stepped out onto the porch, Star stood framed in the doorway behind her.

"Star, make sure you stay inside and be very careful. I can't answer for all the men in the fort."

"I will," Star agreed.

"You'll be all right, Sister?" Small Fawn asked worriedly. "I will not be gone long."

"I will be fine. I'm sure," she added dryly, "that none of these whites want to have anything to do with me."

David didn't answer, the random thought whispering through his mind that Aaron and Star were plagued by the same problem—intolerance.

Star closed the door behind them and stood alone in the quiet room. She could not speak to anyone of the oppressive fear being closed up in this room gave her. She would count the minutes until Small Fawn returned, just to have something to assure her she would be leaving soon.

Caught in her own thoughts, she jerked about when a knock sounded on the door. Fear brought a lump to her throat and made her hands clammy. She reached out and opened the door—and came face to face with Aaron.

"Star, I want to talk to you. . . ."

Chapter 32

Zach had made his decision. Tara's life meant a great deal more to him now than trying to connect Caleb and whomever he was dealing with to the guns. His main thought now was to get the three prisoners away safely. It would be a touch-and-go situation to get them out of the camp and maybe even worse to get them out of the valley once they were free. He needed some diversion, and he needed it while he still had the cover of night to aid their escape. His memory searched the valley, and after a few minutes he smiled a humorless smile. Like a shadow, he rose and melted into the night.

The campfire had burnt low, and since the rim of the valley was reasonably high, it shrouded the valley in welcome darkness. All of the men lay wrapped in blankets, secure that the one guard posted at the narrow section of the valley would be quite enough protection. But he wasn't, for Zach moved swiftly and silently, and soon the guard lay unconscious, his hands bound behind him with a strip of his shirt off to effectively gag the man. Then he moved to the horses, quietly bridling and saddling three. He bridled the others to lead them away, planning to run them off when the time came. He led them as close to the prisoners as he could. They would only have minutes to get from where they were held to where he'd hidden his horse, then to make it through the valley mouth before they would be pursued.

His first inclination was to destroy the guns as a diversion, but that was a futile thought when he saw the guns and the ammunition were stacked too far apart, even though they were all against the back wall. He moved with precision, despite the fact that he could barely see. His memory served him well.

Once he was close enough he studied their positions. Then, knowing the guns would have to remain safe, he knelt by the boxes of ammunition. As quietly as possible, he opened one of the cases and began to remove handfuls of the shells. These he opened, dumping the black powder on one of the cases. In a short time he had a nice pile, enough, he was sure, to blow the rest to oblivion. It had to be condensed, so he carefully separated the shells until he had a deep indentation. Then he used another piece of his shirt to make a bed. He scooped the powder into it and left a trail. He smiled; he'd need an extra shirt when this was over—if they got out. He struck flint and watched the spark catch the tail end of the vein of powder. Then he moved swiftly, wanting to be close to Tara when the powder blew.

Tara slept only from the exhaustion of both mind and body. Mule and Little Raven had put her between them, so in case one of the men got any ideas during the night, the two of them could defend her. Tara may have slept, but Little Raven and Mule did not. They lay awake because they had shared one quiet moment of conversation. They were going to make a break as soon as the camp seemed to least expect it.

A soft sound brought Little Raven to a sitting position, his eyes trying to pierce the darkness about him to pinpoint the direction of the noise. It came again, and this time Mule sat up too. He put out a hand to touch Little Raven and whispered softly, "You think someone can't sleep besides us?"

"I don't know . . . It's strange, but I would swear the noise came from the place where the guns are and not the camp."

There was another moment of complete silence, then Little Raven spoke again, one word and so softly that Mule could hardly hear. "Windwalker."

"I would wager my life. We should be ready for anything. Waken Tara."

Mule bent toward Tara and touched her shoulder. Tara was instantly awake, and Mule had to stifle her cry as she jerked upward, prepared to defend herself.

"Shhh, Tara, be quiet," Mule whispered in her ear.

"What's happening? Mule, they're not—"

"No, girl, be quiet. Little Raven says Zach's here."

Tara's heart leapt. How did he get there? Where was he? How did they know? Her eyes tried to pierce the blackness, but she could see nothing except the dying glow of the fire and the men who lay asleep around it some distance away.

It was then that Zach's voice came ghostlike from inches behind them.

"Horses are by the valley neck. There's going to be one hell of an explosion pretty soon. Be ready to run. We're going to get one chance and that will be it."

She couldn't see him, but just the sound of his voice filled her with hope, as it did Little Raven and Mule. Little Raven reached to take her hand. If they had to make a run for it, he was going to be at least close to one side. He was pretty sure Windwalker would be on the other.

The explosion was resounding, and what shells didn't explode at once began to explode in steady pops, making the sleeping men leap to their feet feeling as if they were being attacked. Their full attention was on the store of guns. At that moment Little Raven leapt to his feet, pulling Tara suddenly erect with him. Mule was already moving. She felt Zach's strong hand grasp her free one and they were running.

Tara felt as if her feet were barely touching the ground. They heard the confusion that had resulted when someone had gathered his senses enough to check on the prisoners, and they knew pursuit was imminent. They reached the horses. Little

369

Raven would have taken Tara before him, but Zach thrust him toward a horse and there was no time to argue. Mule was already mounted. Little Raven mounted quickly and so did Zach, reaching down a stong arm to pull Tara up before him. Nothing felt as wonderful as his arms did when they came about her.

They broke into a run, heading for the valley mouth. They rode past the valley mouth and out onto the plain. But Zach did not stop. He had tried to run the balance of the horses off, but he was not too sure how far they would run. Of course, he wasn't too sure the men would leave the guns before their leaders came, just for the sake of the prisoners. . . .After all, the prisoners were an Indian and a sympathizer, with a woman who had openly claimed she had left her white world behind to become the wife of another Indian. In their minds, it would be hard for those at the fort to believe the prisoners' story of guns and traitors.

They had turned to follow the valley wall, having ridden for a time before Zach reined his horse to a stop.

"My horse is just ahead in the little cut," he said as he slid from the horse's back, leaving Tara still mounted. "Little Raven, get it quickly."

Little Raven nodded and kicked his horse into motion. In the moonlight Tara could see Zach clearly now. All she could think of was that he had come for her.

Mule dismounted and walked to stand close to Zach. They stood together, and Zach reached up to cover Tara's hand with his. "Don't worry, we'll be out of here safely." His voice caressed her, and she felt a quickening mingled with a deep ache of gratitude.

Little Raven came back pulling Zach's horse behind him. Zach walked to it and Mule followed. For a moment they were out of Tara's hearing.

"It is better that we split up, Mule. You and Little Raven ride east, and I'll take Tara with me. If they follow they'll have to choose."

"I knowed you'd come back, boy. I told Tara you would."

"Did you doubt I'd get her out of there safe?"

"I didn't know you was there. I told Tara to say what she could to give us time."

"What do you mean say what she could?"

"Your name isn't exactly scarce around here, and I knowed they was jumpy just thinkin' you might come." Mule chuckled. "So I told Tara to tell them she was your woman. It sure shook 'em up some."

Zach froze, the jolt of Mule's words rendering him momentarily speechless. Tara had not meant the words he had overheard. They had been just a means to keep her safe a while longer. The bitterness of the truth was like a physical blow. He could hardly catch his breath, and when he finally did, his voice grated hoarsely, "And the dress she's wearing?"

"Little Raven's idea. You sent him for clothes and he got the best. Real smart of the boy, and it sure looked good when she stood up and told them she belonged to you. Worked real well. I can still see how they swallowed it."

"Yes," Zach said softly. "Such a lie would be difficult for them to understand."

Before Mule could speak again Zach moved away. "Let's get going, Mule. It's too dangerous to stay here any longer. Little Raven, get mounted, and you and Mule clear out of here. Stick to the high trail and circle around. I'll meet you at the fort in two days. With Tara to prove what happened, at least Aaron will know Little Raven and I are not guilty."

"Be careful, my brother. Autumn Dove has had enough of these men. She is a courageous woman."

"Autumn Dove," Zach said, feeling that Tara had used even the name he had given her to prove she was his, all the while probably detesting the thought that even these renegades would believe she belonged to him.

"It is a name that suits her," Little Raven said in a pleased voice.

"Little Raven, get moving," Zach said shortly. "We have no

idea how much time we have, and if Standing Wolf and Running Fox get on our trail they'll be hard to shake."

"I'll be careful," Little Raven replied, but he frowned as Zach walked to his horse and mounted without even looking in Tara's direction. Something was very wrong. "Windwalker, are you sure we cannot all travel together?"

"No," Zach said in a clipped voice. He kicked his horse, slapping Tara's horse's rump as he passed to force the animal into action.

Before Mule and Little Raven rode in the opposite direction, they both watched the retreating figures, then exchanged puzzled looks.

"He goes through all this, risks getting caught to save our skins, then he treats her like this. I don't know what's wrong but something sure is," Mule said peevishly.

"I could have sworn that when we stopped he was happy to see her safe. He even held her hand. Mule, what changed it?"

"Damn if I know," Mule shook his head. "When that boy sets his mind to a thing, he sure as hell is as obstinate as a mean buffalo. When we get to the fort, maybe we can shake some sense into him."

"I hope so, Mule. I wouldn't want to see him lose her forever. I feel she loves him deeply. Did you hear the pride in her voice when she told them she was his woman?"

Mule stood quiet for a moment, a thoughtful frown on his face. Then he mounted and waited for Little Raven to do the same. "Little Raven, I got a hunch Zach was pretty close when Tara was standing up to 'em. You think maybe close enough to hear what she said?"

"That should please him, not make him so cold and angry."

"Lessen he heard something that made him think otherwise. I was so busy tellin' him I told her to say that and bein' so all-fired happy. It gave us time, and I never thought anything would go wrong when I told him that I was the one who told her what to say. I just let it slip, and now he thinks she lied to protect herself and us."

372

"But he should still even be glad that it saved her."

"You don't get it, Little Raven. He is glad she's safe. What hurts is he didn't want those words to be a lie and now he thinks they are."

"Mule, maybe we should go after them. Windwalker might—"

"No, he won't say a word most likely, just take her home and walk out of her life like a shadow. And he's gonna be hurtin' the rest of his life when he does."

"Maybe not, Mule," Little Raven said thoughtfully.

"Why maybe not?"

"I heard things in her voice, Mule, pride and love. She is not a little girl. She knows her heart. Maybe if he doesn't come to her, maybe she will go to him. I do not think Autumn Dove will give up as quickly as Tara Montgomery might have. Maybe my strong brother will be taught a lesson in stubbornness he never knew before."

"I hope you're right, boy, I shore hope you're right."

Tara was so caught up in the excitement of knowing Zach was so close and they might have the chance to be together before they returned to the fort that it took her some time to realize he rode in a stone-cold silence. He kept their speed just fast enough so they could not talk. But she was so sure he would not push the horses beyond endurance before he let them rest a bit. Then she could say to him what she had said to her captors.

But the ride seemed to go on for hours, as again and again he took precautions to make sure there were no followers. There was a hint of gray on the horizon heralding the birth of a new day before Zach stopped, and he stopped so quickly Tara almost collided with him. "Tara, lead your horse to the shade of those trees and unsaddle her. Be sure you rub her down good and don't let her get to water too fast. I'll find some food."

He disappeared into the shadows before she could even

373

speak, and she stared after him in mute surprise. The warm Zach who had taken her hand so gently in his was gone and in his place was a cold stranger. She had a million questions to ask and set about taking care of the horse while she waited for his return. She had finished what she had to do and, to her pleasure, found some dried meat wrapped in the saddlebags that she had just removed from the horse.

She sat down on a blanket to wait, chewing thoughtfully on a piece of hard dried meat as she did. It took a long time until she could hear Zach returning. He had found some berries and nuts and carried them back in his hat.

When he dismounted he walked to her and set the hat down beside her. "Where did you find the food?"

"On the saddle. It's hard but it's good. Sit beside me and have some."

He reached out, and took a piece, and bit off some, but he did not sit down beside her. Instead he walked to his horse and unsaddled it. Tara was instantly aware that the old Zach was back, and she remained quiet until he finished his work. He returned to sit some distance from her. Tara would never know that he was controlling the need to hold her with an iron will.

"We'll only be here an hour or so. I've checked the trail behind us, there's no sign of anyone. But I want a lot of distance between us just in case."

"Zach, how did you know where we were?"

"I didn't find you, you found me. I was watching and waiting for Caleb and whoever is in this with him to come to the camp. Then I would have had them all."

"And instead you have Mule, Little Raven, and me," she laughed, but the laugh died before his silence.

Tara rose from where she was and walked to Zach, who steeled his nerves with more control than he thought he could master. She dropped to her knees beside him, and for the first time since she had been rescued, Zach met her eyes with his. Tara was met by a cold, impenetrable blue wall. For his peace, Zach could not let her within his guard. He could not be

374

touched by her beauty again, and he smothered the need for her beneath his will.

"Zach, there is so much I want to say to you."

"There is nothing more to be said between us, Tara. I'll take you back to the fort and maybe just once the truth will come out for Aaron and the rest to understand. Once they know for certain what I tried to tell them is true, at least they'll be on guard. Maybe I'll be luckier next time."

"You meant to go after them again! Zach, this time they'll be prepared for you."

"Prepared or not, I have to stop them. This time Caleb and whoever else it is won't be lucky."

"You mean to kill them?"

"There is no other way."

"And what if they kill you?"

"The loss of one Indian will hardly be noticed, and Caleb's plans will be completed."

"You say that so coldly, as if your life means nothing."

"I thought you grew up somewhere along the line, Tara," he said coldly. "One life doesn't mean much. If I succeed, it will be worth it. If I don't . . ."

"I did grow up, Zach, and I won't take your casual words any longer. I can tell Aaron the truth. It's all he will need. I'm sure he and David both will come up with a way to find these men."

"I'm afraid the battle is too personal for that now. You tell Aaron all the truth you want, but I want Caleb Banning." He refused to say that he wanted to hit back at them for what she had been put through. He refused to admit, even to himself, that when he had seen her hurt, a rage had built in him and her betraying words had made it impossible to let go.

"Zach," Tara said softly, "what happened to Autumn Dove?"

"Let's skip the games, Tara. You don't need them. I've promised to take you back, so save your sweet smiles and pretending for someone else."

"I know what you've always felt about me, and maybe at

375

first you were right. But I am not the same woman who came here. I was Tara Montgomery for a long time, angry at you and everything you stood for. Then after a while I became a strange combination of Tara Montgomery and Autumn Dove. But now—now I have given it a lot of thought, and I think I am more Autumn Dove than anyone else."

"Don't think dressing like one of us is going to make a difference. You haven't changed, Tara, it's just your environment. When you're back among your friends and you see their scorn and laughter, you will quickly forget Autumn Dove. She will die a bitter death. You had best hold on to Tara Montgomery."

"It isn't the clothes," she protested. "If you felt this way, why did you send Little Raven to get them for me?"

"My brother can sometimes get a little out of hand. He tends to meddle in affairs that do not concern him."

"You didn't send him for the dress?"

"Yes, I sent him for clothes."

"But not this particular kind of dress?"

"You know what it is?"

"Yes. It was your mother's wedding dress. I—I had hoped that maybe your thoughts had changed toward me."

"The dress makes no difference, Tara," he lied. "Little Raven made a mistake, or he didn't understand what I meant. I sent him for clothes so that you would be more comfortable, that's all."

"Zach, look at me."

Again Zach's eyes met hers. He was shaken by gentleness, by a warm smile, and by a look in her eyes that nearly destroyed his self-control. But Zach was too vulnerable. He could not let her inside his defense. He could not struggle with the pain again.

"Why is it so wrong for me to care, Zach? Why do you think I cannot understand and change? Why can I not be Autumn Dove?" Her voice was a velvet whisper. "And why are you afraid to care for me?"

376

"Tara, your romantic little-girl heart is creating fairy tales again. Prince Charming doesn't have red skin, Tara, and you can't play games with people and walk away." He rose and looked down at her. "I'll saddle the horses. We'd better be on our way. I want to get you back to the fort in a couple of nights."

He walked to the horses, knowing he was running away from all that he truly wanted and knowing once they reached the fort, Tara would be lost to him forever.

Tara watched him closely as he made rapid preparations to leave. There was a glow in her eyes that could well have warned Zach he had pushed Tara one time too often and just a little too far.

"We have to camp tonight, my stubborn warrior. Maybe you can say the words of separation easily, but there are some things that can defeat words. I am Autumn Dove and I am as stubborn as you and I am as determined to get what I want as you. Yes, we will camp tonight. Then we will see just how you can deny what you know the truth is. We will see. . . ."

Zach led the two horses back to her and was relieved when Tara mounted with no argument. He mounted and they rode on, but Zach had the uncomfortable feeling that a storm was pending . . . or something remained unfinished.

Tara smiled. He was right. Something was unfinished . . . and she planned to finish it to her satisfaction and, she hoped, to both their pleasures.

Chapter 33

Zach pushed them on and on, denying to himself that he sensed her every move. That he was so aware of her presence made each moment a hell for him. He was also aware, not only of her silence, but that her eyes were on him, for he would catch the quick look occasionally. The only problem was that he couldn't read what was behind those green eyes.

Was she angry again at being forced to spend so much time alone with him as she had before? Was she uncertain about how he would treat her? What did she expect now?

Sure now that they were not being followed, he knew there was no reason they should not stop soon. She must be hungry and tired, he thought, but if they stopped the hours would be long—too long to be comfortable. It promised to be one of the worst nights of his life.

The sun was a huge red ball just slipping below the horizon when Zach surrendered to the inevitable. They had to stop. He cursed to himself, for the place they finally stopped was a small clearing nested in a grove of trees. He had stopped because the thirsty horses sensed water nearby, and he couldn't deny them. But the spot was certainly a threat to his peace of mind. It was no threat to Tara, however, who was more than pleased with the circumstances, especially since a large gold moon seemed to share her intentions by casting the clearing in a soft

378

mellow light.

Zach busied himself, first caring for the horses, then building a fire out of the wood that Tara was gathering. There was still only the dried meat for them to eat, but this was one night that Tara cared very little for food.

Zach spread her blanket on one side of the fire and very carefully made sure his was on the other. Just knowing she was here was bad enough, but sleeping beside her was just a little too much to ask of any man.

By the time he gave a final check of the horses and came back, Tara wasn't around. He searched the surrounding darkness but didn't see her. Walking to the edge of the firelight, he called out to her.

"Tara!"

"I'm coming!" Her voice came from the darkness. He was relieved and went back to his blanket and sat down. He began to unfasten the leather cords that tied his high moccasins about his legs and removed them. He lay back on the blanket and folded his hands behind his head. At the sound of Tara's approach, he turned his head to look at her.

She stood just inside the circle of firelight. Her hair, loosened and free, reflected the fire's flaming glow. She looked electrifyingly beautiful, and the white wedding dress was enough to disturb what little peace he might have found.

Tara walked slowly toward the fire and Zach had to grit his teeth, wishing she would hurry up and roll in the blanket and go to sleep. At least one of them would be able to get some rest. But Tara only stopped by the fire for a moment, then she circled it and walked toward him. She was shaking within, filled with the fear that he would push her away.

In a reflexive action he sat up, but before he could utter a word of command or protest, she knelt beside him.

"Zach, I want to talk to you."

"This is hardly the time for conversation. Besides, what do we have left to say to each other?"

"We have a lot to say, a lot that needs to be said."

379

"I don't need any gratitude, Tara," he lashed out. "I was rescuing my brother and Mule as well as I was you."

"I wasn't offering you gratitude, Zach," Tara said softly. She reached out a hand and laid it against his chest. She was rewarded by the rapid beat of his heart, which told her he was much more affected than he pretended to be. "We are past gratitude."

He gripped her wrist, meaning to thrust her hand away, but somehow he could only cling to it. "What kind of a game are you playing now?" he snapped.

"I think we are long past games as well. Do you remember asking me what it could mean to me? Whether I'm the courageous white woman who would flaunt her step beyond acceptance to those in the white fort? You told me it would be a lie if I said their rejection meant nothing to me."

"Of course I remember. It is still a truth neither of us can deny."

"You deny whatever you choose to deny," Tara replied in a velvet whisper. "But when I stood before my captors and they asked me about you and me, I said what I know now is more truth than anything else."

"Don't, Tara. Tonight is no time for gratitude that you're going to be sorry for later." He turned from her and stood up, only because he felt his resistance melting like snow before a fire. "We'll be back at the fort in a short while, and you can pick up your life where it was before I disrupted it. I have to finish what I started."

Tara walked up to stand behind him, and for a moment Zach closed his eyes, feeling her presence like a pervading warmth. After a few minutes she smiled, knowing why he refused to face her. She could feel the tumultuous need as well as he. She walked around him and faced him again. He stood with his back to the fire, and she knew very well that the glowing flames brightened her; she wanted just that effect. "Don't you want to know what was said?"

"No," he lied again valiantly, trying to keep from telling her

380

that he knew, that he had heard every word, that he had even died a little when he found them to be untrue.

"Who's running away this time, Zach?"

"Damnit, Tara, what the hell do you want from me? You're safe and you can go back . . ."

"No, Zach, I can never go back. As for what I want from you—" she smiled, "I want you."

"Stop it, Tara, I won't play the game with you. Somehow I always get sliced up in the process. I'm too bloody now to care."

As if she didn't hear his voice, Tara continued to talk, only as she spoke she began to unlace the front of her dress.

"I told them I was your woman, Zach," she whispered, shrugging the dress down over her shoulders. "I told them I belonged to you." The dress moved down, slipping lightly and easily to her hips. Zach watched the firelight kiss her flesh as if he were mesmerized. The dress swished silently to a mound at her feet and she stepped over it to move within inches of him.

Zach could feel the perspiration on his skin. A heat began somewhere in the center of him, expanding until his bones felt like liquid fire. He couldn't allow this to happen to him! His desire warred with logic. He could not touch her only to lose her again. It would be too much to stand. But for the life of him he couldn't move as her hands reached for the ties of his shirt and loosened them. Her hands felt like touches of brilliant heat against his skin. She moved closer, tugging his shirt loose so she could put her arms about him and caress back. "Zach, you told me not to lie. You told me not to deny what there was between us. Well, I've learned not to lie. I want you, Zach. I want you to belong to me, and no matter how I have to fight for you, I will. I can say this more honestly than I've ever said anything before. . . . I love you, Windwalker, Zachary, no matter who or what you are. I love you and I want you. You decide now what your own truths are." She reached up to draw his head down to her, and their lips met in a kiss that battered Zach's senses and assaulted his logic until his head spun. He

381

felt her hands slide down to slip again beneath his shirt and move across his skin. God, he groaned, she could drive him beyond reality. He meant to grip her shoulders and push her away, still sure this was only another dream to be lost. He meant to, but the grip turned to a caress as he felt her soft warm flesh beneath his hands. He held her shoulders, feeling the warmth of her skin and feeling his control slipping. Without knowing he was exerting any force, she was in his arms. From there, all reason was lost as he caught her to him. "Damn you, Tara," he groaned, and was rewarded by a soft throaty laugh as their mouths sought each other. She had won, and if he paid for it until the day he died, he could not let her go now. He kissed her feverishly and she opened her mouth to him, letting their tongues twine, tasting each other with a savoring intimate and rapidly growing passion.

Zach was lost in her. Any thread of rational thought fled before her eager, giving embrace. Tara was drunk with the desire to touch him. She tugged at the shirt again, only this time there were hands to help her. Soon they stood in a renewed embrace where nothing inhibited them. They moved almost as one to the blanket, and he gathered her possessively into his arms again, kissing her temples and stroking her hair.

Slender fingers caressed the flexing muscles of his arms and back, sliding around him to draw him closer. Her body trembled from his caresses and the gentle touch of his hands sent violent shreds of excitement hurtling through her until she could hardly bear the exquisite pain of it all. She arched to seek their joining, but Zach refused to let this miraculous thing end too swiftly.

Through passion-darkened eyes, Zach gazed down at her. Her flame hair caught the moonlight's glow. Her eyes, half closed, were glazed with desire. Moist, warm lips parted and sought with the same need that consumed him. The dam within him burst and his passion flowed without restraint.

The night air was cool on her bare skin, but his hands seemed heated by a smoldering fire and they created electrical sensations as they skimmed her body, capturing her breasts to evoke pleasure. She whispered a soft whimper of delight and arched against his palm. He replaced his hands quickly with his mouth, suckling and licking until she moaned with the exquisite torture. Hardened passion-filled nipples tingled at the touch of his lips and a flame licked through her as his hands sought to explore.

His lips began to torment her, wandering where they would until she could have screamed with the desire that boiled within her.

Tara was oblivious to her surroundings now. Nothing existed in her whirling world but the hands that gently caressed her and the mouth that had ravaged her willing one.

Her hands seemed to have their own will as they slid from the breadth of his shoulders to the broad fur-matted chest. Her mouth tentatively tasted his flesh as his had done, finding the reward stimulating as she felt his iron-hard arms bind her gently but firmly against him.

The shaft of his passion throbbed hard against her belly, and her hands continued to trace a path toward it, drawn by desire as old as time itself, the desire to know and to feel the sweet pleasure of total possession.

His body seemed to be molten liquid as her seeking hands discovered his maleness. A low sensual groan escaped his lips as her hands moved upon his hard muscle-corded body.

He contained the desire to be within her now, easing the aching need of his tormented body. He closed his eyes for a moment to bring the conflagration under control. Then again hard-sinewed arms lifted her, and she felt the power of his possession and was inflamed and completely intoxicated with it. She closed her eyes again as he lifted her against him. Her body seemed to be afire. She had never felt so alive and so sensitive to touch. Each caress of his hands, each touch of his warm lips, made her want to shriek in ecstatic agony, yet she could only murmur soft unremembered pleas for the remarkable awakening to continue.

Her breath was rapid and uncontrolled as again he fed the growing passion that was destroying any restraint she had left. Their bodies came together in a blending that made her cry out in blissful ecstasy.

It was torture, but blindingly beautiful torture. It was pleasure beyond anything she had ever known. She opened to him in a seeking as deep as his own and was filled as his fiery shaft plunged to the depths of her over and over again.

Sweat glistened on their bodies and each strained to give more deeply and capture more completely. It was gentleness enclosing hardness. It was sensitive and wondrous need turning to sheer and overpowering rapture. It was a complete merging of two into one. Something unique and forever unforgettable was formed as waves of pure ecstatic pleasure washed through her, and somewhere within them both was embedded the knowledge that this joy, this belonging, this rightness, could only happen between them. It was the two souls reaching to unite and succeeding with total and absolute consummation.

They lay very still for some time. Their breathing slowed as the primitive force that had captured them and held them beyond reality subsided.

Zach buried his face in the curve of her shoulder, catching her hair in his hand as if to resist the knowledge that their eyes must eventually meet. He was also certain that this loss would be the hardest of his life and never to be forgotten.

But Tara was still lost in the magic of what they had shared. She clung to him, her eyes closed, knowing she had battered his sensual defenses and knowing, just as well, she now had to batter his stubborn logic.

Slowly he lifted his head and turned slightly so he lay beside her. Tara half turned with him, not wanting to let him go. Ultimately their eyes met and held. Zach was shaken to observe a warmth there he had not expected to see. Some deep part of him recoiled in a tentative fear while he struggled for the self-control it would take to be able to let her go.

But Tara was getting much more adept at seeing his reactions and recognizing the shields being put in place. She also knew now the man that hid behind the shields.

"You don't play fair," he said quietly.

"I had no intention of playing fair. If I did, you would walk out of my life, and I can't let you do that."

"You're trying to fool yourself, Tara. This can't be."

"Why? Why, Zach, tell me why. Whether you want to listen or not, I love you."

"Stop it, Tara," he said, half a groan and half a defensive anger. "What can we ever have together?"

"Each other," she replied quietly. Then she added hopefully, "Zach, that's enough. Nothing else matters now. We could have each other and build a life on that."

"Where?" he asked scornfully. "At the fort, or maybe east, in your world."

"Or maybe between both people. Between your village and the fort. But still we'd have each other."

"One day you'd regret it."

"No. The only thing I would regret is if I let you leave my life now. Zach, I will say it again and again until you understand. I love you, and I want to be with you—wherever you want to go. I want to be with you."

"Words said now can be regretted later, Tara. I am what I am. And what I am can never be accepted by some people. Because you are with me you would be condemned in a way you can hardly imagine. If I loved you, how could you expect me to let you sacrifice yourself to a life like that when you could have . . ."

"Have what?"

"A rich life with a man who could give you . . ."

"Could give me what we have? I think not, Zach. You said 'if I loved you.' Look at me, Zach. Fill my heartbeat with yours, remember what we have just shared, then tell me you do not love me."

"Tara . . ."

"Tell me you don't love me, Zach—or tell me that you do. One way or the other, the battle must be finished here."

All Zach's reason told him to lie, to tell her that he did not love her. But his eyes were holding hers, seeing the truth there, and his heart sang a different tune. He could not say he didn't love her, yet he was still tortured by what his love for her could do. He wanted to keep her close to him forever. Did he dare admit to her that his love for her was a raging river that could never be dammed again? That she would possess his soul even if he never held her again?

"Tell me, Zach," she whispered. Her body moved closer to him and her hands caressed him lightly. It was a fragile touch, but one that broke what reservations there were. He caught her to him, binding her against him with arms of iron that told her he would not let her go again. He buried his face against her hair.

"I love you, Tara. How can I deny it any longer when I hunger for you always like a dying man? I love you. I want to fill myself with you, to hold you until life is gone from both of us. I love you, and I dread the pain my love can give you."

She caught his head between her hands, a wild exhilaration filling her. Again their eyes met, hers now filled with tears of happiness. Slowly she drew his head down to hers and their lips met, lingeringly, lovingly, blending in a surge of rapturous joy. Tara was laughing and crying at the same time when the kiss ended and he kissed the tears from her cheeks.

"I heard you, you know," he said quietly.

"Heard me? Say I love you? Well, I'll say it again and again and again! I love you, Windwalker."

"And I love you, Autumn Dove, but that's not what I meant."

"Well, what did you mean?"

"When they held you prisoner and you stood before them angry, proud, and so beautiful."

"You were there all that time?"

"Waiting for the time to get you out. Shall I tell you how

386

felt when you told them you were my woman?"

"How?" she whispered softly as she brushed strands of dark hair from his still-damp brow.

He smiled and kissed her gently again. "I wanted to hold you in my arms. I wanted to come to you and tell you all the things that had been tied up in me so long. I wanted to tell you how much I needed you and wanted you."

"And yet you would have taken me to freedom and let me go."

"For your own good," he protested.

"I will show you what is good for me." Her voice was velvet soft. She took his face between her hands and drew his head down to her, parted lips meeting his in a kiss of flame and desire.

Again they made love with a new kind of passion. Tara was where she belonged, she knew that now, and Zach branded her his in a way that left no denial in either heart.

After a while, when the moon was already on the descent, he put his blanket over them and they slept.

Zach was awake with the first gray line of dawn that touched the horizon. But he lay very still, knowing they should be on the move soon but not wanting to let the moment go. He held Tara close to him, enjoying her reflexive snuggling against his warmth. Her head rested on his shoulder and her hair spilled over his arm. With his free hand he grasped a mass of her tangled hair and drew it to him to inhale the fragrance of it. He spread her hair gently across his chest, letting his hand roam gently down across her shoulder and the curve of her waist. He knew now he had loved her for a long time, yet the knowledge of her love for him and the vibrant giving of her lovemaking stirred him to the depths of his soul.

Tara was stirred awake when he gently drew closer and kissed the soft corner of her mouth. He was more than pleased when she moved so willingly closer and murmured his name as her arm came about him.

"Good morning," he whispered.

"Oh, Zach, is it morning already?" she sighed. "I wish we could hold back the day just a while longer."

"So do I, but there's no help for it. If we want to get you back to the fort by tomorrow, we'll have to get moving."

"Get me back to the fort," she repeated. Then she sat up and looked down on him, giving him a view that gathered his full attention like a tidal wave. "And you are going to leave me there and go after Caleb, aren't you?"

"You know I have to. There are no choices."

"I know," she said, much too quietly, absorbed with his hands that slid up her arms to caress her breasts. "Zach," she continued as he drew her down across him, "take me with you."

He froze, his eyes widening with shock. "Are you crazy? I would never . . ." He paused as she smiled wickedly.

"It's not as though you have not done it before," she chuckled, bending forward and resting her body close to his. "Only the last time was not as promising as this would be."

"You are a delicious, delightful, and wicked little creature and no, absolutely, I will never do a thing like that to you again."

"Zach, why did you take me the first time? For my protection as you claimed?"

"No," he surrendered a truth he felt she already knew. "Because I couldn't let you go. I was afraid I'd ride back one day and find you in the arms of one of the gallant young lieutenants."

"The danger is not still there?" she teased. His arms tightened about her until she protested.

"The danger had better not be there. I would hate to have to eliminate one of the Army's best, but I'd do it."

"Zach, please take me with you. I—I just have a terrible feeling about the fort. I would rather be with you, no matter where it is."

"Tara, you will be much safer at the fort, and your fears are

388

for nothing. You'll be safe and I promise I'll be back as soon as I catch up with him."

"I'm afraid for you," she finally admitted.

"No, Tara, don't be. Remember, I'm safe in this wild place. And I want you safe at the fort."

"But . . ."

"No, Tara, let's not argue," he pleaded softly. "I don't want us to part like that. We have too little time left together. Let's spend it with pleasure rather than anger."

"Zach," she murmured. He drew her close and kissed her fiercely. Tara put aside her fears for the moment. But they lingered in the back of her mind.

Chapter 34

Star had stepped aside and let Aaron come in, closing the door quietly behind her and waiting for him to explain just what he wanted to talk to her about. But Aaron stood with his back to her for several minutes because for the life of him he could not think of adequate reasons to be here. Finally, when he felt he had some control, he turned to face her.

"It seems that you are recuperating rapidly."

"Re—recoup . . . what is that?"

"You're getting well. It's surprising. Your wound was very bad."

"I am very well. My sister goes to talk to our people outside the fort. I shall be leaving soon."

"Yes," he said quietly. "Some of your friends were asking about you."

"Friends?"

"I believe his name is Spotted Fox."

"Spotted Fox came to ask of me?" she smiled. "That is very hard to believe. He is a strong and proud warrior. It is not his way to ask of any woman."

"And that pleases you?"

"Yes," she said, but defiance had sprung to her eyes and something equally as resistant. But he couldn't name it.

"Don't you truly realize you would be a lot better off if you went to the mission school and stayed here? The life you will have to lead out there will be very hard."

"But I would be free," she said softly, "and maybe it is not as 'hard' for me as you think. Maybe . . . it would be much harder here."

"Star, I'd—I'd like to understand you. I'd like to understand your people more than I have." He stopped, knowing his words were lame and not able to explain what he truly meant.

"But our people know that you already think you know us well . . . and hate us."

"Hate . . . It's a strong word," he protested.

"But a truthful one."

"Hate can be changed," he said quietly.

"Hate is like the claws of a bear or the fangs of a snake. Not to be ignored or trusted—and very seldom changed."

"What harm have I done you that you look at me with such fire in your eyes? I am a man who has had as many reasons to hate your people as you have to hate mine." He paused for a moment, then in a voice expressionless and heavy he went on to tell her the story of his family. Star did not interrupt but wished she could stop his words, for she heard things she did not want to hear and felt much more than she wanted to feel. Sympathy and a strange kind of sadness. When he stopped talking there was a stillness that demanded words, words she was unsure of.

"I am not to hate all white men," she said softly, "because of what they have done to my people and still try to do. But you are free to hate all Indians for what a small group of them have done to you. Somehow I do not believe your white justice is fair."

"No," he replied. "Maybe it isn't, but it is all I know."

"And my people and our ways are all I know," she said with a new bitterness. "And there is no way to change our destinies."

"Why?"

"Why?"

391

"Yes, why? Why can people not change and learn from each other?"

"Because there are not enough who care."

"I care!" he said sharply. Again there was a poignant silence. Then he realized that she was not the foe . . . and she could not and would not do battle with him. She would only retreat before him like a wisp of shadow.

He walked to her and her dark eyes turned up to meet his. It was an amber wall, a wall he could not find a way past. It was hard for him to believe how desperately he wanted to remove that wall. He reached a tentative hand to touch her cheek, feeling how warm and smooth her skin was. Very slowly he bent to touch her lips with his. The kiss was a fleeting moment, but when he looked into her eyes the wall remained as high and impenetrable as ever.

He took a step back from her, wanting to say so much more.

"I'm sorry. I know that's not much of an excuse . . . but . . . I am sorry if it seemed I was trying to take advantage."

Star inhaled deeply. She saw before her an honorable man, caught between two forces and struggling with his honor.

"I'm sorry too," she said quietly. She turned her back to him and her voice was gentle. "I think it best that you go. There is little that we can say to each other. Maybe both of us have learned something, that our hatred was not always just. If we can carry that thought with us, it might change the future for many others."

"Can you accept it that I am sorry about what happened to you—and why it happened? Star? . . ."

"Yes."

"If you should ever have need . . . I mean if you should need my help one day, you will not let our . . . differences stop you?"

She turned again to face him. "Because of our differences, I could not do that. Can you see that it would mean I must turn my back on those I love. No, when I go, I must go forever."

"I want you to remember what I said," he declared

stubbornly. "Your people have very little future out there. With the buffalo hunters killing off the buffalo and the trappers growing in numbers, as are the whites that are moving this way, one day there will be a confrontation you can no longer win. I would like you to know you have a friend . . . and if you don't come to me, I will come for you." He tried to smile. "I did not have my doctor nurse you back to health to have you go out there and spoil all his efforts. I—I want you to stay alive."

"Why do you care?" she half whispered.

"I don't have an answer to that. Maybe I will one day. For now, I just want you to know. I know people don't change so fast, not on my side or on yours. . . . God, it sounds like a wall."

"It is a wall."

"Well, wall or no wall, if we want any kind of changes made, I guess it will be like walking . . . one step at a time. This is one step; we can make peace. We can end one part of the battle here. Star, we can make peace."

"With no terms?"

"Unconditional," he replied quietly. "No terms, no demands, no vague promises . . . just some kind of peace." He waited in silence, confused by his hopeful thoughts.

"All right. Peace . . . with no terms."

"Then you will send me word if you ever need my help?"

"I thought we had already agreed to no terms." She smiled for the first time since he had seen her, and the smile sobered him. It changed her coldness to a vibrant glow, and he stood in an almost breathless hope that she would do so again.

"You're right again." He held out his hand and she looked at him, doubt clouding her eyes.

"It's a white man's means of agreement . . . to clasp hands."

Tentatively she slid her hand in his and held it for a moment, then squeezed it gently, enjoying her responding hold. When he released her hand he walked to the door, then he turned. "Peace . . . with no terms . . . for now," he added quietly.

Then he left, closing the door very quietly behind him.

David and Small Fawn had left his quarters and walked across the compound, which was nearly deserted. When they reached the gate, the guards saluted in inquisitive silence and opened it enough for the two to slip out. Then they closed the gate behind them.

Less than twenty feet away Spotted Fox, Buffalo Horn, and Running Deer stood silently waiting. Spotted Fox was the first to smile and speak.

"Always, when I see you Small Fawn, I cannot tell the difference between you and Star."

Small Fawn laughed lightly, "Star would not be so happy to hear that, Spotted Fox. She is one of a kind and would be more pleased if you had eyes for her, knowing who she was."

Spotted Fox's face became serious for a moment. "Is this true, Small Fawn? Would Star be pleased if my eyes were for her alone?"

"I am sure, Spotted Fox," Small Fawn said quietly, "that my sister would find it a great honor should you find her pleasant and worthy of a warrior as proven and as brave as you are. But of course she must speak such words herself. I cannot speak for her."

"It is good," Spotted Fox said shortly. "Come, my father would speak with you."

The three led the way while David and Small Fawn followed behind. The distance of the Indian camp from the front gate of the fort was a little over one hundred and fifty yards, so it did not take them long to reach the first ring of tepees.

Formed into two circles, the tepees surrounded a very large one, belonging to Eagle's Feather.

When they approached the tepee, Spotted Fox asked them to wait as he bent to enter. David and Small Fawn did not speak. After a few minutes, Spotted Fox opened the flap of the tepee and, standing a little to the side, permitted David and Small

394

Fawn to enter.

Eagle's Feather was seated across the fire from them. He raised his eyes to quietly regard them as they came in. He was not a large man, but the atmosphere was filled with his presence. His face was lined with years and yet the eyes were piercing and alert. He sat cross-legged before the fire with a colorful blanket wrapped about him. He motioned to his visitors to take a seat near him. Small Fawn stood aside, allowing David to sit next to Eagle's Feather. Then she sat a few inches behind David and to his side, so that the chief's attention would be on David and she would be more mediator than speaker. Yet, Eagle's Feather's eyes held her for a long moment. He smiled and Small Fawn smiled hesitantly back.

"You are not the chief of this fort?" Eagle's Feather stated. David knew it was most certainly not a humble question.

"No, Eagle's Feather, I am not. But I was the one who found Small Fawn and the rest, and I am the one who saw the village. I am also the one who can claim that there is truth in my chief's words that he did not order this attack. He knew nothing about it."

"If you were not in the fort when the attack happened, how could you know for certain it was not your chief? His feelings for us have been known for a long time. He has never helped us before. Why does he choose to help us now?"

"Aaron is . . . complex. He has reasons for the way he feels, still he is a man of honor. He may make war on you, but never would he slaughter innocent women and children. It is not his way. He would fight you as a man, but never as a coward."

Eagle's Feather's eyes moved to Small Fawn, understanding very easily the look he saw on her face as she regarded David. Then her eyes moved to his.

"Small Fawn, you were there. You saw the men who did this. After your stay at the fort, do you recognize any of these men?"

"No, I do not. I am certain the chief of this fort is not responsible for this terrible thing."

Eagle's Feather nodded slowly, and Small Fawn was more than pleased that he did not question her words.

"Is your sister well enough to travel?"

As much as she wanted to stay with David, Small Fawn could not lie to a man she respected as much as she did Eagle's Feather. "In another day or so she should be. She is very strong and her care was very good."

"Then take these words to her. I will make this camp ready, and we will leave when the sun stands high two days from now."

Small Fawn nodded, feeling David's tension. He would ask her to stay . . . and she knew she couldn't. She was needed now by her people, and she could not live in the fort. The day might come when David made his decision, but she could not say any words to force it. She knew one day he could walk out of her life forever.

"Eagle's Feather, where will you go?" David questioned.

"Back to the village to rebuild," came the firm reply.

"But you are so few, so poorly armed. The men who have done this thing . . . they may come again by surprise."

"No. They may come again. But not by surprise," came the terse reply. It frightened David in a way he had never been frightened. Eagle's Feather would fight, and this time there might not be any survivors. Yet David saw the fierce pride and deep anger that filled Eagle's Feather's eyes and found it difficult to argue. He had to find a way to make Small Fawn understand that she must stay at the fort at least until he could get leave. Then they could have time to talk and make decisions. A kind of panic filled him and he turned to look at her. But her eyes were on Eagle's Feather, and the look of pride and understanding on her face made him shake. She meant to leave with them, and he knew it! He couldn't let her go, but how could he stop her? He knew her quiet logical stubbornness and was completely shaken by it. He had to try to convince her that her place was beside him, or his beside her, whichever they chose.

Again Eagle's Feather's eyes turned to Small Fawn. "You will be ready to travel?" The question was almost gentle. He knew she was being torn between two worlds; at least he was leaving the choice to her.

"I will be ready," she replied quietly, feeling David stiffen beside her. Eagle's Feather nodded in silence.

David looked again into the eyes of Eagle's Feather and knew, whether the Indian leader trusted him or not, that he felt Small Fawn's place was with them and not him. Still it was a sad, rather sympathetic look, assuring David that he felt there was no chance for him to keep Small Fawn. David felt a strange kind of futile anger fill him. Anger because he knew both sides were right and both were wrong, and both could not see any future for him and Small Fawn. He worried that the greatest battle of his life would be now—and most likely with Small Fawn. He had to convince her otherwise. In two days she would leave, and with the tempers growing short and problems building, he just might lose her.

"It is time for us to be going back to the fort," he said to Eagle's Feather. "I will tell Star that you are prepared to leave. I'm sure she will be ready. And I am pleased with the fact that you at least believe Aaron is not responsible for this tragedy."

"He seeks the men who have done this?"

"Nothing would please my chief more than to find these men and punish them for what they have done. He wants peace out here, Eagle's Feather."

"If he wants to keep the peace, then he must give these men to us if he finds them. We are the wronged ones, and we are the ones to punish them."

"These men are white. Aaron will not be able to do that. It is for us to punish our own."

"And that punishment will be just? I do not think so."

"It will be just! On that you have my word, and I'm sure Aaron's as well. He will punish them, but he cannot turn them over to you. Our chiefs in the East would be very angry with him, and they would punish him in return. You must leave

397

justice to him."

"If he catches them," Eagle's Feather said slowly. "We will watch and wait. If they are justly punished, we will come and make peace with your chief. If they are not, we will come and take them from you."

"You can't. You are few and poorly armed."

"We are few here. But our people will gather. There are many ways to arm ourselves. It is told that weapons can be had. There is a way and we will find it. We will not let the men who have done this go free. Tell your chief those words."

David could see the determination in Eagle's Feather's eyes and he knew no further arguments would work. He had to tell Aaron.

"I shall return to the fort now and tell my chief what you have said."

Eagle's Feather nodded and watched David and Small Fawn leave.

David and Small Fawn walked very slowly toward the fort, and they walked in silence. But as soon as they left the range of firelight from the village, David stopped and turned to face her. "Small Fawn, we have to talk, and we can't do it either in the fort or in your village. Come and walk to that stand of trees with me."

She nodded, but David felt she was just a little reluctant. This filled him with trepidation. Could she change her mind and decide to go away with her own people? Her sister and her people had an influence on her, and he was scared that it might be enough of an influence to take her from him. He took her hand in his, and they walked in silence until they stood within the dark shelter of the trees. After a few minutes, Small Fawn spoke.

"David, I have no choice." Her voice was low and he could hear the threat of tears. He drew her into his arms and held her for a long time before he answered.

"You could marry me."

"David . . ."

"No, just listen, Small Fawn. I've thought about this and thought about this until I've come to the only conclusion possible. We stand the chance of losing each other if we go on with the idea that either of our people have a right to make a decision that we should be making. We can't let others rule our lives and tell us how we have to spend a future that should belong to us. Do you love me, Small Fawn?"

"More than my own life but—"

"No buts. I love you and for us that's all that is important. I'm going to leave the Army, resign my commission, and build a small place somewhere close enough to Long and his family, so that we can visit and have friends. Long can teach me all I need to know and you can have Winter Snow for a friend. We'll be happy, Small Fawn, and we'll be together as it should be."

"Will you not regret it one day? What of your sister and your family?"

"My parents are dead."

"David!"

"I didn't know it until I got back to the fort." He went on to tell her what had happened to Tara. "When we get Tara back—and I'm sure we will—I can only hope she can understand, but even if she doesn't, I want to marry you. I cannot let you go, Small Fawn. I just can't. If you leave with your sister the day after tomorrow, fate might find a way to keep us separated forever."

"Because of me you would end the life you have worked for? You would turn your back on everything?"

"Because of you I would begin a life and I turn my back only on a life without you. Can you do that for me?"

"David, I don't want to see you hurt."

"Then say yes."

"I want to be with you no matter what, but I am afraid."

"Afraid?"

"Afraid you will one day look at me with hate and regret in your eyes. That I could not bear. . . . I could not."

"You will never see that because I could not hate you. You're the breath of my life, Small Fawn, and I want you to be part of my life forever. Say yes now and put an end to all the questions. I'll find a way to work everything else out."

He waited in a breathless silence, now knowing what he would say or do should she refuse.

"Yes, David. . . . Yes, I will stay and marry you, and I will pray that I am not making a mistake that will crush you."

He laughed, filled with a wild pleasure. Then the laughter ceased as he caught her soft mouth in a deep, promising kiss. He rocked her against him, savoring the giving response as her mouth opened to him and he felt her surrender.

In an urgency well beyond control, they fumbled to undo buttons, to cast aside unwanted clothing that restricted the touch of flesh against flesh that each desired.

His mouth explored her body, the shadowed curves and taut peaks, until a fire was stirred that raged out of control. Now tomorrows didn't matter, words and games did not matter, only this all-consuming fire mattered.

The sweetness of complete surrender, the ache of what each thought was the bliss of discovery, merged. She took him within her, merging and mingling separate needs into one. With rhythmic movements he blended them into a soaring oneness, and the night dissolved before a tempest that left nothing but their contentment.

Their breathing slowly quieted, their sweat-slicked and trembling bodies grew still, yet they held each other in a silence neither wanted to break.

"David . . ."

"Shhh, love," he whispered against her hair. "There will be time tomorrow to talk. For now, let's not question this. Let's keep this night."

"Tomorrow," she said, "is very frightening."

"Not if we don't let it be," he said with gentle assurance.

"You are always confident," she replied in an exasperated half laugh.

"I'm confident because I have you in my arms and I have

400

your promise. That's all I need."

Gently he held her against him, inhaling the sweet fragrance of her and letting his hands caress her slender hips, drawing them closer. Again and again he touched her soft parted lips with his, stirring a flame he sensed within her. Her eyes were closed and she clung to him, the only stable thing in her recklessly whirling world.

He touched her lightly, caressing her soft, rounded breasts. His lips whispered against her skin, her slender throat, her soft shoulders, then lowered until he captured a taut nipple. His tongue flicked against it, drawing a deep sigh from her.

His mouth returned to hers, hot and demanding, and her mouth responded now, returning his passion with wild abandonment. Tongues warred with each other to draw the deepest fire of their need.

Her mind whirled and crashed against the arousal that blazed within her. The beating of his heart matched the pounding of hers.

She closed her eyes, panting and breathlessly aware that the overpowering magic of his hands and lips had again begun its mystical control of her body and her mind. Her body reacted with instinct to this new and wondrous emotion that shattered her reserves and brought to vibrant life one and only one thought.

David . . . David who reached within her, touching the center of her being and bursting it into a million hot flames that licked at her senses until she felt she could bear the magical beauty of their love no longer.

The ecstasy of their coming together drew a moaning cry from her as her body arched in response to his movements. Her flame matched his. She was a woman, all woman from the beginning of time, and he was the mate ordained for her. Time and place had no consequence as they blended into one, catching the rapture and beauty of the fusing of their love.

She wanted to draw him within her, to hold forever; he crushed her to him as if he could make her part of him by the force of his need. She was his! His mind shouted and his body was released from all thought of anything but her possession.

Their worlds careened out of control, and they filled each other with the timeless possession and flow of love that made them one.

She gasped and nearly ceased breathing as her world seemed to burst into a million fragments and she tumbled among them, lost forever to any other reality but him.

For a while they lay silently together, each unable or unwilling to break the fragile dream that held them.

"This is as it should be for us, Small Fawn," David breathed softly against her hair. "You and I can share a happy life together. It can be so if we work at it and refuse to let others— any others, yours or mine—interfere in our lives."

"You must hold me and give me strength when I fear, David. I would be weak without you."

"Tell me you love me," he demanded gently.

"I do, David. I do love you."

"Then that is enough. It's all we need."

"We'll be happy, Small Fawn, I promise you. I will do everything in my power to keep it so."

"When will we marry. . . . When will we go from the fort?"

"As soon as my sister is returned." He hesitated, "I think she deserves at least an explanation. Besides," he smiled, "I want you two to meet. I think you'll like each other."

"No, we will stay until then. It isn't really fair for you to give up so much for me and not have some small peace of mind in return. We will wait until your sister is returned to you. Then we will go. David, you will be happy away from this life? I always thought you loved the warriors you belong to."

"Love my Army life? Yes, but not half as much as I love you. No, Small Fawn, there are no choices to be made. You will be with me and we'll make a good life together."

"Yes," she murmured softly as their lips touched again and his possessive arms drew her into an embrace she knew she would never want to leave.

Chapter 35

Little Raven sat atop the last hill that led to the fort. He watched Mule hesitate for several minutes before they would ride down to the fort. He was sure Mule shared his own hesitancy. Little Raven might never be listened to, and it was doubtful Mule would be if Aaron were not in the mood to hear explanations.

But their presence had been noted far before either could move again. The huge doors to the fort opened and three riders came out. They rode directly toward Little Raven and Mule, so there was little to do but wait. Before they were joined by the three riders, Mule identified them.

"That one in the middle is Tara's brother, David. The other two are Lieutenant McGiver and Sergeant Murphy. I reckon we got to start explaining pretty quick."

"Are they going to give us time?" Little Raven questioned doubtfully.

"I doubt they got orders to do anything else, 'sides, I don't know iffen we have to worry about the time to explain. We got that. 'Pears to me we got to worry about whether or not they're gonna believe us once we do."

Little Raven licked his lips. He had escaped being given the ignoble death by hanging here once, and he didn't look forward to riding back into the same situation again. He cast a quick glance at Mule, whose face was expressionless, then he sighed. He would have to put his faith in the fact that his brother and Mule knew what they were doing.

David and the two men accompanying him reined their horses to a halt very close to Mule and Little Raven, who both steadied their horses carefully. "Howdy there, Lieutenant Montgomery," Mule began.

"Mule." David's voice was not quite friendly but neither was it threatening, and this relieved Mule somewhat. "Where is my sister? Is she well? What's happened to her?"

"Iffen you'll give me a minute, I'll explain everything."

"Why did Zach take her, Mule? Where is she?"

"Lieutenant, you want me to explain twice, or can we ride on in and I'll explain to Major Creighton. That way we'll only have to go through it once."

"Just tell me if she's well."

"She's right fine. Nobody's harmed a hair on her head."

Both Little Raven and Mule could see David visibly relax. "All right, suppose we ride down and report to the major. Then you and I can have us a little talk. I have a lot of questions that need answering."

Mule nodded, and the five men rode back toward the fort. Little Raven was well aware that all eyes regarding him, as he rode into the fort, were not friendly. If Mule had not been with him, he would have been well on his way across the prairie.

They dismounted before Aaron's quarters. "Maybe you'd better wait here," David said to Little Raven. But Mule was already contemplating the atmosphere and knew Little Raven was more than a little uncomfortable with it.

"Don't reckon so, Lieutenant. Little Raven better come with me. I wouldn't want some damn fool jackass gettin' nervous and hurtin' the boy. It might just be the thing to set this place on fire. I'd say Zach and Little Raven's people are about the only thing that stands between you and an all-out war, anyhow."

"All right," David agreed. He looked intently at Little

Raven, noticing for the first time a strange resemblance to someone, vague enough that he couldn't place where, but he was certain he'd seen that face before. Mule smiled and spoke quietly enough that only David heard.

"Zach's kid brother and maybe one day the chief of Zach's people. Don't make the mistake of doin' the boy any harm."

David was quiet for some time, capable now of seeing the resemblance between Zach and his brother. Finally he smiled, "Come with us—" He looked questioningly at Mule.

"Name's Little Raven," Mule supplied.

"Little Raven. Maybe it would be better if you came in."

Little Raven nodded. He might have been nervous, but his pride would not allow him to hurry. Mule was amused as he slid gracefully from his horse, stood and looked about him for a minute as if casually curious, then walked up to stand beside Mule and David.

"You blamed little rooster," Mule muttered. "Don't get too cocky or you might have us both slapped back in jail." Little Raven only smiled arrogantly, and Mule was still mumbling under his breath when they walked inside.

Aaron replaced the whiskey in his desk. It was his third drink of the day and this was not usual for him. He had to be careful. Getting drunk on duty certainly wouldn't look good when he had a king-sized problem on his hands that could explode at any minute. Star had only been gone for one day and he had begun to miss her in a way he hadn't thought possible. It grated on his nerves and shortened his temper. He had spent the night in sleepless futile anger. He wasn't sure just what he was angry at, unless it was a set of rules he couldn't fight against a society that made his choices for him. He tried to draw on old hatreds for support and was dismayed to find Star's tragedy had killed them. Lost in his thoughts, the knock on his door sounded twice before he noticed it.

"Come in." He had expected almost anything, but not

David's reappearance with Mule and Little Raven in tow. He stood up from behind his desk as the three stopped before it.

"You sure have a lot of nerve, Mule," Aaron said sternly. "Just walking back in here after you helped our prisoners escape."

"Wal now . . ." Mule began.

"Don't bother with excuses, Mule. That's beside the point. What are you doing here with Zach's brother, where's Zach and, most important, where's Tara?"

"She's safe as can be, and her and Zach are pretty close behind us. We came on ahead to warn you and the fort about trouble brewing."

"You said Tara was fine?" David interrupted.

"Last I seen her she was pretty as ever and smiling. 'Course she's changed a bit, but . . ."

"Changed? How?" David asked worriedly.

"Not like you think. She's just more understandin' than she was before she . . . left here. Seems she found out Zach was tellin' the truth all along."

"Truth?" Aaron spoke quickly.

"Truth about Caleb and those guns. She was caught by that bunch and Zach had to get her free. Leastwise she seen 'em for herself and she'll be the first to tell you about them when she gets back."

"Just where are those guns?" Aaron asked.

"Out in Deep Valley, or least wise they wuz. Zach blowed a pile of the powder to hell and back. Still, I reckon they got more. We wuz too busy hightailin' it to do anything about the guns, so I reckon we didn't do old Caleb's plans much harm."

"Tara saw Caleb there?" Aaron questioned.

"Not exactly."

"So it's still Zach's word?"

"And mine and Little Raven's . . . and Tara's when she gets here," Mule snapped. "You sure as hell are a hard man to convince."

"I have to have more proof than that!"

406

"Wal, suppose you just squat here like a stubborn old buffalo and let those hopped-up bucks bring those guns to you—the hard way."

Aaron grit his teeth and glared at Mule for a moment, then he walked to the door and jerked it open to snap orders at the sergeant waiting outside. "Sergeant Murphy, put the fort on full alert. I want double sentries posted, and I want a full patrol to report here on the double."

"Yes, sir." The sergeant moved rapidly, and soon the sounds of rattling harnesses and running feet filled the fort. Aaron returned to his desk.

"Just how soon can I expect Tara and Zach?" he questioned Mule.

"I'd say within a day or so."

"Lieutenant Montgomery, I'm going to send out a patrol to see if we can run across them, then we'll send two others to scout the area. If there's any sign of hostiles, you tell them to get back here on the double. Under no circumstances are they to engage them. Is that understood? This fort needs all the protection it can get."

"I'd like permission to lead the one to meet Tara," David said hopefully.

"Permission granted, Lieutenant," Aaron replied. David was both relieved and puzzled by the subtle changes in Aaron.

"Reckon as how I'll ride with you, boy," Mule said. "Now we've brung a warnin' I reckon we'll be of more use with you."

"I'll be ready to leave the fort in less than an hour. With you to guide me, we should be able to run across Tara much sooner." David's voice still held a trace of worry and strain, enough to annoy Little Raven.

"Your worry for your sister is needless. She would choose to be with my brother if you would ask her."

"Little Raven!" Mule said, half in anger and half in warning.

"Just what did he mean by that?" David demanded.

"C'mon, Lieutenant, let's get ridin'. We can talk on the way. It's better just between us."

407

"Get going, Lieutenant," Aaron said. "You're wasting time here. Maybe Mule is right. . . . Maybe what you have to hear is better done alone."

"Yes, sir." David saluted and left, while Mule continued to watch Aaron for a few minutes.

Then Mule turned to Little Raven, "Suppose you step out and let the major and me do a little talkin', Little Raven. They's some things needin' said that it's best you ain't part of."

Little Raven was reluctant, obviously wanting to say a lot more to Aaron himself. But he nodded quietly, his dark eyes meeting Aaron's for a long moment, if to prove nothing else than his self-control. Then he turned and left. He stood outside Aaron's quarters, watching the activity of the fort as the patrols gathered, He hated to admit a touch of admiration and a well-controlled envy of the bright swords and rifles each man carried.

Inside, Mule watched Aaron as he slowly sat back down in his chair.

"Major, seems to me there's been a passle of things goin' on since I left here. Ain't anything important you could tell me about?" Mule inquired mildly.

"You want to admit you were part of Zach's escape?" Aaron smiled.

"Shore," Mule chuckled, "since it's just between you and me. But I got a feeling a whole lot more has happened here, cause you don't look all fired up about it."

"You're right there, Mule. Eagle's Feather and a group of his people have just left. They've been camped outside the fort for a few days."

Mule remained quiet, sure there was much more to this story than had been said. He was right, as Aaron went on to explain what had happened to Eagle's Feather's village. He reached for rigid control as he spoke, but there were words left unsaid that roused Mule's curiosity. Something had made a drastic change in Aaron, and Mule was puzzled. The self-assured commander seemed to be unsettled and off stride, and more than unwilling to confide in Mule.

"So Lieutenant Montgomery's friend, Longstreet, his wife and kids, and another girl from Eagle's Feather's village have remained behind for a while. David gave Long his quarters for a while and Small Fawn is living there with his family."

"Real decent of you to care for an Injun girl like that."

"What was I supposed to do? Throw her to the wolves? I'm not exactly inhuman, Mule."

"Seems I recollect a gal named Star. Ain't she a twin? Has a sister named . . .ah . . ."

"Small Fawn," Aaron offered.

"Yeah, Small Fawn. Pretty little thing."

"Yes," Aaron said dryly. He had no intention of offering any more. Before Mule could try to dig any more information, a corporal stuck his head inside the door. "Patrols are ready to leave, sir."

"I better get along," Mule said. He walked out on the porch with Aaron behind him. The patrols were all mounted and prepared to leave.

"They have their orders, Lieutenant?"

"Yes, sir."

"You made it specific they are not to engage the . . . enemy under any circumstances?"

"Yes, sir. I made it very clear. There should be no problems, sir."

"Good luck, Lieutenant Montgomery. I hope you find your sister quickly."

"Thank you, sir." David saluted, and the three patrols rode from the fort, separating just outside the doors and riding in three different directions.

Mule rode on one side of David and Little Raven on the other for some distance before anyone spoke.

"Mule," David said quietly, "I think you could be answering some questions."

"Shoot."

David cast one look at Little Raven, straightened his shoulders, and inhaled deeply. Whether Little Raven was Zach's brother or not, he had to have answers.

"What is there between my sister and Zachary Hale?"

"They ain't never told me."

"Damn it, Mule, don't play with words. There isn't a man out here any shrewder than you are. If anyone knows, you do."

"I think Zach's in love with your sister. Is that what you want to know?"

"Not exactly."

"That she's in love with him, too?"

"Not enough, Mule."

Mule turned to look at David, and their eyes met and held for several seconds.

"That they have the same problem you and Small Fawn do?" Mule added softly.

David jerked, "What are you talking about?"

"You said you didn't want to play with words," Mule stated flatly. "If you want the truth, maybe you had better use it yourself."

"What do you know about me and Small Fawn?"

"Ah expects all there is to know."

"How? . . ."

"You forget I been movin' from village to village out here for years. It's not something that Small Fawn's whole village doesn't know."

"Big well-kept secret," David said bitterly.

"Hain't nobody at the fort got any idea about it?"

"Aaron knows now."

"You told him?"

"Yeah."

"What kind of a bug bit him? Seems kind of . . . shaky."

"I don't know. Mule, do you think if Caleb is behind all this that he'd have enough nerve to have the fort attacked?"

"He'd have enough nerve to do anything, and he's got

enough weapons to do it, too. I wouldn't put much past him. Never could stand the skunk nohow."

"What's the point, Mule? Why? If he does do what you think he might, what good would it all do him?"

"Don't have the answer to that. Zach has a few ideas."

"God, this is a mess."

"What are you goin' to do?"

"I don't think you have to ask that."

"You're going to leave the military."

"Not until I know the fort and my sister are safe. I couldn't just walk away."

"There's a lot of trouble brewing. I hope it works out."

"For both white and red," David added.

Little Raven had listened closely to their conversation. He had heard his own people speak nearly the same thoughts. He understood his brother just a little better . . . but wondered if it were possible for red and white to mingle or to wed and live happily.

Caleb stood and looked at the distruction of the powder with a rage written clearly on his face. His rage had grown when he had been told of the capture and subsequent escape of Tara, Little Raven, and Mule. There was no doubt in his mind as to who was responsible. What he couldn't figure out was how Zach had known where they were, and how he had been separated from Tara one moment and appeared like magic to rescue her the next.

"Get the guns loaded up quickly. We'll go to Skull Mountain and put them with the rest. Since you stupid jackasses have botched the whole thing, we'll have to move our plans up. We'll get started gathering the men. We should be able to attack the fort within a week."

No one asked any questions because no one wanted to be in line with Caleb's anger. They moved quickly, packing the guns and leaving the canyon deserted except for the debris that told

411

of Zach's visit.

Caleb rode in a stony silence. Tara had been in his grasp, not to mention the fact that the two people Zach cared for the most had also been at his mercy and slipshod methods had left him none of them. But surely they could not return to the fort, where Zach, Mule, and Little Raven were wanted men. Caleb felt Zach would most likely return to his own village, and since he had kidnapped Tara, he would most likely not stay there very long. No, Zach would be a renegade and nothing he, Little Raven, or Mule could say would carry any weight at the fort, especially with Aaron, who never harbored much tolerance for the Indian anyhow. By the time Caleb was ready to have the fort attacked, he would be safe in thinking Zach and the others were far away. But it wouldn't matter where they ran, they could find no safety. Too much planning had gone into what was about to occur here . . . and too much profit was to be made by too many to let a few destroy all their plans.

Caleb laughed to himself. The intense gullibility of the Indians and the matching stupidity of Aaron and his men as to the real cause of guns being supplied to the Indians was monumental. They were prodding from both sides and soon they would destroy each other. He and the men who were attacking the Indian villages to stir their anger would profit when the blood bath was over.

Still his mind lingered on Tara. He had made plans around her and hated to be thwarted in his desire. Maybe he would make it a point, when all the confusion was over, to fire people up with the idea of a white woman being "taken and brutalized by a savage." He could enlist a lot of people to hunt Zach down, and when he did, he would make sure his demise was slow and agonizing. Then he would have to teach Tara a few lessons of his own. Once he had mastered her, he would be able to make another fine profit by sharing her with men who would more than appreciate her beauty. Yes, Tara Montgomery had a lot to account to him for, and he would make sure the accounting was memorable.

It would take them some time to get to the meeting place, but he had time. He would leave his men there with the whiskey and the slow gathering of Indians, who would be given the coveted guns and enough whiskey-laced enthusiasm to wipe the fort from the map.

While the Indians were being encouraged to the attack, Caleb would meet with the men who were behind this slow insidious plan. There they would discuss the spoils and who would get them. Caleb wanted land—land that future settlers would be forced to cross to the ever-beckoning California. Caleb would hold a large part of the gateway to the West, and he would reap a fortune. Now it was only a matter of time.

They reached the area known as Skull Mountain, so named because of a huge granite protuberance that looked decisively like a human skull. Behind it nestled a cavernous granite boldered area, devoid of any kind of comfort. Still it was a more than excellent place to hide the huge cache of guns already there and to contain the even larger group of men that would soon be filtering in.

Caleb called one of his men aside. "You've never been seen at the fort?"

"Naw, I ain't never had a notion to stop there."

"Well, you're going to now. I want news of everything going on plus, when we do decide to attack, I want someone on the inside to 'encourage' those in the fort to surrender and get out while they still can."

"You ain't going to let anybody walk out of there alive, are you?"

"Hell no, but they don't know that. Once we get them scared enough, we'll promise them freedom if they open the doors and go. Once the doors are open . . ."

The man nodded his total and callous acceptance of this blatant bloodthirstiness. He cared for little except Caleb's promised rewards.

"You saddle up and get going. Make yourself inconspicuous. Take one of the men with you to camp some distance from the

413

fort. He can carry whatever news there is back and forth. Remember, when we hit, as soon as the battle looks hot and heavy, you start talkin' about surrendering the fort and getting out, especially to scared women and kids. They'll be the ones to move the men."

Caleb watched with satisfaction as the two men saddled and left the camp. Before too long the fort would be empty and the land around him would be his.

Chapter 36

David was not too pleased when Mule and Little Raven said they were going to camp for the night and go on in the morning, expecting to meet Zach and Tara the next day. He knew it was getting too dark to travel, but his anxiety over Tara was plaguing him. Mule had said she had changed, but that shook him. How had she changed? Was she scarred from this experience in some way?

Reluctantly he made camp and later, when the men were asleep, Mule and David sat opposite each other across a red-embered fire. Little Raven rolled in his blanket a short distance away, but David was sure he was alert to every word that was being said.

"You think we'll run across them tomorrow, Mule?"

"Should. They was comin' here. Just takin' a roundabout way in case anyone was followin'."

David was silent for a while. Picking up a stick, he prodded the embers of the fire until it crackled and sparks flew. Mule remained silent as well. He knew David had a lot of weight on his shoulders but it was impossible to relieve it unless David wanted to talk. He waited.

"You know Longstreet, Mule?"

"Shore, knowed him a spell back. Good man."

"He's happy living out here with Winter Snow and his kids."

" 'Spects he is. He's a man kin make up his mind to do somethin' then stick to it. Kind you like to have beside you in any kind of a set-to."

"You've seen Tara in the past few weeks, Mule. What do you think she would say if I wanted to do the same?"

"Give up your military career?"

"And marry someone like Small Fawn."

"You know your sister better than I do."

"But you said she's changed."

"Yeah, reckon she has."

"How, Mule?" David questioned quietly. Mule was quiet. "I need to know, Mule. It's important."

"Hard for me to speak for her." Mule was uncomfortable with the conversation.

"But it's not hard for me," Little Raven spoke as he sat up. He'd listened long enough and was half angered that Mule was not defending Zach.

"Little Raven . . ." Mule began.

"What is wrong with my brother loving his sister? He is a better man than most at the fort, and he would make her happy. I have looked into her eyes, and I know she knows this. I also know she is much woman and can make decisions for herself." He looked at David intensely. "And she would understand and respect your wishes. She would accept Small Fawn as sister. I feel this is true."

David was silent again, but it was a relieved kind of silence. He returned his gaze to Mule. Mule had surrendered to the inevitable and smiled. "I reckon as how I think she would, too. But it still ain't our place to say. When we meet them you talk to her, tell her the truth and let her do the same. I reckon that's the best way to get to the heart of all of this."

"Yes," David smiled, "I guess it is." He turned to look at Little Raven again. "Thanks, Little Raven," he said quietly. He rose and walked to his blanket to roll in it and find sleep.

"I know it was not my place to speak, Mule, but I grow weary of Windwalker always having to be expected to feel shame for

416

his mixed blood. He is a man first, and his blood and the color of his skin should not be important if he loves her and she loves him."

"You're right, boy," Mule said quietly, "but that's easier said than done. Seems we can't do nothing but stand by. These people, even if we care for them a whole lot, have to make their own decisions."

"Yes," Little Raven replied as he lay back down. He lay quiet for a moment, then he added softly, "I hope I am never faced with such decisions. I will choose one of my own when the time comes."

Mule remained silent, but he also hoped that things could be that simple for Little Raven.

Zach and Tara rode slowly until the sun was high, then they stopped to rest and eat. They sat together beneath the shade of a tree for a little while, wanting to hold each other and knowing the time would be short. Tara tried again to convince Zach to take her with him instead of to the fort, but he was adamant.

"You need some time to adjust to your thoughts, Tara," Zach said quietly.

"You mean to change my mind, don't you?"

"Maybe," he replied. He refused to hold her eyes with his, and she knew it was a fear he had not yet conquered. It would take time to tear down the barriers he had so carefully built.

"I guess," he laughed softly, "that I still feel maybe this is a wishful dream and that one day I'll wake up and you won't be there."

"But I will," she replied in a half whisper.

"I cannot imagine now being anywhere than with you. Zach, let go of all the past hurts. I know how hard it must be for you to trust again, but I don't want you to just make love to me. I want you to love me, and I guess that has to begin with trust."

He turned to look into her eyes, and she sucked in her breath at the current that leapt between them. Sitting so close to him, she felt the sheer size and power of his body. His eyes were blue crystal and his dark hair was wind-blown across his forehead. She contained the urge to brush her fingers through it, concentrating on a more distinct urge to hold his eyes and transfer her thoughts to him so he would understand. Zach was just as caught in the current. He wanted her touch. He wanted, needed, was desperate for her soft warmth. The bitterness of the past could only be dissolved in her and he knew it. Her hands were folded in her lap and he reached to take one, holding her slender fingers in both his hands. He caressed their soft texture while their eyes melded together. He wanted to convey so much. . . . He needed to bathe himself in the current of her love, to wash away the hatreds and the anger. He rubbed his fingers across her skin so gently that unbidden tears leapt to her eyes. She knew without words what he was feeling, and she wanted to draw him inside and hold him until she knew all pain was gone.

"God, I want you, Autumn Dove. . . . I need you. . . . I love you."

She remained still as he continued to hold her hand with one of his and raised the other to gently brush his fingers over her lips. Her mouth softened beneath his touch, parting on a short breath. The warmth seemed to spiral down inside her to nestle in the depths of her body. Then slowly he stood, drawing her up very gently into his arms, feeling her body mold to his and her hands press against his back. Their bodies memorized each other, feeling heartbeat against heartbeat. He whispered her name against the soft thickness of her hair and heard the breath of his name against his throat with the movement of her lips. He drew her to him, tightening his hold slowly to enhance the powerful feeling of her curves pressed so intimately to him.

When he finally had the ability to release her, he took her face in his hands. His mouth touched hers once, then again in feather-soft kisses that shot wave after wave of agonizing beautiful warmth to the tips of her toes.

Again he wrapped his arms about her, imprinting her body

on his mind. She was washing him clean, and he could drown in the brilliance of the glow that was filling him, wiping away memories of the loneliness in the hostile world where he had always lived. When he looked at her again, she could not control the whimper of sheer pleasure she felt when she read his love-filled eyes. She was lost in his eyes, mesmerized by their magnetic pull.

Then, finally, his mouth took hers in a kiss of possession, given by a man who had spent too many lonely nights dreaming of such kisses. His mouth slanted and sucked, finding warm welcome in hers. His teeth nibbled on her lower lip, then his tongue soothed the ache.

Tara felt drawn into his heat. Coiling her arms around his neck, she pressed closer. She opened her mouth, tasted his tongue, breathed his breath. She gave desire free rein, wanting nothing more than him. The kiss grew deeper . . . and deeper.

Suddenly Zach lifted his head, as if he were listening to something he was reluctant, almost angered to hear.

"Zach?"

"Listen," he cautioned quietly.

"What is it?" She was again sharply aware of how alert and attuned he was. "I don't hear anything."

"Army," he said, controlling his miserable disappointment. "I'd say an Army patrol, and they're not too far away." He gazed down into her eyes, "It looks like you're finally home."

"No, Zach. That's not home," she replied softly. She moved back into his arms, drawing his head down to hers to kiss him again. "This is home," she whispered against his lips. "This is home."

She watched his warm smile and knew the peace and happiness she had been searching for. She responded with a smile of contentment. Zach knew with a certainty that she was his, that she had given herself so totally to him there was no room for his ghosts of denial. He belonged to her as well, and if he had to fight the rest of the world, he would keep her.

"Then I guess we had better go and meet them." He said the

words softly, but she knew that whatever problems had existed for him were gone. She nodded, and they walked to their horses and mounted.

It was still several minutes before Tara could see the long column of blue-clad soldiers that rode in their general direction. Zach stood up in his stirrups, shading his eyes with his hand to study the approaching men.

"Mule and Little Raven are with them, and if I'm not mistaken, the man riding between them is your brother."

"David!" Tara exclaimed excitedly. There had been so much to change her life since she had last seen her brother that suddenly she was a little scared. She realized how extremely different she would look to him. The last time he had seen her she had been a demure and proper lady. Now her skin was tanned, her hair free and loose, and she wore the dress of an Indian bride. Her stomach tightened in a knot and her hands groped the reins until her knuckles were white. Zach reached out to lay his hand over hers. Tara turned to meet his eyes and saw the quick smile of encouragement. She smiled back, knowing that whatever happened between her and David, nothing would ever change what she felt for Zach.

Mule drew his horse to a halt as did Little Raven. David raised his hand in a signal that brought the patrol to a halt.

"Mule, is it? . . ."

"Yessir," Mule pointed, "off there. It's Zach and your sister."

David gave a quick order for the patrol to remain where they were, then the three spurred their horses into motion and rode toward the approaching riders. Within ten feet of them, David drew his horse to a halt and Tara did the same. David could hardly believe what he was seeing. This was not the young little sister he had left at home. She looked as though she had slipped her environment about her like a shawl and belonged where she was. Tara was frightened, unable to read the look in David's eyes.

David dismounted and started toward her. Only then did she

see the white smile. She slid from her horse and ran to him, and with a deep laugh he caught her up in his arms. They laughed, cried, and hugged each other until both were breathless. Then he stood her back on her feet, catching her hands to spread her arms wide and look at her.

"Lord, Tara, you look so beautiful."

"Oh, David, I'm so happy to see you." Tears of joy streaked her cheeks and she could find no more words. He hugged her to him again, rocking her in his arms.

"I'm sorry, Tara, for not being with you when you needed me so badly. I'm sure it was terrible for you."

"I'm fine now, David, really I am. We will have so much time to talk now, and I have so much to tell you." Tara moved out of his arms and turned to look at Zach, who was dismounting and walking toward them.

Zach had watched the tearful but happy reunion. David Montgomery was a man to be reckoned with, and Zach hoped that this first battle for Tara would not be with her brother.

A quick glance down into Tara's eyes, as she watched Zach, told David more than words. Her eyes were deep wells of love. David looked again at Zach, whose face had learned long ago to mask his thoughts. But the mask slipped when Tara extended her hand to his and he reached to take it. It slipped, and David saw past it to the vulnerable man below. He also read a powerful emotion barely revealed but directed entirely at Tara, as if she were the only person in the world.

"David, this is—"

"I know"—he extended his hand to Zach—"Zachary Hale."

Zach was surprised, but he concealed it as he took David's hand.

"Lieutenant Montgomery. I had a notion you might not be as friendly."

"I wasn't until Mule assured me Tara was safe and that you were on your way back."

"I guess," Zach said quietly, "that we have a lot to talk

421

about, too."

"Yes, I guess we do. You could start by telling me why you took Tara from the fort."

"I could say she was necessary for my escape."

"But that would be a lie, and I don't think you're a man who lies."

"David . . ." Tara began.

"No, Tara," Zach smiled, "There is no need for lies of any kind," he said to David. "This is not the place for us to discuss reasons."

"Yes," David said slowly. "I guess you're right. It will be a long jaunt back to the fort. We can talk tonight, when we've settled. Maybe we can share a few . . . thoughts before we reach the fort tomorrow." He hugged Tara to him again as if he hated to let go of her. Then he released her. "Let's get going."

David walked back to his horse, but Zach stood for a minute with a puzzled frown on his brow. Tara moved closer and slipped her hand in his.

"Zach?" she said softly.

"Seems too easy," Zach muttered. "I wonder if Aaron is waiting to stretch my neck."

"David would have said—"

"Maybe, unless he has orders just to bring me in."

"No. David wouldn't do that."

Zach turned to smile down into her eyes. "Well, it really doesn't matter, love, because Aaron, your brother, or the whole Army is not going to be able to hurt us. One way or the other you belong to me."

"I do love you, Zach," Tara breathed.

"Then let's go."

They returned to their horses and mounted, then rode toward the others. Mule and Little Raven met them with enthusiastic smiles.

"Took y'all long enough," Mule complained with a grin.

"My brother grows old and cannot find his way so easily anymore," Little Raven chuckled. "Maybe I should have been with them to lead the way."

"Speaking of leading the way, little brother," Zach replied dryly, "when I send you for something, I expect you to get what I send for."

"You are disappointed in what I have brought, Windwalker" Little Raven asked innocently.

Zach chuckled, "Not disappointed, maybe just a little regretful that I didn't think of it first."

"Mother and Father have many questions to be answered when you return."

"I'll bet," Zach retorted. "I can just imagine the words you have used to encourage their interest. You have a glib tongue, my brother, and one day it's going to trip you up. I just hope I'm close by to see it when it happens."

Tara was not quite sure what their conversation was about, but she liked the way the three laughed together and she was prepared to laugh with them.

Zach, Little Raven, and Mule built their fire a little distance from the rest of the patrol. But it wasn't long before David joined them. Tara had remained close to Zach but was more than pleased when David found a seat beside her near the fire. For a few minutes there was a silence, not a taut and uncomfortable silence, but one that was expectant and filled with waiting.

"Tara, would it be too hard for you to tell me about Mother and Father?" David asked gently.

Tara looked across the fire at David and shook her head. Zach, who was within inches of her, moved even closer, as if to shield her from some hurt. He listened as she spoke of the accident, reaching to take her hand when she choked on the end of the story and became quiet.

"There's nothing back there for either of us, is there, Tara?" David questioned.

"David, we must speak of—"

"I know. Of you and Zach," David smiled.

"We'd rather have your approval," Zach said firmly. "But with or without it, I don't intend to let Tara go."

"Two years ago I would have been angry. I would have fought you in every way possible, and somehow I would have separated you and destroyed your relationship any way possibly could."

"Two years ago," Zach replied, "but not now?"

"That's right."

"Why, David?" Tara asked.

"You're a half-breed, Zach," David stated. "I would have condemned any love you had for my sister because of that."

"David, don't—" Tara began.

"I said that was two years ago," David continued. "I've changed, and I think you've changed too, Tara. Neither of us wants to go back. Neither of us could find back there what we would have to leave here. I have no condemnation, Tara, none at all."

Tara was watching her brother closely. They had always been able to understand each other as children. Now she sensed, rather than knew, that there was much more to this than he had said.

"David, you are trying to tell me so much more, aren't you?"

David ran his fingers through his hair, a sign of nervous frustration she remembered well.

"David?"

"Yes, I am."

"Then tell me."

David cast a quick look, first at Zach, then at Mule and Little Raven. Then he returned his gaze to Tara.

"Tara, I'm in love with a girl and I want to marry her."

"David, that's wonderful."

"It would mean I would have to leave the military."

"Why?"

"Because, unlike Zach, she's not a half-breed. . . . She's

full-blooded Indian, and I love her very much."

Tara blinked in shock, expecting something so totally different that she was taken by surprise and left momentarily speechless.

"I'd hoped you, of all people, would understand," David said miserably.

"But I do, David, I do. Why would you think I would condemn you, or her for that matter, without even knowing her? Tell me about her."

David warmed immediately to the subject dearest to his heart. Soon Tara was smiling at his enthusiasm and his obvious love for a girl named Small Fawn.

"When we get back to the fort, you'll meet her; she's staying in my quarters. I have a friend there, too—Longstreet." He went on to tell her all about Long and his family. "I can build a place somewhere near them, Tara, and we could start a life together that I know could be good."

"We can go back to the fort, but there are still a lot of problems brewing," Zach inserted. He explained that he was going to leave Tara there while he continued the search for Caleb and his men and tried to put a stop to what he was afraid was happening.

"I don't think Aaron is going to believe yet that Caleb is behind all this. No one can give him a logical reason. Caleb has nothing to gain except a little gold or something in exchange for the guns."

"He's not just exchanging, he's leading," Zach said quickly. "And, damnit, he's got an ace up his sleeve and I mean to have the answer to it. To tell you the truth, Lieutenant Montgomery—"

"Don't you think it's time we're on a first-name basis, for God's sake?" David laughed.

"All right. I think Caleb has a goal we just can't see. Besides that, I think he has others behind him; ruthless men who would stop at nothing to get what they want."

David looked faintly puzzled for a minute, as if he were

425

grasping an elusive thought. Then his eyes brightened. "I'll make a wager I could put my finger on the group that's with him in this."

"You know?"

David leaned forward, his eyes holding Zach's, and explained about the raiders who were terrorizing the Indian villages and murdering women and children.

"So they're pushing from both sides," Zach said softly. "And when the battle is over and the smoke clears, they're in possession of everything."

"Then"—Tara's face went pale—"they mean to kill . . . everyone in the fort."

"I'd say so," David replied.

"What can we do?" Her voice was thick with shock.

"Stop him before he can put his plan in action. That means finding him first, and that is not going to be easy. But between Mule, Little Raven, and me, we'll track him," Zach spoke quietly.

"We'd better get some sleep and get an early start in the morning. I don't want to waste any time. Minutes count," David said as he stood and stretched.

"I guess you're right," Zach agreed, even though he would have liked to have shared this one last night with Tara, the last night that they would have for . . . he didn't know how long. He knew this night was lost to them. He stood and looked down into Tara's eyes, reading the same want there. He let his fingers touch her hair lightly. "I've spread your blankets near the fire. I'll sleep between you and the dark. Rest well."

Tara could only nod. Zach moved silently into the night. David knew there was little to say that would ease this long night for Tara. So he rolled in his blanket some distance away and soon fell asleep. Mule and Little Raven had been asleep for a while and the fire was slowly dying. Tara sat near it for a while, deep in thought. She thought about the changes in all their lives and about her future. With the danger beyond the horizon, she had no idea how long they would be together.

426

There might not be very many tomorrows. Slowly she rose, walked around the fire, and picked up her blanket, then walked into the darkness.

Zach knew he wouldn't sleep but he closed his eyes, giving his frustrated dreams free rein. He was startled when Tara suddenly pulled aside his blanket and lay down beside him. He was startled but had no intention of questioning his good fortune. He wrapped his arms about her, drawing her close to him. Neither spoke, and after a while they slept.

Chapter 37

Small Fawn had not found her time at the fort all that pleasant. Her inherent shyness made it worse, for she found it difficult to approach anyone. No one bothered her, but the main reason for that was Long, who made it very clear that if anything out of line happened, whoever caused it would be accountable to him.

To reinforce this Aaron, to even his own surprise, made it clear to all the men in the fort that Small Fawn and Winter Snow were not to be disturbed. It did not have to be told to most of the women because they kept their distance of their own accord, with the exception of Mrs. Braughn, who made tentative friendly approaches.

When the word came that David's patrol was in sight, Small Fawn was excited and ran to the door to watch the front gates swing open and the patrol ride through. She couldn't run to him, as she felt it would not be right and it might shame him before his men. So she stood by the door and watched. It gave her a great deal of pleasure just to watch him as he dismounted. His broad shoulders made him a magnet for her eyes and his whipcord-lean body a strong remembrance for her senses. She knew he must speak to his commanding officer first, but she wanted so desperately for him to hold her. Would they ever be free? she wondered.

"Tara, you can go on over to my quarters if you want. I'm afraid we have to talk to Aaron. We'll be there as soon as we can."

Tara agreed, well aware now of the stares of the inhabitants of the fort . . . especially the women, and even more now of the dress she wore that spoke a million words. She knew now a taste of what Zach must have always felt when he faced the people here.

Zach watched her with worried eyes, but she smiled with more confidence than she really felt. "I'll go, Zach, it's all right. Besides, I think there's someone there I ought to meet."

Zach wasn't relieved—he knew bravado when he saw it—but she had a fine kind of pride and he knew she had to do it her way. He nodded and watched her walk across the compound toward her brother's quarters. At that moment he couldn't have wanted her or loved her more. He watched her until she walked up on to the porch, then the four of them walked into Aaron's office.

Small Fawn stood in the doorway and watched Tara approach. Some instinct told her this was the sister of whom David had spoken so often. She observed the dress and look about this white woman that was . . . different. It seemed to Small Fawn as if Tara stood with one foot in her world and one in another. Her air, her eyes, obviously belonged to the white world, but where was her heart? Small Fawn wondered. She had heard that David's sister had been kidnapped, but David had looked relaxed and easy, so there probably was no anger between him and Windwalker. Her curiosity grew as Tara came closer.

Tara had walked only a few steps before she noticed Small Fawn. She paused only for a second, then moved forward again. It was time to make decisive moves; it was time to breach at least one gap—that between her and the woman her brother loved. Besides, she smiled to herself, who could tell her more about the ways she wanted to learn and more about Windwalker than a woman like Small Fawn? She walked up on the porch and stood just inches from Small Fawn.

"Hello, Small Fawn," Tara said with an easy smile. "I'm David's sister."

The smile was invitingly warm, and Small Fawn paused to try to read any kind of derision or deception in her eyes. But there was none. Small Fawn's smile was a reflection of Tara. She stood aside to let Tara enter, then closed the door behind them.

Zach had watched until Tara disappeared, wishing he could just grab her up and ride away from all the problems. It would be so easy, and for a moment he was tempted. Then he thought of the condemnation he would read in her eyes should he let other lives pay for their happiness. David, who stood beside him, knew quite well what Zach was going through.

"Someday, Zach," he said quietly, "someday."

Zach turned to look at him, smiled, and nodded. Then they walked into Aaron's office together.

Aaron rose from behind his desk, walking around it to face the four men who entered. He was caught between anger and respect. He too knew how uncomfortable and even dangerous it was for the three who had escaped to return to the fort.

From past experience, Zach expected a great deal: distrust, antagonism, or downright hostility. What he didn't expect is what happened. After a long and strained silence, Aaron moved a step closer and extended his hand. "Zach."

Zach was so surprised that for a minute he didn't respond. Then he took the commander's hand, realizing something had happened to Aaron that no one but Aaron knew. "It seems as if we have a mutual problem to settle."

"As far as taking Tara from the fort," Zach began, hoping to end a situation before it developed, "David and I have already . . . taken care of that situation."

Aaron's lips twitched in a half-amused smile. "That's not what I'm referring to, although I'm sure that's settled. I'm talking about the danger to this fort."

"Well, I'll be damned," Zach grinned for the first time. "You don't mean to tell me that you're actually going to start believing what I've been trying to tell you for months."

"Zach, this isn't exactly the time to be amused. You still have no proof that Caleb is involved and I can't move against him unless you do."

"Move against him," Zach repeated quietly. "Aaron, I'm leaving the fort at dawn. If I don't find him, you won't have a chance to move against him. He will have gathered enough men and enough arms to wipe this fort off the map."

"Tell me where he is and I'll stop him."

"If I knew exactly where he was, I'd tell you. He knows I'm on his trail and he thinks I wouldn't come back here, so he doesn't think you'll be warned. The best bet we have is for you to defend the fort, and me and Little Raven—"

"—And me," Mule said firmly.

"And Mule," Zach smiled, "will go on the hunt. It might surprise you where you'll get help from." Zach's eyes held his brother's for a moment, and Little Raven smiled and gave a slight nod.

"I have patrols out yet," Aaron stated.

"They won't find anything," Zach replied.

"You mean the patrols that went out with me haven't returned yet?" David said worriedly. He had been gone overnight, which was most unusual, and not to have the patrols back made the hair on the back of his neck prickle.

"They might have picked up a trail of sorts and followed it." Aaron claimed.

There was no doubt in both David's and Aaron's minds that the three others did not believe this for a minute.

"Damn," Zach muttered. "Aaron, I'm afraid you've shortened the defense of this fort by a lot of able men. It makes it more imperative that you hold here. If you divide your forces any more than you have, this fort will fall and it will mean the death of everyone in it. That includes a life more valuable to

431

me than my own. No matter where you stand personally, Aaron," Zach added softly, "this one time you will have to trust me."

Six months before, Aaron would never have given a thought to trusting Zach, and now he was more than surprised that he did. He was also more than shaken by the vulnerable position the fort was in and the thought that the men he had sent out were. . . The idea appalled him.

"All right, Zach," Aaron's vioce was steady, as were the eyes that held Zach. "Find him, and if you can, find a trace of my men. I—I have to know. . . ." He inhaled deeply. "I'll hold this fort against the forces of hell if I have to, but I have to know if my men have been victims of betrayal by our own kind."

"We'll leave before the first light of dawn," Zach stated. "I'll do my damndest," he continued, "but if I can't find them, I'll bring as many of my father's people here as I can. At least we'll try to help with the defense."

Zach was about to turn and leave when Aaron spoke again. "Zach . . ."

Zach turned to look at him.

"We have a lot to say to each other one day. Don't go and get yourself killed until we can talk."

"I'll do my best," Zach chuckled. "Suppose you do the same."

"I'll make every effort," Aaron returned the laugh.

The three went back out onto the porch while David remained to talk to Aaron.

"Little Raven," Zach said, "you and Mule take our horses to the stable. Make sure they're well taken care of and ready to travel before sunrise. Mule, can you see we get enough provisions for a couple of days?"

"I'll get 'em," Mule replied.

"And I'll be sure the horses are ready," Little Raven agreed. The two left Zach standing on the porch and they headed for the stables, leading the horses. Zach stood for a long moment, looking about him. He was still certain he and Tara could not live here, but the worst thought was that they could not find a place anywhere. He was still caught in his unwelcome thoughts when David came out of Aaron's office and stood beside him. Neither spoke for several minutes.

"I may not be able to go along with you, but I have a friend that I know can be of more help than I—Longstreet. Come over to my quarters and meet him and his family . . . and Small Fawn. Long would be one to understand and he's a fighter who would be an asset. Besides, he knows the area well and he has a lot of friends among the tribes. What men you can't gather, he can." David turned his head from his examination of the fort and held Zach's eyes. "And I have a feeling we're going to need a lot of good fighters before this is over."

"I'm afraid you're right, David." Zach could not help but voice his anger and dismay. "If I take her with me, she could be killed out there. . . . If I leave her here, she may die with this fort and we would never see each other again. . . ."

"I know. . . . I know," David said quietly.

"I suppose you do," Zach said. He ran his fingers through his hair, a habit of frustration. The cold brittle sound of hatred filled Zach's voice again. "We have to find him, David, and when I do, I will kill him and that is a promise I've made to all the gods I know. He's caused all the grief and pain we're going to allow him to cause."

"Zach . . . these men he's involved with. They are very careful. If Caleb fails here at the fort, they will pretend they never knew him."

"And you think that's punishment enough for him?"

"No. But if you succeed here, then you would have to track Caleb to kill him. You know he won't stand and fight. Let the military bring him to justice. Let Aaron punish him."

"And why should I do that?" Zach snapped, his eyes glowing with bitter vengeance.

"For Tara's sake. If you track him—kill him like an animal

433

—then what does it make you? What will it do to you and Tara except justify what everyone wants to say—that you are a savage? Zach, it takes a better man to bring him to justice than to kill him and make everyone believe they were always right."

Zach looked away, reluctant to lose his revenge. Up until now he'd held it like a shield, and David wanted to strip him of this. He wasn't sure now that he really wasn't the savage he'd been labeled. It broiled inside him with a violence that he could taste. He couldn't let go of the years of his torment, not that easily.

"Who gives a damn what everybody believes? At this time I don't think it's important anymore."

"What about Tara?"

"I'll take care of Tara."

"By running when it's all over, and continuing to run for the rest of your life?"

Zach glared at him, knowing he was right but unable to accept that. He pushed everything away from his thoughts and built barriers. David could see; after all, he'd lived with them all his life. He decided to let it drop for now, hoping for Zach and their future's sake that Tara could one day change his mind.

"C'mon, I want you to meet Long. You're two of a kind. I think you'll get along just fine."

Zach wasn't quite sure what David meant but he walked across the compound with him. He was anxious to see how Tara had fared and to talk to her. Their time was much too short to suit him. He doubted very much if they would have one minute alone before he had to leave.

When David and Zach walked into the room it was to the sound of laughter, which surprised them both. Obviously Long's oldest son had said something that had amused everyone, for he seemed to be the center of attraction and seemed to be enjoying it as well. His face was alight with a wide grin. But it was a scene that disturbed Zach. Tara seemed so alive and happy, surrounded by friends and secure here in the

434

fort, amid her people. What would happen to that laughter if he took her from here and they had to live a whole new kind of life, more often alone than with people?

Tara rose from her chair and came to him at once, making matters a whole lot worse, for he knew any kind of separation was impossible for him to face.

Long had risen from his seat as well, and David was quick to introduce them. Long extended his hand to Zach.

"I know you, or rather I've heard a lot about you and I've seen you a few times. I reckon you just don't remember," Long said.

"We've met?" Zach questioned.

"Couple of times, nothing important, but I know you. You've got quite a reputation. It's a real pleasure to meet you."

"Thanks."

The introduction continued with Long's wife and sons, then Small Fawn. The women were quick to offer food and drink, and soon the men were seated and discussing the situation they all faced.

The children were put to bed finally, and Long and Winter now slept in the same bedroom.

"I'll spread a blanket on the floor for me and Small Fawn," David said. "Mule, Little Raven, you, and Zach are more than welcome to spread your blankets on the floor."

Zach rose, "I'll go ahead and sleep in the stable. I'm used to it. Besides, it will give you a little more room."

Little Raven rose and was about to accompany Zach when Mule bumped his arm. When Little Raven looked at him he winked, hoping the young warrior would grasp the purpose quickly. But Little Raven looked at him blankly.

"Me and Little Raven have a few things to talk to Long and David about, Zach. You go on ahead. Maybe we'll just bunk here. Might have a whole lot to talk about."

Zach frowned but continued on to the door. His eyes held

Tara's for a moment, then he left. By now Little Raven had gotten the idea. He smiled but remained seated. Mule walked close to Tara and spoke quietly, letting the words be lost in the bustle.

"Wouldn't be a bit surprised if you couldn't sleep."

"What?"

"Iffen you was to decide to take a walk sometime during the night, nobody'd be payin' any mind. . . . No sir, no mind at all. We're all real sound sleepers."

Tara smiled and laid her hand on his arm. "I knew you were a friend the first day we met. Now I know how good a friend you are."

"He's a good man, girl."

"I know, Mule," she said softly. "And Mule? . . ."

"What?"

"Thank you."

"You're right welcome. . . Right welcome. Tell Zach he owes me."

"I'll do that."

When Mule returned to Little Raven's side he was met by a broad smile filled with enough devilment for three people. But Mule chuckled and bent close to him. "And if you, my red skinned devil, go sleepwalking, I'll wear your hair on my belt. That's a promise."

"Mule," Little Raven said innocently.

"Don't Mule me, boy. Remember, I've known you a long time. Roll your blanket close to mine. This is one night, young shadow, when you're going to stay put."

Zach walked across the compound that was now completely deserted. His energy forbade sleep and his depression promised a long and lonely night.

He lay on the straw and allowed the past to tangle its talons of memories in his mind. He had been so self-assured, so confident of his life and what he could accomplish. Tara had

436

one things to his life he had not expected, and now there was
no way he could refuse to acknowledge that she would still be
better off if he left her life. He just wasn't too sure he was able
to.

The stable was a cavern of shadows, with pale beams of
moonlight casting it in a hazy blue-white glow. It was also so
very quiet that when he heard the creak of the door he was
instantly alert. He could not see the door through the vague
half-light, but he remained very still, gathering his tense
muscles for some kind of an attack.

When she stepped into a beam of moonlight, Zach had been
prepared for anything else but. Something inside him twisted
and turned. She was all his dreams were ever made of and he
couldn't break the cobweb spell her presence cast.

Tara had been a little frightened as she made her ghostlike
way through the shadows to the stable. There was no doubt in
her mind where she wanted to be, and there was also no doubt
this night might be their last.

She saw Zach sit up, saw him blink, and then saw the
recognition flow through him. He rose from the bed of hay and
moved toward her as she suddenly rushed to him and threw
herself into his arms. He caught her to him, swinging her off
her feet and around.

She couldn't talk, her throat choked with soft sounds she
buried against his shoulder. He held her tighter and tighter, his
hard arms crisscrossing her body while he buried his face in the
thick sweet scent of her hair.

"I had to come, Zach, I had to," she cried in a high tremolo
that spoke of something akin to fear. He groaned her name and
pushed her even closer.

"I thought maybe coming home would change your mind,
give you some sense."

"I'll never change my mind," she whispered raggedly. "I
would never change my mind. I love you much too much."

Slowly he let her feet touch the floor, then his mouth took
hers in a kiss that was wild and hungry. They were both finding

437

their breathing difficult by the time the kiss ended. Then between rapid breaths, he kissed her nose, her eyes, her forehead, returning to her mouth with a kiss that reached within to bare her soul and burn his brand to it. The need was spontaneous and inevitable and hot.

He murmured her name again as he felt the searing pleasure of her hands working feverishly as his were; first to touch, to know, and to destroy the barrier of clothes. In moments bare flesh was heatedly touching bare flesh.

Her hands threaded through his hair and Tara let her head fall back, panting softly and surrendering to the heat that was building. He bent his head and caught the peak of one breast, sucking it into his mouth. She began to shake as if her body were disintegrating.

"Zach . . . ahhh . . . please," she sobbed as she moved her hands across his skin. She touched his chest, slid her hand down to his lean waist, across the flat plane of his belly, then down to where he was rigidly hard with desire. He gasped a choked kind of groan, slid his hands down to cup her buttocks and pulled her hard against him. Then he knew he had to be embedded deep inside her, he had to feel her about him, a warm pulsing sheath for the shaft of his passion. They moved to the pile of hay almost as one and without the realization of it. Then he was within her, his possession so full and deep that their sounds of ecstasy mingled. His face was a mask of sweet torment, matching hers, and their bodies glistened with sweat. The need that molded them was like a relentless force. She wound herself about him and lifted to meet his thrusts. He wanted to go slow, to take the time to savor the fine taste of her and the sheer magic of her sheathing, but an urgency within them would not let them wait. She was tightening about him and he could feel, with each deep thrust, the drawing of his very core into her. He felt mindless, as if he could lose himself within her, loving her more with each thrust.

His arms were like iron yet they trembled. He caught her mouth, drinking in her cries until he felt her body arch and

438

urst into a rippling climax. The spasms of his own inside her
made him reel, back-arching muscles quivering and sweat
beading. With a groan he followed her into a prolonged and
powerful climax.

For a long while the huge room held only the sounds of
panting and slowly regained breathing. Still deeply buried
within her, Zach moved slowly to his side, gathering her to him
so they remained joined.

Her arms were tight around him and her face was buried
against his throat. It was then he felt the heat of tears.

"Tara?" He tried to move to see her face, but she only held
him tighter and pressed her face even closer. Zach felt more
miserable with each teardrop that scalded his skin.

"Are these the first tears I'm going to cause you, Tara? Is
this what I'll bring you?"

"Oh, Zach, I'm not unhappy. I don't care what they say, I
have never felt happier. I love you so much, Zach. Oh, Zach,
please take me with you."

"You know I can't, Tara. This trail will be the hardest we've
ever ridden." Slowly Zach lifted her face with one hand. He
took his time examining her features. His fingers gently traced
her features and his eyes followed his fingers, absorbing every
one as if to memorize her. Tenderly he wiped the tears from her
cheeks, then smiled and whispered, "I love you. . . I love you
more than the breath in my body. And that's why I can't take
you with me. For once give me my way, Tara. Stay safe. I
couldn't take your loss. It would be the only thing I couldn't
bear. Tell me, first, that you love me, then that you'll stay
where you're safe."

"I love you . . . deeply, endlessly, and forever. If it's what
you want, then I'll stay."

"And I want you to believe me that I'll be back here as fast
I can."

"Zach? Where—where will we go when you get back?"

"Where do you want to go?" he asked gently.

"I want to be with you, wherever you choose."

"I like the stable," he chuckled as he nuzzled her ear.

She laughed softly. "We can't roll in the hay all the time."

He looked at her in mock surprise, "We can't?"

"Zach, be serious."

"I thought I was."

"Zach," she complained feebly as his lips touched her ski[?] in feather-light kisses.

"I want to take you to meet my family first, then we'll ta[l]k about it. Maybe talk to your brother. I take it he has plans t[o] leave here."

"He does."

"Well, maybe we could build somewhere close if yo[u] like. . . ."

"Is that what you want?" she asked quietly. He sat up an[d] looked down at her.

"What do you mean?"

Tara sat up. Her eyes seemed like deep pools and he bathe[d] in their warmth. She reached to touch his face, then moved h[er] fingers into his hair.

"I mean I want you happy. So we'll wait until this is ove[r]. Then we'll decide . . . together." He bent to kiss her and hear[d] the satisfying deep purr from the back of her throat. His hand[s] were creating a sensual friction upward from her thighs an[d] over her hips. She sighed as the tingling made her quiver. H[e] captured her mouth and gave her a long, thorough kiss. By t[he] time he was done, the tingling had become a slow burn.

Tara didn't want to protest; he brought her too muc[h] pleasure. Soon they were both aflame and all sounds we[re] smothered against his persistent mouth. He wanted to slo[w] down but now it was too late for them both, because as it alwa[ys] could, her fiery climax sparked his.

Tara closed her eyes and gave herself to the pleasure of h[is] soothing caress, and soon she slept. He held her close. She w[as] the balm he would always need. After a while his muscl[es] relaxed and they both slept, holding each other as if they we[re] alone in the world.

Chapter 38

Zach did not sleep long. Even though he'd drawn Tara to his own corner of the stable, dawn would find activity and he didn't want her in the situation she could be found in if he let her remain beside him.

He turned slowly, not wanting to wake her yet, drawing her close to his side to hold her for this last long moment. The time was slipping by too fast. Before long he would have to leave. Over and over he planned the direction he *should* move . . . should move. In the wilderness surrounding them, all his expertise would be needed. He thought carefully. Surely Caleb was not strong enough in numbers to attack the fort yet, but it wouldn't be long until he did. Did he underestimate Caleb? He prayed not.

Caught in his thoughts, he didn't realize Tara had wakened and was lying very still. She, too, wanted to hold the new day at bay, to hold this treasured time with Zach. She was afraid, but the fear was only that somehow something could take Zach from her forever. She could still feel the uncertainty, both in herself and in Zach. The more he admitted his love for her the more dangerous and insecure their position had become. Before, it had been simple to let her walk from his life, she thought; now he might feel it was still the better course because he would not be the means to hurt her.

441

Gently Tara pressed her lips to the flesh of his throat, tasting the warm salt of his skin. She felt his arms tighten, but neither spoke. His hands moved over her slowly, not to elicit passion but almost as if he were indelibly in his memory imprinting every curve and plane of her body.

"Oh, Zach," she whispered.

"Shhh . . . I know, love. But there is no help for it now. We have to get up before this place becomes active. I expect Little Raven and Mule before long."

"You'll have to leave before day really breaks."

"Yes. It's safest. Just in case someone is on watch out there. We wouldn't want them to see us leave."

"Zach?"

"What?"

"You—you must come back to me safe. I think I should die if anything were to happen to you."

He raised up on one elbow, his gaze intently holding hers. A half smile twisted his lips. "It will take a lot more than Caleb or any of his renegades to keep us apart, Tara. I know it took a hell of a long time for me to wake up, but I'm awake now, all right. We stand between two worlds, Tara, and I've fought it all my life. Well, maybe you've taught me to stand up and face it instead of running so hard. If you're willing to give up so much for me, then maybe I'd better start thinking about what I'm willing to do. Together Tara—with you—I guess I can fight just about anything."

He laid his hand gently against her cheek, then he bent to softly taste her mouth again. He closed his eyes, holding the gentleness of her, then he groaned softly. "Damn, we've got to get up." With more resolution than he thought he was capable of, he rose, reached down to take her hand, and drew her to her feet.

They helped each other dress amid kisses, tender touches, and soft muffled laughter. Then Tara stood nearby as Zach began to saddle his horse and make preparations to leave.

The first early rays of dawn were finding the cracks between the boards and dimly lighting the inside of the stable when the door opened. Zach and Tara were not surprised to see Mule and Little Raven, but they were surprised to see David with them.

"David?" Tara questioned.

"I've already cleared it with Aaron," David said. "I'm going along. Neither of our patrols returned last night. I want to help end this, and I want to find out what happened to my men."

Tara was frightened for him as well as for Zach, but she refused to make it any harder for either of them by crying. She remained silent, knowing Small Fawn was doing the same within David's quarters. She watched the men finish their preparations and walked between David and Zach as they led their horses from the stable. The whole fort was wakening now and people were aware that something of great importance was happening. Tara was the one who smiled up at an uncertain Zach, then she slowly and deliberately looped her arms about his neck, kissing him long and thoroughly. His eyes smiled into hers when she finished. He knew her proud defiance and that it was her statement for the world.

"I do love you, woman," he laughed softly. "I do love you."

"Then you had better hurry back," she teased. "Every minute you're gone, those young lieutenants look better and better."

"You'll just start the war we're trying to prevent," he replied. "Not to mention the scalps you might find hanging on my belt."

Her eyes grew serious, "Hurry back, Zach."

He nodded, mounted, and bent to kiss her again lightly. Then she stood and watched the gates swing wide and the five men ride through.

Caleb was ready. He stood with his feet spread and planted firmly, hands on hips, surveying a large group of men whose quantity would have shaken Zach to the core. They were ready to move. All the men were armed and whiskey flowed like water. At this moment he controlled a force that would be difficult to stop.

The men he chose to lead and to be closest to him were sober. He made very sure they stayed that way because when the massacre was over, they would have to help him bring the rest under control. Of course, by the time it was over, he expected Chivington and his picked army to be there to help. Visions of a ruling glory filled him. He would be a power in this territory one day. He'd been promised great things and promised by men of political stature—senators and more important men— men of power.

It was dawn, and they were a savage army on the move. Within a day and a night they would see its destruction. Again he thought of Tara. Another plan had insinuated itself. He was secure with it now, having thought about it for days. He would have Tara Montgomery yet.

Despite their number and their conditions, they moved steadily and well. Each man was prepared for the battle. Each man had a hunger to destroy and to punish. They moved closer and closer to the fort while Zach, Mule, David, Long, and Little Raven moved further and further away.

Tara walked toward David's quarters, joining Small Fawn on the porch where she stood with Winter Snow and the two boys. They suddenly felt as if they were a solitary island existing in a vacuum. Tara sighed. She hoped that she would be able to find one ray of friendliness in the fort, but she had no intention of paying for it with Zach's love. Several minutes after the gates closed Tara and the other women went inside. Tara felt it was wise that they talk together before they had to face whatever the next days might bring.

The women sat and talked for a while but soon realized they had to keep both their worries and their negative attitudes away from Blue Hawk and Small Otter. Both boys were much too astute not to realize something was drastically wrong with their situation. They just had no idea what it was.

"The children need to be fed," Winter Snow said calmly.

Both Small Fawn and Tara were calmed by her serenity. She worried more for her children than for herself.

"Yes," Small Fawn agreed, "we will go to the place where the men eat. David has told me that the man"—she laughed softly, somewhat amused that a man held the position she spoke of—"who prepares the meals will see that we are fed."

"The cook," Tara offered.

"It is a strange thing for a man to do," Small Fawn replied curiously. "Do their women not want to prepare their food?"

"Of course the women who are married prepare the food for their husbands, but for all the men in the fort it is necessary that they eat together, so it must be in one room."

"Oh, I see," Small Fawn said, but her eyes glittered with doubt about this strange activity.

"Come on," Tara said definitely, "we will take the children to eat. Perhaps it would be better if we brought some food back with us so we would not have to return too often." Both women saw the wisdom in this. The less they made themselves visible the less chance there would be for a problem to arise.

As if for mutual support, they walked across the compound in a close-knit group. The atmosphere was less than hostile, but most certainly not friendly. The men were uncertain and insecure. Challenged to fight the Indians and led by a man who, up to now, had no love for them, they were not too sure how to handle the situation and so they tried to keep their distance.

They finished a surprisingly good breakfast, which was served to them by a rugged veteran who was like a gentle bear and just as nervous as Small Fawn and Winter Snow seemed to be. The boys, vitality bubbling in their systems, wanted the freedom of play. There were quite a few other children in the fort and Tara wanted to see if it were possible to break any of the barriers. She knew quite well that children could often destroy such barriers better than adults. She tried to think of the best way around it, but no ideas came to her so the children were returned to David's quarters

After an entire day of confinement, frustration ruled the quarters. In the early evening, Tara walked across the compound toward Aaron's rooms. She was less than halfway across when someone called her name. Tara turned to see Bertha Mendle standing on the porch. Hesitant because of the coldness in most of the women, Tara paused, but Bertha motioned to her to come closer. Slowly she moved toward her, thinking of ways to raise a shield against the possible recriminations. She thought of Zach as a child and of how many times he had had to build shields. No wonder he had found it so hard to drop his protection and leave himself vulnerable to what he expected from her.

"Good evening, Tara." Bertha's voice was much friendlier than Tara had expected. "I have not had a chance to talk to you since you came back to us. I thought you might come in and have some tea and a little chat."

"Thank you, Bertha, I'd like that," Tara replied. Bertha could read the gratitude in her eyes and she became angry again at the intolerance of so many of the people within the fort.

Once inside, Tara sat at Bertha's table while the older woman began to make tea.

"You look tired, child. This has been a very difficult time for you almost from the time we left Ellsworth. People can be so stupid and so difficult."

The relief at Bertha's understanding almost brought tears to Tara's eyes. She gulped back the lump in her throat. She had had no woman's companionship since her mother had died and had not realized until now just how much she had missed it.

Bertha set the cup of tea before Tara and then sat down across the table from her.

"This fort ain't no place for you, Tara."

"What do you mean, Bertha? My brother is all I have. There is no place else to go."

"Yet."

446

"Yet?"

"I'm talking about your own freedom. These people will never forget that Zachary Hale is a half-breed. I also have a feeling . . . that maybe your brother understands better than you think."

"I—I thought . . ."

"You thought no one knew or understood. Well, maybe no one understands, but gossip is like wildfire. Tara, do you want some advice from an old lady who made the mistake of letting someone else decide what her future should be?"

"Yes, Bertha, I do."

"Then when your man gets back you go with him—anywhere he wants to go. And don't let nobody interfere. Do you love him?"

"I do, Bertha. I know that people have been so cruel to Zach. He's been bitter and I don't blame him, but he wants to change that and I want to help him change it."

"It might be a long, hard road you choose, but if you love him, it would all be worth it. I've watched him, all the way out and even when he was here. He's a man to be reckoned with, child, and you'd be happy helpin' him try to change this craziness that seems to hold people apart."

"I guess we can only just take one day at a time. If Zach can find Caleb and those guns before Caleb can gather his men and arm them, then maybe this battle will be over."

"Does Zach think he can?"

"He feels Caleb hasn't had enough time to get all the men together. He's sure he can find them and stop them."

"I'm sure Aaron is nervous, too. If Zach is wrong, Caleb could atack the fort soon."

"Aaron still can't quite believe Caleb is behind this, or even why. What does he have to gain? Zach will have to bring a lot of proof to convince Aaron."

"In the meantime, we must just wait and hope Zach is successful. How are the other women and the two boys faring?"

447

"The women are frightened and insecure," Tara smiled. "And the boys want to be out of these restraining walls. They have lived with such freedom all their lives and . . . without hatred. It is hard for them."

"Maybe I shall bake cookies and go in to see them tomorrow. Boys are all alike in one way—they like sweets."

"I wish they could play in the open."

"Does Aaron forbid it?"

"I was on my way to ask him."

"Why not let me ask tomorrow? If I can find some to agree, I might arrange a little . . . oh, kind of picnic. Children make friends fast. I think the parents would have a hard time stopping them once they began to play together."

"Bertha, you're so kind and understanding."

"And you're a sweet girl that it's not hard to be kind to."

"Maybe I'll come over in the morning and help you make those cookies," Tara laughed.

"Well, if you're going to do that, bring the others with you. Seems we could share a lot of cookin' ways. I have a trunk in the back room. It's—filled with toys. I'll just let the boys open it and go through it. That ought to keep 'em out of mischief for a while."

"Toys?"

"They—they used to belong to my boy."

"You had a son?"

"He died . . . so long ago, it seems. He was just twelve."

"Oh Bertha, I'm sorry."

"I couldn't stand the memories back there so, since I'm a teacher, I decided to go as far away from the bad memories as I could and find some children needing teaching."

"Oh, Bertha," Tara breathed softly. Her eyes glittered with real interest. "I know some children desperately in need of teaching. Do you think you would ever be interested in opening a school where the Indian children could come?"

"Do you think that would be welcome by the Indians, Tara? They resent us so much already. Even though they have good

448

cause, still it would make it hard."

"But no one knows the value of learning as much as Zach does." Tara was excited. "He would talk to them, I'm sure."

"If he gets a chance."

"Zach will succeed. He will find Caleb and those guns and put an end to them. When he comes back, we can try! Bertha, at least we can try."

"Of course we can try, Tara. Maybe teaching children could be a fine bridge between them and us. If you want to try, and," she cautioned, "if your man wants to, then I'd be willing, too." Bertha stood up, "Would you like more tea?"

"No, I think I will go back to tell Small Fawn, Winter Snow, and the boys what you have said. At least I can give them a little enthusiasm for tomorrow."

"This Small Fawn . . . you seem to think highly of her."

"My brother is in love with her," Tara said honestly. "I expect someday we will be sisters-in-law—and I hope friends."

"And your brother will leave the Army?"

"Yes. We both know Small Fawn would not find it pleasant to stay here, and David would not tolerate her abuse."

"What is he going to do?"

"I don't know. I don't suppose he is certain yet. He just wants to start a life with Small Fawn and he has to find a place to do it."

"Maybe he's our answer, too."

"What do you mean?"

"Alone, one person isn't too effective, but if a small group combined, why we might just begin a whole settlement where the Indian children can come as well. Sort of a strong link in a chain."

"Then I'll talk to David. He and Zach could be a strong force for both sides."

"We're getting horses before carts. First we got to find an end to this problem."

"We will. We must have hope. Sometimes it's the only thing

we can build our world on." Tara walked to the door and Bertha went with her. When Tara opened the door they both walked out onto the porch. "My goodness," Tara said, "I didn't realize it was so late."

The moon was very low on the horizon, casting shadows throughout the fort until it looked like a fantasy world.

"Are you afraid?" Bertha inquired.

"Afraid? No, no one will harm me. I'll see you tomorrow."

"Fine," Bertha replied. She re-entered the house and closed the door as Tara stepped off the porch and started slowly across the compound.

Tara's thoughts were on Zach and she was halfway across before her attention was suddenly drawn to a movement by the stable. She paused and watched a man who had been moving toward her. He was acting so strange. When he saw her eyes on him he stopped dead, turned suddenly, and almost bolted for the stable door. There was something about him and the way he was dressed that seemed so vaguely familiar. She walked toward the closed stable doors. Whoever the man was he was acting in a way that roused her curiosity. When she reached the door of the stable she could see the light from an oil lamp beneath the door. Slowly she swung the door open enough to slip inside. There was no one in her line of vision, so she took a few more cautious steps inside. Still she could see no one. She began to move slowly down the line of stalls, peering in each one, but there was nothing but the restless horses.

Then a sharp movement made her whirl about. But at the same moment the lamp, which hung near the door, was extinguished. Fear gripped her. Someone stood between her and the only door to freedom.

"Who's there?" She tried to keep her voice firm and commanding, but even she could hear its thin, frightened sound. She began to move toward the door, fighting the urge both to scream and to run. There was no sound. One step, then another and another. Now moonlight was bringing dark shadows into focus. She could see no one, but the light was so vague that even familiar objects were indistinguishable.

Catching her breath, she suddenly bolted and was only inches from the door when a hard arm caught her, pinning her arms to her side, and a huge calloused hand stifled her scream. She was lifted from her feet, and even though she struggled with all her strength, she was dragged to the back of the stable.

She was thrown down on the straw, and before she could utter a sound he fell on her, one hand circling her throat and cutting off her breath. She heaved and fought, but the relentless hand held and soon a star-studded darkness overwhelmed her. . . . After a few minutes she ceased to struggle and lay still.

Quickly the man rose. He was breathing harshly, but he moved swiftly. He knelt beside Tara, and tore a scarf from about his neck, and gagged her tightly. Then he removed a soft leather belt and bound her hands tightly. Finished, he sat back on his heels and contemplated her, waiting for her to waken. There was no doubt in his mind that she had recognized him. Caleb had not taken Tara into consideration when he had sent him to sabotage the fort. One of the men who had taken Tara from Zach the first time, he was sure she would not forget his face. Now, before she wakened, he had to decide what to do.

Just before dawn a wagon drew to a stop at the gates. Both guards, exhausted by a long night of vigil and not expecting any difficulties from inside, did not move to examine the bundles in the back of the wagon.

"Where 'ya goin'?" one inquired.

"We need fresh meat, so I'm headin' out early. Figure to get me a buck or a doe and get back. I ain't hankerin' to run across any trouble. I should be back by midday."

"Takin' a wagon? Boy are you lazy," one laughed.

"Yeah. I don't aim to haul it back. I'll just park the wagon, track a deer, toss it in the back, and haul it home."

"Well, good luck," the second replied. They swung the gates open and the wagon moved out slowly.

Some distance from the fort the wagon took on more speed. When it was a little over two miles away it stopped. The man on the seat waited, watching the area around him closely. Soon he saw a rider. When the rider stopped, he spoke first.

"What the hell you doin' out here with a wagon?"

"I got a little surprise that you have to take to Caleb," the driver replied as he climbed down. He walked to the back of the wagon, dragged one of the bundles off, and laid it on the ground. He unbound it, and the rider looked down in total shock at a still-unconscious Tara.

"What the hell!"

"She recognized me. If I hadn't taken her, she would have ruined everything. I'm going back to the fort. You take her to Caleb and tell him I didn't have a choice."

"Well, I don't have to take her far. Caleb's about ten miles out. He should be hittin' the fort some time tomorrow morning, so you go on back. They ain't goin' to have too much time to worry about where she is. Caleb will take care of her . . . real good care."

Chapter 39

"Do you think it would be better if we split up, Zach?" Mule asked. "Maybe we could pick up some track."

"No, let's start at Deep Valley first. That's where they had Tara and some of the supplies. Then we'll split and try and track them."

"After all the time?" David questioned. "Won't any kind of trail be gone?"

"Maybe for you, white eyes," Little Raven laughed, "but not for Windwalker and Mule or Long and me. We learn to track well because we like to eat. After a while you can learn it pretty well if you're hungry enough."

"And this critter is always hungry," Mule added as he jerked his thumb toward Little Raven.

"Zach," David said, "have you given any odds against the five of us stopping Caleb? Seems there's not too much we can do."

"You might be surprised," Zach replied grimly. "You're too military-minded. Maybe you need to learn some of the hit-and-run tactics of the Indians."

"They're not in my military manual," David replied with a grin. "I'm used to bugles and formations."

"Well, then you've got a whole lot to learn."

"It's still nearing two days to Deep Valley," Long stated.

"Not if we move fast. There will be no camp. We'll eat on the move. I expect if we push we can be there in the morning."

"Zach, boy," Mule spoke solemnly. "Just how many men do you think Caleb can pull?"

"Well, the young men of my father's village have given Little Raven their word they would not move for at least seven days. That was four days ago. They won't be with him . . . yet. But he has gathered young hotheads from the other villages. I'd say . . . maybe three hundred or so."

"And how many whites?"

"I don't know. I'd say Chivington's group and Long said there was about fifty of them."

"Nice-sized army," Long replied bitterly.

"Enough to take the fort if we give them a chance. But we won't let it happen. By the time he gets organized we'll have found him. The best bet then would be to catch them unprepared, run off horses, blow some of the ammunition if we can, and as for me, I'm going to find my way to Caleb and kill him. A snake without a head soon dies."

"Then let's hope we track him pretty quick," David replied. Zach and Little Raven were silent, and Mule understood the silence all too well as did Long. If his wife were to be at Caleb's mercy, he would feel the same.

From Caleb's vantage point he could make out the vague outline of the fort. He was on a hill, a short telescope in his hand. Caleb gazed at it for some time before he lowered the glass and smiled. The fort was just as good as his. Tonight Chivington and his men would join him, and in the first light of dawn they would attack. Within days the fort would have to surrender to a superior force. Zach had lost and he had won. Tara was there, behind those walls, and it was only a matter of time now until she would have to face him again, only this time he would be master.

He turned his horse and rode back to his camp. Just as he

454

approached it he could see a group of riders coming from the opposite direction, and he knew his coconspirators had come. Of course Chivington and his friends and Caleb would not take part in the attack. No one would be able to prove their guilt in any way. It would be an Indian uprising that would bring about harsh reprisals—reprisals handled by Chivington and his friend. Soon the wide expanse of land he saw before him would be his, and soon after that the railroad, already headed in their direction, would have to cross it. He would have wealth and power beyond any man's dreams.

After this was over he would find a way to trace down Zachary Hale. He had to eliminate such a danger at his back to make his future safe. He knew Zach much too well. There was no way he would leave him as an untied thread to destroy his plans.

Entering the camp, he dismounted, handing the reins of his horse to a young Indian who led it away to see to its care. He walked to one of the campfires and poured himself a cup of coffee, then he squatted close to another man. "Camp ready to move tomorrow?"

"Yeah, boss. Them redskins'll get liquored up tonight and by dawn they'll be frothing at the mouth."

"They have their orders?"

"Yep . . . no survivors."

"How's our inside man working out?"

"He's in and safe. We probably should get some word from him pretty soon. How's he getting in and out?"

"He's a hunter," Caleb laughed. "He can move in and out very freely, he brings their meat."

"Pretty neat."

"Yeah. I also had some orders about the red-haired girl in the fort, Tara Montgomery."

"Nobody's going to do her any harm. We'll find her and drag her out and bring her to you. What about the other women?"

"I don't care. Do as you see fit."

"I'll tell them they can have them. Battle always makes them

455

wild and excited; they need women to sort of get rid of the pressure."

Caleb was about to answer when he saw, in the distance, a rider approaching. He frowned until he could distinguish that there were two riders on one horse. As the man drew closer, the sun glinted on red hair. . . . After a few minutes, Caleb again smiled.

Aaron had been thinking of the group that was sticking so close to David's quarters. He had finally come to a decision. As long as he kept his distance, their treatment would not be exactly the best, but if it were to be made known that they were, so to speak, under his personal care . . . Well, he thought, at least they would get no rough abuse. He could do nothing about the cold atmosphere. For the first time Aaron saw two sides of a story and he didn't like what he saw. He also was unprepared for his thoughts of sympathy for the Indians, not quite grasping just where all the changes were coming from.

He rose early, just before dawn had spread into full day, and dressed carefully. He meant to go and have a talk with Small Fawn and Winter Snow. He meant to also talk to the two boys. There had to be a start somewhere. The subtle draw of Small Fawn's appearance being so much like Star's was on the periphery of his mind and he intended to keep it there—or at least try. He wondered where Star was now, what she was doing . . . and who might be laughing or talking with her. After a while he forcefully abandoned the thoughts. They were disruptive to his peace of mind and most certainly useless, yet he wondered, what if . . . No! He walked to the door and out onto the porch. The occupants of the fort were about their regular daily movements, and he stood for a minute to watch and to think about the beautiful day it was. The fort gates stood open and everyone seemed to be moving at a smooth flowing pace. Sort of like the peaceful quiet before a storm, he thought.

hen laughed to himself at the strangeness of this idea. He was getting old or something.

He started across the compound and in a few minutes was knocking on David's door.

The night before Small Fawn had been slightly worried when it became very late and Tara had not returned. But, she had rationalized, Tara was among her own. If she were in her own village, she would be free to roam where she chose and no one would ever give a thought to bothering her. So, even when it became very late, Small Fawn was not alarmed. The children had been put to bed much earlier, and when it became late the women went to sleep as well. After all, Tara was safer than they were, wasn't she?

When Small Fawn and Winter Snow rose to find that Tara had still not returned they were puzzled . . . but as yet unafraid. After a short while their concentration was on keeping the children under control.

Bertha, too, had risen early, somewhat excited about having children in her house again and anxious about how she would bridge even the language gap. When the morning lingered and no one came, Bertha decided to walk over and expedite matters.

When she arrived and knocked, the door was opened by Small Fawn, who was much more unsure than Bertha. For a minute the women just stood and looked at each other. Still, it was Bertha who spoke first.

"Good morning. Your name is Small Fawn, is it not?"

"Yes."

"I've been waiting patiently all morning. Just when are you and those two youngsters going to come."

"Come—come where?"

"You mean Tara hasn't told you about our plans yet? Well, maybe she wanted it to be a surprise. Are the boys awake?"

"They have been awake before daylight," Small Fawn answered with a slight touch of exasperation in her voice. Bertha had to laugh and Small Fawn responded with a smile

457

that was half surprise.

"Well, I can handle little boys quite well. May I come in?"

"Oh!" Small Fawn was shaken by her own rudeness at making a visitor stand outside the door. She had just never considered that Bertha would want to enter. She stepped aside and Bertha came in. After Small Fawn closed the door, Bertha's words caught her totally by surprise.

"Where's Tara?"

"What?"

"Where's Tara?"

"Why . . . she left here last night and never returned." It was so customary for Indians to move in freedom and share evenings with other members of the family in their lodges that Small Fawn felt this must be the custom of the whites as well.

"She came to visit me last night, but when she left I was certain she was on her way back here. Where else would she go?" Bertha was instinctively frightened.

"Maybe she visited another friend and decided to spend the night," Small Fawn said innocently.

"I'm afraid, Small Fawn, she doesn't have that many friends here."

Before Small Fawn could answer, another knock sounded. Both women looked at the door as if shocked. Who now would be coming? Was it someone bringing bad news? Small Fawn opened the door and Aaron stood there.

"Good morning, Small Fawn. . . . Bertha, what are you doing here so early?" His smile began to fade as he read the worry in Bertha's eyes.

"Major Creighton . . ." Bertha began feebly.

Aaron was looking about the room quickly now, feeling the strange kind of fear knot his stomach. "Where's Tara?"

"We don't know."

"What do you mean you don't know?" he demanded harshly, then he realized he was scaring the women more than they already were. "When did you see her last?" he asked more calmly.

Bertha explained her visit the night before. "But she was on her way back here when she left me."

"When . . . what time?" Aaron pressed.

"Late . . . very late . . . Oh, I should have walked her back," Bertha finished, but by the time she ceased talking Aaron was already out the door.

A thorough search made it clear that Tara was not to be found. Aaron was about to order a search party when a wild shout from one of the sentries drew his attention to the gate. The guards were swinging it closed as fast as they could.

Aaron almost ran up the step that led to the sentry posts on the wall. He stood and looked out over the barricade and his heart began to pound. At least three hundred painted and feathered savages were strung in a long line facing the fort. There were now three reasons for fear: The fort was under attack, he had no idea where Zach and his companions and the other overdue patrols were and, worst of all, Tara had been somehow spirited from the fort and was probably now a captive of the men he faced.

Tara swam up from a black well, feeling first the ache in her head and arms, then realizing she was firmly bound and gagged. Her heart beat in fear, and she slowly opened her eyes and looked up into Caleb's smiling face. She tried to articulate a scathing remark but the gag prevented anything but an angry sound. Now, in the distance, she could hear the sound of gunfire and shrill cries. Her whole being knew Zach had always been right, just as the agony filled her that the fort was now under attack.

She lay on a blanket in a nearly deserted camp. There were only four or five men present besides Caleb and her eyes widened in surprise at their appearance. They were white men, but not the trapper or trader; they were civilized men, yet their eyes reflected the same merciless look that she saw in the depths of Caleb's.

Caleb laughed softly as he loosened the gag from Tara's mouth. "Tara, nice to see you awake. You know, even all roughed up like you are you still manage to look damn inviting."

"What are you doing, Caleb?" she gasped. "This is useless. You'll be caught. . . . Zach will kill you for this."

"Oh, I doubt it, Tara. Listen," he paused, "within a few days your lover and all his friends will be dead and you . . . well, I've got plans for you."

He reached to grasp a mass of her thick hair, sliding his fingers through it. Tara felt the fear do battle with her hatred and her sense of betrayal. Did he believe Zach was still in the fort? she thought desperately.

"You'll never succeed! Never! If it ever comes to that, I'll kill myself before I ever surrender to you."

Caleb laughed again and rose, and as he did he reached to draw Tara to her feet. He unbound her hands. As soon as he did she stepped back from him, but Caleb was unconcerned and Tara sensed his assurance. There was no place for her to go.

Her only thought was that Zach was out there somewhere and maybe . . . maybe he would find her.

The five riders reached Deep Valley and slowly moved around until they found the trail they sought. David was more than amazed, for he had no idea what kind of trail it was; he saw absolutely nothing. As far as he was concerned, the best he could do was follow.

It took less than half a day before Little Raven and Zach exchanged confident glances that David observed quickly.

"Zach?"

"Skull Rock," Zach stated.

"What's that?"

"It's a place not too far from here and I'll bet my life it's where they are. We'll forget tracking. Let's ride."

"What if we're wrong?" David said quietly.

460

"It'll be a damn expensive mistake, but I'm not wrong. There's only so many places a gang like that can be hidden. Let's go."

Little Raven and Zach rode ahead. David looked at Mule and Long. "What do you think Mule . . . Long? Are we making a mistake?"

"So we're all scared," Mule replied. "Zach's the best and pretty near the safest bet to get what you're lookin' for. I'd say, if it comes to puttin' my life out on a limb, I'd do it if Zach said it was a good move."

"Tell me one other thing, Mule," David said as they nudged their horses into motion. "My men . . . those two patrols that went out when I did . . ."

"Come on, David," Mule's reply was blunt, "you and I know damn well ain't none of them comin' back. Out here overdue . . . is dead."

"Christ," David muttered. Long remained silent. David had his answer.

Their riding was at full speed now and the distance was swallowed by the long stride of the horses. It was late afternoon when Skull Rock came into view.

The five sat motionless and looked at the debris strewn about. Hundreds of boxes all, they knew, having once contained rifles, lay about. Obvious signs that a very large group of men had camped here were before them to read. This time David needed no interpretation. What he saw was the base from which a small army had moved, and all five knew the direction in which it had gone.

Zach was, for a second, stunned. He had underestimated Caleb's ability to get his force into control and he knew beyond doubt the price that might have to be paid for his mistake.

"Little Raven," he said grimly.

"Yes."

"Ride as fast and as hard as you can. Get our father. Have him spread the word to gather all the force he can. Tell him to arm themselves well. Then head for the fort. We must be in

461

time to see that Caleb does not succeed." He turned to look at Little Raven. "You and I both know that no survivors will be left to talk of what happened or to name Caleb."

"I will ride as fast as possible."

"Little Raven . . ." Zach said quietly. Little Raven looked at Zach's tormented face. "Tara is in that fort. If she dies . . ."

"Windwalker," Little Raven said firmly, "we will not let it be so. I will bring as many as I can get. What will you do?"

"Mule, you ride in the opposite direction," Zach said before he answered Little Raven. "Stone Heart's village and White Wing's village will hear you. Arm them and bring them. Find the words to tell them the cost of the fort's loss."

Mule nodded. He did not need to question. All three men knew Zach was already suffering the tortures of the knowledge that he had misjudged and the error might just cost him the one person he loved more than his own life. Mule nodded and rode away.

"Go, Little Raven," Zach said quietly.

"My brother, you cannot face these men alone. You are one they are many. You will die for nothing. You must wait. . . ."

"Wait, my brother? For what should I wait? For the moment when I must take Autumn Dove's lifeless body from the burning fort? For the moment that I must see the price she's paid for my stupidity?" Zach smiled a grim and murderous smile and repeated the chant of the Cheyenne. "It is a good day to die, my brother. If I have sent Tara to her death, then it is better I walk the road with her. Now ride; you must bring men in time."

Little Raven could do no more than nod his head. He felt the tearing of his brother's heart and the wound was in him as well. He turned his horse and rode away.

Zach, David, and Long sat for a moment. Then it was David whose hoarse voice broke the silence. "What can we do Zach?"

"We have to get to the fort as quickly as we can," Long began. "One way or the other we have to get past the force outside and into the fort itself. We have to hold them unt

Little Raven and Mule bring help."

"Three of us?" David questioned weakly. "How do we get in?"

"Ride like hell and hope no lucky bullet finds you," Zach said. His horse was already in motion as the last of the words came to them. They followed and soon they were riding like the wind, with a silent prayer in all three hearts that they would not be too late.

Again and again Caleb's force struck at the fort, and again and again Aaron's repelled them, but each time the cost was two, three, or four men. By nightfall, when the enemy withdrew to recap their forces, those in the fort were exhausted. The night grew quiet, then the sound of celebrating drums came to them to fill the rest of the endless night with fear.

The sun had barely sent red streaks into the dark sky when the attack was resumed. They hit again . . . and again . . . and again.

Aaron knew his force was weakening. He was losing men to the accuracy of the new rifles Caleb had brought. If he had had Caleb at his mercy, then he would have quite happily killed him. He thought bitterly of Tara and what she might be going through now, and a new rage filled him. He would fight back to the last man before he surrendered the fort to the animal he now knew in his heart Caleb was.

On the third night, the continuous pounding of the drums had drawn everyone's nerves to a fine, taut line, ready to break.

Aaron had taken Small Fawn, Winter Snow, and the boys to his quarters and set two men to guard them. The emotions in the fort ran high now and he was afraid some violence would be aimed at them.

The next morning the attack was renewed and Aaron stood on the wall platform with his men firing carefully.

463

Suddenly his attention was drawn to three men coming over the crest of a hill some distance away. He squinted his eyes to see through the smoke, feeling he recognized them. Then he saw David's blue uniform.

David, Zach, and Long sat on the hill for a moment, knowing within seconds they would be seen.

"It's going to be some damn race," Long muttered. David simply sat and wished he could stop sweating, while Zach stared at the fort, wanting only to hold Tara one more time and tell her he was sorry.

By this time some of the attackers had spotted them. A small group headed for them to try and intercept what was obviously going to be their race for the fort.

"Well," Long said, "here goes. I sure as hell hope some scared private has the guts to open that gate when we get there or we're going to get pinned to it."

"Let's get to it first." Zach's horse leapt forward and the race was on.

"Get the hell down and open that gate when they get to it!" Aaron shouted to two privates. "If they get to it," he added wearily.

The three men bent low to their horses' backs and urged them to greater and greater speed. The group that chased them was within a hundred yards, then fifty . . . forty . . . twenty and still the gates seemed to yawn miles away. The gates were open and everyone in the fort had their eyes on the three who raced for their lives. Bullets sang about them and one even struck David's hat from his head, causing him to bend near his horse's neck as Zach was doing.

Then suddenly they were through and the gates were closing behind them. Their weary and lathered horses heaved in exhaustion, and the three nearly fell from their backs as they dismounted, anxious to find their loved ones.

Aaron approached them reluctantly. "Aaron," Long said first, but Aaron interrupted.

"Your family is safe in my quarters, Long. They're fine."

Long almost ran the distance to Aaron's quarters. Zach had a grim smile on his face and David a more pleased one. Then they both returned their attention to a scowling Aaron.

"Where's Tara, Aaron?" Zach spoke in a relieved voice. Aaron's silence destroyed any signs of relief at once. "Aaron! Where's Tara?"

"Zach, for Christ's sake, I'm sorry."

"She's dead?" His face paled and his heart felt as if the life were being squeezed from it.

"No . . . not dead . . . she's out there. Someone kidnapped her from the fort."

"Caleb." Zach's whispered voice was now deadly.

Chapter 40

"No!" Zach's cry of anquish was more savagelike than any animal's. He started for his horse again and Aaron moved quickly to prevent him.

"The horse is exhausted, Zach. You won't make it twenty feet."

Zach's lips were pulled back over his teeth in a snarl of savagery. "Get me a fresh horse, Aaron." His voice was warning Aaron he meant to do what he wanted. "Don't get in my way."

"Zach, you can't go out there! For God's sake, man, they'll butcher you. I know how you feel but you've got to at least wait until night."

In all logic Zach knew that Aaron was right. But an unbearable pain filled him. "Damnit! Tara's out there! Can you possibly imagine how she feels!"

"I can," Aaron argued, "and I can imagine how she would feel if you died before you could do anything to help her. Use your sense now, Zach," his voice softened. "This is one time you can't think just with your heart."

"Aaron's right, Zach," David said. "I'd like to go, too, and if we can get out after dark, then we'd better give it a try."

Zach tried to reach for control. He stood very still and inhaled deeply. But the vision of Tara the night he had left, pleading with him to take her along, almost undid him. Again he reached for all the restraint he could find. In desperation he spoke of other things.

"Help's on the way, Aaron."

"From where? There's no military . . ."

"No," Zach's smile was bitter, "some savage redskins are coming. I'd say if you can hold out another two days, they'll be here."

"Jesus," Aaron breathed in relief, "I never thought . . ."

Zach needed some kind of anger, something to fight. "No, I suppose you wouldn't expect these savages to know right from wrong."

"Stop fighting me, Zach." Aaron's voice was much too understanding to suit Zach. "I'm not your enemy, not anymore."

"God damnit!" Zach groaned bitterly.

"Zach, let's get back to protecting this fort, at least until tonight. Together we'll lick Caleb at his own game"—he held his hand out to Zach—"and we'll find Tara. We'll find her, Zach."

Zach held Aaron's eyes and realized he meant every word he said. For the first time Zach took the hand extended to him.

The battle was resumed, with Long, David, and Zach beside the others. Each time Zach fired his rifle his mind held Tara before him, and in a combination of tangled Indian and white deities he prayed that night would come soon.

It seemed to David and to Zach that it had taken forever, but finally the sun set. Zach could hear the message of the drums, the confidence they exuded, the power they claimed. All those outside the fort knew its days were numbered . . . but those inside the fort now knew they had won. Aaron explained, to everyone's shame, that it was Zach and his people who were coming to their rescue.

David was preparing to go with Zach, completely unaware

that Zach did not plan to take him along. Much as he knew David loved Tara, Zach knew her brother could never understand what he intended to do to Caleb. This was one time when the wildness in his blood could not seem to be harnessed. All the ways he could torture and kill Caleb were visions he held before him as he steeled himself for what had yet to be faced.

Zach knew David and Long were together with Aaron in his quarters, expecting him to join them in some kind of plan making. But Zach stood in the center of the stable saddling his horse. Stripped to breechcloth and moccasins, his bronzed skin gleamed in the lantern's glow. No one would see the white blood now. . . . The man setting out to kill Caleb was not white —and he didn't mean to make Caleb's death as pleasantly quick as the whites would do.

He led his horse from the stable after he had extinguished the light, and only the awestruck men on guard saw him. When he reached the gate he spoke quietly and almost pleasantly.

"Open the gate."

"Christ, Zach, you'll get killed out there."

"Hardly," Zach said grimly. "Open up."

"Maybe I should see Aaron first, I . . ." He stopped as Zach turned a frozen blue gaze on him.

"Open the gate, Hank."

Hank Ridges had never looked so closely into the face of death before, not this cold, brutal, and premeditated death. Slowly he opened the gate, and like a stealthy dark ghost, Zach slipped out. In seconds the darkness swallowed him up.

The room in which Aaron had gathered everyone was quiet for some time. Then it was Blue Hawk who posed the question in everyone's mind.

"Father?"

"Yes, Blue Hawk."

"Do you think it is possible for Windwalker to go through all those men again? Will they not kill him before he can find the white woman he searches for?"

"It would not be possible for many men, Blue Hawk, but I have a feeling Zach will be able to do it."

"He is a very brave man," Blue Hawk said with the simple honesty of a child.

"Yes," Aaron replied, "that is so, Blue Hawk."

David looked closely at Aaron, who smiled back. "There was a time," Aaron went on, "that I would have never thought of saying that."

"So things can change," David said softly.

"People make situations change. Maybe you and Zach can do that. I can see with my own eyes that Long already has."

Long rested his hand gently on Small Otter's head and nodded without speaking.

"Did you tell Zach to come here?" Aaron questioned David. "We have to make some kind of plans. Morning comes quicker than you think."

"I told him, but he said he had something to tend to first." David replied. "I suppose he's just checking his equipment or something. He was on his way to the stables a little while ago. Said he'd join me as soon as he could."

Long straightened and looked at both men in surprise, then remembered they were still somewhat ignorant of the Indian ways. He smiled, "I don't think Zach will be here."

"What are you talking about, Long?" David protested. "He and I . . . ." David paused at the look on Long's face.

Simultaneously the three men rose and left, crossing to the stables at a run. But there was no sign of life; the stable was dark. They went immediately to the gate.

"Corporal Ridges, have you seen Zachary Hale tonight?" Aaron snapped.

"Yes, sir, he just left. I tried to stop him, sir, but he just wouldn't be stopped."

There was a paralyzing silence as the three men, powerless now to help, prayed Zach would find his way to Tara. Long was the only sure one, just as he was sure he wouldn't be in Caleb's shoes for all the gold in the world.

Zach moved like a silent shadow. Well experienced, he seemed to become part of the place he crossed so carefully. He cared much less that his life depended on his expertise than the fact that, if she were not dead already, Tara's life did too. He could not allow the thought of her death to enter his mind. The pain of it broke his concentration and he needed all he had. If ever his Indian training was needed, it was now. If Caleb got away this time, he would destroy his trail carefully and Zach might never see Tara again. That thought was beyond bearing. He continued to stalk through the night like a hunting panther . . . a hungry hunting panther.

Caleb had never felt better. He had been assured that in another day the fort would fall. He sat now beside a low burning fire with Tara close enough that he could guard her. She had refused to look at him or speak to him again and his anger at her obstinance was beginning to grow.

Tara had listened to Caleb and Chivington and his other friends talk. She knew now the awful plans they had made and the blood that would flow to help them see their plan turn into power and gold. She prayed for their failure. She also reached for the magic moments she had shared with Zach, to help her face what she knew she meant to do.

If and when the fort fell . . . if she could never see Zach again . . . before she would allow Caleb to defeat her, she would find a way to end her own life and hoped God would forgive her. But she could not face what Caleb's every glance promised.

Caleb watched the firelight burnish Tara's skin to gold. He saw it dance like a brilliant sun in her long, tangled hair. She was so damn beautiful, and he wanted her. What angered him

470

was that he knew where her thoughts were.

Chivington and his men had gone to camp near a vantage point where they could watch the fall of the fort the next day. It left Tara alone with Caleb, and that pleased him. He had thoughts about her all day and now, he promised himself, she would not escape him.

"Tara. . . ." He said her name softly, but she did not raise her eyes from the fire. In anger he moved swiftly, his hand grasping her arm and jerking her close to him. "Look at me," he commanded. Now she did, letting him see the fury and the disgust in her eyes.

"So you still believe he will come for you. How foolish, Tara. When the fort falls tomorrow, Zachary Hale falls with it." She remained quiet, but it broiled within her and Caleb was forcing the barriers of her control.

"I could save him for you," Caleb said softly. Now Tara's eyes held his. "All you need do is put aside the coldness; maybe . . . you could buy his life."

Tara smiled. "Zach would not want his life at such a cost. I love him and I would not shame him like that."

"You are a fool."

"Am I? What do you know of such a love, Caleb? You are not such a man."

"He is a half-breed," Caleb sneered. "The lowest thing on earth."

"No. Those who condemn him are lower."

"With or without your consent I will have you, Tara . . . and I will have you now. I've waited long enough."

"I will fight you with my dying breath."

"Fight as you will," he drew her to him. "No one will come, and eventually you will learn who is master. I will teach you to be what I want," his voice was dangerously soft. "I have so many ways."

He grasped her in his arms, crushing her to him, and his mouth ravaged hers painfully until he heard her moan. He released her and her eyes remained closed while helpless tears

471

scalded her cheeks. "Zach," she whispered, "I love you. . . . I love you."

Caleb's fury was boundless at the call of his hated enemy's name. He forced her backward until he almost crushed her to the ground. "He will not come. I forbid you to say his name again. He will die with the fort! He will die!"

"No! No! He will not."

"I promise you, you will see his charred body tomorrow, and you will know once and for all that he is lost to you."

"He will never be lost to me, you fool! He lives in my heart and in my soul, and your vile touch can never reach there." Tara's anguish bubbled to the surface. "He will never be lost to me, and he won't die with the fort because he isn't there!"

Caleb froze for a moment, then he rose and jerked Tara to her feet. "What do you mean?"

"Zach will not die," Tara spat defiantly. "He is not at the fort!"

"You lie!"

"No. He left the fort before you attacked. He left to search for you. You know him, Caleb," she taunted. "He's free. And if he's free your life is worthless. Any moment . . . any second and he might be here."

With satisfaction Tara saw fear leap momentarily into Caleb's eyes, followed by new anger. "Gather some food together. We're leaving here."

"Where are we going?"

"None of your business. My men will take care of the fort. Once it's finished, I will send them on a manhunt. No matter how good he is no man can outwit or outrun that many men. They'll get him out and let you watch him die. Then we will see what lessons it takes to handle you."

Tara knelt to gather some food and put it in the saddlebags. Caleb walked a few steps away from her and bent to lift a saddle. His hand never reached it. There was a humming sound and an arrow thudded deep into the leather of the saddle. Immediately following that sound was the sharp click of a gun hammer being cocked.

A voice so deadly it made the hair on the back of Caleb's neck stand up cut through the night like a brilliant sword.

"Don't even think of moving, Caleb old friend. I don't want to shoot you. Believe me, I have much better plans."

Caleb turned slowly and a knot seemed to prevent his heart from beating. Zach stood half in shadow, half in light, and he looked like death. His body glistened in the firelight. Tara had never seen Zach this way, either, and she felt her breath catch. He was primeval man fighting for his own. He was the ultimate savage, reverting only to senses and not to logic . . . and he meant to kill. Without mercy or thought and not only to kill but to cause as much pain as he could while doing it.

"Zach." Tara breathed his name. It flowed from her to him like a warm wave of love.

Zach's eyes shifted to her for a moment, taking in her appearance in one raking glance. A low, guttural, almost animal growl came from him as his eyes went back to Caleb, who had now began to sweat in the face of a deadly terror he had never imagined existed.

Tara was filled with panic. True, Caleb needed punishment. But if Zach killed him the way he wanted to, no white people would feel safe with him or want him around. He could never step from one world to the other. The whites would again condemn him, and this time the walls would be too high to climb and too solid to break. She had to reach past the ferocious barrier and find the Zach who understood. She would not let him kill Caleb if it meant he was killing his future as well. "Zach, I'm all right. No one has harmed me."

But Zach wasn't listening. He was contemplating Caleb in an icy blue stare, almost like a predatory beast. "Zach!" she insisted.

His gaze swept to her. "Come over here, Tara," he spoke roughly. She moved close enough that he could reach out and touch her, and he did. In a gentle touch he laid one hand against her cheek and she turned her face slightly to press a kiss against his calloused palm. For a second his eyes were filled with her and hers swam with tears of love. Then he turned his

473

face to Caleb again and she saw the final look of cold and brutal murder grow again in his eyes.

"Zach," Caleb gulped back the fear that tasted bitter on his tongue. He had faced many an adversary, both man and beast, but this time he tasted death.

"I want you to take this gun, Tara, and hold it on him for a moment."

Tara was surprised, but she obeyed. She felt a release of the tension. Maybe Zach wasn't going to kill after all. Even Caleb hoped for a reprieve. But both were wrong.

Zach took a long, wicked bladed knife from the leather band about his waist. It glistened in the firelight as if blood already dripped from it. Caleb licked his lips. He'd been in Indian villages many years. He knew quite well the damage a strong warrior could do with a knife before the victim died. He also knew Zach intended to inflict as much pain as he possibly could.

"Before I begin, Caleb, let me tell you what is happening to your plans for the fort. It seems your small army will soon be getting a surprise." He went on to tell Caleb of the rescue already on its way to the fort. He taunted and teased, enjoying the defeat he saw in Caleb's eyes. But Tara was shattered by a side of Zach she hoped would one day be completely dead. She could not let him continue down the path, for if he did kill Caleb as he planned, it was their love that was going to pay the price for it. Just as Zach started for Caleb, Tara swung to face him again. "No, Zach," she said. Zach stopped and looked at her.

"You don't think I can let him live?" he grated in disbelief.

"Zach, you must take him to the fort and let the military bring him to justice."

"White justice," Zach sneered. "I've seen it; it doesn't work. Tara . . . what he did to them at the fort . . . some have died. I can't let him go when I know what he meant to do to you. . . . I won't, Tara."

"Oh, Zach." The tears she tried to control escaped to form

474

silver drops on her cheeks. "Think what you are doing to us."

"To us?"

"If you kill him here, Zach, you will destroy us. Already the fort must know that you are responsible for their safety. If you bring him to justice . . . if you let Aaron and the court punish him, you will prove so much to them, Zach. That you are a man of honor, that you are so much more than they knew. You can change so much, Zach . . . or you can make it impossible to go on. You are not a savage, Zach. You are a man, the one I love. . . . Zach . . ."

"And if their courts allow him his freedom?"

"Aaron won't do that, not after so many have suffered and died. You have seen a change in Aaron; you know he is trying. You must come halfway, Zach."

Zach looked from Tara to Caleb. His breathing increased its pace and she could see the hand on the knife tighten. A battle raged within him, a wild, tempestuous battle. His bloods warred as the need for vengeance surged through him. It was so hard to let go.

Tara moved to his side, handing him the gun again to make sure his hands were not free. Then gently she laid her hands on his shoulder, letting one caress the hard muscle of his back.

"We have so much that a man like Caleb will never have, or even understand. We can have a life together, Zach." Her voice was soft and awash with her love. "I do love you. I want to be your wife, Zach. I want to have your children and see them grow. I want our life, Zach. . . . Don't throw it away."

She could feel Zach's heart pounding like thunder and she could almost taste the anger he was feeling. There was no more she could say. She had offered him all the sweet promise the future could hold and Caleb stood before him, his death promising all the darkness of disaster.

"Tara." Zach's voice was hoarse with the strain of the war he fought. "Hold the gun on him." It was a command; Tara felt defeated. Had she failed? Was it possible her love was not enough to pull Zach back from the brink of disaster? She could hardly stifle the sob and again she took the gun. Zach walked toward Caleb. Her heart skipped a beat, then began to flutter like a bird trying to escape its cage. Zach had reached for two leather thongs that hung at his belt, pulling Caleb's arms back to tie them firmly. Then he forced Caleb to the ground and tied his feet together. When he stood up again he smiled at Tara, and to her it was the most beautiful smile she had ever seen.

She dropped the gun and ran to him, feeling the joyous pleasure of being caught up in iron-hard arms and crushed against him until she had no breath left. But she didn't care. She cried his name over and over and heard hers murmured in a husky voice against her hair.

When she looked into his eyes she could see the warm tears there. He, too, wept for the overpowering love she had for him. Then their mouths met in a kiss blinding and fulfilling. Their tears mingled and passions soared as again they found the brilliant and all-consuming love that was theirs alone. There would be tomorrow.

Epilogue

Little Raven and Mule had brought enough reinforcements that they shattered the attacking force. In a pincerlike movement, coming from both sides at the same time, they took the attackers by surprise.

So confident of success, Chivington and his men had moved too close and found themselves trapped and captured.

The fort was in a state of euphoria for some time, except for a few. Their minds, hearts, and eyes turned again to the horizon and the wait began.

To those waiting it seemed like hours. Finally Little Raven could stand no more.

"Mule."

"What?"

"I'm going out to search for them."

"Where's your confidence, boy? Don't you think Zach found Tara and is bringing her back?"

"I have faith in him. It's just that . . ."

"Just that you're about as scared as we all are. But we'll wait, Little Raven. It's better that way."

"I don't understand."

"What Mule means, Little Raven," Aaron said with an understanding smile, "is that he thinks Zach will be wise enough not to kill Caleb. He'll bring him in and we'll hang him."

"And if he doesn't?"

"He will."

"How do you know?"

"I think he's learned a lot from Tara, and I think he loves her and wants to build a life together. That's the only way he can do it."

"Mule?" Little Raven said helplessly.

"We'll wait, boy," Mule said softly.

And they waited. Waited until nerves were frayed. Waited and thought from the brightest to the darkest. Waited until Little Raven could have happily beaten Zach if he had had him close enough. When he felt he could wait no more he rose and started for the stables.

"Hey," the guard on the platform called down with a grin. Little Raven looked up at him. "Riders comin'," he shouted.

The gates of the fort swung wide to receive Zach and Tara with their prisoner. But not only did the gates swing open; hearts began to open as well. Zach was overcome by the welcome they received. Tara smiled at him, reveling in his look both of love and intense gratitude.

The wedding of Zach and Tara was held a week later, then Zach took Tara into the wilderness with him, promising to return in two weeks for David and Small Fawn's wedding.

That night Tara lay in Zach's arms beneath a star-studded sky.

"I'm so grateful that fate brought me here," Tara sighed. "This is a beauty that would have been a tragedy to miss."

"I've thanked every god I've ever known that when you came here it was with me. What a fool I was then to try to drive you away. I think I knew the moment I looked into your eyes that I could never love another."

"Ummm . . . you were so hard and stubborn."

"And so much in love I couldn't believe it."

He kissed her gently, and she laughed deep in her throat and looped her arms about his neck.

"Oh, Zach, I do love you so much."

One kiss stopped her words and a short time later their passion stopped all thought.